GIRL
ON
TRIAL

GIRL
ON
TRIAL

KATHLEEN FINE

CamCat
Books

Content Warning: This novel touches upon sexual assault, self-harm, and substance abuse and may be disturbing to some readers.

CamCat Publishing, LLC
Ft. Collins, Colorado 80524
camcatpublishing.com

Hardcover ISBN 9780744306835
Paperback ISBN 9780744306859
Large-Print Paperback ISBN 9780744306873
eBook ISBN 9780744306903
Audiobook ISBN 9780744306934

Library of Congress Control Number: 2023934014

Book and cover design by Maryann Appel

5   3   1   2   4

To Mimi
who showed me it's never too late to write your first book.

———∞◇∞———

"I expect to pass through this world but once;
any good thing therefore that I can do or any kindness
that I can show to any fellow creature, let me not defer
or neglect it. For I shall not pass this way again."

Stephen Grellet

PROLOGUE

JANUARY 12, 2022

———◦◦◇◦◦———

"The only reason I come to this meeting is for my weekly caffeine high," Tiffani with an *i* admitted. Emily nodded at her friend as she took a sip of her lukewarm, watered-down coffee, a taste she'd gotten used to. A taste she now associated with healing.

"I'm not no strung-out addict or nothin'," Tiffani continued and then focused on Emily, remembering that Emily, in fact, wasn't there just for the coffee. "No offense—wasn't tryin' to say nothin' bad about addicts. It's just they don't give us caffeine inside, ya know?"

"No offense taken." Emily smiled as she wrapped both hands around her coffee cup, relaxing her tense shoulders. She'd become used to Tiffani's candor and had grown to appreciate the woman's raw honesty. She watched as Tiffani sprinkled some sugar into her undersized paper cup and stirred it with the plastic spoon tied to a container with blue yarn. Tiffani glanced around the room and then untied the yarn, placing the spoon into the pocket of her gray, state-issued sweatpants. Emily bit her lip, debating if she should stop her, but then decided not to. Tiffani was going to do what Tiffani wanted to do—she always did and always would.

"I gnaw on the edges of this enough and it gives me a sorta sharp blade." She gave Emily a wink as she patted her pocket, keeping the new weapon safe as she took a seat in the circle with the other women.

"One minute, ladies," the guard announced to the group as the chatter quieted down and the women took their seats in the circle. Emily picked up an NA book from the only empty seat in the circle that Nikki left for her as a placeholder. She sat down in its place, shifting uncomfortably in the metal chair. She moved her eyes toward the group secretary, Darlene, as she flipped through a stack of papers on her lap.

"Hello, I'm an addict and my name is Darlene. Welcome to the Lincoln Juvenile Correctional Center's group of Narcotics Anonymous. Can we open this meeting with a moment of silence for the addict who still suffers, followed by the serenity prayer?" Emily closed her eyes and took a deep breath as she tried to stop her palms from sweating. She still got anxious even though she'd been attending the meeting every week for the past year. *How has it been an entire year?* she wondered. *So much has happened in only twelve months.*

"Is there anyone here attending their first NA meeting or this meeting for the first time?" Darlene asked. "If so, welcome! You're the most important person here! If you've used today, please listen to what's being said and talk to someone at the break or after the meeting. It costs nothing to belong to this fellowship; you are a member when you say you are. Can someone please read, *Who Is an Addict?* and *What Is Narcotics Anonymous?*"

"I will," Chantelle volunteered as she reached across the circle, grabbed the paper from Darlene, and began reading aloud to the group.

"Yo, Em," Nikki leaned over and whispered in Emily's ear. "You celebratin' today?" Emily nodded at her timidly. She didn't like speaking in front of people even if it was a group of women she trusted.

"You'll do great," Nikki whispered as she punched Emily lightly in the arm. Emily peered around the circle to make sure no one was paying attention to Nikki's whispers. They weren't supposed to have side conversations during the meeting—the guard would send them out of the room if he caught them.

When Chantelle finished the reading, Darlene thanked her and said, "Now can someone please read *Why We Are Here* and *How It Works?*"

Emily watched anxiously as the paper was passed down to Trina. She closed her eyes and listened to Trina's words, clenching her jaw tightly.

"I used last night," Nikki muttered so quietly, Emily wasn't sure if she was meant to hear her. She glanced over at Nikki, who was staring down into her coffee cup shamefully. Nikki had been the first person to introduce herself to Emily at her initial meeting, making her Emily's OG friend in the group. Emily furrowed her brow and placed her hand on top of Nikki's. She wished Nikki had told her about the relapse earlier—then she could have had an actual conversation with her about it. She wondered where Nikki could've gotten her hands on anything since she'd heard a rumor the guards had been doing weekly bunk checks.

One day at a time, Nikki had told Emily, so many months before when she'd been a broken shell of herself. "One day at a time," Emily whispered, trying not to let the guard hear their buzzing.

Seeing Emily's tentative face, Nikki mumbled, "My roommate snuck some smack up her papusa. Had her boyfriend's kid bring it in when he visited her. Whack, dude. Whack." She shook her head and rubbed her buzzed hair with her rugged hands. "She's a bad influence on me. I gotta get a new roommate."

Emily frowned, aware that there was nothing she could do to help Nikki. Nikki had to want sobriety for herself, just like Emily had wanted it. She squeezed Nikki's hand tightly and whispered, "Glad

Kathleen Fine

you're here." As much as Nikki's relapse upset her, it gave her a tiny bit
of strength to share her story. Maybe she could help Nikki even a little
bit today by sharing her own struggles.

"No touching," the guard yelled from across the room, eyeing
Nikki and Emily. As if being scolded by a teacher, Emily reddened and
instantly pulled her hand away from Nikki's.

Darlene reached below her chair and lifted a shoebox to her lap.
"This group recognizes length of clean time by handing out key tags.
If you have one coming to you, please come up and get it. The white
one is for anyone with zero to twenty-nine days clean and serene."
Darlene opened the box to reveal a white key tag and dangled it in the
air. Nikki glanced at Emily and then hesitantly stood up to collect her
tag. The group clapped and whistled wildly as she crossed the circle
and took her tag. She gave a couple of the women fist bumps as the
group chanted, "What do we do? Keep coming back!" Emily put her
fist out as Nikki gave it a bump. She hoped this small gesture, this
modest group of women cheering for Nikki, would be the reason she'd
quit for good this time.

"The orange one is for thirty days clean and serene." Emily
watched as two women got up, collected their tags, and sat back down.
Applause and chanting, "What do we do? Keep coming back!" vibrated the room.

As Darlene handed out the tags for two months, three months,
and so on, Emily gripped her chair, knowing her turn was coming. Her
palms, damp with her sweat, began to slip along the chair's metal sides.

"The yellow one is for nine months clean and serene," Darlene
announced.

Nikki peered at Emily and nudged her bicep. "Your turn is coming
up soon," she whispered. Emily smiled at her, trying to give the façade
of bravery, but she felt anything but brave. What she really wanted to
do was run as fast as she could out of the room and into the parking
lot.

"The glow-in-the-dark one is for a year clean and serene." *You can do this,* Emily thought as she unsteadily stood up and walked toward Darlene. All the women in the room clapped loudly and chanted as she took the tag and went back to her seat, her face flushing with pride.

Darlene placed the box back under her chair and collected the sheets of readings from the women who had read. "Today, Emily is celebrating her one-year anniversary with us. You ready, Em?"

The women's applause quieted and all eyes turned toward her. Clenching her fists tightly, she felt her beating heart rise to her throat. She scanned the room of women and girls before her. Addicts, inmates, and friends. *My people,* Emily thought as she said, "My name is Emily, and I am an addict. This is my story . . ."

1

TRIAL DAY 1: JANUARY 7, 2019

———◦◦◊◦◦———

The alarm on Emily's phone chimed just as Sophie whispered in her ear, "Wake up, Emawee. Wake up." She opened her eyes widely, her body covered in sweat, her sheets soaked yet again. "Time to wake up." She heard Sophie's whisper get farther away, humming distantly from somewhere in her dreams.

From somewhere in her nightmares.

As she turned off the alarm, she tried to overlook the numerous text messages that'd surfaced from numbers she didn't recognize.

"Die, killer"

"You'll pay in hell for what you did."

"Murderer"

How can people I don't even know want me dead?

With shaky hands, she deleted the texts as a CNN report popped up on her screen, updating her on the "Trial of the Year," that was beginning that day:

CNN Breaking News

The Biggest Trial of the Year Begins Today, January 7, 2019. Emily Keller, also known by the media as Keller the Killer, is accused of causing the deaths of a family of four, two of them small children. Only sixteen years old, Emily is one of the youngest females to be accused of a crime so heinous.

Emily buried her face in her pillow, taking a deep breath. She tried to hold back the habitual tears that were creeping out from the corners of her eyes. *I have to be strong today; no crying,* she told herself as she rubbed her temples slowly. *I need to put on my protective armor, or I'll never make it through today alive.* She reached under her mattress, grabbed her orange pill bottle and gave it a shake, the rattling sound of the tablets comforting her. She poured two pills onto her clammy palm and placed them gently on her tongue. *Protective armor.*

"Emily?" Her brother, Nate, quietly inched open the bedroom door. "You awake? It's time to start getting ready for court."

Without looking up at him, she nodded as she rolled out of bed, trying not to think about how wrong the prosecution had the facts and how she could be sent to prison because of it. As she attempted to walk toward the door, her ankle monitor snagged on her lavender bedsheet. She yanked the sheet off in frustration and dragged her feet to the bathroom to prepare for the first day of her new life.

Debbie and Nate were already waiting for her in Debbie's rumbling Toyota Camry when she stepped out of the trailer.

"It's your turn for shotgun." Emily opened the door to the backseat where Nate was already buckled in.

"You can take it today," he muttered, avoiding eye contact with her.

"I don't need pity shotgun just because I'm on trial for murder, Nate," Emily replied curtly as she reluctantly sat down in the front seat. As she buckled her seat belt, she already regretted scolding Nate for doing something kind. *I'll apologize to him later,* she told herself. Nate had been up with her until three o'clock that morning, listening to her cry and consoling her. *I don't deserve him,* she thought, squeezing her eyes shut.

She rolled down her window and took a deep breath of fresh morning air as her mom lit a Virginia Slim, her hands trembling. "Morning vodka shot hasn't kicked in yet?" Emily muttered under her breath as she turned on the radio. *Or maybe one shot doesn't cut it anymore,* Emily thought.

"What hasn't kicked in?" Debbie asked as she ashed her cigarette into an empty coke can, oblivious to Emily's disrespectful comment.

"Coffee hasn't kicked in yet?" Emily corrected herself as she investigated her face in the cracked side mirror of the car. The face staring back at Emily was swollen from weeks of nonstop crying. Although she'd put on some of her mom's waterproof mascara, she still looked like someone had run her over with a truck. *You're so repulsive,* she thought as she tried to comb her drab chestnut hair with her fingers, squinting at her image through the cracked glass. She wanted to disappear. Sink down into the seat of the car and disappear forever.

As she pinched her upper cheekbones to give her face some color, she glanced at Nate through the corner of the broken mirror, hoping he couldn't tell she was staring at him through the mosaic lens. Since he had headphones in his ears, she assumed he was listening to a news podcast about the trial. The expression on his face looked like it was straining to stay calm, but she could read his emotions no matter how hard he tried to hide them. When you shared a womb with someone, you knew everything they were feeling.

There was actually supposed to be three of them. Her dad had left when he'd found out Debbie was pregnant with triplets. He'd said since he didn't want one baby, he definitely didn't want three. Emily used to sometimes think about how different her life would've been if their other brother hadn't died at birth. Maybe he would've punched Tom Swanson for dumping her two years ago since Nate didn't do a thing about it. Maybe he would've taught Emily to throw a football since Nate was anti-athletics.

Maybe he could've stopped Emily before she lost herself. Maybe he could've stopped this whole situation. Maybe no one would have died.

"Valerie told us to meet her around back when I spoke to her on the phone last night," Emily directed her mom as they pulled up to the courthouse. Debbie nodded as she navigated her ancient car around to the back of the building, avoiding the crowd hovering at the entrance.

"Shit, look at all of the people," Nate announced as he stared at the crowd and cameras surrounding the front of the building. No one seemed to notice their rickety car escape past the swell to the rear parking lot. *Maybe they were expecting some sort of official-looking black SUV like you see in crime movies and not our pathetic piece of tin,* Emily speculated, thinking about how some seniors at her school owned nicer cars than her mom's. She peeked down at her gray dress and nervously picked little lint balls off it as her mom parked the car.

"You look fine, Em," Debbie insisted as she opened a mini bottle of vodka from her purse and took a swig. "That dress looks lovely on you." Debbie had spent her tip money to buy Emily "new" thrift store clothes for the trial. Emily was now pulling at a seam on the edge of the dress, making it unravel.

As she waited for her mom to finish her shot, she felt around for the phone in her purse to make sure it was turned off. She'd turn it on later that night once her mom and Nate were sleeping so she could read through her texts and the news in privacy. That way, if she cried, no one would see her. *Strong people don't cry,* she told herself.

"You need a pill?" Debbie asked as she fumbled through the large purse on her lap. The Valium Emily had taken that morning was beginning to set in, and she was starting to feel unreasonably calm.

"I'm good." *Although I'll need another one soon,* she thought. It hurt her too much to live in reality.

Emily's lawyer, Valerie Anderson, was standing at the back entrance of the building, propping open the heavy metal door with her bright red heel. As Emily stepped out of the car, Valerie waved her hands frantically. "Quick, before they catch on that you're back here!" she shrieked as she lifted her long, hot pink nails to her mouth.

"We better hurry." Debbie grabbed Nate's and Emily's hands, tugging them toward Valerie.

"Wait," Emily urged as she struggled to catch up to her petite mom's gait. Without warning, her black heel wobbled to the side and she stumbled, falling onto the hard concrete. Before she had the chance to assess the damage to her knees, Nate dropped his mom's hand, grabbed Emily up by the arm, and quickly escorted her to the door. As they approached Valerie, all eyes looked to the blood running down Emily's knees. Emily was surprised the wounds stung so badly even though the rest of her felt numb.

"We'll have to find some Band-Aids ASAP before we converse." Valerie's heels echoed in the hallway as she led them to their room. Emily slouched over even more than she had been as she followed Valerie, spying the name *Keller* stuck to a metal door with a yellow Post-it. As they stepped inside, the heavy door slammed behind them with a loud thud.

2

—◦◦◇◦◦—

Emily awoke in the early morning darkness with her heart filled with vivacity. The goosebumps on her skin felt like bubbles forming in a crisp can of newly opened Diet Coke, her favorite drink. The day brought so many promises. It was a new school year. She could be someone brand new.

She peeked out of the modest window above her bed. The moon was still visible, a thick scar in the black sea above her, illuminating the room in an opaque glow. She glanced over at Nate, who was snoring loudly on the other side of their cramped bedroom. She noticed he had drool dripping down the side of his chin, a puddle of spit forming on his gray bedsheet. *How can he sleep so soundly before the first day of school?* she wondered.

Quietly, Emily got on her hands and knees and felt for the vision board she'd made the night before after Nate had fallen asleep. She laid the board out on her lavender bedspread, admiring the cut-out faces of Taylor Swift, Kylie Jenner, and Gigi Hadid. *One day I'll be like you,* she whispered to the women as she rubbed her hands along the words she'd taped below their faces: courage, believe, friendship, happiness, strength, worthy, disciplined, strong, beautiful. She closed her eyes tightly, her bones aching with longing.

I'm going to be popular.

I'm going to be pretty.

I'm going to be happy.

Manifest.

Manifest.

Manifest.

Placing the vision board back under her bed, she tiptoed to the door and stepped into the hallway. As she marched past her mom's room toward the bathroom, she peeked her head in and looked at Debbie's simple space. She resented that her mom had never hung any pictures on the walls or tried to make her room look presentable. *At least try,* Emily had thought, *try to be normal like everyone else's moms.*

"No one's ever in here but me, why would I fancy it all up?" Debbie had replied over the summer when Emily asked if she wanted to shop for decorations with her at the Goodwill. Emily hadn't wanted to say to her mom that plenty of people went in her room: plenty of men. *But then again, the men that go in there are probably too drunk to notice her décor,* Emily had thought.

Emily surveyed her mom sleeping soundly, her leg kicked out from under the blanket, dangling halfway off the bed. Usually by peeking in like this, Emily could tell how intoxicated her mom got the night before. If Debbie had on all her clothes and didn't get in her sheets, she'd gotten drunk. If she didn't come home at all or if there was a strange man in the bed, she'd gotten exceptionally drunk. If she had on her night shirt and looked like she'd washed her face, she'd probably only had a couple drinks. That morning was the latter.

Locking herself in the bathroom, Emily showered then followed a YouTube tutorial on how to perfectly contour bronzer into her cheekbones. She carefully put on the outfit she'd picked out weeks before: faded jeans, a tight white T-shirt, and Vans. Cool in an "I didn't try too hard" sort of way.

Appraising her reflection in the mirror, her big, muddy eyes smudged with makeup, she decided that she'd done the best she could with what God had given her. She wasn't pretty, but she wasn't ugly, and didn't that count for something? She'd read a meme once that if you smiled at yourself every time you looked in the mirror, you'd instinctively give yourself more confidence. She couldn't quite remember when she'd lost her confidence, but she seemed to have woken up one day and it was gone. It was replaced with pimples, drab hair, insecurity, and lanky limbs. She stared at her gloomy reflection and forced a smile back so hard that her cheeks hurt. *I need all the confidence I can get,* she thought to herself.

As she stepped into the kitchen, she opened the bare fridge, scanning its scarce contents: expired milk, mustard, baking soda, and a takeaway container. She grabbed the Styrofoam container and peeked inside to see what leftovers her mom had brought home: a cheesesteak sub and fries. After every night shift, Debbie brought home whatever leftovers the cook gave her from dinner service, no doubt because she'd slept with him a few times, so Emily always had breakfast, even if it was greasy, fried leftovers.

Grabbing a frying pan, she added some oil and a handful of french fries from the container, tossing them into the steamy pan. When they started sizzling, she threw in some cheesesteak bits, breaking up the meat with a spatula. Once it was all cooked, she scooped the concoction onto a paper plate and devoured her breakfast in less than a minute. Satisfied, she tossed her plate in the trash can and placed the pan in the sink to wash after school. Sometimes she daydreamed of loading an enormous, stainless-steel dishwasher, pressing the start button with no worries in the world. Relaxing as her dishes were cleaned without her. *One day,* she thought.

She stuck a mug of water in the microwave for two minutes and then poured it into her handy, reusable Starbucks coffee cup that she'd gotten for Christmas from their next-door neighbor, Miss Jelly. Scooping some instant coffee into the cup, she stirred it quickly before snapping on the lid. Checking the time, she grabbed her backpack, already prepacked for the day, and peeked into the mirror one last time, forcing another smile. *Confidence*, she thought to herself as she headed out to The Pit.

The Pit, a central meeting area in the middle of their trailer park, consisted of some benches, a swing set, and a grill. Nate and Emily, along with most of the teenagers in the neighborhood, hung out there after school and on weekends.

As Emily strolled past their community sign that read, *Blue Crab Cottages*, she thought about how the name made the place sound charming. In reality, the only crabs she'd heard about in the neighborhood were rumors of who gave who STDs.

As she approached The Pit, the sun began to creep up, making for the perfect photo op. She set her steaming hot coffee cup on the bench facing the sun and placed her backpack next to it before snapping a photo. Using her editing skills, she blurred three trailers out so just the sun, her backpack, and her Starbucks cup were in view, adding the *Rise* filter to the photo. She added the caption: "Morning latte and sunrise. Soaking up the last morning of summer," and posted it on her page. It was amazing what some filters and camera angles could do to make her life look more glamorous.

Checking the time again, she hurriedly grabbed her bag and coffee cup and headed back to make sure Nate was up on time. She didn't want to miss the bus on the first day of junior year.

As Emily neared her trailer, she noticed Miss Jelly sitting on her front porch rocking chair, wearing a fluffy purple Ravens robe and pink slippers. She was adjusting a long silver clip that tightly held up curlers against her stark white hair. Emily smiled, impressed how Miss

Jelly had no shame in letting whoever walked by see her dressed in her night clothes.

"Takes your breath away, doesn't it?" Miss Jelly motioned, staring over Emily's shoulder.

"What does?" Emily turned around to see what Miss Jelly was pointing at.

"Why, the sunrise, hon. Weren't you over there lookin' at the sunrise?" she asked gesturing toward The Pit.

"Oh . . ." Emily faltered, realizing she hadn't had the chance to *actually* get a good look at the sun. She turned around and peered at the yellow yolk flirting its way up the horizon.

"It's beautiful," she agreed, looking back toward her neighbor.

"It's your first day of school this morning, right, hon?" Miss Jelly took a sip of coffee from an oversized mug with the word *Mom* printed across it. *Why does Miss Jelly have a mug that says* Mom *if she's never had any kids?* Emily wondered.

"Yup, first day!" Thinking about the possibilities of the day made her heart warm up like Miss Jelly's hot coffee. She was going to make a new friend if it killed her.

"Well, good luck, sweetheart. Why don't you stop by after school and have some carrot cake that I baked last night? I used purple carrots from my garden this time, so it has a lavender hue to it. You wouldn't believe it!"

Emily smiled at Miss Jelly's enthusiasm for the trivial things in life like purple carrots.

"Sure, I'd love to!" she said, happy to appease her.

Miss Jelly was the grandmother she never had. Growing up, Miss Jelly babysat for Nate and her whenever their mom worked, and sometimes when their mom didn't come home at night, they'd creep over to Miss Jelly's house and sleep on her couch. She always left blankets and pillows out in case they ever ended up coming over. Her trailer was their sanctuary.

As Emily opened the door to her own trailer and stepped inside, she heard the shower running and then turn off.

Nate stepped out of the bathroom a minute later, wearing a towel and a gold face mask.

"Thanks for using all the hot water," he teased. As he passed her, Emily handed him the Starbucks coffee cup and he took a sip. "I still don't understand why you make yourself coffee just for your stupid Instagram pics when you don't even like it."

"You should be grateful you get coffee made for you every day," she teased back. "I got twenty new friend requests from last week's post where I was posing in my workout clothes and holding that coffee."

"The one where you captioned it saying you'd gone for a hike and blurred out the trailers?"

"Yup," she boasted. She'd done some research over the summer on editing photos and had been perfecting her skills.

"Guess your followers don't need to know you've never worked out a day in your life then, huh? But wouldn't you rather make real friends than fake Insta-friends?"

"That's the goal," she mumbled under her breath.

"What?"

"Where'd you get money to buy that face mask?" She changed the subject, wishing she'd thought of doing one herself. He smirked at her before scurrying toward their bedroom.

He walked past their mother's room, then turned back to Emily. "What's her status this morning?" he whispered, then pressed his lips together firmly.

Emily's face grew serious. "Seems okay. Looks like she washed her face."

Nate nodded, running his hand through his wet hair, and then headed back toward their room.

"We have to leave here in ten minutes, so you better hurry up!" she shouted, hoping she was loud enough so he would hear her.

She sat down on their pilled, tan couch they'd bought on Craigslist and scrolled through her Instagram feed. She noticed a couple hearts popping up from her post that morning. Five likes so far. *Manifest. Manifest. Manifest.*

Nate stepped out of the bedroom exactly five minutes later, dressed in jeans and a plain, gray shirt. *How can he look so good in five minutes?* Emily marveled at his remarkably handsome face, tanned skin, hazel eyes, and messy, tawny hair. She wished she had inherited just one of the beautiful features that he had—it wasn't fair that they were twins and yet they looked so different. *The girls will go gaga over you today, not that you'll notice,* Emily thought before she snatched her backpack and tossed him his.

"Let's get this show on the road," he exclaimed as he grabbed his coffee and draped his arm around her shoulder.

My first day of eleventh grade is going to be epic, I can feel it, Emily manifested as they stepped out the door and headed toward the bus.

3

TRIAL DAY 1: JANUARY 7, 2019

———◦◦◇◦◦———

Emily clenched her teeth as she followed Valerie into the humble room that smelled like mildew and stale coffee. Her restless legs felt unable to hold her upright any longer, so she quickly sat in one of the six wooden chairs surrounding a rectangular table. Nate and Debbie hesitantly sat down adjacent to Emily, gazes darting around as if planning their escape route.

Breathe, Emily thought as she squeezed her eyes shut and tried to take in a deep breath, but only raspy, short gasps were coming out. She felt outside of her body, like she was looking down on herself and watching a movie play out. A horror movie. And she was the lead actress. None of this was real. As if sensing her anxiety, Nate placed his hand firmly on her shoulder, taking the fatherly role she hadn't realized she was yearning for. She covered her hand on top of his and relaxed her shoulders, allowing herself to open her eyes and take in her surroundings. She glanced down at Valerie's half-filled coffee cup, rimmed with a large lipstick stain, and next to it a notepad covered in scribbles. She leaned over to catch a glimpse of the scribbles, but then realized Valerie had stopped what she was saying and was hovering over her, waiting for Emily to acknowledge her.

Emily looked up and refocused as Valerie paced up and down the eight-by-eight-foot room, motioning her hands rapidly as she spoke, "Please stay focused, Emily. Today we start with our opening statements. Since you're being tried as an adult, it may end up working in our favor as, unlike juvenile court, you have the right to a jury trial. The jury may be more empathetic toward you than a judge. But just remember, since this is an adult trial, you can face the same penalties as adults do, up to ten years in prison for manslaughter."

Emily opened her eyes widely at this early-morning reality check and glanced over at Nate and her mom, who were trying to hide their obvious concern. She remembered having this conversation with Valerie before, but it'd been like she was speaking underwater. She recalled Valerie saying that if she got convicted, she'd never be able to vote. She'd have difficulty getting a job. But Emily had been in such a benzo-induced fog, it'd been too much for her to take in at once. Now, sitting in the courthouse on the day of her trial, she realized that this was her reality. She was being tried as an adult for manslaughter. She could be sent to prison. This was really happening. She closed her eyes and took another slow, deep breath.

Valerie continued. "The prosecuting attorney will say her opening statement first and I'll go second. During this time, I want you to keep your eyes on whoever is talking and act like you're listening. Don't smile and don't cry. You don't want to appear too cheerful or too guilty." She paused for a second and eyeballed Emily up and down. "And thank you for getting appropriate clothes and putting on some makeup," she said. Emily's face grew red. The week before when they'd met up, Emily had been wearing grungy pajamas and hadn't showered for a week. She hadn't been able to wear any makeup since it slid off her face as soon as the tears came, which was almost every hour.

"After the opening statements, the prosecutor will have the initial police officer from the scene of the incident testify as her first witness. After that, they'll call in the medical examiner and then the home inspector. All you need to do is just sit there and appear interested in whoever is speaking or keep your head low. Don't look at the jury. If you hear anything that upsets you, make sure it's an appropriate time to appear upset. If anyone is discussing dead bodies, you can look upset. But appearing too upset will make you look guilty. Do you understand?"

Emily slowly nodded her head. Look upset, but not too upset. Did she understand? She didn't know anymore.

"Mom and I will be sitting right behind you," Nate promised as he leaned over and grabbed both of Emily's shoulders, squeezing them gently.

As Emily let herself relax a little from Nate's assurance, Debbie made a forceful hiccup, causing Emily to tense up again. She turned and watched as her mom sniffled, pulling a compact mirror out from her purse, dabbing the corners of her heavily mascaraed eyes with a crumpled tissue.

"Debbie, this is what you shouldn't be doing during the trial," Valerie lectured her. "You're the adult and need to hold it together. Don't make a scene, this isn't about you. And why are you not wearing waterproof mascara? Didn't I tell you to wear waterproof makeup? No one wants to see a disheveled mother of the criminal crying with black streaks running down her face."

"My baby isn't a criminal!" Debbie interrupted her.

"That's not what I meant, Debbie. Listen, you need to hold it together. Nate, you need to hold your mother together during this trial. Can you do that?"

"Will do," Nate responded, as he robotically lifted his hand off Emily's shoulder and placed it on his mom's instead. "It'll be okay, Mom, shh," he reassured her quietly.

Debbie whimpered, appearing to calm down with his encouragement. She smiled at Nate sheepishly before lifting a pill bottle out of her purse, snapping the lid open, and popping a white tablet into her mouth. Nate frowned at Emily. They both knew what the other was thinking: their mom was going to drown herself in narcotics for the next few days. *Nate's going to have to keep an eye on her, so she doesn't make a scene in court,* Emily thought.

It was silent in the room for a second as Valerie took in the peculiar scene that was occurring between the three family members. She shook her head as if trying to erase the moment. "I think it's best from now on when I meet with Emily to discuss the trial that it's just her and I," Valerie suggested, glancing at Nate as Debbie lifted a silver flask from her purse and took a swig. "It's best not to have distractions from other people, but you can be with her whenever she requests it. Is that okay?"

"Of course," Nate agreed as he stood up and pulled at his mom's arm. "Why don't you go have a cigarette and see when Charlie's meeting us?" Nate knew what incentives would work for her to leave the room.

"Charlie?" Valerie asked.

"My boyfriend," Debbie sniffled as she glanced up toward Emily. "Okay." She warily followed Nate toward the door like a lost puppy dog. Emily tried not to feel hurt when her mom didn't turn around to wish her good luck before leaving the room.

"Now, let's get back to the dos and don'ts of the courtroom," Valerie said, turning toward Emily. "The jury is going to be deliberating whether you caused the deaths of Steven, Brandi, Kathryn, and Sophie." Emily winced at the sound of the little girls' names and closed her eyes tightly. She felt like she was going to collapse. She gripped the arms of the chair to hold herself steady. "Now, some people in the media may think you did this intentionally, but the prosecution is going to spin this as negligence, which is good."

Emily's eyes opened widely at this statement. *Intentionally? Why on earth would I kill those poor girls intentionally?* The room began to spin.

"You may feel uncomfortable seeing the Thomas family sitting on the other side of the courtroom. As you probably know, some of their family members are heavily involved in this court case . . ." Images of the family protesting and holding up signs to send her to prison, appeared in Emily's mind. Her vision started getting blurry.

"Emawee. We're watching Peppa Pig,*"* Sophie whispered in her ear.

Suddenly, there was a knock on the door, and Valerie opened it. An overweight police officer with kind eyes and a seventies mustache handed Valerie something. She closed the door and reached her hand out to Emily.

"Here you go," she said, shoving a wad of bandages, cotton balls, and rubbing alcohol packets into Emily's hands. Emily ripped open an alcohol pack and forcefully dabbed at the scrapes on each knee, feeling a spasm of stinging surge through her body. She relished in the pain.

4

PAST: SEPTEMBER 4, 2018

———⬦⬦⬦⬦———

"Hey, hons, come on in," the bus driver wheezed in greeting as Emily and Nate got on the bus. Since they were the last pickup on the route to school, there were almost no empty seats left. Scanning the seats nervously, Emily was swimming in an ocean with no land in sight.

She felt her cheeks twitch as she caught sight of Steph, her former best friend, sitting toward the back. She shifted her eyes away quickly, hoping Steph didn't see her, and immediately squeezed into an empty seat in the front row next to a freshman. It was safer for her to take a seat designated for lower classes than risk the humiliation of walking to the back and not finding a seat. She observed Nate as he sauntered past her toward the back, not having a worry in the world if people were watching or judging him. It was like they were living on different planets.

While she gazed out the window, her body bouncing up and down with the bus movements, she slid her hand along her forearm, feeling for the four prongs of raised skin. When they'd been twelve years old,

Steph and Emily had made a best friends' pact. Steph had been over at Emily's house for a sleepover while Debbie was working all night, so they'd stayed up until the sun rose. Getting the idea from a book they'd read, they'd placed forks on her gas stove until the metal turned florescent red. Then they took turns branding the forks into their arms as if they were cattle.

"Now we're imprinted together forever," Steph had promised.

Emily glanced down at the raised mark on her arm that still didn't tan with the rest of her body—*her friendship scar.* She wondered if Steph was looking down at her arm at that moment too. They hadn't talked in three months. It was the longest they'd ever not spoken. The longest Emily had been completely friendless and alone.

"Can't you be in the moment anymore?" Steph had mumbled as they were lounging at The Pit. Emily was scrolling through Instagram and had barely even heard her friend speak. "You're obsessed with that thing." She'd pointed toward Emily's phone as if it were a heroin needle.

They'd been quarreling like that for the past few months. Bickering over what was important to each of them. Emily had started getting into being popular and using social media and Steph was still only interested in reading books. Emily had begun to feel like she was hanging out with her little sister, not her friend.

Taking offense to Steph's comment, Emily had replied, "Maybe you need to go on Instagram more to learn some fashion tips since you still dress like you're in the fifth grade." Seeing the hurt on Steph's face, Emily immediately regretted going so far.

"You kiss all of the popular girls' butts. It's pathetic," Steph had countered before Emily had a chance to apologize.

I guess we're really doing this, Emily had thought. "At least I have other friends besides you." She'd stood up to go home, wishing her last statement was actually true. Wishing she'd had a group of friends like so many students at their school.

Then Steph had gone too far. "At least I have a dad who loves me and a mother who isn't a drunk."

And that's when Emily ran home. They hadn't spoken since.

Emily leaned her head against the seat, trying to erase the sound of hatred in Steph's words from her mind. *Even my best friend doesn't love me,* she thought as she stared at the blur of trees passing by her smudged window. She didn't know how she'd get through her junior year stuck at the bottom of the totem pole again . . . especially without Steph by her side. She needed to find a way to make friends this year. She needed at least one friend or she knew she'd inevitably melt away into nothingness.

As the bus approached Crossland High School, she closed her eyes. *Please let me be popular this year,* she thought and then revised her wish, *or at least, please let me find a new best friend.* The bus came to an abrupt stop and since Emily was in the first row, she was the first to exit. As she navigated the steep bus stairs, her shoelace got caught on the door and she fell onto the hard cement, her right knee stinging in pain. She stood up quickly and glanced down to see blood oozing through her new jeans. She turned to see if anyone on the bus had seen her. Luckily, only her seatmate and the bus driver were paying attention. Everyone else was either staring at their cell phones or wrapped up in conversation with their friends.

"You okay, darlin'?" the bus driver asked loudly.

"Fine," she said quietly and quickly rushed toward the building without glancing behind her. She beelined it into the lobby bathroom and hurried into the closest stall.

Setting her backpack on the ground, she assessed the damage to her knee. A quarter-sized blood spot had made a little circle on her jeans. She pulled her pants down and cleaned off as much blood from her skin as she could with toilet paper. Reaching into her backpack, she grabbed her mini pocketknife from her keychain, an item she no doubt would get in trouble for bringing to school if a teacher ever saw her with it. She suddenly heard a person in the far stall sniffle. She hadn't realized she wasn't alone. *Are they crying?* she wondered as she cut a slit in her jeans where the blood was, then stretched the slit around, creating a substantial hole. *Crisis averted.* She could hear the girl blowing her nose and wondered if she should ask if she needed any help. Maybe it was a new freshman with first-day jitters. She remembered her first day of high school. She'd thrown up before she'd even left the house, she'd been so nervous. She felt around in various pockets of her backpack and found a tattered Band-Aid from a few years back. She opened the wrapper, applied it to her wound, and slipped her jeans back up. She'd go check on the freshman really quickly to make sure she was okay before she left for homeroom.

As she stepped toward the sink to wash her hands, she was surprised to see Hannah Patterson step out of the end stall and veer straight to the mirror, mascara streaked down her face as if she'd been crying. *You were the one crying?* Emily thought. She felt starstruck and glanced down at herself to make sure there was no evidence of her fall from earlier. She would've been mortified for Hannah to find out that she'd fallen.

As she dried her hands, Emily glanced over at Hannah, who was rinsing her face in water, erasing the tear-stained streaks down her cheeks. She didn't look like the Hannah who had moved to town right before high school had started—the Hannah that Emily had been intrigued by. She was pretty in a unique *I don't care* kind of way. She'd seemed to make friends immediately. It looked so easy for her. *She's probably never once worried what people think of her,* Emily thought as she gazed at her own drab appearance in the mirror adjacent to Hannah's. But the girl standing next to Emily didn't seem like she had no worries. She didn't seem okay at all.

"Are you okay?" Emily finally got the nerve up to ask when she noticed Hannah reapplying her makeup. Her eyes were still glazed over. *Did she just break up with a boyfriend or something?* Emily wondered. *Why else would she have a reason to cry on the first day of school?* Emily had been following Hannah on Instagram for a year, making comments on her pictures so that she'd notice her. Hannah was so happy in all her photos. She was just the kind of person Emily wanted to be friends with. She was just the kind of person Emily wanted to *be*.

Happy. Confident. Popular. If she could become friends with someone like Hannah . . . her entire world could change. Maybe this was her chance.

"Oh, hey," Hannah muttered, her gaze darting over toward Emily and then back to her own reflection. She applied more black mascara over her swollen eyes. "Sorry, I didn't hear you in here earlier."

"I have some foundation if you need it." Emily reached into her backpack and pulled out her trusty old khaki-colored liquid. Emily knew how to cover up tears. She was an expert at it.

"Is it that noticeable?" Hannah chuckled as she reached over and took the foundation from Emily's hand, opening up the cap.

"I'm just a pro at covering up bad days, I guess," Emily said. "Hell, I just had to rip a hole in my jeans because I fell getting off the bus," she pointed down toward her jeans, deciding to reveal her embarrassing moment.

Hannah glanced down and peered at Emily's jeans and then up to her face, a smile slowly emerging from her frown. "Guess we're both having bad mornings then, huh? Thanks for this, by the way." She began rubbing the tan cream onto her cheeks as Emily admired her from the corner of her eye, trying to think of a way to change the topic to something more upbeat. She didn't want to push her away by asking why she'd been crying. It could come off as intrusive. She decided to shift the conversation to something lighter.

"Super cute top, by the way . . . is it from Nordstrom? I think I tried it on there last week," she said, which was a total lie. She'd seen Hannah post photos the week before on Instagram, as she tried on back-to-school outfits from the dressing room. Hannah had her followers give a thumbs-up or thumbs-down for each outfit, and Emily had wondered at the time how in the world Hannah had managed to get a hundred people to care about an outfit.

"Yeah, good eye. I bought the jeans there too. Well, I stole the top, I bought the jeans. You know, a little giving and a little taking," she admitted and gave Emily a wink. *Why would Hannah have to steal that top?* Emily wondered. It seemed like from her photos Hannah lived in a nice neighborhood, in a nice house. *Can't her family afford to buy her one?*

"You're Emma, right?" Hannah asked as she took out her highlighter stick and rhythmically brushed streaks onto her cheekbones, dabbing her button nose, pierced with a diamond stud.

The sad, mascara-streaked face that had come out of the stall moments earlier was now transformed into a gorgeous, happy-looking girl. The same girl that Emily had swooned over all summer on Instagram.

"Emily," Emily whispered, feeling stupid that she knew so much about Hannah and Hannah didn't even know her name.

"Nice Vans. I need a worn pair like that to wear around the neighborhood." Hannah gestured toward Emily's feet. "And cute jeans too. Love the ripped look, even if it was by accident."

"I got them from a trendy thrift store near my house that has amazing stuff." Emily felt a surge of pride.

"Oh, cool." Hannah applied another layer of sheer lip gloss to her lips, glancing back and forth between herself and Emily in the mirror. "I always love trying out new places to shop. I'm so sick of all the girls in this school wearing the same three outfits. I'm so sick of all the conformity. Aren't you?"

"Totally. I'm happy to meet up with you there sometime and look for some stuff. I think I saw some navy Vans just like these the last time I was there," Emily offered, surprising herself at her boldness.

"Oh really?" Hannah turned her head from the mirror and handed Emily back her foundation. "Would love to find some good deals!" She placed her makeup bag back into her backpack and zippered up the side, assessing her amber colored, blond-streaked hair in the mirror one last time.

"Maybe this weekend?" Hannah turned toward her.

"That'd be awesome!" Emily eyes widened.

"Cool," Hannah said. "And do you mind just not mentioning you saw me crying in here earlier? I'm just PMSing, I guess. You know how it is, right?"

Before Emily could answer her, Hannah tossed her backpack on her shoulders and paraded out of the bathroom, without turning around to say goodbye.

As Emily heard the door close, she stared in the mirror again and saw a girl looking back at her in the reflection with wide eyes and an enormous smile. There was no need to force one this time.

5

TRIAL DAY 1: JANUARY 7, 2019

———◦◦◇◦◦———

Emily was hyperaware of everything around her in the courtroom
as she waited for the judge: the air conditioning vent whistling and
blowing frigid air against her arms above her, the sound of Valerie's
pen scratching at her notepad, the hacking cough of someone behind
her. She tried to drown out the noises as she closed her eyes and waited
for the judge to be called in, allowing the voices to blend together like
background music to her thoughts.

"Emawee," Sophie's voice whispered in her ear. Emily opened
her eyes and turned suddenly. *No, that wasn't Sophie,* Emily told herself,
just your imagination. She scanned the room quickly, seeing that the
courtroom was packed as if they were here to watch the Orioles play
in the World Series. *Glad I can be entertainment for you all,* she thought,
as she spied Nate walking into the courtroom, his arm around their
mom, protecting her from the day ahead. It brought back a memory
of a summer day when they were about seven years old, and their
mom was working a double shift. Emily had decided to go exploring

through different neighborhoods and ended up getting lost for hours. Nate had eventually called the cops because she hadn't come home and he couldn't find her anywhere. A police car located her wandering a side street a few hours later. When she'd walked up to the trailer with the police officer in tow, Nate had wrapped his arms tightly around her, a paternal hold from just a child. She'd felt so much fear that day, but that hug from Nate had made her feel safe, just as seeing him today did.

She peered over at the prosecutor, Mindy Rosenbaum, who Valerie told her was going to "rip her a new one." For sounding so frightening, she was a skeleton of a woman only about five feet tall, and her raven black hair was cut so crisply across her chin, it looked like a wig. Emily shifted her eyes around the room and spied Brandi Thomas's parents sitting directly behind Mindy. She recognized them from protesting on TV, holding up signs and chanting into the camera to put Emily behind bars. She watched as they both knelt in prayer position, gripping bibles. Brandi's mother's eyes suddenly darted toward her and Emily flicked her eyes away as fast as she could, pressing her palm against her chest. Her glare had felt like it burned a tiny hole through Emily's already Swiss cheese heart.

As the judge and jury were called into the courtroom, Emily rose from the stiff wooden chair and glanced down to her ankle monitor. The judge was a heavyset man with a neatly trimmed white beard and glasses. Before he could catch her eye, Emily glanced back down and saw blood beginning to trickle out from the Band-Aids on her knees. She tried to focus on the numbing feeling in her body as the Valium pulsed through it.

Judge Wilson cleared his throat. "Good morning, ladies and gentlemen. Calling the case of the People of the State of Maryland versus Emily Keller. Are both sides ready?" Emily watched as the judge took off his glasses and checked the lenses, using the hem of his robe to wipe away some smudge.

"Ready for the People, Your Honor," Mindy said.

"Ready for the defense, Your Honor," parroted Valerie.

Judge Wilson faced the jury. "Will the clerk please swear in the jury?"

Emily watched as the clerk walked in front of the jury, following the judge's orders. "Ladies and gentlemen of the jury, please stand and raise your right hand."

Emily glanced toward them as they stood up, figuring they were probably looking at the clerk rather than at her. It was an assortment of men and women. One elderly woman reminded her of Miss Jelly, who she knew was sitting somewhere behind her in the gallery, though she hadn't noticed her yet. *That must be a good sign,* she thought. Another juror was a young guy who appeared to be barely eighteen years old and was surprisingly handsome. Emily's face flushed and she looked back down toward her knees.

"Do each of you swear that you'll fairly try the case before this court, and that you'll return a true verdict according to the evidence and the instructions of the court, so help you, God? Please say 'I do,'" the clerk said monotonously. *Does he get sick of doing this every single day,* Emily wondered.

"I do," the jury declared in unison.

"You may be seated," the clerk said, pivoting back to his spot next to the judge.

Emily watched as Mindy pushed her chair out and walked with wide steps over to the jury. She approached them with practiced ease. *She must be really good if she's this confident,* Emily thought. She kept her eyes focused on her hands resting in her lap. She knew if she looked up again, she'd give away a fretted expression, which would make Valerie angry.

"Good morning, Your Honor, ladies and gentlemen of the jury. My name is Mindy Rosenbaum and I represent the State of Maryland in this case. On November 9, 2018, the defendant committed the crime of manslaughter for the entire Thomas family of four." Emily couldn't help but notice that she spoke with the ease of someone who'd done this a thousand times before. From someone who'd sent thousands of guilty criminals to prison. From someone who'd probably send her to prison.

"Let me remind the jury that manslaughter is defined as a killing that stems from a lack of intention to cause death involving an intentional, or negligent, act leading to death." She paused for a second and glanced over at Emily. Emily felt the room begin to spin as Mindy's eyes blazed a laser through her skull. She bit the inside of both of her cheeks as she tried to remain calm.

Mindy held her hands loosely behind her back, and Emily could hear the dangling of a charm bracelet on her wrist that she hadn't noticed before. Clang. Clang. Clang. "Don't be fooled by the appearance and age of the defendant. If you look back in criminal history, there've been many young women who have committed horrendous crimes. Unfortunately, criminals are not one age, race, or face, so there is no way to tell if someone is a criminal by looking at them."

Dammit, why did she have to tell them to look at me? Emily thought. She could feel every single eye in the courtroom on her. Evaluating her. Judging her.

"They come in all shapes and sizes, and you must remember that when listening to the evidence during the next few days. Regrettably, during this hearing, you will not be able to hear from the four victims of the crime, because all four have brutally died due to the negligence of this sixteen-year-old girl. Instead, you'll hear from witnesses describing events leading up to the evening and the morning of the incident. Along with police testimony, I'll prove to you that the defendant, Emily Keller, is guilty of manslaughter." Emily pulled on her tights and shifted uncomfortably in her chair. She wondered who in the jury had already decided she was guilty. Had any of them already ruled her out? The Miss Jelly look-alike most certainly would give her a chance, wouldn't she? She watched as Mindy gave an award-winning smile to the jury one last time before walking back to her seat, her modest heels clicking softly across the marble floor.

Valerie squeezed Emily's leg and gave her a little wink. "Let's do this," she whispered under her breath and then she stood up and approached the jury, her red heels sounding like an elephant's compared to Mindy's. *Why does my lawyer dress like a hooker?* Emily wondered, feeling her face flush. She could hear the quiet hum of the courtroom as the two lawyers switched places.

"Your Honor and people of the jury. Under the law my client is presumed innocent until proven guilty," Valerie spoke boisterously to the group as Emily kept her head low, wishing she could curl into a ball and disappear.

"During this trial, you'll hear no solid evidence against my client relating to the death of any of the victims. You'll come to know the truth: that Emily Keller happened to make a few unwise decisions the night of the tragic incident, but those unwise choices she made do not make her guilty for the deaths of Steven, Brandi, Kathryn, and Sophie Thomas." As Valerie spoke, Emily could feel all eyes from the courtroom staring at her, probably already deciding how many years she'd spend rotting in prison. She thought back to Brandi's mother's angry face. She swallowed hard, too scared to turn her head and see the anger on her face again. Was she staring at Emily? Was she crying?

"Who here hasn't been a teenager and made a thoughtless, selfish decision?" Valerie walked closer and began tapping her hot pink nails against the wooden jury box, causing a few distracted jurors to shift their eyes over toward her nails rather than her face. *Take your fingers off the jury box*, Emily thought, embarrassed by her lawyer's demeanor.

"I deem to say there isn't a juror or a person in this room who hasn't regretted a choice they made during their teen years. Unfortunately for Emily, the imprudent choice she made the evening of November 9, 2018, happened to be the same date and location of the deaths of the

Thomas family." Valerie lifted a hand up, scratching at her chin with one of her long nails before placing it back down on the jury box to rest. "Had Emily not made this choice, would the family still be alive? Had Emily not been at the Thomases' house that evening, would they still be alive? No, the Thomas family would have died whether Emily had been there that evening or not. I intend to prove this to you throughout this trial. Because of this, I ask you to keep an open mind, listen to *all* the evidence, and return a verdict of not guilty. Thank you."

Valerie gave the jury a warm smile and walked back to her seat next to Emily, who still had her head down low, trying not to cry. She rubbed at her elbows and thought about what Valerie had said. Would the Thomases still be alive if she hadn't been there? Yes. They probably would be. If she hadn't babysat, they probably still *would* be alive. It took everything in her not to stand up on her chair and scream to the room, *It's all my fault! Lock me up!* Valerie and the jury had no idea just how bad of a person she was.

"The prosecution may call their first witness," Judge Wilson announced. The doors behind Emily swung open and she could hear the police officer's footsteps approaching the bench.

6

PAST: SEPTEMBER 4, 2018

—◦◦◦◦◦◦—

"**H**ow was the first day?" Nate asked as they stepped off the bus.

Emily had no exciting news besides meeting Hannah in the bathroom, but she didn't want to tell Nate about it. Not yet. She was in no mood for advice. *Are you sure you should be staying up this late before your big test? Did you finish your homework? Have you eaten enough today? Is hanging out with Hannah a good idea? Is she going to be a good influence on you?* She didn't want Nate spoiling her high. She wanted to keep Hannah to herself for now.

"Fine," she murmured as she kicked a rock toward Nate.

"Meet any new people?" Nate found a bigger rock and kicked it toward her.

"What'd you think of the AP Bio teacher? You think he'll be hard?" Emily tried to shift the conversation away from herself.

"Nah, he's an idiot," Nate said as he kicked the rock back toward her, a wordless routine they had during their walks. Someone speaks. *Kick.* Someone answers. *Kick.*

"You always think all the teachers are idiots," Emily teased as she stumbled over to retrieve the rock he kicked too far.

"'Cause they are." Nate pushed past her to get the rock.

"Must be nice to feel smarter than the teachers." She glanced up as they approached their trailer. "Oh, I promised Miss Jelly I'd stop by for some cake. Wanna join? Mom said she's working late so we can grab dinner there later."

"Nah, I wanna review all of my syllabi and chill out." He pointed toward his backpack. "Next time?"

"Okay, nerd." Emily gave him a playful punch on the arm as he veered toward their trailer, walking past their yard and stepping over the grave sites of their cat, Mr. Potato Head, and Pancake, their buried plant.

When Emily was about nine or ten, her mom brought back a Guaiacum officinale, or "tree of life," from a vacation in Jamaica. The Guaiacum officinale is an endangered plant native to the Caribbean, known for its combination of strength, toughness, and density.

Debbie had gone on the trip with her boyfriend at the time and left Nate and Emily for a week with Miss Jelly. During the trip, Debbie had gotten in a fight with her boyfriend, and she returned home with a mysterious black eye and was single again.

She must've brought the plant back to make up for ditching us for a deadbeat boyfriend and a black eye, Emily had thought. Nate and Emily had stared at the newborn tree, which looked a little pathetic like it was about to drop down and die, just like their cat, Mr. Potato Head.

That night Emily had woken up every hour or so and gazed out the window at Pancake to make sure it was doing okay. The next morning, she'd secretly stuffed some of her Captain Crunch bits into her pocket and crammed them in the dry dirt around Pancake. She'd even put blankets out by the tree and spent all morning and afternoon with it. She'd watered it and got out one of her doll's combs, pretending to brush its leaves.

But Pancake ended up only surviving for a few days.

"I guess it just wasn't able to handle the climate here," Debbie told them as Emily wept. She didn't know why she had been so distraught when it died, even more so than when Mr. Potato Head had died. For some reason it was just so tragic that this poor little tree was taken from its home and forced into their backyard where they couldn't care for it or provide it with what it needed. If Pancake was living happily in Jamaica, why would her mom take it away?

She entered Miss Jelly's kitchen and smelled something cooking on the stove. It made her stomach growl for a home-cooked meal. Whenever Emily went into Miss Jelly's home, it brought her a sense of peace. Peace . . . and hunger.

"Hi, hon, how was the first day?" Miss Jelly asked as she diced an onion on a large, wooden cutting board. Emily placed her backpack down and grabbed a seat at the kitchen table, which had the perfect view of the TV. *General Hospital* was just ending, which had been one of Emily's favorite shows to watch at Miss Jelly's when she was growing up. She gave a lopsided grin thinking back to lounging on Miss Jelly's sofa with a big bowl of popcorn on her lap while actors on the show fought over who was the father of whose baby. Life was good then. It was always comforting to see there were other people's lives crazier than hers, even if theirs were make-believe.

"It was okay. Nothing eventful happened," she responded, debating if she should tell Miss Jelly about her new potential friend. She unzipped her backpack and retrieved all the first-day-of-school forms.

"Well, get yourself comfortable and have some cake and a big glass of milk."

Emily grinned as she glanced at the table setting and saw a glass of milk and plate of cake already sitting there waiting for her. *I needed this more than I thought.*

She finished up the forms right as *Dateline* was ending on TV. The topic was women who murder their husbands.

"So, who do you think did it?" Miss Jelly asked as she stirred something sticky in a bowl. The two of them always loved a good *Dateline* murder mystery; it was so fun to figure out if the person was guilty or not.

"Obviously the wife. Who else?" She chuckled as she zipped up her backpack, thanking Miss Jelly for the cake and rising from her seat.

"Why don't you and Nate stay for some supper, hon? I've got all this beef stew and no one to feed it to."

Emily's stomach grumbled, begging her to stay. "We can't today, Miss Jelly," she admitted, regretfully. "We promised my mom we'd stop by C & M and have some dinner there tonight to fill her in on our first day."

"Okay, hon, you stay safe walkin' home from there tonight once it gets dark out, ya hear?" she warned.

"Of course, Miss Jelly. Thanks again!" Emily gave her a hug and headed back to her trailer to drag Nate from his chill time and head to the bar for dinner.

As Nate and Emily stepped into C & M, Emily breathed in the smell of stale beer, Old Bay Seasoning, and fried food: the smell of home. When Emily had been little, she thought it was the coolest that her mom worked there. She waited on tables, bartended, and sometimes even had to run in the back to flip burgers if the cook was taking a smoke break. Her brother and she would sit at a table in the back, do their homework, and dine on unlimited free sodas and french fries. The cook would blast gangster rap and they'd sing along, feeling like they were living the dream. But now that she was sixteen, she was beginning to see it was a little sad. Didn't her mom aspire to work somewhere other than this bar?

"Well, looky who the cat dragged in!" Charlie, a handyman who lived down the street, shouted when he saw them come in.

They shuffled over and took a seat at the bar next to him. Emily scanned the room for familiar faces. It was still the exact same scene it'd been ten years before with the exact same regulars. Three of the tables were filled and five regulars sat at the bar. It was dollar crab night and one family at the table closest to them had about a dozen small crabs piled in front of them, along with several Natty Bo beer cans. Emily rolled her eyes at the bright red MAGA hats on top of the parents' heads.

"How's that oven working these days?" Charlie asked as he took a sip of his beer. Charlie had fixed their oven and every other appliance in their house when it broke, which usually happened at least once a month. Emily had no idea how her mom paid him to do those odd jobs, and quite frankly, she never wanted to know. She glanced over at him and could see why her mom probably found him attractive. Charlie was handsome in a rugged, repair person sort of way. He always had stubble on his face like he'd forgotten to shave, and his hands looked like they had permanent oil stains on them. But he had these eyes that made Emily give him a double take when she first looked at him. They reminded Emily of the blue flames on her gas stove. Eyes that pretty didn't seem like they belonged on a man so worn.

"It's workin' great, thanks, Charlie," Nate responded. Charlie opened his mouth to ask another question when the swinging door to the kitchen opened and Debbie stepped out carrying a tray of fried food. She handed the greasy plates to two men wearing Orioles T-shirts at the end of the bar. They were intently watching the Orioles lose to the Mariners on the screen above the vodka bottles. Emily watched as Debbie grabbed a whiskey bottle from behind her and filled up each of their empty glasses. The two men nodded to her and clinked their glasses together in a toast. Emily couldn't help but wish that Debbie was as stellar a mom as she was a waitress.

Debbie was like the mayor of Crabs & More and was good at what she did; customers loved her. But Debbie always drank while she worked. *It's part of the job, kiddo,* she'd told Emily once. By the time she got home each night, she was too drunk to spend her energy on Emily and Nate and too hungover every morning to give them any attention. It was a vicious cycle.

Her mom gave Emily a wink when she spotted Nate and her sitting with Charlie. Emily noticed that she had dark circles under her heavily made-up eyes. Her caramel hair had a couple grays straying from the sides and she had one of Emily's bobby pins holding up some of the fly-aways.

For being forty, she looked worn and older than she actually was. *Perhaps it's the cigarettes that've aged her. Or the booze. Perhaps both,* Emily had wondered when she'd looked through photos of her parents from before she was born. Debbie had really been a stunning woman. She had Nate's hazel eyes and darker complexion, while Emily had her dad's darker eyes and paler skin.

Debbie leaned against the bar in front of her children, resting her face on her hands as her elbows stuck to the bar top.

"So . . . how was it?" she asked excitedly.

"Fine," Nate and Emily responded in unison.

"Is Steph in any of your classes?" Debbie asked, looking toward Emily.

"No, she doesn't take AP," Emily blurted out quickly, wishing her mom wouldn't ask about Steph. She never mentioned that Steph and she had a falling out over the summer. "She—"

"Ahem . . . waitress!" the family in the MAGA hats called Debbie over.

Debbie rolled her eyes and walked over to their table, handing a check to them. A few minutes later, they shuffled out the door with their whiny kids screaming behind them. Debbie grabbed the money from the table and came back with a wad of cash in her hand.

"Ten percent tip, those fuckers," she cursed. "You'd seriously think that after eating here almost every single week and getting my exemplary service they'd at least tip a little better. The good news is they didn't finish."

She scrounged up four of the small crabs from their table and three mozzarella sticks, placing them on the brown paper in front of Nate and Emily.

"Dinner is served, my dears."

Nate popped one of the cold mozzarella sticks in his mouth as Emily snapped a claw off one of the crabs.

"Thanks, Mom." Nate bit into another mozzarella stick and then wiped his hands on the wet wipe in front of him.

"We haven't had crabs for a couple of months. Usually, the deadbeat customers here take these pathetic little crabs home with them to eat for breakfast," Emily said as she scooped out some crab meat with her finger.

"They're tasty for breakfast. I always like mine microwaved a little though, I can't eat them cold. Oh look, you got a Sally." Charlie pointed down at the female crab's bell shape on its belly.

"Well, I just lost my appetite," Emily muttered in disgust as she put down the crab. "I can only do the Jimmys."

Just then, her mom marched out of the kitchen with a tray of hot, greasy fries and two cups of spicy Maryland crab soup. Emily took a spoonful of the crab soup, trying to scrounge up a morsel of crabmeat from the bottom of the cup and slurped it into her mouth with satisfaction. The salty, Old Bay broth burned as it went down her throat and she dug her spoon in again to see if she was lucky enough to score two bits of crab meat.

"Aren't you sick of eating bar food all the time?" Miss Jelly always asked them when they headed there for dinner. "You can always eat homemade dinner at my house." But Nate and she never got sick of it. They loved it.

As they finished dinner, Emily scrolled through her Instagram feed while Nate and Charlie debated why Trump didn't go to John McCain's funeral on Sunday. Nate was anti-Trump. Charlie was pro-Trump. And even though Nate was much younger than Charlie, he could hold his own in a debate. Emily drowned out the political talk next to her and scrolled through her phone. She had forty-two likes from her morning post and was elated to see Hannah was one of them. She clicked on Hannah's profile and saw a new photo of her with a vape pen in her hand as she leaned against a blue truck. She appeared to be staring off in the distance and a senior from their school was sitting in the driver's seat, smiling at her. Emily thought she recognized the guy from the photo since she'd seen him play lacrosse. She was fairly sure his name was Topper. She wondered if they were dating. She pressed the heart button, hoping Hannah would see she liked the photo.

How can I get her to notice me? she wondered as she looked around the bar. As she caught sight of Charlie and Nate talking, she got an idea. She angled her phone down at the crabs in front of Nate, making sure to get Charlie's beer in the photo and snapped a picture discreetly. She added a filter to make it look retro and captioned it, "Having a cold one and some crabs with the best crew around," and then she posted it. It wouldn't be her fault if anyone concluded that she was the one drinking the beer. Immediately, four hearts danced across her screen. She smiled and put down her phone. She couldn't wait to read all the comments she'd get on it later.

7

TRIAL DAY 1: JANUARY 7, 2019

———⊶◦◦◦⊷———

Gripping the arms of her chair, Emily watched as the middle-
aged police officer with a buzzed haircut approached the witness
stand and was sworn in. Her stomach turned like sour milk when she
imagined what he was going to say. She couldn't bear to hear anything
about the morning the Thomases were discovered. She twisted her
head and glanced toward Nate, feeling like she was going to have a
panic attack. His eyes focused on her and he mouthed, *Are you okay?* She
lowered her eyes, turning back around.

There was nothing she could say back to him. Nothing she could
do. Nowhere she could go. She shifted her focus back to Mindy, who
was already questioning the officer.

"Officer Morgan, what were you doing the night of November
9, 2018, and early morning of November 10, 2018?" Mindy asked,
approaching the witness stand.

Emily tried to concentrate on the questioning, but her brain was
trying to imagine anything other than what he was about to say.

"I was working a night shift patrolling the Crossland areas from eleven p.m. to eleven a.m. I had a petty theft at the local Walmart and had a domestic disturbance call, but other than that, it was a slow night. When I was about to get off my shift, I got a call for a wellness check on the Thomases' house from a neighbor. They were concerned because they had a playdate with the kids that morning and no one was answering the door."

Emily squinted at the gold badge on the officer's chest, skimming her eyes over to the nameplate adjacent to it: M.R. Morgan. She wondered if that meant Mr. Morgan or if his initials were M.R. It made more sense that they were initials, but she bet people called him Mr. Morgan all the time by mistake. She deliberated what his name could be. *Michael Ryan? Matthew Ronald? Miles Andrew?*

Closing her eyes, she envisioned the girls on their playdate that morning. A trip to the aquarium perhaps? Sophie had loved dolphins. Emily remembered her talking about them incessantly at bedtime. Or perhaps a trip to the playground? Emily grimaced at the thought of the girls playing on the playground across the street. The same playground that she . . .

"And what happened when you went to that wellness check, officer?" Mindy asked, tilting her head back.

"No one was answering the door, so I eventually entered the premises to check out the scene. Immediately, I could smell a gas odor so I called for the gas company and an ambulance and fire truck to come for backup. Right then and there, I knew it was going to be a bad outcome. I saw their little dog lying in the dog bed . . ." Officer Morgan moved his palms together, indicating the dog's small size. "And it didn't wake up to bark at me. Looked like she was sleeping. So, I walked over and gave the dog bed a little kick and she still didn't wake. I peeked around the kitchen and it looked like the upper right burner of the stove was still slightly on, so I turned it off. That must've been where the smell was coming from."

Emily shuddered, thinking of Trixie, dead in her bed. *I'm sorry old girl,* she thought as a lump began to form in her throat.

"And, Officer, what was the state the kitchen was in? Did it look like someone had been cooking earlier in the night?" Mindy placed her hands on her hips.

"There was a half full pot of mac and cheese on the lower right burner with a spoon still in it. That must have been what was cooking on the open burner."

Emily envisioned that damn pot of mac and cheese. The thought of eating the cheesy noodles ever again made her want to vomit.

"And what did you do after you turned off the burner, Officer?"

Officer Morgan frowned and sat up straighter before he spoke. "I grabbed a clean-looking dishrag from the kitchen table and put it over my mouth and nose, so I didn't breathe in too much of the residual carbon monoxide. I walked through the hallway and assessed the rest of the main level, but it looked like there was no one down there so I headed upstairs.

The first bedroom I went in was Thomases' room. I could see the couple lying in their bed. I called, 'Hello?' loudly and no one answered so I walked over closely, first to the man, and examined him. I could see his lips were slightly blue and so I checked for a pulse. None. I then did the same to the woman and she also had no pulse. I headed over to the next bedroom and saw an empty twin bed. In the third bedroom, I discovered two little girls sharing one twin bed under the same covers. I checked both for pulses, and they were both deceased as well." He crossed his hands in front of him, lowering his eyes to the ground.

Emily shut her eyes tightly, refusing to process what the officer had said. She didn't want to imagine Katie and Sophie not alive anymore. She couldn't.

"Emawee. Can we have some Flintstone vitamins before bed? Mommy always gives a vitamin to me," Sophie whispered in her ear.

Emily began to rock back and forth, trying to think of anything other than those two precious little girls with no pulse. The people sitting behind her probably thought she looked like a nutcase, but she didn't care. She suddenly felt Valerie's hand reach over and grab her back, forcing her rocking to slow down. She paused and glanced up at her lawyer, who was still facing the front of the room nonchalantly as if her client was not absolutely losing it next to her.

Just as Valerie lifted her hand off Emily's back, the sound of Brandi's mother wailing loudly filled the courtroom. Emily glanced over at the woman and saw she'd slid off her seat. She'd somehow snaked her body like a pretzel on the floor, her arms twisted around her head in a position that Emily didn't know was humanly possible. It made Emily want to join her. *I can't break down and cry, Valerie told me not to,* she told herself as she pressed her finger into her wounded knee and tried to focus on the stinging pain rather than the girls. She refocused her attention back to Mindy, trying her best to keep calm.

"And what did you think killed this family of four so tragically, Officer Morgan?" Mindy asked as she leaned toward him with a concerned look on her face.

"I knew it had to have been the gas stovetop that'd been left on. The whole place reeked of it."

"And why do you think it was left on, Officer?" Mindy asked as she reached toward him, almost touching his arm.

"Objection, Your Honor. The prosecution is asking the officer to speculate," Valerie chimed in.

"Overruled, Attorney Anderson. I'd like to hear the officer's inferences based on the fact that he observed the scene in the kitchen himself," Judge Wilson instructed.

Mindy continued. "Why do you think the stovetop was left on, Officer?"

"Whoever made that mac and cheese must have not turned the burner all the way off when they finished cooking."

"And would you agree, Officer Morgan, that because that person left the gas burner open, that carbon monoxide must have filled up the house, eventually killing not only Mr. and Mrs. Thomas, but also their two little girls and their dog?"

"Yes, I would agree." Officer Morgan shook his head slightly and bowed his head down low.

"No further questions, Your Honor," Mindy said, giving the witness stand a quick tap with her hand.

"Does the defense have any questions?" Judge Wilson asked, glancing in Emily's direction.

As Valerie opened up her questioning, Emily shifted uncomfortably in her seat. She couldn't imagine what it must've been like to find that entire family dead in their beds. They'd gone to sleep and never woken up. It was what nightmares were made of. As the visions of Katie's and Sophie's blue lips and pale skin flashed before her eyes, she could hear the officer telling Valerie that he'd been on the force for eighteen years, but he seemed to be speaking in slow motion. He'd been an officer longer than Emily had been alive. She wondered if he had any daughters. If he was a father.

"And so, do you agree," Valerie said, "that as your job title is police officer, you're not the most qualified person to decide what killed the Thomas family? That there may be more qualified professionals, such as detectives, to make such inferences?"

"Well, I guess, yes, a detective is going to have more time to examine the scene. I was just the initial officer to respond to the call, ma'am." Emily watched as Officer Morgan crossed his arms over his chest and furrowed his brow.

"Thank you, no further questions, Your Honor." Valerie gave him a warm smile and turned toward Emily to take her seat. Emily grimaced, trying not to seem bothered at the lack of questions her lawyer was asking the officer. *I guess I'm getting what I paid for, which is nothing*, she thought. *Maybe I deserve to go to jail.*

"Does the prosecutor have any further questions for the witness?" Judge Wilson asked

"No further questions, Your Honor," Mindy responded, not glancing up from her notes.

"The witness is excused," Judge Wilson declared. Officer Morgan stepped down from the witness stand and slowly exited the courtroom.

Emily noticed Valerie was writing something on the yellow notepad in front of her. When she finished, she slid it slowly in Emily's direction. Emily peered at it and read, "Stop picking at your fingers and enough with the rocking." Emily paused and glanced down at her hands, not recognizing she'd been tearing at her cuticles, and they were starting to bleed. She quickly put both of her hands under her legs and stared down at her knees again. The Valium had her thoughts mushed together. *Is this a dream?* she wondered.

"The prosecution may call the next witness."

"The people call Michael Stevenson to the stand," Mindy announced. All eyes turned as the doors opened in the back of the gallery.

No, not a dream, a nightmare, she decided as she turned to watch Michael Stevenson enter the room.

8

PAST: OCTOBER 3, 2018

———∘◦◇◦∘———

"You need anything else?" Mrs. Walters, the school librarian, asked as she scanned Emily's books and placed them on the counter in front of her. Even though she wasn't her teacher, Mrs. Walters was always checking in on Emily. Always asking what she was working on next and offering to read her essays, making comments in all the margins. She was one of Emily's favorite people.

"Just these today, thanks," Emily said as she grabbed her textbooks on US History and stuffed them into her backpack. She only had a few minutes before biology started and she couldn't miss any second of it since she'd gotten a B on last week's test.

"Any more papers for me to read?" Mrs. Walters' eyes beamed up at her. Emily blushed thinking back to what Mrs. Walters wrote on her final paper last year after she'd received an A+ on it. *You presented your ideas and thoughts really well. You have a talent, Emily. I encourage you to keep writing.* Emily had chosen to write her paper on the reasons for the prevalence of poverty among women. Mrs. Walters had loved it so much, she'd submitted it to a national contest. Although Emily hadn't won, Mrs. Walters was always asking her what she was writing next. Always encouraging her to write more.

"I promise I'll bring you whatever I write next," Emily assured her. As she veered out of the library, she caught sight of someone through the window. She squinted to see Hannah Patterson in the courtyard. She was sitting in a shadow between two brick walls so most people probably wouldn't notice her, but Emily could spot that diamond nose stud from anywhere.

Emily watched as Hannah put a vape pen to her mouth, and then closed her eyes as if she hadn't a care in the world. Emily glanced around her to see if anyone else had noticed her. The library was as empty as the toilet paper section in a grocery store before a snowstorm. She was about to quietly creep out and head into the courtyard toward Hannah when she saw Mrs. Walters step out of a side door and beat her to it.

She watched as Hannah stuffed the pen into her pocket and looked up at Mrs. Walters, her hands crossed in front of her chest as she spoke. *She's definitely getting in trouble,* Emily thought. She hurriedly stepped outside toward the women, loudly opening a candy wrapper while she approached them. They both looked up toward her and stopped talking.

"Hey, Hannah, sorry I'm late for our study session," she lied as she held out her backpack and pulled the US History textbook from it. "You ready to get started?"

Mrs. Walters' eyes lit up in surprise as Emily approached them. "You were going to study with her out here?" she asked.

"Oh, hey, Amelia, what's up?" Hannah looked relieved to see her.

"Emily," she corrected her, embarrassed that this was the second time Hannah had gotten her name wrong, and she'd done it in front of Mrs. Walters. *Maybe all the vaping is messing with her memory,* Emily thought, hoping that was the case and not that Emily wasn't memorable.

"I was just asking Miss Patterson what she's doing out here instead of being in class," Mrs. Walters said, looking at Emily with a stern look on her face she'd never seen before. "You say you're studying?"

"Yes." Emily chuckled. "I'm sorry I'm late, that's my fault." She could see Mrs. Walters raise her eyebrows in surprise and then relax her face. Emily was her soft spot.

"Well, it seems you're so late, the two of you are now missing your next class." Mrs. Walters glanced over at Hannah, whose eyes were now small slits of red.

"Thanks, good point, Mrs. Walters. You know what, Hannah? We better get to class," Emily said, reaching for her arm and pulling her up. "I'm sorry about this. It really is all my fault."

"Don't forget I still want to speak with you about the debate team," Mrs. Walters hollered at Emily as the two of them walked back through the library and into the hallway.

"I can't believe you did that for me!" Hannah whispered as she squeezed Emily's arm tightly. "Mrs. Walters must really love you since she didn't bust me."

Hannah's touch warmed Emily's face. *I need this friendship,* she thought as she imagined the two of them hanging out after school or shopping at the mall. They could do all the things she and Steph used to do together.

"I guess she just doesn't hate me as much as her other students," she lied as Hannah pulled her into the bathroom. She thought about her grade dropping in biology for skipping class, but the opportunity to hang out with Hannah couldn't be missed. Hannah was her ticket to friendship and popularity.

And Hannah made her feel good about herself—and she needed to feel good about herself for once.

"Here." Hannah reached into her pocket and handed her pen over before Emily could respond. "A thank you for getting me out of trouble."

Emily took the pen from her and sniffed it. She'd tried her mom's cigarettes before, so she thought she knew how to inhale, but didn't want to look stupid. She put the pen up to her mouth, took her best inhale, and handed it back to Hannah, feeling her lungs burn with aromatic skunk.

"You used one of these before?" Hannah asked as she put it to her lips and breathed in again.

"Nah, not one of these," Emily responded, not wanting Hannah to think she was a goody two-shoes.

"It's hash oil. My cousin has a medical marijuana card, so he gets me all the good, safe stuff."

"Oh cool." Emily pretended like she knew what hash oil was.

Hannah sucked at the pen some more as Emily sat down next to her, placing her bag down on the tile. Hannah handed her back the pen.

"It's nice to have a little escape once in a while," Hannah admitted, leaning her head back against the painted brick wall of the bathroom. "I'm so sick of feeling alone all the time. Do you ever feel that way? Like no one in the world understands you?"

Emily raised her eyebrows, thinking back to the first day of school when Hannah had been crying in the bathroom. She glanced over at her. "I know exactly how you feel," she said honestly. She couldn't comprehend how Hannah, someone who seemed so put together and popular, could feel the same way as she did. And for some strange reason, the fact that there was someone sitting next to her who also felt this way made Emily feel less alone.

"I usually drink a couple beers to take the edge off. It makes me feel better," she lied, wanting to impress her new friend. She didn't really like the idea of substances after what they'd done to her mom. But being with Hannah . . . doing this right now . . . it actually did make her feel better.

"Oh right, I saw your Insta-post the other week, beers and crabs, right?" Hannah asked.

Emily tried not to show her delight that Hannah had remembered her Instagram post.

"Yeah, I was just having some beers and crabs with friends, no big deal," she lied again, trying to act the part.

"Right on," Hannah exclaimed. "I love crabs with a good Blue Moon. You ever try one of those?"

Emily hadn't but knew a lot of beer brands from watching her mom serve them at the bar. "Of course, it's the best," she agreed.

"We should totally do that this weekend," Hannah suddenly decided, sitting upright, and staring at Emily. "Maybe you could take me to that thrift store then we could get some crabs and beer? Are your parents cool?"

"Sure, that'd be awesome!" Emily responded, probably too quickly. "My mom is chill; she works all weekend so we can total hang at my place." She already started to fret over how she could possibly come up with beer and crabs at her house with no money and no fake ID. *I could always dip into my savings stowed away under my bed from tutoring some of the neighborhood kids. I could make it work.* Hannah took her phone out of her pocket, pressed in her password, and handed it to Emily.

"Put in your number," she directed her.

With shaky hands, Emily typed in her phone number. Hannah took her phone back and punched on the screen with the pads of her fingers. Her nails were purple acrylic with sharp points at the ends, and it baffled Emily how she could type so fast. A second later, Emily's phone buzzed and she glanced at the screen. An unknown number had texted her, "What up bitch." She glanced over at Hannah and smiled.

"Now you have mine too." Hannah grinned. She stood up, put the pen back in her jeans pocket, threw her backpack around her shoulder, and sashayed out of the bathroom without saying goodbye. Emily stared at the closed door and then glanced down at her phone again, blinking her eyes repeatedly to assess what'd just happened.

She peered up to the sky and whispered, "Thank you, God."

9

TRIAL DAY 1: JANUARY 7, 2019

———◦∞◇∞◦———

The bailiff led an elderly-looking man with thick glasses and a lousy combover to the witness stand. He looked like Christopher Lloyd from *Back to the Future*; one of Nate's favorite movies. Emily thought back to the days when Nate used to make her watch that movie day after day—he'd try to reenact the time travel scenes with his little match box car on their coffee table. She wished she could time travel back to being that little again. She wished she could time travel back to before she ever met Hannah.

As the man was sworn in and took his seat, Emily peered down at her cuticles and quickly pulled a little skin from her thumb, watching it bleed. She glanced up as Mindy stood to begin her questioning, holding a notebook firmly in her hand.

"Hello, Mr. Stevenson. May I ask you what your profession is and what your job entails?" she asked.

"I'm a medical examiner," he stated. "I examine bodies during an autopsy in order to determine the cause of death." Emily remembered

Valerie saying something about him being the top examiner in the state, but he looked more like a crazy scientist to her.

Oh God, this is going to be worse than the last witness, Emily thought to herself as her quivering hand pulled on a cuticle and she felt the skin rip away.

"And how long have you been in this career?"

"About thirty-five years."

Mindy glanced down at her notebook. "And in those thirty-five years, about how many dead bodies have you examined?"

"Geez Louise, I don't know. Maybe ten bodies a week? You do the math . . . what is that . . . fifteen thousand?"

"That's certainly a lot of bodies. You obviously are very experienced. Of those fifteen thousand or so bodies, about how many of the deaths were affected by carbon monoxide poisoning?"

Mr. Stevenson looked up at the ceiling, deep in thought. "Maybe about thirty or so? It isn't so common around these parts. Or any parts, really. Usually, bodies we see that've been affected by carbon monoxide poisoning have been burned first from a fire. Although we do get some suicides using motor vehicle exhaust," he added.

Emily glanced over at the jury as he spoke. Some were on the edge of their seats, alert and curious. Others were slumped over, looking revolted by the topic of dead bodies.

"Thank you, Mr. Stevenson. So just to be clear here, did you examine the bodies of Steven, Brandi, Sophie, and Kathryn Thomas on November 10, 2018?"

"Yes, I did," he said before clearing his throat.

"And what did you find after examining all of the bodies?" Mindy asked as she glanced down at the notebook in her hand.

Emily held her breath, trying her best not to imagine the dead bodies of the Thomas family. She'd never seen a dead body besides her cat, Mr. Potato Head. But he'd just looked like he was sleeping when he died. She closed her eyes and imagined playing with Mr.

Potato Head on a sunny morning as she drowned out the medical examiner's voice. "You're a good boy," she whispered as she petted his orange-and-brown striped fur.

He purred and rested his soft face on her lap. Her mom was home and safe, resting in bed. Nate was doing homework in their room. Dinner was in the oven. Everyone was alive.

Everyone was okay. *Good kitty.*

"During the autopsies, the first thing I noticed on each body was the ruddy appearance of the face. Carbon monoxide poisoning is notable because embalmed bodies are normally bluish and pale, whereas deceased carbon-monoxide poisoned bodies may appear unusually lifelike in coloration." He turned toward the jury as he matter-of-factly explained this, and Emily watched as the jurors' eyes filled with horror, disgust, and dread. "All four of the Thomas family members appeared to have the lifelike coloration like I've seen before in cadavers. I then tested the ratio of carboxyhemoglobin to hemoglobin molecules in each body. In an average person it's around 5 percent. The Thomases' values ranged from 30 to 90 percent, which indicates that the cause of death was most definitely carbon monoxide poisoning."

"Thank you, Mr. Stevenson. No further questions," Mindy said, closing her notebook and heading back to her seat.

"Does the defense have any questions?" Judge Wilson announced.

"Not at this time, Your Honor," Valerie responded.

Startled, Emily turned her head slowly toward Valerie, angered she wasn't going to ask him any questions. *She should at least try!* Emily screamed in her head. Valerie gave her a side eye and Emily closed her mouth and looked back to her feet, remembering that she just broke her rule of appearing calm to the jury.

"Then if that's the case, we'll take an hour recess for lunch," Judge Wilson announced to the courtroom.

As people in the room filed out, Valerie whispered in Emily's ear, "You better stop with the facial expressions. I better not see this happening when all your little teenage friends get up there to testify against you."

Emily took a giant gulp and let what she said sink in. She'd tried so hard not to think about who'd be testifying during the trial. She closed her eyes, imagining all the dreadful things they'd say about her.

10

PAST: OCTOBER 6, 2018

———◦◦◇◦◦———

"Just stay in there and go to sleep!" Emily instructed her mom, closing the bedroom door softly behind her. Her mom had worked a day shift and had come home so plastered from enjoying the morning mimosa special, she couldn't even speak clearly. Emily had been debating about calling it off with Hannah, but figured since her mom was so drunk, she'd be dead to the world until the morning.

Emily had spent two hours vigorously cleaning the house inside and out. Masking the stale smell of her mother's cigarettes, she'd put a scented plug-in in every socket she could find. The house was as ready as it could be. She didn't have crabs, but the fridge was stocked with her mom's beer, and she was hoping that would be good enough for Hannah.

Waiting outside on a fold-out chair, she scrolled through Instagram on her phone, trying to appear nonchalant, as Hannah pulled up. She secretly hoped that maybe they could stay outside so she could avoid any embarrassment of Hannah seeing her home life but knew that was probably wishful thinking. Hannah waved toward Emily as she parked her burgundy Kia sedan in front of the trailer.

"Totally retro," Hannah exclaimed as she stepped out of her car and slammed the door behind her. She was wearing a loose tie-dye shirt, jeans, and a bandana tied around her head like a hippie. "I love that you live here. I've always wanted to look around this trailer park whenever I've driven past it." She leaned against the front of the trailer, held out a peace sign, and snapped a selfie. "This'll be a perfect vibe photo to post later." She glanced around as if she were a kid visiting an amusement park.

Emily felt her face turn beet red as she tried to act cool. "Yeah, it totally sucks living here." She closed her eyes, not sure if that was the right thing to say or not.

"No, it's so gnarly! I love seeing how other people live," Hannah exclaimed. She marched past Emily and opened their creaky front door without asking if she could go inside. Before Emily could run ahead of her to let her in, she heard her squeal.

"Flowered wallpaper and brown carpet!" she hollered as if she'd won a prize at the fair. "It's like stepping into a seventies movie!" She peered around the family room and kitchen as her eyes opened widely in disbelief.

Emily crossed her arms, surprised that she was starting to feel protective about the home that Nate and she grew up in. When Nate and she were younger, they used to love that flowered wallpaper. Once when they were about twelve, they'd found Debbie's old Polaroid camera in a box of things in her closet. They'd spent the afternoon taking headshots of themselves in front of the wallpaper because it made for the perfect modeling backdrop. *Was it possible to hate and love something all at once?* she wondered.

"Yeah, we're only here temporarily until we find a bigger house," she lied. "We just haven't found one that fits all of our criteria yet." That wasn't a total lie. She *had* been looking on Redfin almost every day at houses in the area for sale. The only catch was, they had no actual money to move anywhere else, but Hannah didn't have to know that part.

"No, I love it!" Hannah exclaimed. "It's such a comfortable feel. Nice and homey." She plopped herself on the couch and put her feet up on their stained coffee table.

"So, should we go check out that thrift store?" Emily suggested, hoping to get her out of the place as soon as possible. She knew her mom wouldn't wake up but didn't want to risk anything.

"Can we just chill here?" Hannah asked. "I'm in the mood to just hang. Do you have any beer?"

Having prepared for this question, Emily nodded and headed to the fridge. Her mom was so intoxicated that even if Emily drank the whole case of beer, she wouldn't notice. She grabbed two Natty Lights: her mom's beer of choice. She tossed Hannah a beer from across the room and they clinked the cans open in unison, giggling. Nate and Emily had shared a beer occasionally with crabs when her mom was tipsy enough to let them, but she'd never sat down and drank a whole beer by herself. But plenty of people her age did it all the time, right?

"Cool, thanks! You have any cards?"

"I think so." Emily walked into the kitchen to search through their junk drawer, filled with everything imaginable from batteries to hand sanitizer. She found a pack of unopened cards shoved way back in the drawer that had Niagara Falls photos printed on the front. Miss Jelly had brought them back for Nate and her when she went there five years ago.

"Let's play drinking War," Hannah exclaimed to Emily with a gleam in her eye. "Every time I win a hand, you take a sip and every time you win a hand, I take a sip."

"Okay," Emily said hesitantly as she tossed Hannah the card pack so she could shuffle. Emily didn't want her to know that she'd never learned how to shuffle. *That's what happens when your childhood is missing family game nights; no one teaches you to shuffle,* she thought.

Hannah shuffled the cards and passed them out. As they started to play, Emily came to realize that Hannah's rules required them to drink pretty much after every other card was dealt. When they finished their first beer, Hannah headed into the kitchen and grabbed them two more. Emily was starting to feel buzzed, not even caring that Hannah could see how scarcely her fridge was stocked. Hannah must have been buzzed too because she didn't make one of her observant comments about it like she had about the rest of Emily's house.

"Where's your bathroom? I gotta pee," Hannah said, placing a card down on the stack.

Emily pointed across the kitchen and watched as Hannah got up and walked over to it, closing the door behind her. She sat back and gave a sigh. It was going okay.

Everything was going okay.

"Emily?" a slurred voice came from the hallway. Emily's eyes widened in horror as she saw her mom step into the hallway and toward the family room wearing only a T-shirt and underwear.

"Mom, go back to bed," Emily whispered, standing up quickly and ushering her mom back to her bed.

"My bedsss isss wet," her mom slurred as Emily shuffled her toward her bed, seeing a big urine stain where she'd been laying. Emily's face flushed and her eyes watered. *Not today, Mom. Not today.*

"Just lie down on top of the comforter and I'll clean it up later. Okay?" she asked as she guided her mom carefully back on top of the bed.

"Emily?" Hannah's voice called from the hallway.

"Be right there!" Emily shouted. "Don't leave this room again!" she whispered to her mom. Her mom lay down, eyes already closed, falling asleep instantly. Just as Emily turned to head back to the family room, Hannah's head poked in from the doorway.

"Is . . . everything okay?" Hannah asked, glancing down toward her mom and then at the big wet stain on the bed as Emily tried to cover it up with the comforter.

Emily rushed toward the door and closed it quickly behind her, her face feeling like it may melt off from embarrassment.

"Fine, everything's fine. My mom's just . . . not feeling well."

She walked back to the family room as Hannah followed.

"It's . . . okay you know," Hannah said. "My uncle drinks too. He once drank so much on Thanksgiving, he passed out right on the table, his face completely covered in gravy and cranberry sauce."

Emily smiled, relieved that Hannah was attempting to make her situation feel more normal.

"What I'm saying is, don't be embarrassed. We all have skeletons in our closet. Okay?" Hannah reached out and hugged her. A real hug. A hug that could squeeze the juice out of a lemon. A hug that made tears come to Emily's eyes. A hug that made Emily think that maybe sharing her pain with Hannah could actually make it feel less hurtful inside of her.

"Thanks," Emily said as Hannah unleashed her arms and sat back down on the couch. "That really means a lot. More than you know." She picked up her beer and took a long swig. And then she took another. And then another.

"Can I tell you something?" Hannah asked as she placed a card down and took a sip of her beer.

"Anything." Emily was all ears.

"I feel really connected to you. I feel like you aren't like all the other girls at school. All they talk about is who's given who a blow job and who took whose boyfriend. It's all so petty, ya know? But you . . . you're real. You aren't concerned with all that drama. You are the real deal, Emily."

Emily felt her face flush. She wasn't used to people complimenting her. "Thanks, I feel connected to you too," she said. "And no, I don't really know what that crowd is like . . . I've never had that many friends I guess."

"Ugh, you're so lucky. That's probably why I like you so much. You're so . . . easy. I guess you haven't heard the rumors about me then, have you?" Hannah asked as she placed a card down on top of Emily's.

Rumors? Rumors would have required Emily to have friends. And Emily didn't have any friends anymore. She'd lost the only one she had. "No, I haven't."

"You must be locked in a cave then," Hannah chuckled. "Savannah's basically told the entire school that I fucked the whole football team, which is an utter lie. Just because her boyfriend dumped her and tried to hook up with me means she thinks she can try to destroy my life. It's total BS."

Emily raised her brow and took a sip of beer. Savannah was the captain of the lacrosse team. And if she didn't like you, that meant no one on the team did. "I'm sorry," she said, placing a card down. "In total truth, I don't have many friends myself. My best friend and I had a falling out over the summer. We just . . . grew apart. So I've been a loner lately. It's been really difficult."

"Yeah, high school fucking sucks, doesn't it?" Hannah laughed before chugging the rest of her beer. Emily couldn't believe that the person she thought seemed the happiest felt the same way she did about high school. Was it just a rule that high school was supposed to be terrible for everyone? And if you made it out alive, you won the prize of a shitty life?

Hannah raised her beer in the air. "Cheers to high school fucking sucking. Ha, that rhymed, didn't it?" She lifted her can up and clinked it against Emily's. "Sometimes I wanna just run away. Do you ever think about doing that?"

Emily chuckled. "I mean, if I miraculously won the lottery, I'd be long gone. But if I ran away now, where would I go? I don't have any money, as you can see." She gestured around the family room. "But yeah . . . in my dreams I'd be somewhere else. Someone else."

"For real. Sometimes I just wanna marry some old geezer who's gonna die any day for his money instead of going to college."

"I don't know about sleeping with some old man." Emily winced, trying not to imagine the gross image.

"You ever been with an older man? They know what they're doing."

Emily paused. "Yuck, no. Have you?"

"Who's the guy I saw you walking down the hallway with earlier today? Do you have a boyfriend?" Hannah asked, avoiding Emily's question.

Emily hadn't even noticed Hannah earlier that day in the hallway and wondered why she didn't say hi.

"That was Nate, my twin brother," she replied, feeling like a loser for not having a real boyfriend.

"Is he home now?" Hannah asked, looking around the room as if he'd miraculously appear. "Is he single?"

"No, he's at a study group . . . but yeah, he is single actually."

"Not that I'm looking for anything serious or anything. I'm so over guys right now, ya know? I just hate dating. Are you dating anyone right now?"

"No, not right now." *She doesn't need to know that "not now" means "barely ever,"* Emily thought to herself. The only boyfriend she ever had was Tom Swanson two years ago who dumped her during gym class, but they'd only dated for two class periods, so did that really count?

"What about you?" Emily asked, pretending she didn't already know Hannah had just posted photos of herself with that senior guy, Topper.

"Talking to a couple guys," Hannah admitted. "No one really special. I mean, why is it that guys think they're entitled to us, ya know?" Emily didn't know but didn't want to let Hannah think that no guy had ever wanted her.

"My parents don't let me date anyway. They're über-strict since I'm their only child," she added.

Emily lifted her eyebrows in surprise. *She sure is rebellious for having such strict parents,* she thought.

"How do you see the guys then?" Emily asked, placing a card down on the table.

"If I tell you this, can you pinkie promise not to tell anyone ever?" Hannah asked.

"I swear."

"For real, like you can't tell anyone ever or I'd be arrested."

Emily opened her eyes up wider. "Pinkie promise."

"I sneak out," she whispered with a devious smile as she took another sip of her beer.

"Oh," Emily said as she began to think that she'd have no need to sneak out if she wanted to. Her mom was passed out every night and wouldn't notice if she was home or not. *Why does the fact that I have no one to care if I sneak out make me jealous? Doesn't every teenager dream of having free rein to come and go as they wish?* she thought as she took another sip of her beer.

"Your parents never wake up?"

"They did once," she responded. "So, they got this fancy alarm system and put sensors on every window. I'm trapped in there now." She laughed and sipped her beer.

"So how do you get out?" Emily asked as she placed down a card.

"I've got other ways," she admitted and gave Emily a wink as she threw down a card on top of the pile. She stared at Emily with a quizzical look as if deciding whether she should tell her secret or not.

"The only reason I'm telling you this is because I really trust you, okay?"

"Okay . . ."

"I sneak out of the house I babysit in," she blurted out suddenly, chasing the secret with a sip of beer.

"You what?" Emily asked in astonishment.

"It's not like that," she added defensively. "I've been babysitting this family for a couple of years. The parents get drunk every weekend. The kids all have baby monitors in their rooms, and the monitors are hooked up to an app on the parents' phone and my phone. So, after I put the kids to bed, I turn on the baby monitor app and sneak out the back to meet guys in the playground by their house. I'm close enough where if I hear one of the kids wake up on the app, I can just run back inside and take care of them. The parents don't get home until past midnight every time, and most nights, they're so blacked out they just hand me a wad of bills and thank me in oblivion."

Emily stared at her, trying to keep her mouth from dropping open.

"You're judging me, aren't you?" Hannah asked as she placed down a card and chugged her beer.

"No . . . I just . . ." Emily didn't want to lose her trust already. She was finally beginning to feel like she'd made a friend for once. "Genius!" she thundered, even though she was thinking it sounded immoral to leave kids alone in a house while she was out making out with guys.

"Yeah totally," Hannah agreed. "It's a win-win for everyone. The parents get their night out, the kids are put to bed safely, and I get my freedom for a couple of hours. Everyone is safe and taken care of. If anything, I worry more for those poor kids the next morning because their parents are probably so hungover, I don't know how they function enough to take care of them! The mom is kind of a bitch but the dad is hot, so that makes up for it! And it's great money. I get at least a hundred bucks a night."

"Sounds like a great situation," Emily said cautiously.

"You should totally come with me next time," Hannah suggested as she crushed the second beer can in her hand and laughed.

"Oh, that'd be great. I totally need to make some extra money," Emily said, which was true, although with all her AP classes she really had no extra time to work. Studying took up 99 percent of her life. *More money would be nice to buy some more clothes,* she thought, glancing down at her boring outfit and then glancing up at Hannah's cool clothes.

"I'm babysitting them next Friday and I've always wanted a friend to keep me company if you wanna join?" she asked. "We could split the money. I was going to have this guy, Topper, meet me once the kids go to sleep and I'm sure he could bring a friend for you!"

"Awesome, I'd love to!" Emily exclaimed quicker than she intended to.

"I gotta go after this beer," Hannah mumbled. "My mom's making pot roast and freaks if I'm gone for over two hours. You're so lucky you don't have to worry about that."

Am I? Emily wondered.

"Do you want me to get you an Uber?" she asked Hannah timidly as she placed a card on the table. She questioned if Hannah should be driving after all they'd had to drink.

"Nah, I'm okay. I do this all the time," Hannah replied as she took another sip from her beer.

"Won't your parents notice you're drunk at dinner?"

"Drunk? Who's drunk, lightweight?" she laughed as she leaned over and punched Emily lightly on the arm.

I guess maybe it's just me; she must have a high tolerance, Emily speculated, embarrassed by her assumption.

As they finished their final beers and card game, Emily tried to avoid the nagging fear beginning to creep into her head: *What exactly will I be expected to do with Topper's friend Friday night, and why do I feel so guilty already for something I haven't even done yet?*

11

TRIAL DAY 1: JANUARY 7, 2019

———◦◦◇◦◦———

"It's supposed to rain later," Nate said, biting into the first half of his sandwich.

Valerie's team had provided them with a bag of deli sandwiches wrapped in tin foil, each one labeled with marker. Five Styrofoam sodas cups and five bags of Utz chips were lined up in a row next to the sandwiches. Emily eyed the black marker scribbled on the sandwiches and grabbed the one labeled TPH for turkey powerhouse. She was feeling nauseous but figured that the turkey would be the least likely to go bad if she put it in her purse to eat later that night for dinner. Since her mom wasn't working at the bar that week with the trial going on, food would be scarce at home and she wouldn't have many other options.

She stuffed the sandwich in her purse and grabbed a bag of chips and a soda as she sat down. She watched as Nate grabbed the tuna sandwich and opened his mouth to announce that he was a pescatarian out of habit but then realized it was just Emily in the room.

"How many cigarettes are Charlie and Mom actually smoking?" he asked as he took another bite of his sandwich. "They're not eating lunch?"

"Liquid lunch," Emily muttered as she sipped her Coke. She heard Valerie barking to someone on her cell phone outside the door as Nate took another bite, chomping loudly. The smell of the tuna made Emily queasy, and she took a bite of a chip to try to ease the nausea.

Emily listened to the ticking of the clock on the wall as she sipped her drink while Nate ate his lunch, neither of them looking at the other. She tried to pretend this was just a normal day, although if it were a normal day, they wouldn't be so silent. *I guess there isn't much to talk about,* she thought, trying to conjure up conversation.

"Do you think the jury seemed friendly? Like, they'd be willing to give me a chance?"

Nate shifted uneasily in his chair. "Yeah, sure," he responded, although Emily knew he was obviously saying what he thought she wanted to hear. "That older lady in the front row reminds me of Miss Jelly. She looks like she'll definitely say not guilty."

"I was thinking the same thing!" she said. It was amazing how they had the same thoughts sometimes. She looked down at her chips and pretended to concentrate on eating rather than addressing the awkward silence in the room. After a few more minutes of uncomfortable quiet, Nate took his cell phone out of his pocket and opened his daily cross-word app. *I take that as a sign that we're going to do the cell phone quiet game,* Emily thought as she grabbed her phone out of her purse and turned it on. Right away, twenty text message notifications popped up and she swiped her finger across the screen to hide them. Instead, she opened her Candy Crush app and began to mindlessly play.

"What'd you think of that young juror in the back left row?" Nate suddenly asked, keeping his eyes on his phone.

"The guy?" Emily asked, wondering why he was bringing him up.

"Yeah." A crimson color emerged on his cheeks.

"He was hot. Looked like Harry Styles," Emily admitted, a grin creeping up on her face.

"He smiled at me." Nate's face was so red by now, it matched Valerie's stilettos.

Emily gave him a blank stare. Nate and she had never had the talk about his sexual orientation, but in all their sixteen years, he'd never mentioned liking girls. She remembered one time, when they were about thirteen, Steph and Nate had been alone in their bedroom while Emily was watching TV in the family room. Nate had been showing Steph his records or something, Emily couldn't remember exactly. But when Emily approached the door, she saw Steph lean in and it looked like she tried to kiss him. Nate turned his head away and when he did, Emily had quickly scurried back to the couch so she wasn't caught. A few minutes later, Steph had come out of the room, teary eyed, and said she'd forgot she had to go home to help her mom make dinner. That was the closest Emily had ever seen Nate get to a girl and he seemed repulsed by it.

"Maybe you can get his number after all of this is over. But *only* if he finds me not guilty," Emily added.

"Maybe." Nate pretended to inspect the labels on all the sodas in front of him.

Emily smiled, and then realizing what he was doing for her, she said, "Thanks for getting me to think about something other than the trial."

"You're welcome," he muttered, his face still beet red.

They continued playing their games in silence for the rest of lunch.

12

———◦◦◦◦◦◦———

It'd taken Emily three days to get over her hangover, having gone to sleep immediately after Hannah left. She hadn't even heard Nate come home that evening or Debbie get up. *I must've passed out like my mom,* she thought in disgust. She couldn't believe her mom put herself through that almost every day. When Friday finally came and she was feeling more like herself, Emily raced home from the bus drop-off and hurried into her house to get ready. She was starting to get more apprehensive about that evening, not sure if she should be excited or nervous.

"Apply foundation that blends with your skin type. If you have pimples, you can use high-coverage foundation. Just make sure you don't apply a lot of foundation, which will give a cakey look," the influencer on the YouTube video instructed her. She looked at her reflection, at her dark gray eye shadow and black eyeliner, approving the result. She'd decided for tonight she needed a bolder look rather than her normal school makeup. She'd even gone to the thrift store and secretly shoved a cute black sweater into her bag. If Hannah could steal, she could too. Taking the sweater out of the bag, which was shoved in the corner of her closet, she ripped the tags off and tried it on. The good thing about the thrift store was that there were no hard-to-take-off sensors like real department stores, which made stealing easier. *Probably because no normal person would steal from a thrift store; they'd go for quality stuff in an actual store,* Emily thought as she posed and stared at herself in the mirror.

She heard her door open slightly, and Nate popped his head in. "Pit?" he asked as he took a bite of an apple. "Everyone's grilling out."

"Can't tonight, I'm babysitting, remember?" Emily reminded him as she sat down on her bed and put on her socks.

"Oh, right. People from the neighborhood?"

"Yep." She felt a little guilty for not telling the whole truth. *They technically live in a neighborhood, just not* our *neighborhood so I'm not totally lying,* she thought, trying to defend the fib to herself. She wasn't ready to share her new friendship with Hannah with him yet since she knew he'd be in her business as soon as he found out.

"All right, see ya. Have fun. The kids will love you."

Hearing those words only sent the guilt deeper into her stomach.

As she clasped large gold hoops into her ears, she heard a man's laughter coming from the family room. *Oh right, Mom said Charlie was coming over.* Emily remembered that her mom was off that night. Debbie claimed they were just friends, but Emily suspected something more might be going on.

She could smell cigarette smoke creeping out from under her door and flinched. *Please don't get cigarette stink on my new sweater,* she thought. The last thing she needed was the family she was about to babysit for to think she smelled like smoke.

As she finished curling her hair, she heard a ping on her phone.

"Pulling up," Hannah texted.

Emily grabbed her purse and slammed her bedroom door behind her.

"Where ya headed, kiddo?" Charlie asked, leaning against the kitchen counter as if it were a bar. Her mom was on the other side of the counter, pouring him a drink. *I guess old habits die hard,* she thought.

"Babysitting tonight," she muttered, trying not to give too much information.

"Lookin' like that?" he asked, eyeing her tight sweater and jeans.

Emily rolled her eyes. There was no way her mom would've noticed what she looked like if he wasn't there to point it out.

"Looking like what?" she asked, innocently.

"Just looks like you're more done up than usual." He took a sip of his whiskey.

"Oh, stop it, Charlie," her mom chimed in as she reached across the counter and smacked him playfully on the arm. "You look beautiful, Em. Don't you pick at her when she's off to make some money for herself." She gave Charlie a wink and then headed over and planted a kiss on Emily's forehead.

Before Charlie could say anything else, Emily shuffled out the door, letting it slam behind her. Hannah's high beams were on, and Emily had to squint as she headed toward her. She opened the passenger door and smelled a hint of weed. As she sat down, she saw Hannah had her vape pen in her hand, and she passed it to Emily.

"Hey, girl," Hannah said without mentioning the odd fact that she was handing Emily a vape pen on their way to go babysit little kids.

"Oh, no thanks," Emily stammered. "I probably shouldn't if we're about to babysit."

"No, you're going to need this," she warned. "Believe me, these girls are a handful and their parents are usually drunk around them most of the time. It'll just take the edge off a little."

Emily shrugged as she put the pen up to her mouth, inhaled, and passed it back. It went down smoother this time and she felt an instant calming effect go through her body. "So where does this family live anyways?" She glanced around the car, curious about what Hannah kept in there. The first thing her eye caught was a pack of condoms next to Hannah's lip gloss in the center console. Her eyes widened and she looked away quickly. The only time she'd seen a condom was during health class freshman year. Mrs. Winston had passed them out, teaching the class about safe sex. *Condoms?* she thought, feeling like a major prude. She felt her face turn red as she took the pen back from Hannah and inhaled deeply.

"They're on the water in a totally nice house." Hannah was talking, oblivious to Emily's discovery of her condoms. "Mr. Thomas renovates houses, and he fixed up the one they live in."

As they pulled up to the house on Oak Hill Road, Emily gaped at the Thomases' spruced-up house that sat on stilts facing the water. It wasn't enormous but was a hell of a lot nicer than her trailer. As Hannah pulled into the graveled driveway, she dropped the pen into her glove compartment and checked her makeup in the mirror.

"I'll do most of the talking, okay?" Hannah instructed as she applied lip gloss to her already pink lips.

"Okay." Hannah held the lip gloss out to her and she gladly grabbed it and began to apply it to her own lips.

As they exited the car and headed up to the house, the front door flung open. Emily watched as two little girls with platinum blond hair ran down the front porch stairs toward their car.

"Hannah Banana!" they screamed in unison as they each clung to her legs.

"Emily, meet Sophie and Katie," Hannah said as she embraced them both.

"Hi, Sophie and Katie." Emily smiled at the adorable girls, wondering why Hannah had ever complained about babysitting such cute kids. Both girls peered up at her and smiled back, shyly hiding their faces behind Hannah's legs. Sophie appeared to be a little older than Katie, maybe by a year or two. "How old are they?" she asked Hannah.

"How old are you girls?' Hannah asked, looking down at them.

"I'm six!" Sophie shouted as Katie nuzzled her head into Hannah's leg, refusing to look up.

"Katie's four," Hannah informed her. "She can be a little shy at first."

"Nice to meet you both," Emily said and gave a curtsy. Sophie and Katie giggled at this silly gesture.

"Girls, get in here right now and let Hannah and her friend come inside!" a woman hollered from the front door. She had bleached blond hair and wore a thick layer of makeup. She was dressed in tight black jeans and a black top. Emily thought she looked like she could be pretty but had so much makeup on, it was hard to tell what she was hiding behind it all.

As they approached the front door, Hannah introduced her. "Mrs. Thomas, this is my friend, Emily." Mrs. Thomas eyed Emily up and down before giving a fake smile, showing her bright white veneers. Without saying hello, she headed toward the kitchen.

"I told you she was a bitch," Hannah whispered under her breath.

"I'm going to run upstairs and finish my hair," Mrs. Thomas announced as she walked back into the foyer holding a glass of white wine. "The girls are finishing up their pizza and watching *Frozen*. Steve should be down soon." She headed up the stairs and Emily let out her breath, not realizing she'd been holding it.

She glanced around the foyer that led into the kitchen and the family room. The kitchen was shiny and clean: black kitchen cabinets, marble floors, granite counters. Her nose was flooded with the smell of apple pie and she could see a large, red candle burning on the kitchen island. As she followed Hannah into the family room where the girls were watching a movie, she was blown away by stuffed animals, and not toy stuffed animals. Physically, stuffed dead animals. Over the TV, there was a colossal taxidermy deer with large antlers and glazed-over eyes mounted to the wall. Scattered across the room were more deer mounts, and Emily spied a stuffed squirrel eating an acorn on the shelf across the room.

To the left of the TV overlooking the kitchen was an enormous taxidermy bear posed like it was about to attack someone. It must have been over six feet tall. *Nate would die if he came into this house,* Emily thought. He hadn't eaten meat since he was little. When he was around eleven, he made signs saying, "Everybody is Somebody's Baby" with photos of dead baby cows and chickens below the words. He'd spent a whole Saturday outside the local butcher's shop holding up the signs and protesting until the shop owner called the cops on him.

"Wow, someone likes to hunt, I guess?" she asked Hannah as she pointed toward the animals.

"Yeah, Steve is a huge hunter, apparently," Hannah muttered nonchalantly as she picked up a piece of pizza and took a bite. "I've gotten used to them all by now. My dad has a couple deer mounts in our house, so I see this kind of stuff a lot."

Emily had seen taxidermy deer and squirrels in houses around the neighborhood before also, but she'd never seen a huge, lifelike, taxidermy bear.

"And the bear?" Emily asked, wondering where Mr. Thomas could have killed a bear that considerable around Baltimore.

"Daddy killed that mean bear with Uncle Tommy in Alaska and Tommy killed a cheetah in Africa," Sophie chimed in with a proud smile across her face.

"Oh, cool," Emily replied with a strained smile. She understood killing deer for meat and displaying it; people did it all the time around there. But to kill a bear and cheetah? Something didn't feel right to her about that. She glanced to the side wall and realized there was an enormous window overlooking the entire bay. She strolled over to peek at the view, happy to leave the dead animals behind.

"What a view!" she exclaimed to Hannah as she stared at the moon hanging above the bay.

"It's fantastic, isn't it?" a raspy male voice responded from behind her. Startled, she turned around and saw who must have been Mr. Thomas standing directly behind her, holding a petite dog in his hands.

"Oh, hi," Emily said shyly.

"Don't worry, I don't bite," he smiled wryly. Emily thought he sort of looked like an Italian model from the neck up. But when she looked down at his tight button-down Nautica polo, ripped jeans, and overly gelled hair, his look changed from Italian model to Jersey Shore salesman. Even though he was far from her type, she couldn't help but find him attractive.

"You must be Emily," he said, smiling at her.

"Yes," she murmured, nervously. "Nice to meet you."

"This is Trixie," he said, gazing down at the geriatric chihuahua shaking in his arms. "And I see you met Yogi." He motioned to the bear. "I shot him on a hunting trip in Alaska. He watches over our family." He paused and gave Emily a wink, causing her to blush. "Hannah Banana told me about you. I always say the more pretty girls in my house, the merrier!"

Emily glanced over at the girls to see if they heard him hit on her, but they were deep into the movie and hadn't seemed to notice. She watched as he meandered out of the room and into the kitchen, whistling a tune she didn't recognize. She could see his muscular, tanned arms begin pouring a bottle of brown liquor into a plastic kid's cup and then he took a hefty swig. For just one second, she imagined his tanned arms wrapped around her body and then chided herself. *He's an old dad, for God's sake, Emily,* she thought. *How can I be attracted to someone who's such a tool bag?*

She sat on the couch and Hannah handed her a piece of cold pizza from the box sprawled on the coffee table in front of them. The girls were nuzzled up on Hannah's lap and were intently watching the movie, loudly chomping on their pizza. *She really is good with those kids, I must admit,* Emily thought. She heard Mrs. Thomas's heels clinking down the steps and glanced over as Mrs. Thomas pulled a white beaded jean jacket from the coatrack in the foyer and put it on.

"We'll be back before one, Hannah!" Mrs. Thomas yelled. She watched as Mr. Thomas placed Trixie in her dog bed by the back door and bent down to give her a kiss. Then, he headed to the foyer and grabbed a black leather jacket rimmed with silver studs from the coatrack.

"Have fun!" Hannah yelled to them both without taking her eyes off the TV.

"You know we always do!" Mr. Thomas yelled back, and he caught Emily's eye again and smiled. She looked away quickly, her face flushed. *Don't have a crush on the man you're babysitting for,* she told herself.

"Boy, you weren't kidding about them both," she whispered to Hannah as she heard the front door close.

"I know, right?" Hannah agreed. "Total hottie and total bitch. But it's all worth it for the money. And, of course, these cutie patooties!" She giggled as she pinched both girls' cheeks.

The girls squirmed on her lap and giggled with her. Emily took a gigantic bite of the pizza and smiled. *Tonight's going to be a good night,* she thought with a grin.

13

TRIAL DAY 1: JANUARY 7, 2019

———∞∞∞∞———

"The prosecution may call their next witness," Judge Wilson announced as he glanced up toward Mindy. Emily nervously sat on her hands and then turned around to see Miss Jelly and Steph sitting in the last row together, chatting. She wondered if they'd been there earlier; she hadn't noticed.

"Here," her mom had said during their lunch break after she came in from smoking with Charlie. She'd handed Emily another Valium and Emily had affably accepted it, even though she was still feeling the effects of the two pills she'd taken that morning.

"The people call Fredrick Babcot."

All heads turned as a short, middle-aged man in worn jeans and a denim shirt walked into the room. As he was sworn in, Emily closed her eyes and felt the Valium oozing through her body. She felt her hands relax . . . then her toes . . . then her feet. The buzzing in front of her wasn't real.

None of this was real.

"Mr. Babcot, can you tell the jury what your profession is?" Mindy asked as she approached the witness stand.

"I own a company called Chesapeake Home Inspections," he replied in a surprisingly high-pitched voice. Emily wondered if he was ever teased for it growing up. *Teenagers can be so cruel,* she thought.

"What does Chesapeake Home Inspections do, Mr. Babcot?"

"We inspect the structure and components of a home and look for any immediate or potential problems. We also provide a written report to homeowners or buyers looking to buy a home with a description of problem areas in the home." Emily could hear the man's voice quiver, a hint of anxiety detected. *I guess even adults get nervous to speak in front of people,* she thought.

She opened her eyes and looked up as Mr. Babcot sat in the witness stand. She spied a piece of his hair that he must have missed during his comb-over bobbing up and down on the top of his head. It reminded her of Alfalfa and between that and his quivering, high-pitched voice, she suddenly felt sorry for the man. Sorry that he'd been dragged out to her trial when all he wanted to do was inspect homes. She looked up at his comb-over and watched it bounce, deciding to focus on that while he spoke. It distracted her from what was really happening.

"And did you find anything wrong with the stove on the morning of November 10, 2018?"

"No ma'am, the stove is a gas-burning oven. It was running as it should." He fidgeted with the cuffs of his worn shirt.

"So, if someone were to leave the pilot running, let's say, for an extended period of time, would you say that it would produce a significant amount of carbon monoxide?"

"Yes, ma'am. Any gas burner that is left on by accident emits carbon monoxide."

"And can these burners just ignite without someone physically turning them on?" Mindy twisted her hands as if she were turning on a stove.

"No, ma'am, they have to be turned on by someone in order to run."

"So, if one of these burners was left on, do you conclude that was probably because someone turned it on and forgot to turn it off all of the way?"

"Yes, ma'am. That happens occasionally to burners. Especially when the user is not familiar with operating gas stovetops."

"Emawee, can you make us mac and cheese?" Sophie whispered in Emily's ear. Emily leaned over and scratched at her leg, adjusting her ankle monitor. *Not now,* she thought, trying to push Sophie's voice out of her head.

"And when gas burner is left on, does it leave an odor behind that one can smell right away?"

"Carbon monoxide is odorless, but the gas provider adds mercaptan, an odorant additive, to alert homeowners of leaks. It's a sulfur-like smell."

"Thank you, Mr. Babcot. No further questions."

Emily shifted in her chair and glanced over as Valerie scribbled in her notepad next to her.

"Emawee, you're the best!" Sophie whispered. Emily shook her head and smoothed her hair out with her hands.

"Does the defense have any questions?"

"Yes, thank you, Your Honor." Valerie rose from her seat and walked to the front of the courtroom, taking her notepad with her. "Good afternoon, Mr. Babcot."

"Good afternoon." His Alfalfa hair bounced to the left side of his head and Emily stared at it intently, trying to drown out Sophie's whispers in her head. *"Emawee,"* her voice repeated. Emily squeezed the skin between her brows tightly, trying to force Sophie's voice out.

"Thank you for explaining to us the findings you observed with the stove. I'm glad it was working in fine condition."

"You're welcome."

"You mentioned that the gas provider adds mercaptan to alert homeowners of leaks. Do people usually smell this right away?"

"Sometimes right away."

"Sometimes not?"

"It depends what other smells are in the house. Were they cooking food that had a lot of odor? Did they light scented candles? Were there cleaning products in the house that smelled? It really depends on the situation."

"Were you aware there appeared to be recently used candles in the kitchen? Would that have interfered with the mercaptan odor?"

"Possibly, sure."

"Did you happen to notice if there was an exhaust fan above the stove, Mr. Babcot?"

"Yes, the exhaust fan was not the standard size for that type of stove. The basic range hood fan size is about 250 CFM, but the burners on a gas stove produce a lot more heat than those on an electric range, so a kitchen with a gas stove requires a larger capacity range hood vent fan. A gas stove range needs to have a 400 CFM range hood fan or higher. This house's range hood fan was only 250 CFM and looked original. It looks to me that maybe the owners replaced an electric stove with a gas stove without replacing the hood range. This was not up to code."

"Interesting, thank you, Mr. Babcot. So, without a strong enough fan exhausting any smoke or, let's say, carbon monoxide, would you say that could be a problem?"

"Correct. There wouldn't be enough ventilation flowing the unwanted air out of the house."

"And do you think that if the homeowners had installed a range that was up to code, let's say, it could have prevented a possible carbon monoxide poisoning incident if someone had accidentally left the burner pilot running?"

"I suppose it could have, yes." He shifted in his seat.

"Thank you. During your inspection of the house, did you look for carbon monoxide detectors?"

"Yes, I did."

"And what did you find?"

"There weren't any in the house. The law is to have one on every level."

"Interesting, it is the law to have one, yet the Thomases didn't?"

"Yes, it looked like they had the house renovated and didn't install the detectors like they should have."

Emily raised her eyebrows in surprise. *How could they not have any carbon monoxide detectors in the house?* she wondered. Even her measly old trailer had three detectors and it was an eighth of the size of the Thomases' house. *Maybe if they'd had one, none of this would have even happened,* she thought. *Damn that Mr. Thomas.*

"So, there was no detector in the house at all that could pick up if there was carbon monoxide in the house, even though the law requires it?"

"No, ma'am."

"And if there were those detectors in the house, would they have alarmed if there were poisonous levels of carbon monoxide in the air?"

"Yes, ma'am."

"And whose job is it to make sure they're installed in the house?" Valerie crossed her arms in front of her chest.

"Well, the homeowners should have done it and whoever did the renovations."

Valerie paused, looking over at the jury as she spoke. "Oh, whoever did the renovations! Mr. Babcot, were you aware that the owner of the house, Mr. Thomas, was an unlicensed contractor? His occupation was flipping homes in Baltimore?"

"No, I wasn't aware of that."

"Well, now you know, Mr. Babcot. So, do you think, since Mr. Thomas, the homeowner of 1428 Oak Hill Road, was a contractor who worked on homes almost every day, he'd know that the law required him to have a working carbon monoxide detector in his house, and he should have put a range above his oven that was at least 400 CFMs?"

"I'd think he would definitely know that, but I know a lot of these guys who flip homes just do half-ass jobs, pardon my French. And if he was doing his own house, he probably took even less care with following the rules since he knew he would have no one inspecting it after he finished." Emily saw him sit up a little straighter, appearing to gain some confidence as he spoke.

"Interesting point, Mr. Babcot. So, would you agree that with working carbon monoxide detectors and a range up to code for the gas stove in the house, the house would be pretty safe if someone had left a burner pilot on by accident for a certain period?"

"Speculation, Your Honor!" Mindy interrupted.

"Sustained."

The gallery was quiet. So quiet, Emily could almost hear the murmur of possibility.

"No further questions, Your Honor," Valerie said, and walked back to her seat with her chin held high.

14

PAST: OCTOBER 12, 2018

———◦◦◇◦◦———

"Is Trixie dead?" Emily asked Hannah, only half joking, as she petted the stiff dog. Trixie seemed to be mostly deaf and was asleep in her dog bed in the corner of the room. As Emily petted her on the back, she didn't even flinch.

Hannah laughed as she headed into the kitchen. "No, she's just old and sleeps like ninety-nine percent of the time. The only time I see her awake is when Mr. Thomas is toting her around."

Emily spied a little blanket next to Trixie's bed and wrapped it around her. "There ya go, little girl," she whispered before heading into the kitchen.

"You think the girls are asleep?" she asked as Hannah poured herself some of the liquor that Emily had seen Mr. Thomas pour himself earlier. Emily watched as Hannah took a substantial swig and placed the cup down.

"Yeah, they should be," she said. Emily watched from the corner of her eye as Hannah adjusted the sleeves on her top. She caught sight of a few small scratches on her wrist that looked like a cat had attacked her. *How have I not noticed those before?* Emily wondered. *Maybe she always wears long sleeves to cover them up?* Emily recognized those scratches. She'd seen enough teenage movies about cutting. And those looked like self-induced cuts. She debated if she should say anything or not, but felt like they were close enough now after everything that'd happened with her mom the other day.

"Is everything okay, Hannah?" Emily asked as she slowly reached her hand over and laid it on top of Hannah's wrist, feeling the lines of scabs forming, still new.

Hannah blushed and glanced down at her wrist, brushing Emily's hand off hers as she poured more liquor in the cup.

"It's really not what you think," she said. "I just . . . I just cut sometimes when I . . . when I feel like I don't have any other way to get the pain out."

Emily frowned and placed her hand on Hannah's forearm above the cuts. "How long have you been doing it?"

"A few years. Ever since we moved here. I don't do it a lot. Just a few cuts with a razor blade. And never deep, either. I'd never try to kill myself or anything. I'm not crazy."

Emily wasn't sure what the right thing to say was. Tell her parents? Tell the school? Ignore it? How was a broken person supposed to help a broken person?

"Next time you get the craving to do it, will you promise to call me first? Maybe if you call me to talk about how you're feeling, maybe you won't feel like you have to."

Hannah wiped a tear from her eye and leaned over to hug Emily. "You're the best, Emily. You always understand me."

Emily felt a heaviness in her chest as if Hannah had just added a pile of cement books on top of her fragile heart. She wasn't sure if she was being a good friend or a bad one. This was unfamiliar territory to her, and she didn't want to mess it up. Then Hannah reached over and squeezed her hand, giving her the reassurance she needed. A small book lifted off her heart, leaving a lighter pile behind. She glanced up as Hannah handed her the cup.

"What's this?" Emily asked, although she already knew the answer. She'd seen people drink it a million times at the bar. She'd seen her mother drink it a thousand times at home. The familiar, ethyl odor smelled like something she'd take her nail polish off with. It smelled like her mother.

"Who cares what it is! It does the job!" Hannah chuckled with a devious smile, the tears now gone.

"But . . . I mean . . . we can't really get drunk while we're baby-sitting," Emily murmured. She didn't want Hannah to think she was a loser, but how far would she go to act cool? "What would happen if the girls woke up or the Thomases see we've been drinking?" she asked, beginning to think that maybe babysitting with Hannah wasn't the best idea.

"Believe me, it's fine," Hannah assured her. "We'll just have a couple swigs. Not enough to get us drunk and by the time the Thomases get home in five hours, it'll have worn off."

Still hesitant, Emily sniffed the brown liquid in the Snoopy cup and took a little sip.

"Come on," Hannah urged her. "That's not going to do anything. Take a big sip."

Following Hannah's orders, Emily took a bigger gulp and gagged. She grabbed a random Diet Coke can from the counter and guzzled it to chase away the alkaline taste in her mouth.

"Good girl," Hannah praised her. Just then, her phone pinged, and she picked it up and glanced at the text.

"The guys will be here in ten minutes," she announced. "They're meeting us at that playground across the street." She tapped her long, pointed fingernails on her phone and turned it over to show Emily the baby monitor app. Emily squinted at the screen and saw that it was split in half with two images of the girls sleeping soundly in their beds. "The app is open on my phone and ready to go. It works at the playground so if the girls as much as turn over in their beds, I'll be notified with a vibrate." She staggered across the room and grabbed her gray suede purse from the foyer floor. She reached in and grabbed something that looked like candy and tossed it at Emily.

"Oh thanks," Emily said, not looking down at the object in her hand. "I'm crazy about anything with sugar in it."

Hannah laughed.

"What?" Emily asked defensively.

"It's not candy, dummy." Hannah giggled. "It's a condom in case you need it for tonight."

Emily squinted down at the foil in her hand. "A condom?" she asked. *Why in the hell would I need a condom for tonight?* Emily thought, suddenly yearning for an excuse to stay at the house. *Even if it's Harry Styles coming tonight, I still wouldn't have sex with him!* She tried to play it cool.

"Thanks, girl, but I don't think I'll be needing this quite yet," she said, trying to act easy breezy. Hannah stared at her with an expressionless look, so Emily added, "But I'll put it in my pocket just in case." When Hannah grinned, Emily felt like she'd passed the test.

"Ya never know when you'll get lucky!" Hannah informed her. "It's always best to be prepared 'cause God knows those immature high school boys certainly aren't!"

Emily nodded in agreement as if she knew anything on the topic. Hannah glanced down at the baby monitor on her screen again. "Looks like they're dead to the world. Time to go!" She grabbed the Snoopy cup from Emily's hand and took another long gulp before leading Emily to the back door.

"Why are we going out this way?" Emily asked her.

"Security cameras. Mr. Thomas has one on the front of his house in case any moron robber wants to come steal the gaudy crap inside. But I found a way to get out unnoticed."

Emily followed Hannah to the back deck and down the stairs. There was a narrow strip of grass in between the house and the dock leading to the bay that they carefully treaded along.

"Make sure to step lightly," Hannah warned Emily. "We don't want to make any foot tracks."

Emily lifted her feet up one at a time, wondering how on earth she was supposed to step lightly. *How can I change the heaviness of my own body weight?* she thought. Hannah led her behind the neighbor's house, which was void of any light besides the moon.

"Don't worry, an old lady lives here, and she goes to bed super early every night. She's never noticed a thing," Hannah said. They walked across the street and headed into the playground. Emily glanced back at the Thomases' house. She saw the security camera propped up on the corner of the house facing the driveway and front steps. Turning back, she could just make out two people sitting on the swing set at the far end of the playground.

As they approached the playground, a memory suddenly flashed into Emily's head. When Nate and she were little, her mom and one of her boyfriends had taken them there once. The boyfriend's name was Micky and he'd driven a massive black pickup truck with wheels that seemed to be as big as Emily. He'd taken them to McDonald's and then they all came to this playground and had the whole thing to themselves.

It felt like they were in Disney World for the afternoon. Her mom and Micky canoodled on the bench with their six-pack and cigarettes, while Nate and Emily ran wild through the jungle gym. They'd all been so happy. *I wonder whatever happened to good ole Micky. He was only around for a few months,* she thought.

"Looks like he brought Chuck," Hannah noted, gesturing toward the guys.

"Chuck?"

"Yeah, he's cool."

Emily squinted as she tried to get a better look at the guys. She stared as Topper lifted a cigarette to his lips. She watched him lower his jaw slightly, blowing out a beautiful, thick ring of smoke. The dark hood on his sweatshirt was covering his head so only his deep blue eyes shined through the darkness. *He really is hot, in a badass sort of way,* Emily decided.

She glanced next to him at what must be Chuck, who was Topper's polar opposite. He had fiery red hair and cinnamon freckles covering his face. She guessed he must be a football player because it seemed like his pale arms were about to pop right out of his tight T-shirt. He was holding a liquor bottle with clear liquid in it, and she watched as he took a long swig, burped, and handed the bottle over to Topper. Topper passed him the cigarette and unscrewed the cap to the liquor bottle. Emily tried her best not to be repulsed by Chuck's vulgarness. *Maybe he has a good personality deep down,* she thought.

"Hey, sexy," Topper said, smiling at Hannah as they got closer.

"Hey, loser," Hannah replied with a grin as she kicked his foot playfully. "Topper and Chuck, this is Emily."

"What's up," both guys chirped in unison.

"Hey," Emily said, trying to sound cool. The burning in her esophagus from the liquor was starting to give her some confidence. "Can I have some?" She gestured toward the liquor bottle, surprising herself at her boldness.

"I like her already." Chuck laughed as he took a long drag of the cigarette and squinted to check out Emily. Emily forced a laugh as Topper stood up and reached over to hand her the bottle. She grabbed it from him and tipped it up to her mouth. She felt another burning sensation as the alcohol oozed into her throat, giving her more liquid confidence.

She smiled as she handed it over to Hannah and watched as she took a large mouthful.

"What's your deal?" Topper asked Emily.

"Me?" Emily asked. *Of course, he means me,* she thought, feeling stupid. She needed to play it cooler. She grabbed the bottle from Hannah and took another sip. Before she could answer Topper, Hannah did for her.

"She's my friend," Hannah informed them. Emily tried to conceal a smile creeping across her face as Hannah spoke about her. "She's totally cool and retro. We drank beers last weekend at her house." Hannah smiled flirtatiously at Topper and then leaned over and linked her arm with Emily's, resting her head on Emily's shoulder.

"Right on," Topper said. "Glad you ditched that prude." Emily wondered who he was talking about but didn't say anything. Savannah from the lacrosse team who was spreading rumors about her? Or someone else?

Hannah sauntered over to Topper and casually sat down on his lap on the swing. Emily put her hands in the back pockets of her jeans, unsure of what to do with them as she was now the only one standing in front of the three of them as they sat on the swings. She wondered if they expected her to sit on Chuck's lap. Just then, Hannah's phone vibrated, and she took it out of her back pocket.

"Oh shit," she announced, glancing down at the baby monitor app shining up from her phone.

"What?" Emily asked, secretly hoping that one of the girls may have gotten up and they could say goodbye to the guys. She didn't know where the rest of the night was going, but with the alcohol sinking in, she was starting to not trust her own judgment.

"Ugh, Sophie just got out of her bed and walked into the hallway," Hannah complained, rolling her eyes.

"Oh no!" Emily exclaimed, trying her best to act annoyed even though she was relieved. "I guess we have to go back now!"

"Em, do you mind just running over there really quick and putting her back to bed? Pretty please?" Hannah pleaded. "I would hate to leave the guys here all alone when they drove all the way out here."

"Sure, of course," Emily proclaimed too quickly, thankful that at least she'd get some time away from the guys for a little bit. "I'll be back soon!" She veered toward the neighbor's house, trying to remember the path they'd taken on the way out. She was having a little difficulty walking straight, feeling wobbly after all the booze. She turned back around one last time and watched as Topper held a lighter to Hannah's face as she lit a cigarette dangling from her lips.

"Hurry back, hottie!" Chuck yelled out at Emily. Emily's eyes darted over to him and through the blurry, alcohol-lens coating over her eyes, she thought she saw him laugh as he high-fived Topper. She grimaced at the thought of hurrying back to that drunk creep. Her head was woozy as she turned back toward the house. As she crept up the back stairs and opened the sliding glass door into the family room, she saw Sophie poke her head around the corner at the bottom of the stairs.

"Hannah?" Sophie whispered as she rubbed her eyes wearily.

"Hey, sweetie," Emily whispered to her as she walked toward her, trying not to trip on the toys the girls had left scattered all over the floor earlier.

"Where's Hannah?" she asked with a disappointed look on her face.

"She's in the bathroom," Emily blurted out, not able to think of a better excuse. "What's wrong?"

"I had a nightmare," Sophie whined. "Can you come get in bed with me till I fall asleep?" Emily glanced around the room, not sure what to do, but realized there was no one to tell her what to do. *I'm the adult and decision maker here,* she told herself.

"Of course," she said with conviction. She leaned down and picked Sophie up.

"I like you, Em," Sophie simpered as she nuzzled her face in the corner of Emily's neck. A pang of guilt in the pit of Emily's stomach hit her and she felt like she was going to throw up.

"I like you too, Soph," she responded. The deep regret descended into her alcohol-fused body. *What kind of person am I to leave these two adorable and innocent girls in the house by themselves?* she thought as she carried Sophie up the stairs and walked her into her room. She placed her down carefully and watched as Sophie patted the spot next to her dolphin blanket, directing Emily to lie down. Emily realized that more than anything, she wanted to be resting in that bed next to her and not be at that playground with Chuck. She lay down and they stared up at the constellation of star stickers on Sophie's ceiling above them. Sophie cuddled up closer next to Emily and rested her head on her shoulder.

"Will you sing me a song, Em?" she whispered. Emily tried to think of a song to sing and the memory of her mom singing "Rock-a-Bye, Baby" came into her mind with a warm comfort. Her mom used to sing that to Nate and her until they were probably in kindergarten. When she started working later hours and they began putting themselves to bed, Emily missed those nights of her mom playing with her hair and singing her that song.

"Rock-a-bye, baby, on the tree top . . ." she began to sing softly to Sophie. Closing her eyes, she listened to Sophie's breathing slow down.

Emily was awakened by a vibration in her pocket, and she sat up suddenly. She took her buzzing phone out and glanced down at a text from her mom asking how it was going. Rubbing her eyes, she looked at the time: 11:45. She'd been asleep for over an hour. She glanced down at Sophie, who was innocently slumbering next to her, and smoothed her hair.

"Sleep tight," she whispered as she shut the door quietly. She hurried downstairs past Trixie, to the back sliding door. The nap had made the alcohol wear off a little bit and she was feeling more stable on her feet. The last thing she wanted to do was go back to the playground to see Chuck, but she didn't want to jeopardize her newly found friendship with Hannah. *Hopefully, I can avoid Chuck for the next twenty minutes or so and talk to Hannah and Topper the whole time,* she thought as she veered around the house.

As she marched across the street toward the playground, she noticed that Hannah and Topper were nowhere to be seen. Instead, Chuck was sitting on the wooden bench next to the slide, staring down at his phone with a lit cigarette in his hand.

He glanced up as Emily approached him and gave her an irritated smile. "What happened to you?" he asked, placing his phone in his pocket.

"Sorry," she said. "One of the little girls had a nightmare so I had to sit with her till she fell asleep, and it took forever," she lied. She didn't want him to know that Sophie had fallen asleep right away and so had she. "Where's Hannah and Topper?" she asked, glancing around, hoping they weren't too far away.

"They took his truck out in the woods to have some private time," he slurred. Emily realized then that he must've gotten drunk during the time she was gone. She gazed down at the empty liquor bottle resting under the swing set where he had been sitting earlier. He got up from the bench and stumbled over to her. "We'll just have to catch up quickly." Emily's eyes widened as Chuck leaned down, planting a sloppy kiss on her lips. He tasted like stale cigarettes and liquor, and she tried not to gag as he shoved his tongue in her throat. She stumbled back as he forcefully grabbed the back of her head, sucking hard at her face. His free hand reached over and squeezed at her breast, powerfully. For a moment or two, her heart pounded in panic through her chest, and she had mental flashes of what could happen next.

"It's getting late," she finally managed to say in between kisses as she tried to push him away.

"Then we better be quick," he responded as his hand reached down, trying to unzip her jeans. He was swaying badly, clearly unable to multitask kissing her and unzipping her jeans at the same time. After a minute or so, he seemed to give up on trying to open her pants and grabbed her hand, putting it forcefully on his jeans. She tried to move her hand away, but he pressed harder. She could feel a tear creeping out of the corner of her eye and realized she wasn't a physical match for him if she decided to fight him off.

All she wanted to do was crawl back into that safe bed with Sophie and her pink princess sheets. Just as Chuck started moaning and pushing her toward the ground, she saw headlights and heard car tires approaching. She looked over and saw Topper's blue truck pulling into the parking lot.

"Dammit, Topper!" Chuck exclaimed as he pulled away from Emily and adjusted himself through his jeans. The car doors slammed shut, and Topper and Hannah stumbled over to them, holding hands. Hannah's hair was a bird's nest, and her mascara was running down her face.

"Looks like you two are getting to know one another," Hannah said, giggling, as she glanced back and forth between Chuck and Emily.

"Yeah, thanks for giving me blue balls, Topper," Chuck responded as he punched Topper in the arm. "Guess you were saved by the headlights, huh, Em?" He peered over at Emily and smiled a cunning grin as if he knew he had been pushing her too far and would have gone farther if they hadn't shown up.

Emily opened her eyes widely and looked over at Hannah for help. "Guess we better get back since the Thomases could be home any minute," Emily suggested, trying to get the hell out of there.

"Good call, girl," Hannah agreed. She leaned over and tugged Topper's shirt toward her, giving him a sloppy kiss. "Night, boys." She swaggered over to Emily, grabbed her hand, and pulled her toward the house without glancing back at the guys.

"Sorry we left you, but you'd been gone for so long and Topper wanted some private time with me, if you know what I mean," Hannah whispered as they tiptoed around the neighbor's house and back into the Thomases' backyard.

"Don't worry about it," Emily replied, not wanting to make Hannah think she was upset. *Should I tell her about Chuck going too far?* she wondered, but then decided it would only make her appear prudish.

When they headed into the house, Hannah started to pick up the girls' toys and throw them into the toy bin across the room. She grabbed the remote and put on HGTV, then trudged into the bathroom. Emily glanced over at Trixie, still tucked in and sound asleep as she'd left her earlier in the evening.

"I'm going to make myself look like I didn't just get fucked." Hannah chuckled as she closed the bathroom door. She gestured toward the couch. "Sit down and make yourself look like you can't wait to find out how these people decorated their new bargain beach house."

Emily sat down on the couch and watched the screen, wishing she could trade places with the people on the show and be the one picking out her own new bargain beach house. She heard the toilet flush and the water running in the bathroom.

A few minutes later, the front door handle jiggled. Emily glanced over to the foyer as Mr. and Mrs. Thomas stumbled inside. Emily smiled and got up from the couch to say hello. Mrs. Thomas staggered into the family room as Mr. Thomas stumbled into the kitchen and opened the fridge, searching intently inside. Emily inspected Mrs. Thomas carefully and suspected she was very drunk.

"Hey, Chica!" Mrs. Thomas slurred sweetly to Emily, indicating that she was, indeed, very drunk. Just then, Hannah opened the bathroom door and shuffled into the foyer to join them. Mrs. Thomas stumbled over and put her arms around Hannah, giving her a big squeeze. "She's my favooorite, favoooorite little babysitterrrrrrr!" she slurred.

Hannah giggled and hugged her back. "And you're my favorite MILF," she teased.

"You hear that, baby?" Mrs. Thomas yelled into the kitchen to Mr. Thomas. "Hannah thinks I'm a MILF!"

Emily glanced over at Mr. Thomas as he turned the oven on and stuck the entire box of leftover pizza in it. His eyes were glazed over, and he was intently gnawing at a cold chicken wing he'd produced from the fridge. He sluggishly glanced toward them and appeared to process his wife's words. "Hell yeah, let's have a threesome," he yelled back as he bit into his chicken.

"Steven! Stop joking around!" Mrs. Thomas snapped at him. "Sorry about that idiot," she apologized and rolled her eyes. "Pay the poor girls so they can get home," she scolded him as she leaned over and took off her high heels.

"Oh right," Mr. Thomas said to no one in particular as he reached for his wallet in his back pocket. He took out a wad of bills, flipping the cash through his hands. He staggered into the foyer and handed Hannah the bundle of bills. "Here ya go, lil' lady," he slurred.

Acting as if nothing was out of the ordinary, Hannah grabbed Emily's hand and pulled her toward the door. "Thanks, guys!" she shouted as she led them out onto the front steps and closed the door behind them.

"They were plastered!" Emily whispered to Hannah as they headed toward her car.

"I told you," Hannah said. "I've seen them way worse than that."

Emily glanced over at the Thomases' yellow Mustang and saw that it was parked halfway on the grass and halfway on the gravel driveway. The center console light had been left on and their car keys were on the gravel next to the driver's side of the car.

Hannah noticed the car the same time Emily did. "Idiots," she muttered under her breath. They hopped into Hannah's car and sped away.

15

TRIAL DAY 1: JANUARY 7, 2019

⸻◦◦◇◦◦⸻

Emily was drowning in fatigue. She felt like she was lying at the bottom of a pool, held down with fifty-pound weights. Between taking Valiums, drinking beer her mom had given her when they'd gotten home, and the lack of food she'd eaten, her body felt worn and spent. She'd never ended up eating the turkey sandwich for dinner. She'd given it to Nate to eat and told him she wasn't hungry, so he'd picked off the turkey and eaten the rest. She knew there wasn't anything in the house for him to eat, and he deserved to eat more than she did. *I don't deserve anything,* she thought.

Rolling over, she glanced at Nate who was snoring softly even though he'd just gotten into bed. *How can he fall asleep so fast every single time?* she wondered. She pulled her phone off the bedside table and turned it on for the first time since their lunch break. She was allowing herself twenty minutes of privacy in case she needed to cry. She clicked on the news app and was confronted with photos of Nate, her mom, and herself heading to their car after the trial. In one photo, Valerie was holding a folder in front of Emily's face, unsuccessfully blocking the photographers from capturing a good shot. She noticed she had some mascara running down her cheeks and her face looked swollen. *Had I been crying and not realized it?* she wondered. She glanced at the article and skimmed it.

Before she could carry on reading, a text popped up from Valerie. She opened it up and read: "Don't read the news. Don't read your text messages. In fact, go find your mom and hand her your phone. You can get it back when the trial is over. It's not benefiting you to read anything negative during the trial as it may reflect on your behavior and the appearance you emit to the jury."

How does she know that's what I'm doing right now? Emily wondered. She sighed, peeling herself out of bed, and trudged into her mom's bedroom. Debbie was sitting upright with a glass of red wine in her hand and was watching the tiny TV propped on her dresser. Next to her, Emily saw the box of wine she'd be drinking for the night. *At least she's at home and not out,* Emily thought.

"Hi, hon," Debbie purred. She patted the spot next to her in bed and Emily sat down and handed her the phone.

"Valerie said I had to give you my phone until the trial is over," Emily admitted, not hiding the tears from her face. Debbie grabbed the phone from her and leaned over to store it in her bedside drawer. As she did this, she pulled out a pill bottle.

"Good idea," she agreed as she opened the bottle. "How're you doing? You look tired; you should go to bed and get some rest." She reached over and handed Emily two oval pills and her glass of wine.

"I know," Emily agreed, as she placed the pills on her tongue and took a sip of the wine. She glanced around her mom's room, trying to take it all in. *What if the jury convicts me and I go to jail for the rest of my life? What if this is one of the last nights I sleep in this house? How can I ever live with myself again for what happened to those little girls? Does one mistake make me a bad person even though I've lived all my life being a good person? Can good people do bad things to good people? Why did those little girls have to die? Where are those little girls now? Is there a heaven? Is there a God and, if so, why would God kill those little girls?* She took a deep breath and closed her eyes. *God didn't kill those little girls . . . I did.*

She wanted to tell her mom all her worries. She wanted to tell her that she hadn't been able to sleep for the past two months and when she did, all she saw were Sophie's and Katie's faces. She wanted to tell her mom that all she wanted to feel was nothing at all. But instead, she closed her eyes and tried to stop the tears from falling.

As if she were reading Emily's mind, Debbie whispered, "Worrying doesn't take away tomorrow's troubles. It takes away today's peace."

Emily raised her brows at her mom's words of wisdom. She wished her mom had been there for her a few months before when she'd needed her. She wished they could've done this then. Now it was too late. Emily thought back to her favorite childhood book that her mom used to read to her, *The Runaway Bunny.* No matter where the bunny went, the mommy rabbit was always going to find her.

But didn't everyone know that rabbit mothers immediately leave the burrow after giving birth and only stop by for a few minutes each day to feed the litter? After less than a month, the bunnies are left to fend for themselves.

Debbie patted the pillow next to her, gesturing for Emily to lie down. She placed her wine glass down and leaned on her side facing Emily, her fingers reaching over and twisting Emily's hair into a loose braid. Emily closed her eyes and tried to summon strength from her surroundings.

Her thoughts felt so heavy that her head felt like it might explode. Just then, Debbie started singing "Rock-a-Bye, Baby" softly and Emily felt a tear creep out of her eye. She could faintly smell the wine and cigarette scent of her mom's breath. *She's five years old again and her mom is playing with her hair, singing "Rock-a-Bye, Baby." She'd just taken a bath and she's in her Cinderella pajamas. Her mom cooked Nate and her spaghetti, and they played Twister and watched* Toy Story 2. *Her mom didn't drink at dinner and no boyfriend came over. Just the three of them.*

Emily felt her eyes get heavy as she listened to her mom's voice begin to hum the tune quietly, sipping her wine in between verses.

When her breathing deepened, Debbie stopped and whispered into Emily's ear, "You need to forgive yourself. You're human, you're flawed. Know that I love you no matter what." Emily was the bunny and her mom's voice was going to save her. She fell into a deep sleep of oblivion.

16

PAST: OCTOBER 19, 2018

———◦◦◇◦◦———

"Sour Patch Kid?"

The chubby freshman sitting next to Emily dangled a yellow bag in front of her eyes.

"No thanks," Emily said, but seeing the disappointed look on the girl's face, she grabbed a red gummy out of the bag. "Sure, I love these." She popped it in her mouth and saw a smile begin on the girl's face. Kneeling up on the seat of the bus she pinched the metal window levers at the same time, and opened the stubborn glass. She breathed in some fresh air, trying to ignore the smell of the students who hadn't seemed to have learned about deodorant yet.

She was relieved that it was finally Friday afternoon. She could see Hannah again. That week, she'd only seen her once, leaning up against Topper's truck after school, hardcore making out with him. She'd also seen Chuck three times in the halls that week, and each time he ignored her. The first time she saw him, he was walking past her with two football players. She'd thought maybe he hadn't seen her, even though there was no one else around. The second time, he was walking with a lacrosse player and he most certainly did make eye contact with her, but he looked away immediately. The third time, he was holding hands with a cheerleader with fake blonde hair and long pink fingernails. Right as they passed her, he tickled the cheerleader and gave her a kiss on the cheek. She was so baffled because she was repulsed by him but was secretly hoping that their make-out session would have at least scored her some popularity points. Maybe he was embarrassed by what he'd done to her. Instead of dwelling on it, she decided to use the week to focus on school and keep up with her Instagram posts, but she couldn't help feeling lonely without Hannah.

When Hannah had finally called Emily the previous night, she'd felt relief surge through her body.

"So, this weekend?" Hannah had asked when Emily answered on the second vibration, trying not to act too eager. "You have any plans?"

"Hm, I don't think I've confirmed anything yet," Emily had lied, trying not to sound too enthusiastic since she had zero plans whatsoever.

"Great, we're going to a party!" Hannah had exclaimed. "Okay if I tell my parents I'm sleeping at your house since my curfew is super early?"

"Of course!" Emily had replied, hoping that Hannah didn't really want to sleep over since there was nowhere for her to sleep except their uncomfortable, cheap couch.

"Awesome! I'll pick you up at eight tomorrow!" Emily had heard the click on her side of the phone and felt a nervous tingle in her stomach.

As she stepped off the bus behind Nate, she meandered slowly, hoping he was too busy talking to friends to notice she was lagging behind. He stopped and turned toward her when he realized she wasn't following him.

"Why are you taking so long, Em?" he asked, holding his backpack straps tightly. He headed over to her with a worried look on his face.

She felt remorse that she'd been secretive with him about her new relationship with Hannah.

"I'm going to the thrift store to spend some of that babysitting money I made last weekend," she said casually, deciding to omit the fact that she needed a new outfit for the party with Hannah that night. "Wanna come?" she asked, knowing he'd rather die than thrift shop. She knew Nate would rather save up his money and buy one new quality item at a real store than buy cheap, used stuff from the thrift store.

"No thanks. Why don't you come to The Pit when you're done?"

She looked down and picked at her cuticles, trying to think of a way to tell him about her plans for the night. "Well . . ." she hesitated. "I already have plans."

"Plans? With Steph?" He searched her face as he spoke.

"No, a new friend," she said cautiously.

"Who?" He gripped his straps tighter.

"This girl . . . Hannah," she murmured as she looked up to the sky.

"Patterson?" He furrowed his brow.

"Yeah, you know her?" Emily asked in the most innocent voice she could muster.

"I know she seems like bad news," he huffed as he crossed his arms authoritatively. "I see her smoking outside of school and hanging out with older guys all the time."

Emily rolled her eyes and crossed her arms in front of her chest to match his.

"You do you, Em, but just be smart, okay?" he warned.

"Thanks, Dad," she teased and playfully punched him in the arm, although Nate really was the closest thing she'd had to a dad. "Have fun at The Pit."

He nodded and turned to catch up with his friends. Emily spun herself around and walked as fast as she could to the thrift store. She calculated that it was a mile away, so she didn't have much time to find something presentable for the party. She had thirty-five dollars left over from babysitting so she figured that should be more than enough to get something adequate to wear.

As she approached the building, a sense of nostalgia filled her. Her mom used to take Nate and her there every year when they were little to buy their back-to-school clothes. The last Sunday of the month was always half off so that was the day they'd go. Debbie would give them each twenty dollars and it felt like they'd won the lottery. Emily would usually peek at the price tags and buy as many items as she could for the twenty bucks, adding the total in her head carefully. She'd leave the store with her arms full of shopping bags, feeling like Julia Roberts in *Pretty Woman*.

As she entered the thrift store, she breathed in the scent of used clothes . . . the smell of old attics and cedar closets. Inside, the store looked like a vast warehouse with rows and rows of clothes to be picked through. Emily veered straight to the women's section in the far-right corner of the store. Instantly, she found a pair of black Steve Madden boots with a kitten heel and a tight black shirt from H & M. It wasn't the perfect outfit, but the combo would go well with her ripped jeans and would blend in enough with the other girls at the party. She didn't have enough time to spend picking through the racks for anything else since she had to walk a whole mile back home and get ready. As she glanced down at the price tags, she realized she was two dollars short.

"Shit," she whispered. Grasping both items, she headed casually to the men's section to work her magic. She pretended to browse at men's dress shirts intently, keeping her eyes down as she bent down and faked tied her shoe. She discreetly shoved the H & M shirt into her backpack and stood up, swinging the backpack back over her shoulders. Turning quickly to go purchase the boots, she was startled to see Mr. Thomas at the end of the row, staring at her with a playful grin on his face.

"Well, what do we have here?" he crowed with a grin. "What do you think you're doin' over here in the big boys' section? You buyin' something for your boyfriend?"

Emily blushed, racking her brain with excuses as to why she was in the men's section. *Did he see me shove the shirt in my backpack?* she worried.

"It's my dad's birthday this weekend and I was just looking for a shirt for him," she blurted out quickly and then wondered why Mr. Thomas, who had enough money to afford nice clothes, was shopping in a thrift store.

"What are you doing here?" she asked him, trying to change the subject from herself.

"We have a costume party comin' up and Brandi picked out our outfits, as usual. I'm going as a pimp, so I'm lookin' for a big fur coat." He gave her a wink and Emily couldn't hide her smile, embarrassed that she probably looked like an infatuated girl with a crush.

"Your dad, huh?" he asked as he put his hands in his jean's pockets. "Looks like you only found something for yourself." He pointed toward the boots in her hand.

"Looks like it!" she chuckled. "I better go buy these so I can try to find him a present somewhere else!" She trudged past him to the cashier.

"Why don't you let me buy them for you?" he suggested, tugging the boots out of her hands.

Emily juggled the offer in her head. "No, don't worry about it," she told him, not releasing the boots from her hands. "I have that money from babysitting last weekend, remember?"

He grabbed the boots out of her hands and smiled. "Let me. I'm happy to help out," he said. "The girls loved you and I want to keep my babysitters coming back." He winked again.

She could feel her cheeks singe bright red and tried to hide her mortification. "Why, thank you, Mr. Thomas, that's very kind of you," she stammered, trying to keep her cool. She followed him to the cash register and stood behind him as he pulled out his credit card and paid for the boots. The jaded-looking lady behind the register glanced up at them as she handed him the bag. *Does she think he's my boyfriend or my dad?*

she wondered. After paying, Mr. Thomas handed Emily the bag and put his hand on her back as he escorted her to the door.

"Thanks again, Mr. Thomas," she said as she exited the store and headed into the parking lot. She felt guilty for stealing and then allowing Mr. Thomas to buy the boots for her.

"How you gettin' home?" he asked as he glanced around the parking lot for her car.

"Walking," Emily replied quickly before she realized she shouldn't have told him this. "I don't live far, it's okay." She didn't want him to drive her home and see where she lived; it was too embarrassing.

She watched as he strolled over to his yellow Mustang and opened the passenger side door. "Get in. I'll take you home," he instructed. Emily hesitated, but then got in to the car, figuring at least he'd save her the twenty-minute walk home so she would have enough time to get ready for the party.

"What's your address?" he asked her as he started to back out of the spot.

"My address?" Emily asked, deciding she was too ashamed to let him see where she lived. "Sixty-one Meadow Lane," she instructed him, which was actually Steph's address down the street. Steph's trailer was one of the bigger ones in the neighborhood, which would be less humiliating for her to have Mr. Thomas to see.

He nodded as he put Maroon Five on the radio and turned the volume up, full blast. Emily tilted her head toward the window and rolled her eyes in silent embarrassment for him. He may be hot, but his choice in music made it clear he was about two decades older than her. He bounced his head to the beat of the music as he drove the mile toward Steph's house.

"Do you like babysitting for us?" he asked her as he swerved his Mustang into her community.

"Yes, Mr. Thomas," she replied. "Your girls are really adorable."

"Yeah, they are, aren't they? I really lucked out."

Emily smiled, wishing she had a dad who said that about her.

As they approached Steph's house, Mr. Thomas slowly pulled the car to a stop and turned the music down.

"Thanks so much for the ride home and for the boots," she said as she opened the door. "You really shouldn't have."

"Of course, Emily," he grinned as he rested his hand on the clutch. She jumped out of the car and waved goodbye as a cue for him to leave, but he didn't pull away. *He must be waiting for me to go inside,* she thought. Left with no other options, she slowly turned and approached Steph's trailer.

She put her hand on the front door lightly and waved again, but he just waved back and remained in his car watching her. *Guess I'm really doing this,* she thought. She took a deep breath, pushed the front door open, and walked in.

"Emily?" Steph asked in surprise.

Emily was faced with Steph and three of her brothers all squeezed on the couch watching TV. Steph lived with her five siblings and it was a tight fit, even in their larger trailer. Emily thought she may have seen a little bump on Steph's mom's belly when she saw her walking the dog over the summer, but she couldn't get a good enough look. For Steph's sake, she hoped not.

"Oh, hi!" Emily said, hesitating as she tried to figure out a reason why she would've just barged in. She glanced down and saw their dog, Cheeky, sniffing at her shoes as it waited to be pet. Quickly, she came up with an excuse. "I thought I saw Cheeky get hit by a car and ran to your house to tell you, but thank goodness, she's here and okay!"

Steph glanced at Cheeky and then back to Emily with a confused look on her face. "You saw a dog get hit by a car?" she asked as she got up from the couch. "Where? Is it okay?"

"I thought I did," she lied. "But I guess I didn't since Cheeky's here!"

"But a dog got hit by a car, right?"

"Well, I thought it did, but I guess it didn't!" Emily squeaked, realizing she wasn't making sense. "Anyways, I better get back home! I'm glad Cheeky's okay and I'm so sorry to barge in on you all!"

She quickly let herself out, taking in a huge sigh of relief that Mr. Thomas's car was gone. She headed down the steps toward her house as she heard Steph's door quietly open behind her.

"Are you okay, Em?" Steph asked gently. Emily turned her head and gave her best smile.

"I think so," she replied honestly as she shrugged and kicked the gravel with her Vans.

"I know we had a falling out, but I'm here if you need to talk about anything," Steph responded. Emily nodded and gave another smile as Steph softly closed the door behind her. She felt a wave of guilt about not being friends with Steph anymore. A wave of guilt that Steph had to share that trailer with all her siblings squished in like sardines. A wave of guilt for all the terrible things she'd been doing ever since she met Hannah.

She shuffled back to her house with a pit of shame in her stomach. As she approached Miss Jelly's trailer, she ducked her head and tried to walk fast so Miss Jelly didn't notice her passing by, but like always, Emily heard a voice chirping from the window that was halfway open.

"Is that my little Emily walking past my house not stopping in to say hi?" Miss Jelly shouted from the kitchen.

Emily half smiled, pivoting toward Miss Jelly's door. As she stepped inside, an aroma of something cooking from the crockpot hit her and her belly growled, wanting whatever was stewing inside of it.

"Hi Miss J," she said. "I'm sorry, I was hurrying home since I'm having a friend over and wanted to get ready."

"Oh, Steph? Since when do you get all dolled up for Steph?" Miss Jelly asked as she stirred the pot with a wooden spoon. She was wearing the apron Nate and Emily had gotten her for Christmas, a cartoon woman's body in a bikini. Miss Jelly had thought it was the funniest thing in the world when she'd opened it.

"No, not Steph . . . a new friend. Her name's Hannah. I go to school with her."

"Oh, isn't that lovely. You'll have to bring her around sometime. I'd love to meet her," Miss Jelly said with a sparkle in her eye. She picked up some garlic salt sitting on the counter next to her and shook it into the pot.

"Oh, she isn't that kind of friend," Emily said and then stopped herself. "What I mean is . . . she isn't like Steph. She doesn't really like to hang out the way Steph and I used to."

Steph, Nate, and Emily used to love to hang out at Miss Jelly's house growing up. It was like they had a shared grandmother. Miss Jelly had a little cabinet in her living room filled with toys just for them and they'd spend hours playing Monopoly, Clue, and every other primitive board game she had in there. She'd let them all try on her costume jewelry; even Nate tried on the jewelry too.

They really were inseparable. *Three peas in a pod,* Miss Jelly used to call them.

"Well, that's too bad to hear." Miss Jelly frowned as she lifted the spoon to her lips and took a sip. "I haven't seen much of you and Steph together in a while. Did something happen?" she asked.

"We just . . . grew apart the past couple of years. We like doing different things now. And we sorta got in a fight and said some things to each other we can't take back now," Emily admitted. What she meant to say was that Steph was stuck in the past and had no desire to grow up and be a teenager. That Steph said things that scarred Emily's heart. But Emily didn't tell any of this to Miss Jelly.

"Friends fight. They say things they don't mean. Friends make up. That's life. I think Steph doesn't *want* to have the same likes as everyone else, Emily. Did you know she still visits me sometimes when you and your brother get dinner at the bar?"

"She does?" Emily asked. She didn't think Steph saw Miss Jelly anymore.

"She sure does," Miss Jelly informed her as she opened a drawer and retrieved a can opener. "She knows you have your own path to follow. I just want you to remember that the biggest challenge of life is to be yourself in a world that's always trying to make you like everyone else," Miss Jelly said as she placed the can opener on a can of kidney beans. "I don't think Steph wants to do all the things those teenagers do, especially watching what alcohol has done to some of the people closest to her. And that takes courage to just be herself when everyone else is trying to fit in. Just remember that." She winked at Emily and smiled. *You mean what alcohol has done to my family?* Emily questioned.

"Thanks for the chat, Miss Jelly, but I really do have to get ready," Emily said as she gave her a hug before heading over to her trailer.

She headed straight to the bathroom and took a long, hot shower, trying to wash away the guilt and shame from earlier. *Tonight is going to be a fun night. Manifest. Manifest. Manifest,* she thought as she rinsed the shampoo out of her hair.

17

TRIAL DAY 2: JANUARY 8, 2019

———⸺◦◦◇◦◦⸺———

"Coffee?" Charlie asked as they filed into his beat-up, mahogany Ford Bronco. He had four coffees from the local Royal Farm Store resting on his lap.

"Awesome, thanks, Charlie," Nate said as he grabbed a cup, sat back, and buckled his seatbelt. Emily took a cup to be polite and handed it to Nate, giving him a wink. She watched from the back seat as Charlie took two little brown bottles of liquor and poured them into Debbie's and his cups. *It's crazy how things can just become normal to people,* she thought as Charlie handed Debbie her spiked coffee.

The four of them stared out of their windows in silence during the drive since Charlie's radio was broken. *What could we really talk about besides the trial, anyways?* Emily thought, grateful for the quiet. As they approached the courthouse, Debbie rummaged through her purse, grabbing her pill bottle and giving it a shake. Then without glancing back, she reached her hand behind her toward Emily's knee and opened her palm, revealing two small white pills. Emily grabbed the pills, placed them on her tongue, and stared back out at the passing cars on the highway, wondering where all the people were headed to that morning as she swallowed.

Once they sat down in the courtroom, she tried to distract herself from the tense day ahead. Valerie had already gone over with her what would happen. The prosecution was going to be questioning the Thomases' next-door neighbor, the security camera installer, and Madison Harris. Emily had debated about telling Valerie the truth about what was on the cameras. The truth about the night she'd gone over to Mr. Thomas's house.

But she just couldn't say it aloud. If she said it aloud, that would mean it really happened. And maybe somewhere deep down inside of her, she hoped it'd been a nightmare.

She heard Mindy announce that she'd like to call Noreen Moore to the stand and watched as an elderly lady with a walker snailed down the aisle, not lifting her head off the ground in front of her. Noreen was a tiny woman with white hair and kind eyes. She was wearing an aubergine button-down cardigan and orthopedic-looking walking shoes. Emily thought the old lady appeared extremely nervous, her eyes darting around the room from person to person as she got settled in her seat.

As Noreen was getting sworn in, Emily glanced over at the jury and noticed the good-looking juror in the back row. He was staring at someone behind Emily and appeared to be blushing. She remembered that Nate was sitting directly behind her, and she could almost feel his eyes burning through her and into the hot juror's eyes. She tried to conceal a smile at this little revelation.

Mindy stood up and began to question Noreen.

"Good morning, Ms. Moore. I'm sorry to have to meet you under these dire circumstances."

"Good morning." Noreen coughed into her wrinkly, pale hand.

"Can you please tell the jury your address, Ms. Moore?"

"1426 Oak Hill Road."

"1426 Oak Hill Road. Why, isn't that right next door to 1428 Oak Hill Road?"

"Yes, it is. Isn't that why I'm here?" Noreen asked, not trying to sound sarcastic at all, although it did make someone sitting somewhere behind Emily snicker.

"Yes, it is, Ms. Moore. And so, your neighbors are, I'm sorry, your neighbors *were* Mr. and Mrs. Thomas, is that correct?"

"Yes, so upsetting what happened to that poor family," she whimpered as she wiped a tear building up from the corner of her eye with a tissue.

"How long have you lived at 1426 Oak Hill Road, Ms. Moore?"

"I've lived there for fifty-five years."

"Wow, that's quite a long time, you must know all of the neighbors then, huh?"

"Yes, I know pretty much everyone in the neighborhood, although nowadays I don't get outside too much to converse with them."

"And did you know the Thomases, your next-door neighbors, pretty well?"

"Pretty well. We'd chat if I was outside watering my garden. But we didn't spend much time together. Their daughters were always sneaking over to my house and trying to pick my flowers, poor dears, may they rest in heaven." Noreen stared up to the ceiling and made the sign of the cross before folding her hands together as if in prayer. Her hands were delicate like a birds, appearing as if they'd snap in two as she moved them.

"Will you sing me a song, Em?" Sophie whispered quietly in Emily's ear. Emily scratched at her head sluggishly. She needed another Valium.

"And they lived next to you for about six years, is that correct?"

"That's correct. It was pretty run-down when they bought it; I was happy to have a family finally move in and make it presentable."

"Yes, that must have been a nice change. I know they did take such good care of the house, didn't they? Did you ever see babysitters coming to the house to help with the two little girls, Ms. Moore?"

"Why, yes, I would sometimes see a girl driving up to their house to babysit at night when the Thomases would go out. I didn't know her, though."

"And did you ever notice anything peculiar going on while she would be babysitting, Ms. Moore?"

"I did. Two or three times I would notice her sneaking out and walking over to the playground across the way to meet some teenage hoodlum. It was always when the girls' bedroom lights were off in the house so I figured she was just sneaking out for a little bit and would head back. I never tried to butt my business in it too much." Emily's eyes widened to discs. She wanted to interject that she must be talking about Hannah, not her. She sat on her hands, anxiously hoping that Noreen would say that it was Hannah that she saw babysitting and not Emily.

"And do you see that girl you saw babysitting anywhere in this room, Ms. Moore?"

"Yes, she's sitting right there."

Noreen Moore pointed her wrinkly finger directly at Emily, and Emily opened her mouth wide. *She has me confused with Hannah!* Emily thought. She felt a pit growing in her stomach. Little old Noreen couldn't be the woman to send her to prison, could she?

"No further questions, Your Honor," Mindy concluded and headed back to her seat.

Valerie stood up and began to question Noreen immediately. Emily glanced around the room, her eyes darting from left to right, not sure where to look. She felt wrongly accused. She needed Valerie to fix this.

"Good morning, Ms. Moore. Can you please tell the jury how old you are? I know a woman hates to tell her age, but we'll need to know for purposes of this case."

"I'm eighty-two years old."

"And I see you're wearing glasses, is that correct?"

"Yes, ma'am."

"Are those for seeing far away or up close?"

"Both, these are bifocals. Once you reach a certain age, everyone needs them."

"And when was the last time you had your eyes checked at the eye doctor, Ms. Moore?"

"I don't recall . . . maybe ten years. I don't need to get them checked often. I can see simply fine out of them."

"Were you aware that optometrists recommend getting your eyes checked annually as people wearing glasses can have vision changes as often as once a year?" Valerie asked as she glanced over toward the jury.

Emily peered over and saw a couple people writing down notes, eyebrows lifted.

That could be a good sign, she thought.

"No, I was not aware. But like I said, my vision is simply fine as it is."

"Ms. Moore, do you remember seeing the defendant, Emily Keller, sitting right here, sneak out of the Thomases' house the night that the incident happened on November 9, 2018?"

"I can't always remember dates, ma'am, but I think that is when it was, yes."

"And she would drive up to the house when she babysat?"

"Yes, ma'am."

"What color was her car? Was it a sedan? A truck?"

"It was red . . . a small car, I don't know what model."

"Thank you, Ms. Moore. And you're sure that this person you saw getting out of the car those few times was the same girl you saw sneaking out the back of the house?"

"Yes, ma'am, that is what I said."

"Okay, just making sure. And you stated earlier that the girl you saw getting out of that car and sneaking out of the house was this girl sitting here before us, Emily Keller. Is that correct?"

"Yes, ma'am. That is her. That's what I said." Emily could see Noreen's pale face grow red in frustration.

"And were you aware that Emily Keller does not have her driver's license?"

"No, why would I know that?"

"You wouldn't know that, would you? Did you know that she doesn't own a red car, not any car, since she doesn't drive?"

"No, I was not aware."

Thank you, Valerie, Emily thought as she glanced up toward the ceiling. *Please let the jury see that she's confused.* Emily saw more jury members scribble down some notes and felt a small glimmer of hope.

"And were you aware that the Thomases had another babysitter that they'd been using for the past year who does drive and own a little red car? Were you aware of that?"

"Well, no, I thought that was her. All these teenage girls all dress the same and look alike with those streaks in their hair and their ripped jeans . . . no care about what they look like, like we used to back in my day."

"So, it sounds like you may be mistaken and have the two girls mixed up. Is that a possibility, Ms. Moore?"

Yes Valerie, yes, Emily thought, trying not to show a smile on her face. She glanced down at her trembling hands and folded them, trying her hardest not to pick at her cuticles.

"Well, it sounds like that may have been the case."

Valerie grinned as she headed back to her seat.

"No further questions, Your Honor."

Emily sat back in her chair and breathed a little sigh of relief.

18

———◇◇◇◇◇———

"Coral reefs . . . dying," Nate explained as Charlie took a sip of his frothy beer. Emily stepped out of the bathroom, fully dressed, primped, and ready to go, wearing her new shirt and boots. Nate appeared to be talking to Charlie about the effects global warming was having on the ocean. He nodded at Emily midsentence and resumed his conversation.

The Who was playing loudly on the kitchen radio, and Emily could hear her mom singing along in her bedroom. "Whoooo are you? Who? Who? Who? Who?" Emily peeked her head in. Debbie was staring at herself in the mirror above her dresser as she applied red lipstick to her thin lips. She was wearing black jeans and a pink mesh top that needed to go back to the eighties.

Whenever Debbie dated someone new, she always got all primped up for them like she was going to a club, whether they were staying in or going out. Emily noticed a cocktail glass and a beer can sat on the dresser next to her makeup bag.

"Double fisting tonight, Mom?" Emily asked her as she leaned against the door and crossed her arms.

"Oh no, hon," Debbie exclaimed with a chuckle as she dabbed at her lipstick with a tissue. "I was already drinking this beer when Charlie got here, and he walked in and handed me this drink since he didn't know I already had one!"

"Mom, you're still double fisting if you're drinking them both, even if you didn't intend on it."

"Leave the attitude in the other room, missy," her mom teased her and then smiled as she picked up a drink in each of her hands and tried to take a sip of both at once, spilling a dribble down her chin. Emily rolled her eyes as she headed out of the door. *The good thing about new relationships is that my mom's always happier at first. Hopefully, Charlie won't end up like the rest,* she thought.

"What time is Hannah getting here, hon?" Debbie asked.

"When she gets here," Emily teased before giving her mom a grin. She headed into the kitchen and sat down next to Charlie and Nate at the table.

"I think we're going to get pizza and watch a movie, Em," Nate offered with a little glimmer in his eyes. He seemed excited; the atmosphere in the house was like there was some sort of hope of normalcy. "Do you and Hannah wanna hang out here with us?"

Nate's desire to stay in with Debbie was news to Emily. They never usually hung out as a family, and she could tell in the tone of Nate's voice that he also knew it was a special night. Nate, their mom, and Charlie all hanging out as a pretend family would feel special. *But not tonight,* she thought. *Tonight is my night with Hannah and my chance to get in with the popular crowd.*

"Sorry, not tonight, Nate," she said. Nate shrugged and then lowered his brow as Emily felt a wave of guilt go through her. Nate had always been the one to try to warm up to all their mom's boyfriends, whereas Emily had always kept her distance, not bothering to get close to someone who wasn't going to stick around. Whenever Debbie used to give them the bad news that things were over with Joe or Don or Mike or Tim or JR, Nate would lock himself in their room and play their dad's ancient records. Once, when Emily was snooping through his stuff, she found something under his mattress.

At first, she thought it was a porno magazine, but once she pulled it out, she realized it was a notebook. When she'd opened it up, she saw a family photo of Debbie, Emily, and Nate with a cutout of a man from a magazine pasted next to Nate. They were all posed in front of a huge Christmas tree cutout. Emily had thought the man was handsome; he looked a little like Nate. She'd flipped the page and saw another photo of Nate from when he was little. He was sitting on a swing and next to him was another cutout of a different man who was laughing so hard his eyes were closed.

As she flipped through the notebook, she found all different photo creations Nate had made of himself and a father he didn't have. A family he didn't have. *We aren't this family, Nate,* she'd thought, regrettably.

"Too bad, kiddo, we're going to have some fun without you," Charlie said. He strolled to the fridge and opened a can of cold beer and then opened the junk drawer that contained all their delivery food menus. He scrambled through the menus until he found what he was looking for, holding it high in the air. "Ah ha!" he exclaimed. "Tony's! I'm going to order us all my specialty pizza surprise!" Debbie stumbled into the room just as the radio changed to a Tom Petty song.

"My favorite song!" she shouted. Charlie took her hand and spun her in a circle, leaning her into a dip.

"Well, she was an American girl. Raised on promises," they both sang in unison.

Nate rolled his eyes at Emily as they observed the two of them dance. *Maybe they really could be something,* Emily thought. *I wouldn't mind Charlie as a stepdad, really. It'd be nice to finally have a dad in my life.* She heard a knock on the door and before she could head over to open it, Hannah turned the knob and stepped inside.

"Looks like the party's already happening in here!" Hannah exclaimed as she danced over toward Debbie and Charlie. The three of them took one another's hands and began belting out "American Girl" at the top of their lungs, not even caring they hadn't been introduced. Emily sat down next to Nate and picked up her mom's half drank beer that was sitting on the counter, taking a swig. Nate turned and gave Emily a surprised gawk as she shrugged and gazed back at the dancing trio. When the song was over, Hannah sashayed over to Emily and whispered, "You have the most awesome family ever!"

19

TRIAL DAY 2: JANUARY 8, 2019

———◦∞◦◦∞◦———

"The people call Landon Biggs to the stand, Your Honor."

Emily shifted the mint on her tongue that Valerie had given her when they'd sat down. It was hard for her to eat lunch again; they'd ordered crab cakes from Jimmy's Seafood and the fishy smell was getting to her stomach. She'd picked at a side salad, but there was ranch dressing on it, even though she'd asked for a vinaigrette, so she really couldn't stomach that either.

She focused her attention as a tall, thin man was sworn in. He was wearing a lemon-yellow polo shirt and blue glasses. *He looks like a minion,* she thought. She wished Katie and Sophie could've been there to giggle at him with her. They would've laughed. She felt her eyes begin to well up with tears and looked down at her feet.

"Mr. Biggs," Mindy began after he sat down, "can you tell the jury where you work?"

"For Home 4 U Safe Security, ma'am," he replied in a thick Baltimore accent.

"And how many years have you been working there, Mr. Biggs?"

"For about eight years."

"And what does your company do?"

"We install security systems, doorbells, and cameras in people's homes."

Emily thought back to the cameras in front of the Thomases' house. Why had they gotten them installed in the first place? Were they worried about break-ins? It seemed like a pretty safe neighborhood to her.

"And did you install any of your products in the Thomases' house at 1428 Oak Hill Road?"

"Yes, ma'am."

"What products did you install?"

"I installed a doorbell with a camera and a motion detector with a camera above the Thomases' garage door."

"And how long ago did you install this?"

Landon reached into his pocket, pulled out a receipt, and handed it over to Mindy. "As you can see here, I have the receipt from when I installed it." Mindy took the receipt from him and handed it over to the clerk.

"Please note to the court that the receipt is dated December 5, 2017," Mindy announced to the judge and jury. "And can you tell the jury and court how these devices work?"

"Yes, ma'am. Both devices are hooked up to an app on the owner's phone. If the doorbell is rung, for example," Landon pointed his finger as if ringing a doorbell, "the owner would get an alert on his or her phone and could view whoever was at the door. Also, both devices pick up motion. If either camera picks up motion, the owner will get alerts as well. The owners can also access live views from the cameras whenever they want."

He puffed up his chest proudly as if he'd been the one to invent the technology himself.

"So, these devices pick up any motion in their range and send the videos to the owner's phone, is that correct?"

"Yes, ma'am."

"So, what you're telling me is that anytime anyone has come or gone from the house, the Thomases have documentation of it on their phones?" Mindy furrowed her brow.

"Yes, they should, ma'am."

"And do they work at night?"

"Yes, they work at night. If they pick up a motion, a light will click on and the camera will record in the dark." Landon crossed his arms in front of his chest as he finished explaining.

"Thank you, no further questions."

"Does the defense have any questions?" Judge Wilson announced to the court, staring at Valerie. Mindy headed back to her seat and Valerie shuffled some papers around to the left of Emily and then stood up.

"Not at this time, Your Honor," Valerie responded and then sat back down. She turned and gave Emily a sheepish smile.

"We'll take a fifteen-minute break," Judge Wilson announced before slamming down his gavel.

During the break, Valerie turned to Emily with a serious expression on her face. "You said you snuck out of the back, right, Emily? Is there a chance you showed up on the cameras? I just want to make sure there aren't any surprises."

Emily felt like she was going to throw up at the thought of her showing up on any cameras. She couldn't tell Valerie the truth until she knew for sure she was seen.

"Yeah, I snuck out of the back like Hannah showed me," she responded. "So, I shouldn't be on the cameras . . . but either way they're going to have a witness saying they saw me outside."

"Yeah, but drunk teenagers may not be as reliable as video foot-age," Valerie informed her. "I just want to make sure that you're confident you didn't get yourself caught on camera that night or this is going to be hard to get you out of. I know the prosecution is still waiting on the footage from the cameras. I don't want any revelations I don't know about."

Emily picked at the cuticles on her fingers and grinded her teeth. There was a lot she hadn't told Valerie, but she hoped she wouldn't have to. Valerie glanced down, shuffling through papers again and then picked up her phone and started texting. Emily hadn't realized the footage from the cameras would be more than just from the night of the incident.

When they'd spoke before, Valerie had said they were looking through footage, but Emily just assumed it was from the night they'd died, not the whole month before. *That means the cameras will show the court every time I've gone to the house, including when I was there the night of Madison's party. How will I explain that to the court?* she worried. She debated if she should tell Valerie the truth.

She turned around to find Nate and her mom, but they weren't in the room anymore. *Mom must have gone for a smoke break and Nate probably went to the bathroom*, she thought. She reached into her purse and pulled out a Valium. She slipped it on her tongue and took a sip of the water bottle sitting on the floor next to her. She was hoping the second pill didn't make her too woozy, but she had more knots in her stomach than a sailboat. She needed something to calm her down.

"Can I go to the bathroom really quickly before break is over?" she asked, interrupting Valerie from her texting. Valerie nodded without glancing up from the screen, so Emily got up and rushed to the bathroom. She rushed into the stall closest to the door, thanking God the bathroom was empty, and immediately threw up the water and Valium she'd just swallowed.

I must really be feeling nervous if I'm throwing up right now, she thought as she dabbed toilet paper against her mouth and washed her hands. She grabbed another Valium from her purse and swallowed it dry as she investigated her face in the mirror. *"Look, mommy! Emawee is here!"* Sophie whispered from the bathroom stall behind her.

Emily wiped her running mascara from under her eyes and pinched her cheeks a little to get the color back. She grabbed a mint from her purse, popped it into her mouth, and exited the bathroom, hurrying to the conference room. She sat down and took a sip of her Diet Coke, hoping it would help with her nausea. The last thing she needed was to vomit in front of the entire courtroom.

20

———∞◇◇∞———

"You sure you don't want a slice of my famous specialty pineapple, bacon, and onion pizza, ladies?" Charlie asked with a chuckle, "It'll be here any minute!" Emily glanced at her phone and saw it was time for Hannah and her to head out to the party. They'd be late if they didn't leave soon.

"No one's gonna want to make out with me if I eat that so I think I'll pass, Charlie," Hannah said and laughed. Emily reddened, hoping Nate and her mom hadn't heard Hannah's comment.

"See ya, kiddos!" Charlie and her mom yelled.

As Hannah and Emily headed toward the car, Emily glanced back through the window at Nate sitting on the couch, watching TV alone. She felt a pang of guilt that she was leaving him when he had wanted so badly to have a family night. She shook her head and tried to refocus on the evening ahead.

"So, whose party is this, anyways?" she asked as Hannah started the engine.

"This girl Madison from the field hockey team," Hannah replied. "Do you know her? Blond hair, big boobs?"

Emily did know who Madison was. She'd once gone to a sleepover at Madison's in the fourth grade and from what Emily remembered, Madison lived in a nice neighborhood with big houses that had beautifully landscaped yards. The kind of neighborhood that she dreamed of living in. Madison had invited ten friends over for the slumber party. They had pizza and ice cream cake, and stayed up watching movies in her huge basement. At about midnight, Madison's mom had come down and told everyone to set up for bedtime, so all the girls had gotten their bags and set up their sparkly, princess-themed sleeping bags and pillows like the slumber party pros they were, unlike Emily. Emily did not bring a sleeping bag because she didn't own a sleeping bag, much less a sparkly, princess-themed one. She felt so mortified about not having one, she pretended she felt sick and went upstairs to tell Madison's mom that she'd thrown up in the bathroom. She had gripped her stomach pretending to be in pain to prove her point. Madison's mom had to call Debbie at the bar, and Emily had to wait an hour for her to come pick her up. Once she was in the car, Emily had cried the whole way home and kept pretending she was sick. She didn't want to tell her mom that she was embarrassed about the sleeping bag situation. That Monday at school, all the girls were talking about the fun things they did after Emily had left the party, and she'd felt so left out. She was never invited to a slumber party by any of those girls again. *Maybe they didn't want me to throw up in their big houses like they thought I did in Madison's,* she'd assumed. *Or maybe they only wanted friends who had enough money to own a princess sleeping bag.*

"Yeah, I know her," Emily answered as she gazed out of the window, starting to get nervous about being in a room full of people she wasn't friends with.

"Open the glove compartment," Hannah directed her. Emily opened it and took out a plastic bag filled with mini vodka bottles.

"Where'd you get these?" Emily asked, her eyes narrowing.

"I have my sources. Hand me one." Hannah grinned.

Emily took a bottle out and handed it to Hannah warily, wondering if she was planning to drink it while driving. Her curiosity ended as soon as Hannah grabbed the bottle out of her hand, unscrewed the cap, and downed it.

"I got four bottles, two for each of us," she told Emily. Emily examined the bag on her lap and took another bottle out. It reminded her of the mini bottle from *Alice and Wonderland* that said "Drink me." She unscrewed the cap and smelled it, twisting her head away quickly from the strong alcohol smell.

"Here," Hannah said, handing Emily a small bottle of apple juice she was holding between her legs. "Chase it with this."

Emily forced a smile and then poured the warm, burning liquid into her mouth and quickly took a sip of apple juice.

"One more to go and we'll be the perfect amount of relaxed for the party."

They each took the last two shots from their tiny bottles and finished off the apple juice. As they approached Madison's house, Emily started to feel the effects calming down her body and nerves. She opened the passenger mirror and double-checked her makeup as Hannah spritzed herself with some perfume and popped some gum into her mouth. They got out of the car and approached the party, their boots clicking on the newly paved driveway. Madison's party was in the same house that Emily remembered, and it looked just as scary as it had when her mom picked her up in the middle of the night so many years before.

Hannah approached the front door first, and Emily was happy to let her take the lead. When they entered, she scanned the living room to the left of the foyer, dining room to the right, and kitchen straight ahead through the hallway. It wasn't tremendously crowded but had a good amount of people inside. As they walked to the drink station in the kitchen, a couple of people said hi to Hannah, completely ignoring Emily.

"Here we go," Hannah announced as she took two red solo cups off the stack and filled them with ice, ladling some mysterious-looking juice from a punch bowl into each of them.

"Jungle juice, my favorite!" she exclaimed as she handed Emily her cup. Emily took a sip and was surprised by how good it tasted. Fruity, like Kool-Aid.

"Hannah!" a girl called from the family room adjacent to the kitchen. "Come play some drinking games with us!"

Hannah grabbed Emily's hand and tugged her over to the group of people crowded around a coffee table scattered with cards. Hannah introduced Emily to the group: Steve from the football team, Ben from the lacrosse team, twin cheerleaders Stacy and Mackenzie, and Brody, who was a male cheerleader. Brody, who was super bubbly, turned to Emily and explained the rules of the game, Cards Against Humanity, and whispered details about each player.

She learned that Ben was dating Stacy, Steve was dating Mackenzie, and Brody was dating a guy named Miles, an aspiring Broadway dancer who was at an audition in D.C. that very weekend. Emily glanced at their mouths, noticing they were all stained burgundy from the jungle juice.

As she began to play with her new friends, she allowed her worries to melt away. She started to loosen up, and her nerves disappeared. Everyone was so nice and friendly, and she laughed so hard, her belly hurt. She could hear "In My Feelings" by Drake playing on the speakers and unconsciously began bopping her head to the beat, singing along as she sipped her drink. *Look, the new me is really still the real me, I swear you gotta feel me before they try and kill me.*

During the second round of the game, she spied Topper and Chuck in the kitchen making themselves drinks. Hannah must've seen them too because she got up from her seat and veered over to give

Topper a kiss. Chuck smiled at Emily as he started toward her just as Savannah, the captain of the lacrosse team, approached him and put her arms around him. He turned to her and kissed her on the cheek. *I thought Topper and Chuck were calling her a slut at the playground?* Emily thought as she watched Savannah grab his hands and lead him outside to a group of people standing around a firepit. She glanced around the room to see if Hannah had seen Savannah, her frenemy, but Hannah was now nowhere in sight.

Without Hannah or Chuck around anymore, Emily decided to focus on the game. She was happy she didn't have to worry about Chuck shoving his tongue down her throat. And she didn't need to be glued to Hannah at all times; she could make new friends.

Ben flipped over a card and read it to the group: "In return for my soul, the devil promised me_____."

Emily scanned her cards before placing down the one she thought would be the most appropriate. Ben read the responses: "Dead babies. Keg stands. Doin' it in the butt. Five-dollar footlongs. Superhero dildos." Everyone was laughing as Ben's face became serious while reading Emily's card: "Acceptance."

Everyone looked confused and Emily blushed, hoping they didn't realize she'd been the one to put down that card.

"Well, I think the winner is Doin' it in the butt!" Ben yelled as Brody cheered and gave him a high five.

Emily continued to play for what must have been an hour as someone continuously filled up her cup. She'd lost count of how many drinks she'd had, and Hannah had never come back. *She's probably somewhere with Topper,* she thought, annoyed that Hannah had ditched her again. Her head started to spin, and she stood up to go to the bathroom, trying to remember where it was. When she finally staggered her way into the powder room, she closed the door and immediately threw up bright red jungle juice into the toilet. *Well, there you go, Madison. I threw up for real in your house this time,* she thought.

She flushed the toilet twice and tried to clean up any red marks before glancing in the mirror with blurry vision. She realized she probably needed to get home before she made any bad decisions or got sick again.

She fumbled in her purse and took out her phone to text Hannah. Squinting, she saw that she had a missed text from Nate. She opened it to see a photo he'd taken of Debbie and Charlie cuddling on the couch and another photo of himself holding a huge bowl of popcorn. The text said, "Wish you were here" below the pics and the pang of guilt she'd felt earlier in the night crept its way back into her heart. Trying to erase the remorse, she went back to searching for Hannah's number and texted her, asking where she was.

"Sorry girl Topper wanted some alone time are you ok?" Hannah texted back.

"Not feeling too hot do you think we could head home soon?" Emily texted, hoping she didn't sound too much like a loser. She didn't want Hannah to know she'd thrown up.

"We went for a drive and will be twenty or thirty more minutes if you know what I mean. I can send a car to take you home?"

"Okay, thanks," Emily texted back. She stumbled out of the bathroom, trying not to sway back and forth, and staggered toward the front door. She wobbled to the front porch, hoping not too many people noticed her leave. The night was cold and crisp, and she could smell the bonfire and weed drifting from the back of the house. She sat down and started rummaging through her purse for some gum, hoping that when the Uber arrived, she wouldn't barf in the car.

After about ten minutes passed, headlights approached, almost blinding her. She put her arm up to shield her eyes as the beams flashed, indicating they were there to pick her up. She got up and hobbled toward the Uber, then realized it was not an Uber. It was a bright yellow Mustang . . . and Mr. Thomas was driving. The passenger window rolled down and he smiled at her from the driver's side.

"Your chauffeur is here, madam," he yelled over the lousy music blasting from his radio.

"Oh, hi, Mr. Thomas," Emily murmured. "What're you doing here?"

"Hannah texted me that you needed a ride, and I was just coming home from getting some drinks with my buddies down the street. Hop in," he yelled as he leaned over the center console and opened the passenger side door for her. She felt a surge of panic go through her. *Why would Hannah text Mr. Thomas of all people to come get me? I can't let him see me drunk,* she thought.

"It's not a big deal," Mr. Thomas assured her as he lowered the music. "I give Hannah Banana rides whenever she needs one." He reached over and patted the passenger seat, indicating for Emily to get in. She hesitantly glanced around, hoping someone would see her and tell her what to do. She felt a wave of nausea come over her again. Not knowing what else to do, she got in the car.

"Atta girl," he squealed in delight. "I don't bite." He turned up the music and backed his car out of the driveway and into the street.

"So, not feeling well, huh?" he asked her. "Have too much to drink?"

"Um, a little," she replied hesitantly. *I guess the cat's out of the bag,* she thought.

"I feel ya. I used to get at it when I was your age too."

She leaned her head against the seat and gazed up at the moon, trying to keep her focus on something stable. Closing her eyes, she attempted to keep the nausea from creeping back into her stomach as she listened to Mr. Thomas sing along to Jason Derulo. Eventually, she heard the Mustang signal and turn into her neighborhood. As the car slowed down, she opened her eyes to see that they were not, in fact, at her house, but instead, pulling up to Mr. Thomas's house.

"What're we doing here?" she asked, disoriented as she jolted herself upright. "Can you take me home?"

"You don't want your parents to see you in this condition, do you? You and Hannah can sleep at my house tonight and let the alcohol wear off for tomorrow."

"I don't think that's a good idea," she said, shaking her head. "My mom will be worried, and I don't want to disturb your wife and kids."

"No disturbing at all. They're at our condo in Ocean City this weekend."

She touched her temples and closed her eyes tightly, trying to process the situation. *Is this really happening?* she wondered as she got out her phone with shaky hands. She texted Hannah, asking if she knew Mr. Thomas was taking her to his house.

"Yes, it's totally fine," Hannah texted back. "I'll be there soon and we can share the guest room."

Emily breathed a sigh of relief. She clicked on Nate's text from earlier and replied back: "Can you tell mom I'm just going to crash at Hannah's tonight?"

Nate didn't text back right away. He'd probably already gone to bed. She stumbled out of the car and Mr. Thomas led her up to the house.

"Guest room is upstairs, next to Sophie's room," he directed her. He walked into the kitchen and grabbed a beer out of the fridge. "You want a beer?" he yelled.

She hesitated but then said, "No, I think I'll just go upstairs if that's okay with you."

"Fine by me, darlin'," he said as he took a sip of his beer. Emily watched him rummage through the fridge, searching for food to eat. She staggered up the stairs and found the guest room, next to Sophie's room as Mr. Thomas had indicated. She closed the door quietly behind her, kicked off her boots and peeled off her sweater and jeans. She opened one of the dresser drawers and found a stack of seasoned T-shirts. She grabbed one and threw it over her head. Exhausted, she got under the sheets and glanced at her phone again, checking to see if Hannah had texted back. Still nothing. She put the phone down and closed her eyes, trying to make the room stop spinning.

She must've fallen asleep right away because when she felt Hannah get into bed next to her, she realized she hadn't heard her come into the room. She turned around to ask her where she'd gone with Topper and realized it wasn't Hannah in bed with her at all. Facing her in bed was Mr. Thomas, leaning his head down to kiss Emily's neck.

"Mr. Thomas!" she said, startled. "What're you doing in here? Get out!"

"Shh," he whispered. "Don't worry, baby, I'm not going to hurt you." He reached toward her shirt and ran his hands down to her underwear.

"Mr. Thomas, please," she whispered, trying to push his hands away. "Hannah will be here soon."

"Good, then maybe Hannah Banana would like to join us." He snickered. "Hannah likes to have fun with me too, you know."

He tugged at her underwear hard, and she felt them rip. As he kissed her neck, she felt him push his entire weight on top of her. *Is this a dream?* she thought. How could you ever be perfectly sure when you were dreaming or when you were awake? *Wake up, Emily! Wake up!* She started to feel nauseous, and her head felt like it was spinning. She felt a tear rolling down her cheek as she tried to push him off, but he was more than double her weight.

"Don't act like you don't want it, Emily," he whispered. Her head was spinning. *Is this happening? Maybe Hannah already came in and this is an awful nightmare. Is this what happens when you drink too much jungle juice and throw up, you have terrible nightmares like this?* She closed her eyes hard and opened them again to see if it was really happening. When she did, she saw Mr. Thomas's dark, beady eyes looking down at her. She closed them tightly again, deciding to keep them shut.

"Please," she begged him. "Please don't!" More tears started streaming down her face as he advanced and then suddenly, she felt a lightning bolt of pain between her legs. *I'm dreaming. I'm dreaming.* She squeezed her eyes hard and start singing "American Girl" in her head, trying to drown out the grunts coming from Mr. Thomas.

When he finished, he rolled off her to the other side of the bed. Emily lay as still as a rock, not knowing what to do, praying for him to get out of the room immediately. He leaned over and kissed her forehead. She winced as if he'd hit her. Then, she heard him give a little laugh as he headed out of the room.

She curled her body toward the window, trying to ignore the oozing stickiness and stinging pain coming from between her legs as she cried herself silently to sleep.

21

TRIAL DAY 2: JANUARY 8, 2019

———◦◦◇◦◦———

"The prosecution calls Madison Harris to the stand."

All eyes turned as Madison entered the room, her big boobs jiggling out of her tight, low-cut top. Her bleach blond hair was pulled up in a ponytail, and it bounced along with her boobs as she made her way to the witness stand.

As Madison was being sworn in, Emily couldn't help but think that she must not have gotten the memo about court attire since she looked like she was going to a Post Malone concert in her ripped jeans and brown hooker boots, but then admonished herself for thinking about Madison's outfit at a time like this.

"Hi, Madison. Can you tell me where you go to school?" Mindy began to question her.

Madison gave an award-winning smile and looked around the room as if she were a contestant for Miss Maryland and was about to be asked what her best quality was and why she should win the crown. "Crossland High School," she said and then glanced at the jury. Emily saw Madison's eyes catch on the attractive juror in the front row. She smiled inwardly to herself, knowing that he preferred Nate to her, which gave her a happy feeling like she'd won a little.

"What grade are you in, Miss Harris?" Mindy asked, smiling warmly at Madison.

"Eleventh," Madison replied as she bit on her lower lip.

"How do you know Emily Keller?"

"I've known her since elementary school," Madison said, looking disappointed by this fact.

"Elementary school? Wow, that's a long time! Are you still friends with Emily?"

"No, not really. We were friends when we were little, but now have different friends. I play a lot of sports like field hockey, so I hang out with a lot of those people. And Emily . . . I'm not sure what Emily does . . ." Her sentence drifted off and then she smiled and glanced over at the hot juror again.

I don't do anything, Emily thought as she picked at her cuticles.

"Have you talked to or hung around Emily at all this school year since you say you're not really friends?"

"Only two times . . . not in school."

"Can you tell me about the first time?"

"The first time I saw her, I had some friends over at my house and she showed up uninvited with my friend, Hannah. She ended up playing a card game with some people at the party and got really drunk and left."

"Do you remember the date of that party?"

"I do. My parents were in Deep Creek at my aunt's cabin that week. It was October 19. They got home the next morning after my party. I got in trouble because some kids had left beer cans in our bushes outside. I got grounded for a week and couldn't go to any parties the next week for Halloween and was totally bummed about it."

"And you said Emily got really drunk? How do you know that?"

"I saw her drinking during the party while she was playing a game. A little bit later I saw her swaying as she was walking to the bathroom, and I went into the bathroom after she came out and there was puke on the toilet seat and it reeked of throw-up." Madison wrinkled her nose up and closed her eyes in disgust.

"What happened after she left the bathroom?"

"I don't know. I didn't see where she went. I think she left."

"Thank you, Madison. And you said you saw her a second time this year, is that correct?"

"Yes, that is correct," she said flatly.

"And what was the date of that occurrence?"

"It was November 9."

"And where did you see Miss Keller on November 9?"

"There was a bonfire party outside in a field by the Crossland Fire House. I saw Emily there with a drink in her hand, and it seemed like she was getting cozy with a guy."

Mindy approached an easel that was set up to the left of the judge's stand that Emily hadn't noticed before and flipped a piece of cardstock around to reveal a map of the Thomas's neighborhood.

"People of the jury, I want to show you all a map of the Crossland community in case any of you are unaware of the neighborhood. Here is the Crossland Fire House." She pointed to the firehouse on the cardstock with a little laser pointer that she pulled out of her blazer. "And here, eighteen blocks away, is the Thomases' house on Oak Hill Road." She turned back toward Madison. "Madison, you said you saw Emily Keller at this bonfire party on the night of November 9 in a field behind the Crossland Firehouse, is that correct?"

"Yes, that's what I said."

"And what time would you say you saw her?"

"Maybe around eleven or twelve?"

"And you said she had a drink in her hand? Was it an alcoholic drink?"

"Yes, it was a beer."

"And why do you say she was getting cozy with a guy? Who was this guy?"

"A guy named Chuck Bailey from our high school. I could see her from across the fire and he was all over her, it looked like. I could see them holding hands and she pulled him away from everyone to go have sex with him."

Emily's mouth went agape, not remembering seeing Madison at all at the bonfire. *Is she lying?* Emily wondered. Either she was lying or she was hiding somewhere too.

She heard buzzing from the crowd behind her and turned to Valerie, hoping she'd yell "objection," but she didn't. She just scribbled away at the notepad sitting in front of her. Emily stared down at her hands and started to pick frantically at her cuticles again.

"How do you know they were going to have sex, Miss Harris?" Mindy asked with pursed lips, trying to keep composure in the court-room.

"Because Emily's a slut, that's why."

"Objection, You Honor," Valerie said, standing up.

"Sustained," Judge Wilson said as he gave Madison a stern look.

Emily heard gasping and chatter behind her, and she grimaced. *If they only knew the truth,* she thought.

"Sorry, Your Honor," Madison said. "But also, Chuck came back afterward and told everyone they had sex. He clearly looked like he'd been rolling around. His pants were still unbelted, and his hair was disheveled. Looked like sex hair if I've ever seen it." Madison grinned, innocently.

"Thank you. I have no further questions, Miss Harris." Mindy headed back to her seat and sat down. Emily faced Valerie, hoping she could telepath the right questions for her to ask Madison so she could prove to the jury that she was lying. Valerie ignored Emily, scribbling something on her notepad.

"Does the defense have any questions?" Judge Wilson asked, glancing their way. Valerie smoothed out her black skirt and rose from her chair confidently.

"Hello, Miss Harris. You said you saw Emily Keller the night of October 19 at your house, is that correct?"

"That is correct."

"And you said she was drunk? So drunk that she threw up in your bathroom and was swaying?"

"Yes, it was gross." Madison made a face of disgust as if that were the worst thing anyone could've ever done.

"And had you been drinking that night, Madison?"

"Well, yeah, it was a party."

"What type of alcohol did you drink?"

"Um, well, I guess I had a beer or two and some jungle juice. I had some White Claws too. And a shot or two of tequila."

"Wow, a beer or two, some jungle juice, a couple shots of tequila. That would put you at a minimum of five drinks, and I'm being forgiving here. Is that about right?" Valerie raised her brows.

"Well, yeah I guess." Madison looked down at her hands, her face flushing.

"And you're a petite girl, about one hundred and ten pounds?"

"One hundred and eight." Madison glanced up quickly, smiling grandly to the room.

"I'm sorry, one hundred and eight. A person who weighs one hundred and eight pounds ingesting five alcoholic beverages is considered to be highly intoxicated. I'm surprised you noticed everything going on with Emily at that party considering how much you had drank yourself. You said she was very drunk. Did you see what she was drinking?"

"She had a red Solo cup, so I'm assuming jungle juice or beer."

"Did you pour her anything to drink?"

"No."

"Did you get close to her and look at what she was drinking?"

"Well, no."

"So, could you be one hundred percent certain she was drinking at all?"

"Well, I guess not one hundred percent, but I mean, come on, she was playing a drinking game. Of course she was drinking."

"You're assuming. But again, you can't be one hundred percent sure. And you said you went into the bathroom right after her. Was someone in the bathroom before Emily?"

"What do you mean? I mean, I'm sure someone was, it was a party."

"So, someone could have vomited in the bathroom before she went in there?"

"I guess someone could have."

"So, since you didn't see her throw up and didn't see her drink, are you one hundred percent sure she was drinking at all?"

"No, I guess I'm not one hundred percent sure."

No, you're not, Emily thought as she shifted in her seat.

"And since you were apparently heavily intoxicated, could it have been you swaying rather than Emily swaying since you were drunk?"

Emily tried not to burst out laughing as Madison became flustered, something she clearly wasn't used to.

"Well, I don't know, everyone was drunk."

"Okay, thank you, Madison. Let's talk about the night of November 9, 2018. You said you saw Emily at a bonfire behind the Crossland Fire Department, is that correct?"

"Yes, that is correct."

"Had you had anything to drink that night?"

"Yes, it was a party."

"Of course, of course. So, would you say you had about the same amount to drink as you did at your party on the 19th?"

"Um, I mean, I don't know. I probably had a few beers."

"A few? How many is a few?"

"Maybe four or five."

"Okay, so four or five beers for a girl who weighs one hundred and eight pounds again would put you at a highly intoxicated state. You said you saw Emily at eleven or twelve at night? That must be dark at that time, right?"

"Right, but there was a bonfire."

"Of course, a bonfire. And she was across from it, so maybe fifteen feet or so away from you?"

"I guess so," Madison shrugged.

"So, after having five beers, it being eleven or twelve at night, would you bet your mother's life that you're one hundred percent certain that it was Emily across from you? Or is there a slim chance it could have been a girl that looked like her?"

"I mean, I guess it could have been a girl who looked like her, but I know Emily had a thing going on with Chuck and this girl was with Chuck."

"Ahhh. Okay. So, you're basing this on who she was with?"

"Well, Emily hooked up with Chuck before."

"Okay, so this girl looked a lot like Emily, and you thought it must be her because you thought Emily hooked up with him before?"

"I know she hooked up with him before."

"And did you have anything romantic going on with this Chuck character?"

"No, he was hooking up with a few girls I know, though. He's not the boyfriend type, if you know what I mean. I mean, sure, I made out with him a few times, but who hasn't?"

"So, did you have hard feelings because you believed Emily hooked up with him and he didn't want to date you?"

Emily could see Madison was getting flustered as her face flushed, and she couldn't help but feel happy. She did her best to conceal the grin beginning to form on her face.

"Me? Hard feelings. Hell, no. Emily is a slut, and that's a fact."

"Keep the crude comments to yourself or I'll remove you from the stand," Judge Wilson chimed in, giving Madison a death stare.

Emily felt her face turn as beet red as Madison's.

"So, it sounds like you have some resentments here, Miss Harris. Remember, lying in a court of law is a federal crime. You cannot just say you saw her because you're angry that she may or may not have hooked up with someone you were interested in."

"I'm not lying!" Madison interrupted. "I really did see her that night!"

"Madison, you had had five beers, it was around midnight, and you were looking in the dark from about forty feet away. Can you be one hundred percent certain you saw Emily Keller the night of November 9 at the bonfire behind Crossland Firehouse?"

"Ninety-nine percent certain," she said, her face turning sour, clearly not liking to be questioned in this way.

"Miss Harris, that's not what I asked. What I asked is if you were one hundred percent certain. Would you bet your mother's life on it?"

Madison gave a humph sound and crossed her arms. "Well, I guess not one hundred percent."

"No further questions, Your Honor."

22

PAST: OCTOBER 20, 2018

————⟡————

"**D**on't worry baby, I'm not going to hurt you," Mr. Thomas whispered as Emily woke up with a throbbing in her head and aching between her legs. As she rubbed her eyes, she came to the realization that she was still in the guest bedroom of Mr. Thomas's house. She glanced over and saw that Hannah was sleeping soundly next to her. *Was it a dream?* she wondered. No, it wasn't a dream. She wished it were. She peeled herself out of bed and stared down at the blood-stained sheets from where she'd been sleeping. She put on her clothes from the night before and tried to shake Hannah awake.

"Hannah," she whispered, not wanting to wake up Mr. Thomas from down the hall. Hannah stirred and opened one eye at Emily, wearily.

"What?" she groaned, groggily. "What time is it?"

Emily peered down at her phone and saw the time: 6:04 a.m.

"It's six," she replied. "Sorry, can you take me home? I really need to get home now."

"Come on, Em, it's a Saturday, let's sleep in," Hannah pleaded as she rolled onto her stomach.

"I really need to get home now," Emily repeated herself urgently as she shook Hannah's arm.

Hannah groaned again and sat up. "Fine, but you owe me one, bitch," she whined and then smiled at Emily, indicating she was joking.

"I'll be in the car," Emily whispered before tiptoeing down the stairs, trying not to make a sound. She snuck through the front door and quietly opened Hannah's car door, relieved that she'd left it unlocked the night before.

She closed the door gently behind her, as to not wake up Mr. Thomas. It was still mostly dark outside, but the sun was just beginning to creep up.

Five minutes passed and then she watched as Hannah dragged herself out the front door and down the steps. Her mascara was running down her face and she looked really hungover. She plopped herself next to Emily and started the car.

"What's the deal anyways?" Hannah asked as she backed out of the driveway.

"I just didn't tell my mom we slept out and I want to get home before she notices," Emily lied. As Hannah drove toward Emily's house, she lit a cigarette and Emily tried not to gag at the smell. She opened her window a crack, watching the sun mock her as it rose from the horizon, too bright and cheery for the somber day.

"Where'd you go last night?" she asked Hannah, annoyed at her suddenly.

"Topper wanted to go have some alone time, I told you," Hannah reminded her. "I got you a ride home, didn't I?"

"I really didn't feel comfortable seeing Mr. Thomas and sleeping at his house," Emily explained, not caring about clashing with Hannah this time. "He's really a creep."

"Oh, come on," Hannah said. "He's creepy in a kinda hot way!"

"Maybe if you like old creepy men," Emily said, shuddering. "He made me feel . . . uncomfortable." She wasn't sure how much she should tell her.

Hannah slowed the car down and glanced over at Emily warily. "Uncomfortable how?"

Emily shook her head. *I can't do this,* she thought.

"What happened with you guys last night?" Hannah asked as she blew smoke out of the crevice of her mouth.

"Don't act like you don't want it, Emily," Mr. Thomas whispered.

Emily hesitated, trying to decide how much to tell her. *What did happen with us? Did we hook up? Was I raped? I didn't want it, but I had gone inside his house, knowing it wasn't a good idea. Why would a dad with kids do this to someone my age? Did I say no? Maybe I didn't say no.* The night was so foggy.

"Nothing," she replied slowly as she gazed at the clouds drift in front of the rising sun ahead of them, making the sky dark again. "Nothing happened with us."

"You don't seem like your normal happy self, Em," Hannah said as she veered into Emily's street.

"I'm always happy," Emily said. "Sometimes I just forget."

23

TRIAL DAY 3: JANUARY 9, 2019

———◦◦◇◦◦———

E mily hovered over the toilet and dry heaved. She'd felt too nauseous to eat breakfast that morning, so she didn't have any substance in her stomach to throw up. Madison speaking the day before was just a foreshadowing of witnesses to come, and Emily's body was feeling way off. She couldn't seem to keep food down anymore and was feeling queasy all the time. That morning, the prosecution would question Topper, Chuck, and Hannah. Emily couldn't think of three people she'd rather see less. *Well, I can think of one person, but he's dead,* she thought as she unscrewed the bottle of Valium in her purse and placed two pills on her tongue. She couldn't risk showing her emotions in court and wasn't sure if she could handle it without the Valium.

She rinsed her face with cold water and patted it dry then applied some waterproof mascara and blush to make herself appear more presentable. *Crap,* she thought as she peered down at a run in her black tights that she must've snagged while she was in the bathroom. They were her mom's nylons and were too small for her, and to top it off they looked ridiculous with her ankle monitor. *Screw it*, she thought, too tired to take them off, and not caring what she looked like anymore. She stepped out of the bathroom and found Nate standing outside waiting for her. The sight of him made the knot in her stomach loosen up a centimeter. He narrowed his hazel green eyes and took her arm in his, undoubtedly seeing how disheveled and upset she was.

"It'll be okay, Em," he assured her as he squeezed her arm. "I'm here."

She followed him through the courtroom, her body rigid. All eyes were on her as she headed down the aisle, the quiet conversations humming from different directions pausing briefly at the sight of her. As they passed by Brandi's parents, she thought she heard someone whisper *murderer*. Or maybe she was imagining it . . . she wasn't sure what was real and what was only in her head anymore.

The room fell silent and everyone stood as Judge Wilson entered the room. As he went through the expectations for the day and the jury entered, Emily braced herself for the first witness, Topper. She couldn't anticipate what Chuck could've told him happened the night of the bonfire. She rubbed her sweaty hands down her legs, trying to calm herself.

"The people call Thomas Mitchell to the witness stand."

Emily cocked her head to the side, trying to process the name. *Have they called in a new witness I didn't know about?* she wondered. She shifted in her seat as the courtroom doors opened and Topper sashayed coolly into the room as if he were Justin Bieber on the red carpet. He was wearing tight black jeans and had on a red flannel button-down with the collar popped. His hair was gelled up just enough as if to appear like he just woke up with it that way.

As he was being sworn in, Emily glanced at the jury as they studied him intently, probably examining how attractive he was. His vivid blue eyes appeared bright in contrast with his red shirt, and his eyebrows were thick and furrowed.

"Mr. Mitchell, can you tell me what name you like your friends to address you by?" Mindy began.

"Everyone has called me Topper since I was little," he explained. "When I was two, I couldn't say my name, Thomas, and the name Topper always came out, so it just stuck." He grinned toward the jury looking like he thought he was the lead singer in a boy band and the jury was his fan club.

"Thank you for explaining, Topper. That'll help when speaking with my next couple of witnesses as well, so we don't get confused about names and who is who here. So, can you tell me where you were the evening of Friday, November 9, 2018?"

"I was with my girlfriend, Madison Harris, and we were driving around for a while hanging out, if you know what I mean," he said. Emily was stunned to hear Topper call Madison his girlfriend and frowned, thinking of what Hannah would think of his statement. He was definitely Hannah's boyfriend that night, not Madison's.

"We ended up going to a lame ass bonfire behind the Crossland Firehouse late that night."

"About what time did you go to the bonfire at Crossland Firehouse on the night of November 9, 2018?"

"Maybe like 11:30. I'm not sure."

"And did you see Emily Keller"—Mindy pointed her finger at Emily—"at the bonfire that night?"

"No, I didn't." Emily gave a sigh of relief, eased that he was telling the truth. She knew he didn't see her that night. She hadn't recognized anyone at the bonfire.

"But I know someone who definitely did," he continued.

"And who is that?"

"My buddy, Chuck." Topper smoothed his hair with his hand. Emily wondered if his hand was now greasy from all the product.

"Is that Chuck Bailey you're referring to?"

"Yep."

"And how do you know Chuck saw Miss Keller at the bonfire?"

"Because he made me take him to the ER afterward. He made me swear not to tell anyone."

Emily shifted in her seat, her heart rate accelerating as she anticipated what he was about to spill to the court.

"The ER?"

"Yeah, she did a number on his, excuse my French, dick," Topper said bluntly. Emily heard chatter behind her, and she put her head in the palm of her hands, trying to keep the embarrassment from forcing her to collapse onto the floor.

Mindy didn't blink and showed no emotion.

Emily didn't know how she could keep such a straight face during this questioning, while she felt like her armpits were going to sweat through her blazer.

"What do you mean, did a number on it?"

"I don't know, ma'am. All I know is he told me they had sex. He said she was so rough and crazy with that shit, he needed to get it looked at. I had to leave Madison at the bonfire to drop Chuck off at the ER so he could get help."

"Did you go into the hospital with him, Mr. Mitchell, to see what was wrong?"

"No, he wanted to go in alone," he explained. "But he texted me later and said she almost broke it or something, she didn't know what she was doing with it." The jury, Emily realized, was on the edge of their seats, eyebrows raised and alert. It was almost impossible to keep a neutral face during this part of the trial.

"Did he say anything else about that night to you, Mr. Mitchell?"

"Just that she was, pardon my French again, a skank and didn't know how to suck dick. He told the whole football team to stay away from her."

"Objection, Your Honor," Valerie said, gripping Emily's arm as she stood up abruptly.

"Sustained. Keep the language clean, son," Judge Wilson glared over at Topper.

"Thank you, Mr. Mitchell. No further questions." Mindy walked back to her seat grinning in Emily's direction. Emily immediately looked down at her feet feeling partly horrified, partly nauseous, and partly numb from the Valium. She could only wonder what her mom and Nate were thinking. Everyone would be talking about this at school if they weren't already.

Emily held her breath as Valerie stood up and began to question Topper.

"Good morning, Mr. Mitchell. You're fairly good friends with Chuck Bailey, is that correct?"

"Yeah."

"About how long have you been friends with him?"

"Maybe ten years, since we were kids."

That was pretty much as long as Emily and Steph had been friends. She wondered if male friendships had the same special bond as female ones, and if he and Topper were anything like she and Steph.

"So, you have been through a lot, huh?"

"You could say that."

"And what kind of things do you like to do with Mr. Bailey when you're together?"

"Oh, you know, usual guy stuff." He smiled at her sheepishly. That same sheepish grin he used on Hannah. That same sheepish grin he probably used on all the girls at the school. At least all the pretty ones. Not Emily.

"No, I don't know, Mr. Mitchell. Can you tell me?" she asked, her expression rigid.

"I don't know . . . we hang out. We drink . . . and have fun. You know."

"So you like to hang out and drink?" Valerie furrowed her brow.

"Well, yeah, you know."

"No, again, I don't know, Mr. Mitchell. That is what I'm trying to find out. So, you like to drink together. Do you like to smoke weed together?"

"Sure, I mean it's basically legal now."

"Do you like to do other drugs together?"

"What, am I on trial here or something or is Emily?" Topper shifted uncomfortably in his seat.

"No, I'm just trying to find out what kind of things you do with Chuck since you're not being specific. Have you ever done any other drugs with Chuck besides marijuana?"

"Well, yeah, sure."

"Like what?"

"Um, like Coke sometimes. We've done shrooms a couple times and some Molly and some acid. But only recreationally, you know. We aren't drug addicts or anything. Everyone at our school does them." He smiled again reassuringly, but his bright blues eyes looked a little faded.

"Of course." Valerie smiled back at him. She paused and looked at the jury, waiting for them to soak in his words. "Only recreationally. And the night of November 9, 2018, were you and Chuck on any drugs or had you drank any alcohol?"

"Well, I mean, sure, I'd smoked a bowl and had a beer or two but nothing crazy. Chuck had quite a few too it seemed, but like I said, I was with Madison earlier in the night, so I wasn't with Chuck at all before I saw him at the bonfire and he told me about screwing Emily."

"Right, you had said that, hadn't you? So, you said Chuck was pretty drunk?"

"Yeah, I guess, but I could clearly see he was in pain."

"Does Chuck always tell you about his personal . . . experiences with girls?"

"Well sure, don't all guys?" he asked with a grin.

Emily tried not to roll her eyes. Guys were horrible, disgusting human beings. They deserved to be removed from the planet entirely.

Except Nate, of course.

Valerie hesitated, pursing her lips. "I wouldn't know, Mr. Mitchell. As you can see, I'm not a guy." She smiled. "So yes, he tells you about all the girls he's intimate with?"

"Yeah, he does."

"And do you think he ever stretches the truth a little about how far he may or may not have gone with a girl to impress his friends?"

"I mean, sure. I guess some guys may exaggerate the truth at times." He shifted again in his chair as he adjusted his shirt collar. "But just for the record, I don't do that."

"I wasn't asking about you, Mr. Mitchell. I was asking about Mr. Bailey. So, you've known him to exaggerate things?"

"Well, I guess Chuck can exaggerate sometimes, but who knows? I'm never in the room with him and the girl he's banging."

"But do you think there is a possibility of him exaggerating what happened with him and Emily that night?"

"Look, I don't know what happened with him and Emily. But I *do* know Chuck. And Chuck was in *pain*," he raised his voice and frowned. "He would never have had me take him to the hospital if he didn't need to go. Why would he lie about that? All I know is someone definitely did *something* to him down there."

"Someone," Valerie interrupted. "But not necessarily Emily, since you never actually saw her that night with your own eyes, is that correct?"

"That's correct. I never actually saw Emily that night with my own two eyes," he agreed.

"So, another person could have done something to Chuck, and he could have blamed it on Emily?"

"That's possible, but again, I don't know why he would make that up. What in the world would he be trying to hide?"

What he's trying to hide, Emily thought, *are the actual details of what I did to him the night of the bonfire.*

24

PAST: OCTOBER 24, 2018

———◦◦◇◦◦———

The week following Madison's party passed by in a fog. Emily avoided responding to Hannah's texts and refused to look at her Instagram or social media. She'd cried herself to sleep every night, rummaging through her mom's medicine cabinet for sleeping pills to help get her through her restless evenings. All she kept imagining was Mr. Thomas's beady eyes above her. She wanted to roll over and blurt out to Nate what'd happened but lost her nerve every time she got close to telling him.

That afternoon at school, it took everything in her to force a smile and not break down and cry. She'd gotten her first D on her US History test because she couldn't concentrate on anything other than Mr. Thomas.

As she headed out of the building when the final bell rang, she felt a tap on her shoulder and turned around to see Chuck standing behind her smiling. She felt her stomach drop, ready for something terrible to happen.

"Hey, Em! How are you?" he asked, grinning. *Does he seem nervous to talk to me?* she thought as she eyed him suspiciously, trying to figure out if he was being sincere. She stared at the freckles covering his face, reminding her of a cheetah . . . or a leopard.

"Fine," she muttered as she turned toward the bus.

"Wait." He stopped her, grabbing at her shoulder. "Do you want a ride home?"

Surprised by his kindness, she lifted her eyebrows. *A leopard doesn't change his spots,* she thought to herself. "No thanks," she said, before turning toward the bus again.

"Are you sure?" he raised his voice as she walked away. "I just want to let you know whatever happened that one night at the playground . . . I was drunk . . . and if I made you feel any sorta way, I didn't mean to."

She eyed at him suspiciously. *What is he trying to get out of me right now?* she wondered.

"So anyways, maybe we can start over? Want me to give you a ride home?"

She turned and smiled unenthusiastically at him. "Maybe next time." Then she turned and headed for the bus, passing Brody and Stacy from the party who were standing nearby in their cheerleading uniforms. They both waved, and Emily waved back.

As much as she would've loved to be friends with them, seeing them only reminded her of that night at Madison's party. Of Mr. Thomas's house. Seeing them made her remember it all.

And all she wanted to do was forget it all. She hadn't realized that when she'd manifested all these things for herself, they'd come with a price. A hefty price.

When she stepped on the bus, she noticed that most of the seats were empty and then remembered there was a pep rally after school. She looked for Nate but recalled him telling her he was staying after school to tutor someone for some extra money. As she headed down the aisle, she spotted Steph sitting in the back row, gazing out the window. She wandered back and sat in the empty seat adjacent to her.

"Hey," Emily chirped, leaning toward her former best friend.

Steph turned from the window and smiled. "Hey, Emily."

"Wanna go over to Miss Jelly's this afternoon?" Emily asked, surprising even herself. She realized that she needed to go back to her old normal. She needed an afternoon of Steph, Miss Jelly, and homemade cookies.

"Sure, I could for a little," Steph said, grinning. "I could use some help with my stat homework actually."

Emily smiled back at her. She was an ace at math. "Well, you're in luck, I just got a ninety-eight on my stat test."

The bus dropped them off and they walked side by side to Miss Jelly's house in silence. As they approached her trailer, it was as if Miss Jelly had a sixth sense and the door opened before they knocked.

"Are those my girls?" she asked, welcoming them both into the house with hugs like a grandmother who hadn't seen her grandkids in a year. She set up some hot tea and a bowl of potato chips on her kitchen table and Steph and Emily got out their notebooks to begin their homework.

"I'm going to run to the store to get some butter for my cookies, girls," Miss Jelly informed them. They nodded at her as Emily showed Steph probability density functions in her textbook.

"Ah, I'm starting to get it now," Steph said as she scribbled away in her notebook. Emily smiled at her and took a sip of her tea. She took a deep breath and began to feel a little calmer. As Steph continued to work on her homework, Emily took out *In Cold Blood* by Truman Capote.

She had an eight-page essay due next week about the murder of the American dream and hadn't started it yet. As she flipped through the pages, thinking about where to start her thesis, Steph stopped what she was doing and peered up at her.

"Listen, Em, I'm sorry for everything I said about your dad leaving you and your mom being a drunk," she blurted out, her face turning red.

Emily glanced at her and smiled sympathetically at her apology. "I'm sorry for all that I said too. I *was* up those popular girls' butts and was neglecting you. Can we start over?" she asked her hopefully.

"Definitely," Steph agreed, and went back to scrawling in her notepad.

They remained silently working for a few minutes side by side. "So, you and Hannah have gotten pretty close this year, huh?" Steph asked, without glancing up from her notebook.

"Um, yeah, sorta," Emily admitted, trying not to blush.

"That's cool. She seems nice."

"Yeah, she is." Emily wasn't sure where she was taking the conversation.

"I see her in the bathroom sometimes," Steph continued. Emily stared at her quizzically trying to figure out why she was telling her this. Then she said, "She cries a lot in there."

Emily gawked at her, trying to act surprised. "Cries?" she asked, feeling a little like she should protect Hannah's privacy.

"Yes, cries. She always hides in the last stall during fifth period. She doesn't know that's usually when I use the bathroom too, but now I just go out of habit to see if she's there. And I always see her navy and hot pink backpack on the floor under the stall. She always cries so quietly, most people would never notice. But I do. She must be an incredibly sad person somewhere deep down."

Emily knew that Hannah had her demons. But she hadn't realized she cried in the bathroom every single day. She hadn't realized quite how sad Hannah just might be. She seemed so happy and flawless with the picture-perfect life compared to Emily's.

"I guess you never know what people have going on behind closed doors. Sometimes the people with the biggest smiles are struggling the most," Steph said as she flipped the page of her stat book, looking like she wanted to say more but hesitated. "One time I stepped out of the stall and even saw she had cut herself."

Emily peered up at her in shock remembering what Hannah had confided to her about cutting. Remembering the marks on her wrist. She hadn't realized Hannah was cutting in the bathroom at school. She hadn't realized she was doing it that often.

"Cut herself?" she asked.

"She had a little razor in her hand when she stepped out and when she was washing her hands, I could see some blood coming from her wrist. I asked if she was okay, and she said she was. I wasn't sure if I should've said something to a teacher or not."

"Oh wow," Emily exclaimed, glancing out the window that overlooked her trailer next door. She could just make out Nate sitting on his bed putting in his earphones. He must've just gotten home. She'd never noticed you could see in their bedroom from this window in Miss Jelly's house.

She wondered if Miss Jelly ever investigated their lives from this window. Probably not. She wasn't a nosy type of person. She directed her focus back to Steph.

"Did you ever ask her what was wrong?" she asked Steph, not wanting to tell Steph Hannah's secret. It wasn't her secret to tell.

"Yeah, but she said I wouldn't understand," Steph explained. She turned her head and focused on Emily seriously. "I just think whatever Hannah is going through, it's something serious, even if she acts like she's okay on the outside. And I just want to warn you before you get mixed up in all of that."

Emily stared at her, wanting to tell her that she understood what Hannah must've been going through. She began to feel nauseous, thinking back to Mr. Thomas and Hannah.

"Good, then maybe Hannah Banana would like to join us." Mr. Thomas snickered. "Hannah likes to have fun with me too, you know."

She wanted to tell Steph that all she wanted to do right then was put a razor to her wrists like Hannah must have that day. She wanted to tell her that all she wanted to do was to feel some kind of pain other than the pain she felt remembering what Mr. Thomas did to her. *Maybe Hannah cut herself because Mr. Thomas did to her what he did to me. Maybe she never really wanted it.* She was beginning to understand that maybe Hannah had been masking a lot more from her than she'd realized. Before she got up the nerve to tell Steph all she was feeling, Miss Jelly opened the door and stepped in, carrying two bags from the grocery store.

"I hope you're hungry, girls," Miss Jelly announced. "Because I'm making my famous chili baked potatoes for dinner." Steph and Emily looked at each other and a smile lit up their faces.

"I'm just going to walk over and invite Nate too," Emily said, as she headed to the door. *Maybe,* she decided, *instead of using a razor like Hannah did, I can use these three people to heal this deep wound inside of me.*

25

TRIAL DAY 3: JANUARY 9, 2019

———◦◦◦◦◦———

"What little weasels," Debbie huffed as she blew out a puff of smoke from the corner of her mouth. During the short recess, Emily had gone outside with her mom and Charlie while they smoked. Nate refused to inhale their secondhand smoke so he was waiting inside with Steph and Miss Jelly. "How dare they say my Emily would do something like that." She focused her eyes on Emily, her brow furrowed as she put her arms around Emily's waist. She leaned her head against Emily's protectively.

"You didn't do anything sexual with that boy, Chuck, right, Em?" Debbie asked as she flicked her cigarette with her finger. Her expression transformed to surprise when she saw Emily didn't respond right away. "It's okay if you did, I mean . . . I've made my fair share of mistakes with men, and believe me I started way earlier than you."

"Nothing sexual happened with us that night, I swear," Emily told her honestly.

"I knew it." Debbie grinned at Charlie.

"Of course, she didn't," Charlie responded. He blew out a puff of smoke and it hit Emily directly in the face. She gagged and immediately turned to the side of the stair rail, throwing up the water she'd drank from the fountain earlier.

"Oh no, honey!" Debbie leaned over and patted her back. "Charlie, don't blow smoke in her face! Have some decency!" She grabbed a bottle of water from her oversized brown purse, unscrewed the cap, and handed it to Emily. "Poor thing, you're a bundle of nerves." She tipped the bottle into Emily's mouth and poured the water in.

"I'd be throwing up too if I were you," Debbie pointed out. "All these people lying and judging you for things you didn't do." She reached into her purse again, took out a small flask, and unscrewed the cap. "Forget that water, you need some of this to calm your nerves." She handed Emily the flask. "Take a couple sips, hon, and calm your nerves."

Emily glanced back and forth at the two adults in front of her, casually offering her a flask of liquor before ten in the morning in front of a courthouse. She shrugged as she grabbed the flask and took a long swig, flinching as the potent taste of the whiskey sliding down her throat. She quickly grabbed the water and chased the sip down with it hoping she wouldn't throw up again.

"There ya go," Debbie said coolly as she grabbed the flask from Emily and took a sip herself. She screwed on the cap and placed it back in her bag. "We'll have more for lunch, okay, sweetheart?" Emily nodded and turned to go back into the courthouse, not sure of who her mom really wanted to help in this situation, Emily or herself. They took their positions back in the courtroom and she anxiously waited for the next witness.

"The people call Charles Bailey to the witness stand."

All eyes turned as the doors opened and Chuck marched into the courtroom and sat down at the witness stand. As he was sworn in, his fiery hair and pale skin appeared iridescent in the bright courtroom lights. His huge muscles bulged out of his tight-fitting white shirt, and he looked as if he could bench press every one of the jury members at once.

Mindy began the questioning. "Hello, Mr. Bailey. You like to be called Chuck, is that correct?"

"That's correct, ma'am," he responded politely. Emily had never heard him speak when he was sober, besides the one time he'd offered her a ride home after school. He was either surprisingly polite or good at pretending to be polite.

"Thanks, Chuck. Can you tell me where you go to high school?"

"Crossland High, ma'am."

"And what year are you in?"

"I'm a senior, ma'am."

"Have you ever met the defendant, Emily Keller, previous to today?" Mindy pointed at Emily, and Chuck's eyes slowly veered in her direction. Emily looked him in the eyes for one quick second and immediately darted her eyes down to her shoes. She gripped her chair tightly, thinking back to his lips on hers. The thought of him close to her made her want to throw up.

"Yes, ma'am, I've met Emily."

"About how many times have you met Miss Keller?"

"We've hooked up a couple of times." He clenched his jaw tightly and folded his arms in front of him.

Emily flashed her eyes up toward him in alarm. *Liar,* she screamed in her head.

"Where did these, what you call hookups, take place?" Mindy walked over toward the jury box.

"The first time was a few months ago. We met Hannah and Emily across from the Thomases' house at a playground while they were babysitting. They went off somewhere and Emily and I hooked up."

"Who is 'we'?" Mindy asked, leaning an elbow lightly against the wooden jury box. Emily began to feel sweat drip down her back. *Was it getting hotter in the courtroom?* She glanced around to see if anyone else was sweating as much as she was.

"Me and Topper."

"And you said Emily and Hannah were babysitting that evening?"

"Yes, ma'am."

"Do you happen to remember the location or address of the house where they were babysitting?"

"Yeah, the Thomases' house on Oak Hill Road."

"Do you remember when this hookup occurred?"

"Um, lemme think . . . it was probably around the beginning of October or something. About a month after school and football season had started."

"Do you know if Miss Keller and her friend left the children alone in the house to meet you in the playground across the street?"

"Yes, ma'am, they did. They said they had a baby monitor to keep an eye on them."

Emily could see Valerie scribble something down on her notepad next to her as he spoke.

She wanted to take off her blazer to cool down but didn't want to bring any more attention to herself than she needed to.

"And what did you all do in the playground across the street?"

"What do you think?" he asked with a sheepish grin. When he realized Mindy wasn't smiling back, he shifted a little in his seat, coughed into his fist, and continued. "Well, we drank, and we hooked up."

"You and Miss Keller drank?"

"Yeah."

"What were you drinking?"

"Vodka."

"Do you remember how much of the vodka Emily Keller consumed that night?"

"Oh, I don't know, but I'm sure a bunch of shots, I'd guess."

Emily closed her eyes and tried to contain her anger.

Not only was he lying about how much she drank, but he also was leaving out anything about Hannah and Topper drinking at all.

"Wow, I'd assume that'd get a teenage girl pretty drunk then, huh, Mr. Bailey?"

"I guess so," he conceded.

"And can you tell me what you mean by hooked up?"

"Well, you know," he scratched the back of his head. "We went into the woods . . . and we . . . had sex."

Emily squeezed her hands together tightly. She couldn't believe he was lying. *Wasn't lying under oath illegal?* she thought. She closed her eyes and felt the whiskey she'd drank ooze into her blood and mix with the Valium already drifting in her bloodstream. She imagined herself sitting on a raft as it floated through her body, numbing each part. She wished she could pop another Valium into her mouth right then, but too many eyes were on her.

"And after you had sex, did Miss Keller go back to babysitting the children that night?"

"Yeah, her and Hannah went back."

Mindy paused and looked at the jury as she spoke. "So, you're saying Miss Keller left children alone in a house while she was in charge of taking care of them, got drunk, had sex with you, and returned to the house and continued to babysit the children while intoxicated?"

"Yeah, that's what I'm saying, ma'am." His eyes sharpened as he spoke.

Emily glared at Chuck's face, willing him to look at her. She couldn't believe he was lying this much. She stared into his eyes and flinched when all of a sudden his eyes darted to hers and he gave the quickest smirk and then looked away. His dark eyes had appeared almost black. A signal only she would know: this testimony was him getting back at her for what she did to him the night of November 9.

"And you said you saw Miss Keller another time?"

"Yeah, I hung out with her one other time."

"Do you happen to recall the date of the night you hung out with her?"

"Yes, ma'am. It was the night of November 9. I know that because I had to go to the ER that night."

"And can you tell me what happened on that night?"

"I was at a bonfire behind the Crossland Firehouse. I was minding my own business when I saw Emily out of nowhere. She looked like she was drunk or something and seemed to really want it from me bad. She pulled me away, so we could be alone."

"And what happened when you were alone with her?" Mindy asked, raising an eyebrow.

"We had sex and she pleasured me." Emily watched as two jury members raised hands to their mouths. She thought of Miss Jelly sitting behind her.

Of Steph.

Mindy nodded. "Can you tell me why you would have to go to the ER after that happened? One does not usually have to go to the ER after having intercourse."

"Let's just say, she didn't know what the hell she was doing, okay? I'm not going to give you all the details on my personal manhood, ma'am. But that girl, she's an amateur slut."

Emily heard chatter begin from behind her. Was it her mom and Charlie? Or someone who'd never even met her?

"Now, Mr. Bailey," Judge Wilson interjected, "we won't be using that language in my courtroom."

Chuck peered up at the judge nervously. "Sorry, sir," he apologized, setting his jaw.

"Mr. Bailey," Mindy continued, "do you have a copy of the ER bill or receipt for the jury to see?

Chuck stood up and pulled out a folded wad of paper from his back pocket and then handed it to Mindy. She unfolded it, skimming it quickly.

"Your Honor, I'd like to let the jury know that there is a medical statement here from Franklin Square Hospital dated the morning of November 10, 2018, at 1:30 a.m. It states that Charles Bailey was treated for corpus cavernosum."

She handed the piece of paper over to the clerk who then walked up to hand it to the judge.

"Can you please tell the jury what corpus cavernosum is, Mr. Bailey?" she asked, looking at the jury as she spoke.

"Before you respond, Mr. Bailey," said Judge Wilson, as if anticipating the spectators' reactions, "I'd like to remind the courtroom that if people cannot act like adults in here, you will be asked to leave."

Chuck blushed, glancing down at his feet. "Penile fracture, ma'am." A gasp went through the crowd behind Emily, and she put her hand up to her mouth in astonishment that he was revealing this to the courtroom.

"Order in the court!" Judge Wilson slammed down his gavel. "If the people in this courtroom cannot contain the noises or chatter, I'm going to have to ask you to leave. This is the last warning."

"Thank you, Mr. Bailey. No further questions, Your Honor." Mindy glanced toward Emily quickly before heading back to her seat.

Emily glanced at Valerie as she jotted away on her notepad before standing up and heading over to Chuck.

"Mr. Bailey, can you tell me when you first met the defendant, Emily Keller?"

"I told the other lady already." He folded his arms in front of his chest and frowned.

Valerie paused, cocking her head in amusement as if she wanted the jury to see his true personality. "Can you remind me again, please, Mr. Bailey?"

"Yes, at the playground on Oak Hill Road across from the Thomases' house when she was babysitting."

"Oh right, so you say that was the first time meeting her?"

"Yes, didn't I say that about a hundred times already?" he huffed. Emily tried to hide a smile, glad that he was showing his true colors.

"How would she have planned to meet up with you that night if you had never met?"

"Well, my buddy Topper set it up with Hannah."

"Topper as in Thomas Mitchell?"

"Yeah."

"So, you and Topper went to meet Hannah and Emily, is that correct?"

"Yes, ma'am, that's correct."

"Were Topper and Hannah dating at that time?"

"At that time, they were, yeah."

"So, Hannah was going to sneak out and meet Topper and since Emily was with her, she brought her, and Topper brought you?"

"Yes, ma'am."

"Had you ever met Hannah or anyone else there before?"

"No, ma'am."

"Do you know if Hannah and Topper had met there before?"

"From what Topper said, him and Hannah met there a few times."

"A few times while Hannah was babysitting for the Thomases?"

"Yes, ma'am."

"So, was it Hannah babysitting for the Thomases that first night you met Emily or Emily babysitting?"

"Well, I don't know. I guess Hannah was babysitting and Emily was with her."

"So, in fact, Hannah was the person in charge of the children that night and had snuck out like this before with her boyfriend Topper?"

"Well, I don't know who oversaw the kids that night, ma'am. All I know is they were together."

"But you can't confirm that Emily had ever babysat for the Thomases before or if she was actually babysitting that night at all, because it seems likely that the recurring babysitter, Hannah, would more likely be the babysitter that night and not Emily?"

"No, I can't confirm that."

"Thank you, Mr. Bailey. And now to the night of November 9. You say you saw Emily at the bonfire? Can you tell me who she was with?"

"She was alone."

"She was alone at a bonfire? Isn't that a little strange?"

"I guess, yeah."

"What was she doing at the bonfire when you saw her?"

"Well, she wasn't actually at the bonfire. She was nearby behind a tree."

"Behind a tree, you say. So, it doesn't sound like someone who was at a bonfire at all? Maybe just a girl observing a bonfire?"

"I don't know, ma'am. All I know is I saw her there that night and we hooked up."

"Right, you hooked up. For the . . . second time, you say, correct?" Valerie hesitated, clearly wanting the jury to see she didn't believe his words.

Emily held her breath. *Fix this, Valerie,* she thought.

Chuck eyeballed the room nervously. "Correct," he said, coughing into his hand again.

"Did you have to go to the ER after you hooked up with her that first night on the playground at Oak Hill Road?"

"No, ma'am"

"But you say you had the same intimacy level with her both nights?"

"That's correct."

"That's odd to me. That the first time you were intimate with her, you had no complaints. And then all of a sudden, she was so inexperienced and didn't know what she was doing that you had to go to the ER! Seems like a big change up, doesn't it, Mr. Bailey?"

"It does, I guess," he admitted as he shifted in his seat uncomfortably.

"Are you aware, Mr. Bailey, that lying under oath is a federal offense? If you're lying about what you say about what Miss Keller did to you, that is a crime."

"I'm aware and I'm not lying," he demanded, his voice rising a little as he crossed his arms in front of his chest.

"I should hope not, for your sake. No further questions, Your Honor." Valerie headed back and sat down next to Emily as Chuck gave her one last satisfied smile before he was dismissed.

26

———◦◦◇◦◦———

Heaviness, now familiar and almost welcoming to Emily, filled her chest. She lay down on her bed and scrolled through her Instagram feed, trying to imagine herself in someone else's life. *Acceptance*, she thought, *that's all I wanted.* When she'd gone through everyone's posts twice, she finally opened the fifteen un-responded-to texts from Hannah asking Emily what was wrong. Her final text had asked if Emily wanted to go to a party on Saturday. Emily closed her eyes and then pressed delete on each one.

She'd spent the last week of October quarantined in her trailer. She couldn't fathom going to another party or having another drink of alcohol again, yet somewhere deep down, she couldn't help but yearn for something to numb the thoughts going on in her mind. She was still sore from the night with Mr. Thomas, which was a constant reminder of what happened to her, even though she was trying her hardest to forget it. She couldn't tell anyone what happened and wouldn't allow herself to think that was how she had lost her virginity, with a thirty-something-year-old drunk married man. To get her mind in the right space, she'd attempted to avoid social media all weekend, she'd rewatched old episodes of *Friends* on Netflix, and she'd even worked a bit on her big essay due the following week.

Glancing back down at her phone, she finally caved and texted Hannah back, deciding that Hannah didn't do anything intentionally wrong to her. Hannah wasn't the one who raped her.

"Sorry, been having major period cramps and have felt like crap," she lied. Her period had been a couple of weeks before.

"Oh, I hear ya girl!" Hannah texted back right away. "What are you up to this weekend? Wanna babysit with me?"

Emily looked down at the question and felt her heart begin to palpitate just thinking of ever stepping back into that house again.

"I can't this weekend I have a big essay due next week," she texted back with trembling hands, which was the truth, she did have a big essay due. But Hannah didn't need to know that Emily only had one page left and would probably be finished by tomorrow.

"Oh darn, I thought we could just hang out there and have a girls' night? Popcorn and soda?" she texted back. *She obviously knows something is up. Otherwise, there's no way in hell she'd want to stay in and have a girls' night. Especially because I heard in the hallway there's supposed to be some big bonfire party this weekend and I think it's near the Thomases' house. There's no way Hannah would want to miss that,* Emily thought.

"Bummer, maybe next time? Wanna come over one night next week?" Emily texted, hoping to appease her.

"Def! Lemme know which night!" Hannah replied. It seemed to satisfy her enough, so Emily put down the phone and let out a sigh of relief. She needed to somehow think of an excuse to never babysit for the Thomases ever again. She saw her bedroom door open slightly from the corner of her eye and Nate's head popped in.

"Wanna head to C & M for dinner?" he asked. Emily realized she was famished.

"Yes!" she exclaimed as she grabbed her purse and slipped on her shoes that were sitting by the door.

As they walked the familiar route to the bar, Emily zipped her jacket up and examined her breath as it exited her mouth, reminding her of her mom's cigarette smoke. The extended summer they'd been having was over and it officially felt like winter.

"How was the party with Hannah last weekend?" Nate asked. Emily had expected him to bring this up. She'd been avoiding him since the night of the party so he hadn't had alone time with her to ask any questions.

"It was good," she muttered quickly as she rubbed her hands together and blew on them to keep warm.

"You slept at . . . Hannah's?" he asked casually as he kicked a rock toward her. She opened her eyes wide and stared back at him quizzically. She felt terrible lying to her brother.

"Hannah's . . . friend's house," she said, hoping that the shorter the answers she gave, the less he'd ask.

"Which friend?" he asked. She kicked the rock to him, trying to think up a person he would believe. Nate could always tell when she lied.

"Come on, Em," he urged, stopping their walk as he turned toward her. "It's me. I don't give a shit where you slept. I just want you to tell me the truth." He kicked the rock back in her direction.

"The place where we babysat the other night," she admitted honestly. "Mr. Thomas's house." She kicked the rock back to him and it hit his shoe. She couldn't see his face so she didn't know what his expression might be.

"Why would you sleep there?" he asked in surprise as he slowly started walking again. "That seems really weird to have two teenage girls sleeping with a whole family at home."

"Hannah had asked Mr. Thomas for a ride home and instead he took us to his house," she revealed to him, omitting the fact that he took only her there because Hannah was out having sex with Topper. "His wife and kids were at their condo in Ocean City for the weekend, so he let us sleep in the guest room."

"Why wouldn't he just take you guys back here? You know Mom doesn't care if you guys were drunk."

She tried to think up an excuse but was starting to have trouble coming up with lies. "Hannah didn't want to sleep on our couch. She wanted her own bed," she blurted out the best excuse she could think of.

"Seems weird to me for a grown man to have two teenage girls sleep at his house. Did his wife know?" He kicked the rock toward her.

"I'm not sure," she lied and kicked an empty beer can sitting on the side of the road as she passed by it instead of the rock. She watched as rancid beer spattered out.

"Did he try anything on you guys?" He kicked the beer can away and slowed down.

"Try anything? No."

"Just seems creepy, Em, for a married guy with kids to have two teenage girls over. If he didn't try anything then he might another time. If I was you, I'd steer clear of sleeping there. Tell Hannah she can sleep in my bed next time, and I'll sleep on the couch."

"Okay," she agreed. Nate stared at her with a concerned expression as if he knew she wasn't telling him the whole truth. She felt guilty as if she'd done something wrong. She wanted to tell him what happened but if she did, she was worried he'd tell someone or he'd judge her. All she wanted was for him to hug her and tell her it would be okay. Instead, she kicked another rock as she hugged her arms across her body, trying to keep warm.

They approached C & M and stepped inside, feeling a rush of warmth hit their frigid bones. Charlie was sitting in his usual seat and patted the barstools next to him when he saw them enter.

"Do you ever leave here?" Nate asked him as he gave Charlie a fist bump.

"I have the prettiest bartender in all of Baltimore waiting on me. Why would I leave?" Charlie jeered with a grin. Debbie was across the room, serving crabs to three men with matching camo hunting vests on. Emily observed as one man grabbed her mom's butt while she walked away from the table and the other two men laughed. Debbie swatted his hand away without looking behind her and then held up her middle finger in the air for them to see.

"Hi, honeys," she said as she approached them, leaning over to give Nate and Emily each a kiss on their foreheads. "How was school? You both almost finished with your essays?"

"I finished mine," Nate boasted.

"I have a few more sentences but should be done tonight," Emily said. She'd been trying to work hard to get her schoolwork back on track since her grades had been dropping the past couple of weeks. It'd been so hard to focus when all she could think about was Mr. Thomas.

"Great!" Debbie exclaimed with a smile. "How did I raise such smart kids?" She poured herself a shot glass of brown liquor and slugged it back as she gave both her kids a warm smile. "Guess you got it from your father and not me. At least he was smart enough to get out of this place." She put the shot glass down and walked over to the elderly man at the end of the bar, handing him a new beer.

At least he was smart enough to get out of this town, Emily thought.

27

TRIAL DAY 3: JANUARY 9, 2019

———◦◦◊◦◦———

"The people call Hannah Patterson to the witness stand."

Emily felt the hair lift from the back of her neck as Hannah walked into the courtroom and was sworn in. She had puffy red eyes and was holding tissues in her hands. She appeared so different from when Emily had last seen her. Her hair was dyed ombre pink, and she had a new gold stud in her nose. She still looked as beautiful as ever but just sad and beautiful.

As Emily stared at Hannah, she felt a surge of resentment build up inside of her that she hadn't realized was there before. She understood she was on trial for her own poor choices, but Hannah was the reason she'd made those choices. *I wish I never met you,* she thought as she glared at her former best friend. She thought about where she would be right then if she hadn't met Hannah. *At C & M with Steph? Doing homework with Nate at The Pit?* The possibilities were endless.

Mindy began the questioning. "Hello, Miss Patterson. Can you please tell the jury where you go to high school?"

"Crossland High," Hannah replied in a somber tone, not sounding like herself whatsoever.

"And do you know the defendant, Emily Keller?" Mindy asked, pointing toward Emily.

From the witness stand, Hannah's eyes made contact with Emily's for just a moment before slipping away. "Yes."

"Can you tell the jury how long you have known her?"

Hannah sighed, the lines on her forehead deepening. "Since the beginning of the school year."

"What would you say your relationship is with Miss Keller?"

"Is or was?" she asked hesitantly.

Mindy looked at her for a second and then answered, "Both."

"Well, we were best friends in September and October. But we had sort of a falling out. And we haven't talked since . . . the incident." She slumped over in the chair as she spoke, her shoulders gravitating heavily toward the ground.

"And can you tell the jury what sort of things you did with Miss Keller during your friendship? Did you, let's say, play any sports together? Go shopping? Do your makeup?"

Hannah paused, glancing up at the prosecutor. "Um no . . . well, we spent time together. We went to parties. We babysat together."

"What did you do when you hung out?"

"We would hang out and drink together at her house."

"Drink what together? Alcohol?"

Hannah paused before taking a deep breath. "Yeah, we drank beer together."

I wish I never fell off that bus and saw you in the bathroom, Emily thought, staring at Hannah's sad face as she spoke. Before Hannah she'd never been drunk. Never done drugs. Never smoked. Never had sex. What had become of her? Who had she become?

"And you say you went to parties together?"

"Yeah . . . well, just one."

She scratched at her wrist and Emily squinted, trying to make out if there were any fresh cuts, but she was too far away. She wondered if Hannah had stopped cutting or was still at it. *She's not my problem anymore,* Emily tried to tell herself, willing herself not to care about her anymore.

"Did this party have alcohol?" Mindy asked, walking closer to Hannah as she spoke.

"Um . . . yeah," Hannah replied nervously, clearly worried about getting in trouble for underage drinking. Emily wondered how much her parents knew about everything their daughter had done. She wondered if they were sitting in the courtroom right then.

"And did you see Emily drink at the party?"

"Yeah . . . I mean everyone drank at them. That doesn't make us bad people," Hannah said defensively.

Mindy smiled softly, clearly trying to ease the witness's nerves. "No one said you were a bad person, Hannah. So, you say you babysat with Emily?"

"Yeah."

"Hannah, banana!" Emily heard Sophie and Katie whisper from behind her. She shifted in her chair, rubbing the back of her neck. *Not now,* she thought, willing the girls to disappear from her mind.

"Was the Thomas family the only family you babysat with her?"

"Yeah."

"And did you ever sneak out of the Thomases' house while you were babysitting with Emily?"

"Yeah, I did that once with her."

"And where did you go when you snuck out of their house with her?"

"We went to the playground across the street." Hannah sniffled, wiping her nose with a tissue. "But we had a baby monitor app on our phone the whole time and could see the house. We knew the girls were okay or we wouldn't have done it. We could see the house from the playground and the girls were safe. I swear I'm not a killer!"

Mindy grinned. "No one said you're a killer, Hannah. I'm just asking you about your relationship with Emily. Can you tell the court who you met on that playground the night you snuck out of the Thomases' house?"

"We met my boyfriend at the time, Topper, and his friend, Chuck."

"Topper Mitchell and Chuck Bailey, is that correct?"

"Yeah."

"And what did you do with these boys on the playground while you were supposed to be babysitting?"

Hannah's eyes darted around the room as she sniffled. "We just hung out." She began to cry a little and wiped her eyes again with tissues.

"And were any of you drinking while you were hanging out?"

Hannah looked up at Mindy with melancholy eyes. "Yeah," she whispered and then a sob belched out of her. "I'm sorry, okay? I didn't think it was important because we could see the house from where we were, and we had the baby monitor app on our phones and really, we weren't gone that long, and everything was okay that night. The girls were okay, and everything was fine."

"I had a nightmare," Sophie whispered. *"Can you come get in bed with me till I fall asleep?"* Emily closed her eyes and tried to stop the tears from running down her cheeks, but it was useless. She thought of Sophie cuddling with her in bed. She saw her peeking her head around the stairway, rubbing her eyes tiredly. *Sophie, Katie,* she thought. *Oh God.*

"And what were you doing the night of November 9, 2018?"

Hannah sniffled again and straightened herself in her chair. "I was in Virginia with my family because my grandmother had passed away and we were attending her funeral." She blotted the wet tissues under her swollen eyes still streaming with tears.

"So, you were not in town that night. Were you supposed to babysit for the Thomases that night?"

"Yeah, but Emily ended up doing it for me."

"What a nice friend she is." Mindy smiled warmly. "And did you communicate with Emily at all that evening while she was babysitting?"

"Yeah, we texted."

"What did you text about?"

"That she was going to go to the bonfire at the Crossland Firehouse for me."

"Why would she do that?"

"She was going because I asked her to." Hannah broke out into another sob.

"Why did you ask her to?" Mindy turned toward the clerk. "Can we get her more tissues, please?" The clerk grabbed a box of tissues from a table behind him and handed them to Hannah. She took a few, honking her nose loudly into them.

"Because I thought Topper was cheating on me and I wanted her to spy on him," she mumbled through sobs. "I'm sorry, Emily, this is all my fault. I made you do it." Hannah's eyes shifted toward Emily and gave her a sympathetic look. Emily couldn't help but feel a slight empathy for Hannah.

"And did she confirm with you she went to the bonfire?"

"She texted me she was on her way and that she was there, yes. But then I didn't hear from her for the rest of the night."

"To be clear, she told you she left the Thomases' house that night? Leaving the children unattended?"

"Yeah."

"The court has obtained the transcripts from your text messages that evening." Mindy marched over to her desk, pulled out a stack of papers, and headed over to Hannah. "Your Honor, for the court's records, I'd like to ask Hannah to read the highlighted texts that occurred between 7:00 p.m. and 10:30 p.m. on November 9, 2018." She handed the papers to Hannah, and Hannah nervously looked down at them.

"Can you read the parts that are highlighted?" Mindy asked.

Hannah cleared her throat.

"Emily: 'Leaving now'

Hannah: 'Great!'

Emily: 'Here'

Emily: 'Looking for them now. No sign of his truck in the lot.'

Hannah: 'Do you see them?'

Emily: 'Can't see that far'

Hannah: 'Get closer!'

Emily: 'They aren't here'

Hannah: 'Are you sure???'

Emily: 'Yes, I don't really know any of the people there, they're all seniors it looks like'

Hannah: 'Maybe they're coming later'

Emily: 'Maybe. But I can't wait here to find out'

Hannah: 'Or maybe they're in the woods hooking up!'

Emily: 'Maybe, but again, I can't wait here to find out. It's going to take me 30 minutes to run back to the house'

Hannah: 'Wait'

Emily: 'Sorry'

Emily clenched down hard on her teeth, shifting her jaw from side to side. The thought of Hannah from that night made her want to punch a hole in the wall. No, it made her want to do something worse than punch a hole in the wall. What Hannah made her do that night . . . it changed the trajectory of her entire life. And it possibly ended the Thomases' lives.

"So, to summarize, she confirmed to you in the text messages that she was at the bonfire, and it would take her thirty minutes to get home so we can assume it took her at least thirty minutes to get there, which would leave the children alone for at least sixty minutes unattended with a potential gas burner lit in the house, is that correct?"

"Yeah," Hannah confessed and stared down into her tissue woefully.

"And that is assuming she didn't stay and hang out at the bonfire. Do you know if she ended up staying and hanging out there for any amount of time?"

"No, I don't know. I didn't hear back from her after that last text."

"Thank you, Hannah. That's all I have for today. Your witness," Mindy said, looking at Valerie.

Valerie stood slowly, smoothing out her skirt. "Good afternoon, Hannah. How are you doing today? Not very well, I guess, huh?"

Hannah made a pouting face and looked down. "No, not very well."

"About how long have you been babysitting for the Thomas family, Miss Patterson?"

Hannah stared up to the ceiling as if calculating in her head. "Since I was fourteen. Two years."

"And about how many times do you think you've babysat for them in that two-year period?"

"Oh, I don't know. I'm not good at math," Hannah confessed with a frown.

"Give me your best estimate. Ten? Fifty? One hundred?"

"Maybe thirty?"

"Okay, thirty times. That's a lot. You must really have gotten to know the family well, is that correct?"

Hannah sat up straighter and her face shifted into a more serious tone. "Yeah, I knew them well."

"And you said you snuck out across the street that one time with Emily, correct?"

"Yeah."

"Did you ever sneak out of the Thomases' house any of those other thirty times when you were babysitting by yourself?"

Hannah glanced around the room uncomfortably and reddened. "Yeah." She looked down at the floor and started to wail again. "And I just feel horrible about it now. I could be sitting where Emily is."

"About how many times did you sneak out of the Thomases' house when you were babysitting alone? Can you give me another estimate? Was it one other time? Five? Twenty?"

Hannah shifted again in her seat. "I didn't start till last year. So maybe only like ten or fifteen times . . ." she hesitated. "But I didn't realize it was going to hurt anyone! I had the baby app on my phone! I swear I never was trying to hurt anyone and really, if anything bad happened to the girls, I could be back in the house in five seconds for real! I feel so sick about it now! I can't believe it could've been me what happened to Emily." She broke down in sobs again, blowing her nose loudly into her tissues.

"So, Miss Patterson, the first time Emily babysat with you, you say you snuck out with her and met Chuck and Topper, correct?"

"Yeah," Hannah said, blowing her nose again loudly.

"Can you tell me whose idea that was to sneak out? Your idea or Emily's?"

"It was my idea," Hannah admitted softly.

"Your Honor, can I please have Hannah read the beginning of the text messages from the evening of November 9, 2018, including from 5:00 p.m. to 7:30 p.m.?"

Hannah fumbled in her lap and picked up the papers Valerie placed down.

"Just start from when Emily got to the Thomases' house, please," Valerie instructed her.

Hannah began to read,

"Emily: 'I'm putting the girls to bed at eight then will head over around nine or whenever I'm done. Putting phone down now until then.'

Hannah: 'Ok hurry'

Hannah: 'Have you left yet?'

Hannah: 'Where are you?'

Hannah: 'Answer me!'

Hannah: 'Did you finish putting the girls down?'

Hannah: 'Hurry up! You need to leave now!'

Hannah: 'You promised me you would do this for me! You better not break your promise!'

Hannah: 'Emily where are you?'"

Hannah glanced up toward Valerie to see if she should resume reading or not. A single tear was dripping down her cheek. Her eyes shifted from Valerie's to Emily's, and they looked soft with apology. Emily looked away quickly, feeling her breath catch in her throat.

"Thank you, Hannah. I have one last question for you. The night of November 9, 2018, when Emily is accused of leaving the Thomases' house to go to a bonfire. Whose idea was that for her to leave? Her idea or your idea?"

Hannah sniffled again and looked Emily in the eyes as she spoke. "It was my idea. It was my fault. It was all my fault." She broke down in loud, convulsing sobs.

"Thank you, Your Honor," Valerie said with a smile. "No further questions."

28

———◦◦◇◦◦———

The room was filled with sunlight, and Emily's heart was filled with cautious hope when she awoke. She made herself a tea and sat down on the couch to try to relax before school. Holding the hot mug in both hands, she breathed in the wild scent of chamomile. After the previous night at C & M with Nate and Charlie, she felt rejuvenated and ready to start over. When Nate and she had arrived home from dinner, they'd set up their school laptops in the kitchen and she was able to finish her big essay. She'd been on the verge of telling Nate about what had happened with Mr. Thomas but kept chickening out. So instead of talking, she'd typed. It was nice just having someone to work next to. Nice not feeling so alone.

As she took a sip of piping hot tea, she heard her phone ping from the coffee table. Glancing down, she read the text message from Hannah.

"OMG, my grandmother died last night Em I can't BELIEVE this!"

Emily frowned, remembering Hannah telling her that her grandmother lived in Virginia and wasn't doing well. *I think she had colon cancer,* Emily thought as she typed back.

"OMG I'm so sorry!" Emily texted.

"I'm DEVASTED! Can you skip school and come meet me somewhere today? I need a friend!"

Emily hesitated and glanced around the room, wishing someone would tell her what she should do, but no one was awake yet. This was an important week at school, and skipping wouldn't be the smartest thing to do.

But she also felt sorry for Hannah. Even though she never met her own grandmother, she could understand how upsetting it would be to lose someone you loved.

"Of course, anything you need!" she texted back and then immediately regretted it. *I guess I can just stop by, console her, and be in school in time for second period,* she thought, reassuring herself.

"Great my parents leave for work at 8. Come over then? My address is 16 Bay View St. a few blocks from the school. You can walk there if you get off at the bus stop."

"Okay see you soon," Emily texted. *I wonder why her parents are okay enough to go to work, but she's not okay to go to school?* Emily thought but shook her head and figured everyone had their own ways of coping with death.

On their walk to the bus, Emily explained to Nate the situation.

"Do you think this is the smartest idea, Em?" he asked her. "Finals are coming up and with these classes it really isn't the best idea to skip a day. Can't you just see Hannah after school?"

"She really needs me," Emily replied, realizing she sounded pathetic.

"Your decision, Em, but don't come crying to me when you flunk the AP finals. Just remember what my good old friend Ed Sheeran says, 'I can't tell you the key to success, but the key to failure is trying to please everyone.' Sometimes you need to put yourself first."

She gave him an eye roll and grimaced. "Thanks for the advice, Ed."

When the bus dropped them off at school, Emily veered left and headed toward Hannah's house. She put the address in the GPS on her phone and started on her journey, which thankfully only took a few minutes like Hannah had promised. Emily admired Hannah's split-level house in her cookie-cutter neighborhood. Her front yard had a giant Raven's flag out front, and a pretty leaf wreath hung on her sea green front door.

Emily rang the doorbell, and Hannah opened the door a second later, grasping at a box of tissues. She was wearing worn sweatpants and her face was red and puffy.

"Oh, Hannah," Emily said as she lifted her arms to give her a hug. Hannah collapsed into Emily's arms and began to sob.

"Emily, it's just so awful! We were supposed to go there for Thanksgiving and see her, but she took a turn for the worse and I didn't get to say goodbye. The last time I talked to her was a month ago and she seemed to be doing okay."

"I'm so sorry," Emily comforted her, patting her hair as Hannah tears fell onto Emily's neck. She led Emily into the family room, which Emily noticed had framed family photos scattered all over the walls and pumpkin decorations left over from Halloween. Maury Povich was playing quietly on the TV. It looked like there were some paternity tests being done. Emily's favorite. They sat down on Hannah's coffee-colored leather sofa, and Hannah wrapped a furry blanket over her legs. "So, your parents went to work?" Emily asked as she glanced around the room, taking in the space.

"They had to but are both getting off early tonight and we're driving up to Virginia around eight."

"Oh, that's good," Emily said. "When's the funeral?"

"It's Saturday, but we're going to stay at my uncle's house and help him plan everything."

"Well, let me know if you need me to get any assignments or anything from school." *I can't imagine taking a whole week off school during midterms week. I'd be screwed,* she thought.

"I'm not worried about school," Hannah said. "Fuck school." Emily could see that's where Hannah and she differed. *I don't think no matter how much I tried, I could force myself to think, "Fuck school." It's my only chance to get out of this life,* she thought.

"Okay, do you need me to do anything else for you then?" she asked, trying to be supportive.

"Just keep an eye on Topper while I'm gone. Make sure you don't see him hanging out with other girls!" Hannah laughed before quickly furrowing her brow and sniffling.

"Of course, I'll let you know if I see anything suspicious. But I'm sure I won't. Topper loves you. He'd never cheat," she lied. She had no idea how Topper felt about Hannah; she didn't know the guy at all. But she wanted to say anything that'd make Hannah happy right then.

"Thanks, girl." Hannah grinned. "Oh," she recalled, as if just remembering one more thing. "I'm supposed to babysit for the Thomases on Friday night. Can you cover for me?"

Emily felt as if a lightning bolt hit her. "Friday?" She swallowed hard, trying to think of an excuse quickly. "I totally would, but I can't. I have a big essay due, and I haven't started."

"Please, Em?" she pleaded. "They have a wedding and I promised them like a month ago. It should be good money, and they'll be drunk!"

Why is she pushing me so hard? Emily wondered. She didn't want to think about Mr. Thomas being drunk ever again. She didn't want to think about Mr. Thomas ever again. She felt like she was going to throw up.

"I'm really sorry, but I can't Hannah. I have this essay and it's really important. Can't they find someone else to babysit? I'm sure there're plenty of high school girls who'd love to go babysit for them and make a hundred bucks." She got up from the sofa, trying to conceal the tears beginning to form in her eyes. She'd tried to block any thoughts of Mr. Thomas from her mind and suddenly, she was overcome with the emotions she'd been trying to bury.

"If they hire someone else then we risk them replacing us for good. You don't want that happening, do you?" Hannah asked, following Emily across the room.

That's exactly what I want to happen, Emily thought as she picked at her purple nail polish, chipping it off her half-bitten nails. "I don't want to babysit for them anymore."

She worriedly glanced over at Hannah, who was glaring at her, mascara smeared underneath her eyes.

"Em, if they find someone new to replace me, I mean us, then I won't have a way to get out anymore. How will I meet Topper? How will I have any fun in my life ever again?" She walked over and grabbed Emily's hands tightly. "Please, Em, please just do this for me. If Mr. Thomas finds some shiny new babysitter, I'll be stuck in my prison of a home for the rest of high school. It's the only way my parents let me leave. You'll never see me again. You don't want that, do you?"

Emily pulled her hands away and looked down at the floor. She felt the room begin to spin. Hannah was not going to guilt trip her into this. She was not going to risk putting herself in a dangerous situation with Mr. Thomas again just so Hannah could have a place to sneak out of.

"Are you still mad or something about last weekend?" Hannah asked, reaching out and grabbing her hands again.

"No, I'm not mad." Emily looked down, trying to decide how much she should tell her. "Mr. Thomas just creeps me out."

Hannah laughed. "Why? He's a hottie."

"Yeah, but he's like an old man," Emily replied. "And . . ." she hesitated.

"And what?"

"And he . . . hit on me when I slept there the other night." She slowly glanced up at Hannah, expecting to see an expression of surprise appear on her face.

Hannah smirked. "Yeah, that's Steve for ya. He does that when he's really drunk."

Emily blushed and looked down, debating if she should tell Hannah more. "It just . . . made me uncomfortable. How can a man his age have girls our age sleep over?"

Hannah's smirk shifted into a scowl, and Emily could feel the tension in the room shift. "Well, if he makes you uncomfortable, why did you let him buy you those shoes at the store? He told me about it. You weren't uncomfortable then, were you?" She headed into the kitchen to pour herself a cup of coffee. *I don't think I'm making it clear to her what he did to me and now she's angry. How do you tell someone you were raped?* Emily wondered.

"Hannah, I'm not trying to fight with you," she demanded as she followed her into the kitchen. "I'm just telling you how he makes me feel. And I just don't want to babysit there anymore."

Should I tell her? Should I tell her? Should I tell her? Emily repeated in her head.

Hannah poured some vanilla creamer into her coffee and took a sip. "Emily, my grandmother just died, and you come in here like you're miss goody two-shoes. I don't need this today!" Her voice rose.

"I'm sorry for your grandmother," Emily said, putting her hands in her back pockets. She couldn't bring herself to bring up the *R* word. Nothing she was saying was making sense or coming out the way she wanted it to. "I—"

The doorbell rang, and Emily turned her head to the sound of the door opening, then Topper entered with flowers in his hands.

"Oh, Topper!" Hannah burst into tears and ran over to him. He picked her up and pulled her into a bear hug.

"Baby," he whispered and then kissed her forehead.

She lifted her head and sniffled as they started making out sloppily, as if Emily weren't there.

Emily glanced away embarrassed as she pretended she wasn't witnessing a moment meant for just the two of them. She stared at the TV as Maury announced to the man that he was *not* the father. The man on the TV was doing a touchdown dance as the crowd cheered. *I bet my dad would've loved to go on this show and have that happen to him,* she thought. She grabbed her backpack and headed toward the door to leave.

"Hey, Topper," she muttered, awkwardly, not sure of what to say. Topper gave her a blank stare as if just realizing she was in the house.

"She was just leaving," Hannah informed him, not looking at Emily. Emily reddened and lowered her head as she squeezed past them and shut the door behind her.

29

TRIAL DAY 4: JANUARY 10, 2019

———◦◦◦◦◦◦———

Emily fiddled with the beaded bracelet on her wrist Miss Jelly had given her for her birthday, as Valerie prepped her for the day. She'd found it in her bedside drawer, and even though it was childish, it felt lucky. After yesterday's witness questioning with Topper, Chuck, and Hannah, today seemed like it'd be somewhat of an emotional break.

"First thing we have this morning is a review of the security cameras that have finally come in." Valerie stood in front of Emily with her arms crossed, clenching her jaw so tightly, Emily wondered if she'd crack a tooth. She blinked hard and waited for her to continue.

"After that, we have our two character witnesses: Steph and Miss Jelly. I think they'll be great on the stand, since they both spoke so highly of you to me when I met with them."

Emily turned her head and stared down at the table, not knowing what to do with this information. She wasn't used to hearing good things about herself, especially in the past couple of months. "Okay, sounds good," she said, wondering why Valerie was still hovering over her.

"Is there . . . something you want to tell me about the cameras? Something I might have been surprised to find on them?"

Emily swallowed hard. How much had the cameras recorded? She thought she'd done a pretty decent job staying out of their view. She watched as Valerie reached over and grabbed her coffee, which reeked of burnt hazelnut. Emily swallowed the bile building up in her throat from the smell and reached down in her purse for a Valium, not caring that she was blatantly taking it in front of her lawyer. She slipped the pill into her mouth before cracking open the small can of ginger ale in front of her. Bouncing her knees rapidly she replied, "Did they see me sneaking out or something? What did it record? Why don't you just tell me?"

Valerie's nostrils flared and Emily gripped the sides of her chair tightly, not prepared for what was coming.

"What the actual fuck, Emily?" Valerie shouted as she paced back and forth in front of her. Emily glanced down at her hands and started to pick at the cuticle on her thumb until it began to bleed. "Why didn't you tell me you slept over at the Thomases' house alone?"

Emily's eyes widened. She'd forgotten the footage was going back that far. She was so sure they'd only show the night of the incident. She should have told Valerie everything.

"I didn't realize the footage would go back that far," Emily explained, defensively. "We were at a party, and Hannah left me there and I didn't have a ride home. Hannah texted Mr. Thomas and asked him to drive me home, but he took me there instead. I don't know why. I didn't wanna go there." Emily looked down shamefully before taking a sip of the ginger ale. "Look, I'll explain everything to you, but not today. If you want to know what happened with everything, put me on the stand tomorrow. Forget about Steph and Miss Jelly. They can say the kindest things in the whole entire world and that won't make a difference. I need to tell the jury my side of the story. I'm certain if they just hear what I have to say, they'll understand that it's not my fault that family died. You just have to give me a chance. Please, Valerie. Let me testify tomorrow." Emily didn't know exactly what she was going to say to the jury. All she knew was that she never intended for that family to die.

Emily imagined herself sitting in front of everyone in the courtroom to testify. She imagined herself barfing all over Judge Wilson. She imagined herself blurting out, "It's all my fault!" She imagined herself fainting, cracking her skull open and dying right then and there. Maybe all of those things would happen or maybe none of them would. Maybe she'd be able to defend herself. Maybe she'd be able to explain to the jury that none of this was intentional. That she was not a murderer. That she was a good person. A good person who made one bad decision.

"Hell, no," Valerie said abruptly. "That's going to throw the whole trial away. I told you before, no one does that, Emily."

Emily took another sip of her ginger ale and stared at her lawyer intently. "But I want to. I think I could do a decent job defending myself and explain why I did what I did. I'm tired of listening to what people tell me to do. The last time I did that, when Hannah told me to sneak out of the house, look what happened. I have to go with my gut. And my gut is telling me to testify."

"Bad idea, Emily. No," Valerie demanded. Just then, Emily heard a knock on the door and an officer entered.

"Five minutes, ladies," he announced, quietly shutting the door behind him.

"I'll see you in there." Valerie quickly packed up her things and marched out the door without saying another word.

Emily glanced around at the empty room and felt her head start to weigh down with the Valium she'd swallowed. She'd also taken two that morning with a sip of her mom's coffee laced with Bailey's, but it hadn't done much. *Am I becoming dependent on them like my mom is?* she wondered before shaking the idea from her head. *I just need to get through this trial and then I won't take one ever again.* She grabbed a mint from her purse and popped it into her mouth to help with her nausea before heading into the courtroom.

As she walked to her seat, she tried not to sway as she felt all eyes on her. Lifting her head, she noticed a TV screen in front of the jury. *That must be where they'll show the footage of the security cameras.* She felt a wave of panic begin to wash over her, knowing what they'd find on the cameras. She leaned over and whispered, "I really want to testify." Valerie didn't acknowledge her at first, but then gave the slightest shake of her head as she directed her attention to Judge Wilson.

Emily peered at Nate, her mom, Steph, Miss Jelly, and Charlie whispering to one another behind her. She wished she could talk to Nate about testifying. She needed someone to advocate for her and didn't want Valerie to be the one making decisions.

As the jury was being called into the room and sworn in, she reached over and grabbed Valerie's pen from the table in front of her. She scribbled on the notepad, "I want to testify."

Valerie picked up the pen and wrote next to it, "NO." Then she put the pen in her blazer pocket, not giving Emily the chance to write back. Emily gave her a glare and crossed her arms in front of her.

"The people call Tyler Pratt, Your Honor."

A burly man wearing a navy blue uniform with the label Homes 4 U Safe Security on the chest was sworn in as Emily turned her head back toward Nate again. He tilted his head and furrowed his brow, seemingly curious as to why she kept glancing at him. Her palms were sweating badly so she wiped them on her legs and lowered her head to the floor.

"Hello, Mr. Pratt. Can you tell me where you work?" Mindy began as she rubbed her hands together and approached the stand. Emily noticed that Mindy had a slight smirk on her face. *Probably because she already knows what's on the tapes. She knows, and I know, and soon everyone else in this room will know.* Emily felt bile rising in her throat.

"Home 4 U Safe Security, ma'am."

"And it's my understanding that your company provided the security cameras for Mr. and Mrs. Thomas at 1428 Oak Hill Road. Is that correct?"

"That's correct." Emily watched as he leaned back in his seat, practically taking up the entire witness stand with his body.

"And you have the footage here from the evening of November 9, 2018, is that correct?"

"That's correct, ma'am. We have the twenty-four-hour footage recorded and I've submitted it to the court."

Mindy took a remote out of her pocket and clicked on the TV. It was already paused on a screen split in two: one from the doorbell camera and one from the garage motion camera.

"Can you tell me what views we're seeing here before we review the tapes?" Mindy asked as she pointed toward the screen.

"Yes, ma'am. The screen on the left is the doorbell camera. This camera is installed to the right of the front door of the house, and it records anytime anyone rings the doorbell or if it detects motion up to thirty feet away. The screen on the right is the garage motion camera. This detects and records any motion up to thirty feet away as well."

"Thank you, Mr. Pratt. I'm going to hand over the remote to you now so you can navigate the footage for us since I'm a novice at this." Mindy grinned and walked over to Tyler, handing him the remote. Tyler grabbed it from her and leaned over so he could see the TV. "Can you play for us what footage the camera got at 3:58 p.m. on the evening of November 9, 2018?"

"Yes, ma'am." Tyler directed the remote toward the TV and pressed a button on it. Emily observed the fuzzy black-and-white screens as they showed her mom's car pulling up to the house and Emily getting out of the car.

She could feel herself blush as she scrutinized herself on the screen, a close-up of her face on the doorbell camera as she approached the front door and pressed the doorbell. The screen showed the tops of two little platinum heads open the door.

"Emawee!" a little voice echoed into the camera.

"Emawee!" another voice mimed right after. The screen displayed Emily shuffle past the camera before closing the door. Then it was silent. It was an out-of-body experience, sitting right there, in plain sight, while everyone in the courtroom watched her on the screen.

"Emawee," Sophie whispered in her ear. Emily could feel the girls nuzzling up to her legs. Could feel their soft cheeks resting against her arms. *Sophie, Katie, Sophie, Katie.* Emily bit her lip to cut the panic short. The bile was rising. Her palms were sweating. She wanted to leave the courtroom right then. Leave and run home and never come back.

"Thank you, Mr. Pratt. I'd like to point out to the jury we have the footage here that Emily Keller arrived at the Thomases' house at approximately 3:58 p.m. and entered the house. We can see here that both girls were present and alive." Mindy turned toward Tyler. "Can you please play for me the footage at 4:15 p.m.?"

"Yes, ma'am." Tyler clicked on a button as the screen fast-forwarded slightly and then he pressed another button, and it began to play. Emily viewed the TV as the front door opened, and Mr. and Mrs. Thomas headed down the front steps toward their car. As they approached the yellow Mustang, Mr. Thomas slapped and then grabbed Mrs. Thomas's butt before pulling out a pack of cigarettes from his back pocket and lighting one up. Emily heard a few snickers from behind her in the courtroom. Seeing Mr. Thomas for the first time since she'd babysat made Emily feel like she was spinning. She shook her head so hard, her hair fell into her eyes. She felt Valerie's hand rest on her back, stilling her. She hadn't realized she'd been rocking.

"Thank you, Mr. Pratt." Mindy faced the jury again. "And as you can see, the Thomases left their house at approximately 4:15 and were very much alive and well." Mindy turned back toward Tyler. "Now, Mr. Pratt, can you please play the footage from 9:07 p.m.?"

"Yes, ma'am." Tyler fast-forwarded and clicked play. Emily stared at the blank, dark screens and saw and heard nothing but crickets. The courtroom was dead silent as everyone's eyes stared at the screens. Then about a minute in, the screen on the right showed a slight movement in the left-hand corner.

"Stop!" Mindy yelled. Tyler scrambled with the remote in his hand and pressed "stop" quickly.

Mindy walked up and put her finger up to the image on the garage motion camera. It was a blurry image that could have easily been an animal or a person. "Mr. Pratt, can you tell me what you see here?"

Tyler cleared his throat. "It looks like the camera detected a motion at about 9:09. It must be right at thirty feet away and seems to be in the neighbor's yard next to the Thomases' house."

"Thank you, Mr. Pratt. Can you now play the footage of 12:27 a.m.?" Tyler picked up the remote and fast-forwarded before pressing play. Emily stared as the same image in the same spot appeared and then disappeared from the screen quickly. "Stop!" Mindy yelled. "Can you rewind a little and pause it back on that image for me?"

"Yes, ma'am." The screen froze on the same blurry image that was there earlier.

"As you can see," Mindy turned toward the jury, "it appears that at 9:09 and then 12:27 the same image was captured in the neighbor's yard, indicating that Emily may have snuck out of the back of the house like she had done previously with Hannah and then came back that way. This indicates that she was out of the house for three hours and twenty minutes, leaving the children completely alone during that time. The house could have burned down, been robbed, or worse, been filled up with carbon monoxide during that time and Emily would have never known since she was out at a bonfire during those three precious hours."

Emily tried to compose herself. She didn't know how much longer she could sit through any more images of the Thomas family. Any images of the past. She wanted to crawl under the table. Run out of the room. Be anywhere but where she was.

"Now we could go back and look at all the footage of Emily and her friend Hannah sneaking out while they were babysitting, but we already know that Hannah Patterson has admitted guilt to that. What I'd like to play now is another piece of interesting footage that the security cameras caught in the early morning hours of October 20, 2018. Mr. Pratt, can you please play the footage from 1:15 a.m. on October 20, 2018?"

Emily balled her fists and sat on both of her hands. *"Don't worry, I don't bite,"* Mr. Thomas whispered in her ear. She bit down harder on her lip, tasting metallic saliva as she watched Tyler press play. The screen showed Mr. Thomas's car pulling up to the house and he and Emily got out of his Mustang. Emily could see herself sway on the screen as she hobbled toward the front door and Mr. Thomas's hand was on her back leading her there. The screen darkened as the door began to close and then Mr. Thomas's voice came through: "You want a beer?"

Emily heard buzzing behind her and felt bile begin to rise in her throat. Before she could grab a mint from her purse to subside the nausea, she turned her head and threw up the ginger ale and Valium all over the floor.

"No further questions, Your Honor," Mindy concluded, oblivious to the spectacle behind her.

Valerie let out a yelp and leapt up as she exclaimed to the judge, "Your Honor, the defense would like a recess!"

30

PAST: NOVEMBER 7, 2018

———◦◦◇◦◦———

Emily peered at the back of Nate's head as he leaned against the seat in front of her. Since Hannah was in Virginia for her grandmother's funeral, it'd been restful for Emily the past couple of days not having to worry about running into her in the hallway or having to respond to any of her texts.

"Hey." Emily tapped Nate on the back of his head. He turned around and glanced at her and Steph. "Do you two wanna go to C & M for one of our usual afternoon snacks like old times?" she questioned, eyebrows raised. Nate and Steph glanced at each other and grinned; no words needed to tell Emily their answer was yes.

They got dropped off at the bus stop and strolled to the bar side by side, talking about memories from their childhood. It was like nothing had changed at all. Emily was delighted to see that they had the whole bar to themselves when they arrived. She glanced around for her mother but figured Debbie must be in the back restocking condiments, like she usually did during the slow parts of the day. Instead of sitting at the bar, they headed to the back corner booth they used to sit at when they were little.

"Steph!" Debbie exclaimed when she come out and saw them all placing their backpacks onto the sticky floor. "What a nice surprise!" She glanced back and forth at the triad, waiting for some sort of explanation as to why they were suddenly together, but the three of them simply smiled back at her mutely.

"So, how's your family, Steph?" Debbie asked as she took a rag out of her apron, wiping leftover crumbs on the table from previous customers.

"They're good," Steph replied shyly. She sat on her hands and looked around the bar as if viewing it for the first time. "Gee, this place hasn't changed a bit!"

Debbie's eyes darted around like she was trying to see the bar from Steph's point of view. "No, I suppose it hasn't, has it?" Emily could see a slight color forming on her mom's face, before she quickly shook it off and took a pen out from the loose bun on top of her head.

"So, what can I get ya?" Debbie asked eagerly as she lifted a pad of paper out from her apron. "You hungry?"

"Starving," Nate replied, rubbing his stomach dramatically.

"You're always starving," Emily teased as she gave him a wink.

"I'll take an old bay veggie burger with fries," he grinned without picking up a menu.

Emily watched as her mom jotted his order down on the pad of paper. *Is she writing our orders down for show or is she really not able to remember three orders?* Emily wondered. *Maybe all that booze has gotten to her memory.*

"I'll have a shrimp salad wrap, no fries," Emily said. Debbie nodded as she wrote her order down carefully. All eyes turned toward Steph.

"I'll just have a side of fries," she muttered, hesitantly.

"Just a side of fries?" Nate asked. "Come on, Steph, you gotta get more than that."

"You know you always eat for free here, hon," Debbie informed her, giving her a wink. "Get what you want." Debbie had always let Steph eat for free whenever she was there; she was like family.

Steph scanned each of their faces and grinned. "Okay, I'll take the same as Nate then, but a real burger. Medium well, please."

"Atta girl!" Nate exclaimed as he gave her a light punch on the arm. As soon as Debbie headed back into the kitchen to put in their orders, Emily could sense Nate's and Steph's eyes burning into her. She glanced back and forth between them as they silently stared at her.

"What?" she asked, not sure why they were gaping at her.

"Em," Nate began.

"We're worried about you," Steph interrupted him. Emily glanced back and forth between them, feeling like she was in the middle of an intervention.

"What do you mean?" she asked as she took a straw from the canister in the middle of the booth and popped it out of its wrapper.

"You just seem like something has been wrong lately," Nate explained as he folded his hands in front of him.

"You seem unhappy," Steph chimed in.

Emily felt herself becoming defensive. "I'm fine," she said, not wanting to tell them the truth. "Just stressed about schoolwork."

"It just seems like ever since you've been hanging out with Hannah, you haven't been okay," Nate said.

"I'm fine, Nate," she repeated. She needed to keep her feelings buried deep down. *If I let them out, the dam will break,* she thought.

"You know the acronym for fine is Fucked Up, Insecure, Neurotic, and Emotional, right, Em?" Nate asked, teasing her.

"Just know we're here if you need to talk," Steph assured her as she took Emily's hand in hers. Emily forced a smile as Debbie approached them and dumped a basket of fries in the middle of the table. Emily was relieved to be saved by the fries and popped a few in her mouth.

When the rest of their food came, they devoured their plates as if it were their last meals.

"I forgot how good this food is," Steph announced, wiping grease from her burger with a napkin as it dripped down her chin. "Remember when we were little, and we would get Shirley Temples and pretend they had alcohol in them and would giggle and act like we were drunk?"

Nate and Emily laughed in unison. "Yeah, and remember when we dared Nate to go into the women's bathroom and he walked in on Mrs. Watson taking a dump?" The three of them burst into laughter. Emily's stomach hurt from laughing so hard.

"Oh my God, I literally still cannot look her in the face when I see her," Nate snorted. Just then, Debbie approached them with three plates.

"Berger cookies, one for each," she said as she put a plate in front of each of them. Emily picked up the vanilla cookie covered in a thick layer of chocolate fudge and bit down as Steph and Nate did the same. She felt like she was ten years old again and wished they could be like this forever.

"I get off at eight tonight," Debbie announced as they were finishing their cookies. Emily glanced around and noticed that the bar was starting to fill up with customers. "Tammy needed some money so she's coming in."

"Sounds good," Nate said. Emily grinned. Her mom hadn't gotten off work early in a while; it would be nice to spend time with her.

"Thanks again for all the tasty food, Mrs. Keller! It was all so delicious!" Steph exclaimed as she grabbed her backpack from the floor.

"Of course, hon. Tell your mom I say hello. Do you guys still have to finish your essays?" Debbie asked, turning toward Emily and Nate. "Charlie said he could stop by and bring a board game if you're up for it."

"Yup," Nate said.

"I'm finished. Sounds like fun," Emily agreed.

"Great!" Debbie exclaimed, giving them each a kiss on the head. Emily felt for the first time in a long time that maybe things could go back to how they used to be.

31

TRIAL DAY 4: JANUARY 10, 2019

———◦◦◇◦◦———

"She cut off the footage before Hannah came in later," Emily mumbled, wiping throw up from her cheek with a tissue.

Valerie stared at Emily and ran her hands through her hair before covering her face with them. "Jesus, Emily. This doesn't look good, but honestly, I think you're in a lose-lose situation here. I'm sorry, but none of this is looking good for your character."

"I know," Emily admitted. "Just let me try to get my side out. If the jury still can't agree with me that it wasn't my fault, then I guess I deserve to be in jail."

Valerie rubbed at the back of her neck and wrinkled her nose. "Finish those crackers and put some blush on your face," Valerie directed her as she gathered her things to leave the room. "I'll see you back in the courtroom in ten minutes." Emily watched as Valerie grabbed her briefcase and headed toward the door.

A few minutes later, Emily walked back into the courtroom, noticing right away that it smelled like disinfectant mixed with a lingering throw-up scent. She tried to keep her face down as she felt Nate and her mom's eyes burning a hole in the side of her neck as she meandered past them. She had asked them not to come on the break when she spoke to Valerie because she didn't want to have to explain herself to anyone. *They'll all find out in court tomorrow; there's no point in reliving it all twice.*

She turned her head toward her lawyer as she stood up and apologized to the court and the jury for the incident. "As we all know," Valerie explained to the jury, "nerves can make us sick sometimes." She turned her head toward Tyler Pratt and began her questioning.

"Mr. Pratt, I see that Attorney Rosenbaum had you play the footage from the evening of October 19 going into the morning of the 20th, but had you stop it as soon as we saw Miss Keller and Mr. Thomas enter the Thomases' house. Can you do me a favor and fast-forward in a setting where we can watch a couple of hours go by?"

"Sure can, ma'am." Tyler nodded, pressing a button on his re-mote. Emily watched as the TV fast-forwarded the footage to about 2:35 a.m. and she could see car lights approach on the screen.

"Please stop fast-forwarding and press play now, Mr. Pratt," Valerie directed him. Tyler pressed play and all eyes in the court stared at the screen as Hannah's burgundy Kia sedan pulled up to the house and parked. Emily watched as she got out of the car and went to the door, then paused in front of the camera with her phone to her ear.

"Steve, lemme in, you locked the door," Hannah shouted into her phone and then placed it in her pocket. "Ugh, dumbass," she muttered under her breath.

The courtroom viewed the screen as the door opened and Mr. Thomas appeared, his arm grabbing Hannah by the waist and pulling her inside. "Ah, hahaha," Hannah's voice could be heard as the door shut behind them and the screen went black.

Emily felt a wave of nausea, thinking of the possibility that Hannah might have slept with Mr. Thomas the same night he raped her. *"Maybe*

Hannah Banana would like to join us," she could hear Mr. Thomas snicker. *"Hannah likes to have fun with me too, you know."*

Emily felt ill. *Could she have slept with him? It was possible,* she thought, *or did he rape her too?*

All eyes shifted back to Valerie. "Thank you, Mr. Pratt. I just wanted the jury to see that yes, Emily Keller did get a ride home after a party from Mr. Thomas, but her friend Hannah slept over as well." Valerie faced the jury. "I also want to point out to the jury that the events that Attorney Rosenbaum had you watch on the night of October 19 are totally unrelated and have nothing to do with the events that took place the night of November 9. We're not here to judge what went on during previous nights that had nothing to do with babysitting at all, we're here to judge one single night." Valerie turned back toward Tyler. "And so, Mr. Pratt, instead of going back and watching all the tapes of Hannah Patterson sneaking out of the Thomases' house like I could have you do, I'd like to go back to the footage of the night of November 9. You showed the court two images, one at 9:09 p.m. and one at 12:27 p.m. Can you please get me the image of 9:09 p.m. first?"

Tyler pressed a button on the remote and the image of a blurred figure appeared on both camera screens. "Here ya go."

"Thank you, Mr. Pratt. I can't make out a face, though. Is that a person or an animal?"

"It's too hard to tell, really. It's really right over the limit of how far the camera can detect. It's definitely something living and moving, though."

"Yes, definitely," Valerie agreed with him. "But could it be a deer?"

"Sure, it could be."

"A dog?"

"I guess if it was a big dog." He shrugged his shoulders.

"Or I guess it could be a neighbor taking a walk?" she suggested.

"Sure, any of those things."

"So, there's no way the camera can show who or what that image is?"

"No, there's no way. Like I said, it's just too far away to get a clearer image."

Valerie nodded. "And can you please get me the image from a few hours later at 12:27 a.m.?"

"Sure, can do." Tyler pressed the remote and the same image reappeared on the screen.

"Thanks, Mr. Pratt. Could this image be a deer?"

"Yes, it could, ma'am."

"A dog?"

"A big dog."

"A neighbor taking a walk?"

"Yes, ma'am."

"I'll ask you again. There's no way the camera can show who or what that image is?"

"No, there's no way. Like I said, it's just too far away to get a clearer image."

"Thank you, Mr. Pratt. No further questions."

"The witness is excused."

Mindy cleared her throat and stood up. "Your Honor, the People rest their case," Mindy announced and sat back down.

"Is the defense ready with its case?" Judge Wilson asked Valerie.

Valerie cleared her throat and stood up. "Your Honor, due to recent events, in addition to my two character witnesses for this afternoon, the defendant has requested to take the stand as well. I would like the rest of the afternoon to prepare for this, so I'm requesting that the defense be postponed until tomorrow."

Emily's eyes widened at this surprise and relief washed over her like waves on the sand.

Thank you, Valerie, she thought to herself, making a mental note to give her lawyer a hug later.

"Is the defendant aware that the fifth amendment guarantees any person accused of a crime the right to not take the witness stand in their own trial and that if she should choose to exercise that right, not taking the stand is not an admission of guilt?" he asked Valerie, eyebrows raised.

"She's aware, Your Honor, and she would still like to take the stand."

"Okay, then let's convene for the day and reconvene tomorrow morning at 9:00 a.m. sharp for the character witnesses to take the stand, followed by the defendant." Judge Wilson hit his gavel on the table just before Emily began to dry heave into her purse.

32

———◇◇◇◇◇———

"You have a lot of homework?" Emily asked Nate when they arrived home from their afternoon snack at C & M with Steph.

"Nah, it'll only take about an hour," he informed her as he retrieved his books from his backpack and set up his assignments on the kitchen counter. As Nate completed his work, Emily reread her completed essay to make sure it was A+ material. She was looking forward to spending some quality time with her mom and Charlie later that night. After she reread her essay twice, she swept the floor and vacuumed the rug to keep herself busy. She went through all the cabinets and found a fall-scented candle: Autumn Delight. She imagined what her autumn could've been like if she hadn't met Hannah. Maybe Steph and she would've carved a pumpkin or gone trick-or-treating. She lit the candle, breathing in the fresh, seasonal scent. The house was ready for board games and family time.

"Mom texted me that she's going to be thirty minutes late," Nate murmured as he zipped up his backpack. Shoulders hunched, he trudged over to the couch and clicked on the TV. Emily frowned and plunked herself on the couch next to him, trying to stay optimistic. When 11:30 came and Debbie still wasn't home, Emily felt too drained to keep her eyes open anymore.

"Wanna just go to bed?" she asked him, knowing he was probably even more let down than her. Before he could respond, the front doorknob jiggled, and Debbie and Charlie stumbled in, giggling to themselves. Nate and Emily glared at them like angry parents whose teenage children had come home after curfew.

"Where've you been?" Emily asked, trying not to sound too angry. "I thought we were playing a game tonight?"

"We are, sweetie," Debbie slurred her words. She held up a box of Scrabble and Emily heard the wooden letter pieces rattle together in the box. "We had to go pick it up from Charlie's house."

"So, it took you three hours to get it from Charlie's house?" Emily asked, crossing her arms in front of her.

"No, kiddo. I wanted to take your momma out for a celebratory drink for getting outta work early," Charlie said as he hobbled into the kitchen and opened the fridge, searching inside for a beer.

"Looks like you had about five or six celebratory drinks," Nate pointed out as he rose from the couch and walked to their bedroom. "I'm going to bed." He stepped into their room and closed the door behind him. *I don't know how Nate can just do that. He doesn't like conflict and either brushes it off or shoves it deep down. Either way, he never fights with my mom,* Emily thought, wishing she could be less confrontational.

Debbie watched Nate close his bedroom door and then turned to Emily. "Wanna play, sweetie? We didn't mean to come home late. I'm sorry."

"No, Mom. I'm tired too. I finished my essay and homework and I'm beat," Emily mumbled as she headed toward her bedroom, trying to take an example from Nate and not start a fight with her mom this late at night. *I can talk to her about it when she's sober tomorrow,* she told herself.

As she was about to open her bedroom door, Debbie interrupted her. "Oh, I forgot to tell you who we ran into at Big Eddie's," she bellowed. Emily tried to hold her tongue to tell her that Big Eddie's bar wasn't anywhere near Charlie's house.

"Who?" Emily asked, humoring her.

"Steve and Brandi Thomas! Such a great couple! You didn't tell me you were babysitting for such a fun couple!"

Emily felt her stomach drop and her knees go weak. "You did?" she asked, quietly. Her heart was pounding so hard in her chest, she thought it would jump out of her throat.

"Oh, Big Stevo!" Charlie exclaimed loudly. "We did some shots together! Boy, can he put them back! He said you're a star babysitter!"

"Yeah, he said you're just the best!" Debbie chimed in, cracking a beer. Emily stared at them both, frozen, not sure what to do. She couldn't tell if she was going to throw up or faint.

"And Brandi, why she's just so stunning. Isn't she stunning, Charlie?" Debbie asked, turning toward Charlie. "And Steve is just so handsome. An Italian stallion!"

"Not as stunning as you," Charlie purred before grabbing her and giving her a sloppy kiss on the cheek.

"So anyways," Debbie continued, "Brandi mentioned that your friend Hannah was supposed to babysit Friday, but her grandmother died! Poor girl, you didn't tell me! Anyways, he mentioned you couldn't babysit because you had a big essay due, but I told him you were finishing it tonight and you would be happy to! They have a wedding and it's important! He said he'd pay you a hundred bucks! You can't beat that!"

"No, you can't! I should become a babysitter with what they pay now!" Charlie laughed. "Big Stevo paid for all our drinks tonight too. Looks like he does well for himself! Looks like he's a keeper!"

"Oh, I don't think I can, Mom," Emily muttered, trying to think of an excuse since her essay justification wouldn't work anymore. She leaned her hand against the wall to keep herself from falling. She needed to find a replacement. She debated about asking Steph, but she couldn't risk Mr. Thomas doing anything harmful to her friend. *There's always Nate*, she thought, but then she shook her head. She couldn't let Nate find out what happened to her. And if he babysat for her or even if he came with her, there was a chance he could find out. She couldn't handle the shame of either of them knowing what she'd gotten herself into. Would they think what happened with Mr. Thomas was her fault?

"Oh, hon," Debbie slurred, "I already told him you could do it! Of course, you'll do it! They're in a bind, and you need to help them and your friend Hannah out!"

"But, Mom . . ." Emily hesitated, racking her brain for something to say. "I really have to edit and revise my essay, I think. It isn't up to par with where I would like it to be." She squatted and put her head between her knees, not caring if her mom and Charlie thought she looked crazy.

"Oh, bananas!" Debbie yelled. "You get A's on all your assignments. This is a hundred bucks. That's more than I make in a bartending shift. If you don't do it, I will, and you can come bartend for me. Besides, I already told them I'd drop you off there on my way to my shift at four since their wedding is on the Eastern Shore and they have to leave early to get there on time."

"I'm not doing it, Mom," Emily demanded sternly, yearning to tell her why she really couldn't do it. She stood up and puffed out her chest. Charlie glanced back and forth between them and then, taking a hint, he stepped outside to have a cigarette and let them fight in private.

"Emily, I don't ask for much from you," her mom slurred. She staggered into the kitchen and pulled out a drawer full of opened envelopes. "But look at these bills! Water bill, electric bill, cable bill! They all keep piling up, and I'm strapped for money. It would be nice for once if you thought about someone other than yourself and tried to help out the family." Emily peered at her mom and the bills and felt resentment begin to build up on the dam of her piled-up emotions.

She felt tears begin to burn her eyes so she walked toward her bedroom door before her mom could see them. "Good night," she mumbled.

"Good night, hon!" Debbie yelled back as Emily heard her open the fridge and crack open another beer.

Emily closed the door quietly behind her, thanking God that the lights were out already, and Nate couldn't see the tears streaming down her cheeks.

33

TRIAL DAY 4: JANUARY 10, 2019

———∞◇∞———

The drive home was silent. *My family may be a lot of things, but they know when to shut their mouths when I need them to,* Emily thought, thankful for the quiet. She opened her window slightly to air out the smoke filling up the car as Debbie and Charlie puffed on their cigarettes. Wondering if this would be one of the last times she would see it as a free woman, she leaned her head against her window and gazed at the city skyline. She felt nauseous again and decided that she'd been ignoring what was happening to her body for too long. Her period had always been irregular, heck, she didn't even get it until she was fifteen. But the previous night when she was trying to fall asleep, she realized she hadn't gotten her period in a couple of months. *Maybe this isn't just trial stress or teenage irregularity? Maybe this is all something else?* she'd worried.

"Mom?" Emily blurted out, surprising even herself, as Charlie veered off the highway onto their exit.

"Yes, sweetie?" Debbie asked as she lowered the Steely Dan song playing from the front speakers.

"Can we stop at CVS on the way home?"

"Sure, hon," Debbie said quietly. Emily could see her mom and Charlie glance at each other from the rearview mirror, but neither said anything. Charlie pulled up to the CVS, conveniently located next to a Herman's liquor store, and Debbie and Charlie got out at the same time as Emily.

"Meet back here in ten minutes?" Debbie asked as she grabbed Charlie's hand and pulled him toward the liquor store.

"Sure," Emily said warily. She headed nervously toward the CVS as she heard Nate roll down his window.

"Want me to come in with you, Em? Are you okay?" he asked, his eyebrows furrowed. He didn't ask what she was buying, and Emily wasn't sure if he instinctually knew or not. He certainly was acting like whatever she was going in there for was serious. And as much as she loved having a twin brother, it was times like this it would've been nice to have a sister. Nate would never understand missing a period or the woes of having to buy a pregnancy test at sixteen.

"I'm okay, thanks," she said, grateful for his offer, but needing to do this on her own.

She trudged inside and scanned the aisles until she came to the diapers, feminine products, and pregnancy test section. Searching through her choices, she tried to decide which one was best. There were digital ones, two-packs, and cheap-looking ones. *I wonder if they all work the same?* She grabbed the one that said it showed two blue lines if you were pregnant and one blue line if you weren't pregnant. *Seems clear enough,* she thought as she headed toward the cashier.

As she approached, she saw a group of guys about her age buying cigarettes and she veered past them and marched into the makeup aisle. *I need to stall until they leave. I can't let them see what I'm buying.* She scanned the Cover Girl display and grabbed some waterproof mascara; her mom and she could use some more for the trial. Surveying the guys as they left, she casually walked up to the cash register and put down the pregnancy test with the mascara balancing strategically on top of it. The cashier licked his greasy fingers as he opened a plastic bag and scanned both items, placing them in the bag without peering up at her. She mentally thanked him for not giving her a judgmental look for buying a pregnancy test and handed him the exact change due. As she headed out of the store, Debbie and Charlie were already outside the car smoking another cigarette, each holding a brown bag of liquor.

"You good?" Debbie asked, knowingly stepping lightly on the situation.

"Yeah," Emily mumbled as she veered past her and got into the car. She sat next to Nate and could feel him watching her as she leaned her head back against the window. Her mom and Charlie sipped from their brown bags as Charlie drove them home, and finally they pulled into their neighborhood.

"Do you want me to come back to the house with you or do you want space?" Nate leaned over and whispered so quietly, Emily barely even heard him. She looked at the concern on his face, wondering what was going on in his mind. All of this couldn't be easy for him.

"Space," she mouthed, reaching over and placing her hand on top of his so he knew that she appreciated his act of kindness.

As they passed by The Pit, Nate asked to be dropped off.

"I'm meeting some classmates for a project," he announced, hopping out of the car.

As soon as they pulled up to the house, Emily unbuckled her seatbelt and went straight to the bathroom. She ripped open the box and read the directions carefully, huddling over the toilet and peeing on the stick with her full bladder. She carefully put the stick back in the box, then placed it back in her purse. As she exited the bathroom, carefully making sure not to shake the test inside of her purse, she passed by her mom and Charlie sitting on the couch watching TV with their bottles in hand.

"You want us to order pizza for dinner, hon?" Debbie asked as she shuffled past her toward the bedroom.

"Yeah, sure, whatever," Emily said quickly as she slipped past them and closed her door. She swiftly locked the door behind her and took the test out carefully, making sure not to look down at it yet. She placed the test on her dresser and counted: "One Mississippi, Two Mississippi, Three Mississippi . . ."

34

PAST: NOVEMBER 9, 2018

———◦◦◊◦◦———

"**D**on't worry, I don't bite," Emily heard the whisper from a faraway dream as she opened her eyes. Her sheets and nightshirt were entirely soaked in sweat, and she immediately stripped the bed, wanting to be rid of the evening's nightmares. She was dreading seeing Mr. Thomas and didn't know how she was going to get through the school day knowing she was going to have to see him that night. During her morning shower, she tried to plan out the best feasible way to go about the evening: *My mom is going to drop me off at the Thomases' house and then I can go straight inside to see the girls and start playing with them, avoiding any contact with Mr. Thomas. Mr. and Mrs. Thomas will leave for their wedding right away and not really talk to me at all. When they get home, I'll tell them my mom is outside to pick me up, even though she'll be working, and then I'll walk a few blocks away and call an Uber to get me.*

She took a deep breath and turned off the shower. She could do this; it was just one night and then she never had to see the Thomases ever again.

She sat with Steph on the familiar bus ride to school and read over the paper she was handing in early for AP Psychology. The bus abruptly pulled into the school parking lot as Steph glanced out the window behind her, tilting her head curiously.

"What?" Emily asked, twisting her head to see what she was gaping at. She peered outside and saw Topper resting against his truck and Madison Harris leaning very closely against him.

"Isn't that guy dating your friend Hannah?" Steph asked warily.

Emily squinted her eyes to make sure she wasn't seeing things. She watched as Madison slid her hands into the pockets of Topper's jean as he appeared to whisper something in her ear. Then he kissed her neck as she laughed.

"I thought so," Emily said. "Maybe they broke up. I haven't talked to her in a few days." Emily didn't want to tell Steph about the argument she had with Hannah after her grandmother died. She slipped her phone out of her pocket and took a picture of Topper and Madison as evidence before placing it back securely. She wasn't sure what she'd do with the information. She wasn't friends with Hannah anymore, Hannah had made that clear. But didn't Hannah have the right to know that Topper was cheating on her with Madison?

"This is why I don't date," Steph admitted as she put her backpack on and stood up to head off the bus.

Me either, Emily thought.

During first period of US History, Emily couldn't concentrate on anything except Madison and Topper getting cozy in the parking lot. If she were Hannah, she'd want to know if Topper was hooking up with Madison. She raised her hand and asked Mr. Johnson if she could go to the bathroom. When she got into the bathroom, she slipped into the first stall and snuck her phone out of her back pocket to text Hannah.

"Hey, I know we're not on the best of terms right now and I'm not sure if this is my place to tell you. But I saw Topper and Madison getting pretty comfortable in the parking lot this morning and I would want to know if I were you. Please don't get angry with me." She attached the photo she'd taken and pressed send then held her breath. She immediately saw dots on her screen, indicating that Hannah was responding.

"WTF?!?!?! ARE YOU KIDDING ME?? WHAT A FUCKING LIAR AND SHE'S A WHORE!" she texted back immediately.

"I'm sorry," Emily texted back, not knowing what else to say. "I have to get back to class now. Text me later if you want." She turned her phone off, deciding that she'd look again at lunch. *I did my due diligence and now I need to learn US History. Hannah can hash it out with Topper if she needs to. I need to think of myself first for once,* she thought as she headed back to class.

At lunch, she sat with Steph and Nate in the cafeteria and turned her phone back on. She glanced down to see she had eleven missed text messages from Hannah and four missed calls from her. She scanned through the texts:

"He said that you're lying he wasn't with her"

"He said she's seeing Chuck not him, are you sure it wasn't Chuck?"

"Who am I kidding, Chuck has bright red hair, this is obviously Topper!"

"I don't think Madison would go for Topper she doesn't like bad boys"

"I texted Madison and she's denying it"

"Can you please call me?"

"WTF, call me please?"

"I really need to talk to you"

"Are you sure that wasn't another guy? It's hard to tell in the pic!"

"Topper is denying it."

"Madison is such a slut it probably was her the minute she found out I was gone she pounced on what was mine."

"Call me please!"

Emily glanced up from her phone to Nate and Steph, who seemed to be in deep discussion about the lack of chip assortment in the cafeteria. They appeared to have both decided that the school needed to have the Utz brand instead of Lays.

"Sorry, guys, I'll be back. I gotta make a quick call," she informed them. They both nodded in her direction, resuming their conversation. She snuck into the bathroom and dialed Hannah's number.

"Emily, where've you been!" Hannah sobbed into the phone, picking up before the first ring.

"Sorry, I was in class," Emily apologized. "I'm in school still so I really can't talk long."

"Topper is totally denying it," Hannah cried into the phone. "I just don't know who to believe!"

"It was one hundred percent him, Hannah," Emily whispered. "Chuck and Topper look nothing alike, and you know that. That photo I sent you is Topper, you can clearly see."

"I knowwwww," she whimpered. "But it's so hard because he's saying all of these nice things to me and says it wasn't him!"

"Well, do what you need to do," Emily replied, trying to take the high road and not get sucked into her drama. "I told you what I saw. That's all I can do."

"Ugh, now I'm going to be worried all weekend during my grand-mother's *funeral* that they're hooking up!" She started crying again. "I can't do this, Emily!"

"I'm sorry, Hannah, I really am. But I don't know what I can do for you," Emily said, trying to sound helpful but also hoping to end the phone call soon.

She wanted to go back and talk about simple things like potato chips at the lunch table with Steph and Nate.

"A bunch of seniors are having a bonfire behind Crossland Fire-house tonight and I know Topper and Chuck are going!" Hannah said, as if a lightbulb popped on in her head. "You *have* to go and see if he's there with Madison! Can you please do that for me, Emily? Please??"

Emily opened her eyes widely. "I can't, Hannah. I'm babysitting the Thomases for you since you're away."

"Oh perfect! They live a couple blocks from there! You can run over and peek and then run back!"

"No, Hannah, I can't. I don't feel comfortable doing that." Emily raised her voice, trying not to talk too loudly.

"Emily!" she pleaded. "Please just do this for me! If you put the baby monitor app on your phone, you can run over there for five minutes after you put the girls to bed, look to see if he's there with her, and then run back. The whole thing will take ten minutes total. Pretty please, Emily? You don't have to say hi to anyone or even let anyone see you. Just sneak up and take a peek and get a photo if you see them together and then run back."

Emily thought about it for a second and hesitated. She couldn't help but feel sorry for Hannah that Topper was cheating on her. Emily was tired of guys thinking they could get away with anything. *Mr. Thomas. Chuck. And now Topper. Maybe if I can prove Topper is cheating on her, there will be one less guy treating a girl badly.* When she thought about going to the bonfire, it didn't sound too awful. Running over for a minute without anyone seeing her and running back seemed harmless.

"Alright, I'll do it," she agreed, hoping she wasn't making the biggest mistake of her life.

"I love you, Emily, you're the best!" Hannah exclaimed enthusiastically. Emily ended the call and turned to the toilet behind her and immediately threw up. Her nerves had already started.

35

TRIAL DAY 4: JANUARY 10, 2019

———◦◦◇◇◦◦———

"One hundred eighty Mississippi," Emily whispered. She stared down at the test and rubbed her eyes. She blinked and looked back at the package insert from the box. One blue line meant not pregnant. Two blue lines meant pregnant. The stick had two clear blue lines. As blue as Topper's eyes. She stared at the test, willing the second line to vanish, but the harder she stared at it, the darker it appeared. She could already picture the headlines in the news: *Keller the Killer is Pregnant with the Victim's Baby.*

With trembling hands, she picked up the test and carried it carefully to her bed as if it were an uncooked egg, one crack away from breaking. She had to lay her head on her pillow for a minute before she could think of what was happening. She needed to feel the comfort of the bed beneath her, the soft cotton sheet against her cheek. She needed to grasp her reality. Grasp that what happened had really happened.

I. Was. Raped. I. Am. Pregnant.

She couldn't stop thinking of all the possible scenarios in her head and what she should do about the baby. *Is it too late to get an abortion? Can I get an abortion in jail? Certainly, I should be able to get one if I was raped, right?* She should've paid more attention in her AP Government class on state laws. She thought it might be legal in some states and not legal in others, but she wasn't sure. She'd heard rumors around school of girls getting abortions, but no one that she knew had gotten one. She stood up and paced around her room, suddenly realizing tears were streaming down her face. She heard a jiggle on the doorknob and before she could run to move the pregnancy test off her bed, her mom's face peeked in and looked at her and then down at the test on the bed.

"Mom!" Emily yelled more harshly than she needed to. "I thought I locked that! Ever heard of knocking?"

"Oh, sorry, hon, you must not have twisted the lock on the knob all of the way," Debbie said sheepishly after realizing what was on the bed.

"Please leave me alone!" Emily demanded sternly as she crossed her arms protectively in front of her. "I need privacy right now." She sat down on her bed and threw a blanket over the test. Her mom opened the door wider, stepped in, and closed it behind her. She walked over to Nate's bed and sat down. Emily could smell the whiskey on her breath from across the room.

"I think I've done a really decent job giving you all the privacy you need the past few months, Emily, haven't I? I've even had your cell phone this whole time and haven't looked at it once," she said in a surprisingly calm voice. She stood up slowly, moved over to Emily's bed, and sat next to her. "I know I'm not perfect, but maybe what you need right now is an imperfect mother to talk to because I can understand anything you're going through and won't judge you because I bet whatever you've done, I've done worse."

Emily looked up at her mom's glazed-over eyes and sniffled. "I didn't do anything wrong though, Mom," she whimpered as she started crying softly. "I didn't. I didn't!"

"Shh. I know you didn't. I know you're innocent," her mom whispered, her voice calm. "Do you want to tell me whose baby it is, hon?" she asked as she put an arm around Emily's shoulder.

Emily opened her eyes widely at her mom's candor and shook her head. "Everything will come out tomorrow, Mom. I just want to feel normal tonight. I just need to escape." She turned toward her mom's face and was alarmed to see teardrops trickling down her cheeks.

Her mom nodded and closed her eyes. "Okay," she assured her. "I can do that." She lifted Emily up by her arm and led her into the kitchen. Charlie was sitting at the table with a handful of delivery menus in front of him and a fresh can of beer. He saw them approach him and beamed.

"What are you ladies in the mood for? Chinese? Pizza? Mexican?" he asked with a grin as he tossed the menus onto the table in front of him. Debbie and Charlie both stared at Emily and waited for an answer.

"Chinese," she announced as she forced a smile. "I'll take a shrimp toast and pork lo mein."

"Atta girl!" Charlie exclaimed as he picked up his cell phone to call it in.

"Oh, and can you see if they have those string bean pancakes too?" Emily asked. She suddenly felt starving.

36

———◦◦◇◦◦———

Debbie pulled up to the Thomases' house at four o'clock sharp. She let out a long whistle when she surveyed the house.

"What a house! What a view!" she exclaimed, putting the car into park. Normally, Emily would agree with her, but since this was the Thomases' house, she rolled her eyes.

"Thanks, Mom," she said as she stepped out of the car.

"Have fun, sweetie!" Debbie yelled. "Wish I could switch places with you!" *Little does she know,* Emily thought. Debbie started backing out of the driveway before Emily got to the front door and then waved goodbye before speeding away. Emily slowly approached the door and glanced down at herself to make sure there was nothing promiscuous looking about her. She was wearing jeans, an oversized hooded sweatshirt, and her Vans. Her hair was in a messy bun, and she had absolutely no makeup on. *There's no way Mr. Thomas will hit on me looking like this,* she told herself. When she was about to ring the doorbell, the door swung open and Sophie and Katie burst through.

"Emawee!" Sophie shouted as she grabbed Emily's right leg.

Katie looked at her older sister and mimed her. "Emawee!" she bellowed, clutching Emily's left leg. Emily tussled the hair on both of their heads and grinned. *They really are adorable and sweet. It's too bad they have such awful parents,* she thought.

"Hi, guys!" she chirped, cheerfully. She stepped into the foyer and glanced around warily. No sign of Mr. or Mrs. Thomas. The house smelled like pumpkin pie and she thought gleefully for a second that Mrs. Thomas had baked one, but then saw an orange candle burning on the kitchen island.

"Mommy and Daddy are getting ready so they said we could let you in," Sophie announced as she pulled Emily's hand and led her into the family room. "We're watching *Peppa Pig.*"

She followed them both into the family room and sat down on the couch. The girls jumped up and sat on either side of her. As they watched Peppa try to think of a talent for her class talent show, Mrs. Thomas sauntered into the room wearing a long formal navy blue dress.

"Hi, Emily!" she said cheerfully. Her demeanor was much friendlier than the last time Emily had come over. "Thank you so much for helping us out tonight. I don't know what we would've done without you!" As she was speaking, she clipped large silver hoops in her earlobes, which made the formal dress look more trashy than classy, Emily thought.

"No problem," Emily replied hesitantly. Katie nuzzled her head on Emily's shoulder and hugged her arm.

"Look, Mommy!" she shouted. "Emawee is here!"

"I can see that," Mrs. Thomas glanced at her. Emily watched as she walked into the kitchen, listening to the sound of cabinet doors opening and closing. The pumpkin pie candle scent was wafting into the room and was beginning to give her a headache. She wondered if they'd mind if she blew it out after they left.

"Emily!" she called from the kitchen. "Can you come in here a sec so I can go over the evening?"

Emily looked down at the girls who were nuzzled up on each side of her. "Sorry, kiddos, I have to go talk to your mommy." She peeled herself loose and shuffled past the creepy bear eyeing her as she entered the kitchen.

"Sorry, Steve is being a prima donna and taking forever so we need to run out of here as soon as he comes down. I won't have time to go over dinner and bedtime with you if I wait for him."

Emily breathed a sigh of relief knowing she'd only have a brief encounter with Mr. Thomas when he came down. "It's okay," she said, sounding more cheerful than she had before.

Mrs. Thomas placed two bowls and two spoons on placemats in front of her, along with a box of Kraft Mac and Cheese. "You know how to make this, right?" she asked. Emily nodded her head. "Okay, good, because that's about all we've got right now. So just make this for them and then they can have some cookies from the pantry afterward." She pointed to the pantry door to the right of the oven. "After they both eat, tell them they can skip their bath tonight and you can play with them and let them watch TV until about eight and then put them to bed. Sound good?"

"Sure," Emily agreed, not really knowing if there was anything else she needed to know. When she had been there before with Hannah, she hadn't really been paying attention at the girls' bedtime since Hannah had taken the lead. *I'm sure I can figure it out, I'm not stupid,* she thought confidently. Just then, she heard footsteps coming down the stairs and Mr. Thomas's loud voice booming on his cell phone, and she startled at the sound.

"I know, Phil," he boomed loudly to the person on the other line. "You tell him I'll be there in the morning, but I'm on my way to a wedding right now and I'm not working tonight!" His voice got louder as he approached. Mrs. Thomas headed toward him in the foyer, and she grabbed both of their coats from the coatrack. Emily turned awkwardly toward them, not sure if she should join them in the foyer or not. She could hear them talking to each other before they both popped their heads into the kitchen and glanced at her.

"Hey, Em." Mr. Thomas stared at her with a smirk on his face as he buttoned up his Raven's puffer coat on top of his pinstripe suit. He picked up their dog, Trixie, who was dressed in a pink sweater and had a bow in her fur.

Emily looked at him in surprise and then looked over to Mrs. Thomas as she was buttoning up her black peacoat.

"Hi, Mr. Thomas," Emily responded reluctantly as she felt her face turn red. She felt the lightheaded as he opened his mouth to say something, but Mrs. Thomas grabbed him by his coat.

"Come on, Steve, we're *late*!" she shouted. "I swear, Emily, he takes longer to get ready than me!" She tugged him toward the door.

"Wait!" he bellowed as he ran Trixie over to her dog bed, placed her in it, and gave her a long kiss on the head before running back to the foyer.

"So long, kiddos!" Mr. Thomas yelled to the girls before Mrs. Thomas dragged him out the door.

The door slammed behind them before the girls could even register they'd left. *What kind of dad gives his dog a kiss goodbye and not his daughters?* Emily wondered before answering her own question. *The kind of dad who rapes his babysitter.* She walked into the family room and sat back down in her designated spot between the girls.

"Did Mommy and Daddy leave?" Sophie asked without taking her eyes off the TV.

"Yes, they did, sweetie."

"They didn't say bye," Sophie whimpered, continuing to keep her eyes glued to the screen.

"They were really late and in a rush, but they told me to tell you they love you both," Emily lied. Sophie gave a slight nod, acknowledging that she heard her, and then leaned her head on Emily's shoulder as they continued watching *Peppa Pig*.

At around 5:30, Emily realized that Mrs. Thomas never told her what time dinner usually was, so she got up from her seat and announced, "Who's hungry for dinner?"

"Me!" both girls exclaimed in unison.

"Can you make us mac and cheese?" Sophie asked as she began to bounce up and down on the sofa.

"Definitely! Wanna come help me make it in the kitchen?"

Both of their eyes lit up in surprise. "We could help you?" Sophie asked. "Mommy never lets us help her!"

"Of course! I think you'll make great helpers," Emily replied and patted her head. "Plus, you need to show me where you keep everything in the kitchen since I don't know where anything is!" She hoisted both girls up on the bar stools and stood behind the island so they could both watch her. "Okay, ladies. Welcome to Emily's home cooking show. Today we'll be making gourmet mac and cheese all the way from Italy!"

The girls both giggled. Emily smiled, delighted that she was entertaining them. Nate and she used to love watching cooking shows growing up.

One Christmas Eve, Debbie had to work at the bar, and there was a snowstorm. Nate and Emily didn't want to trudge all the way over there for dinner in the snow, so they decided to pretend they were on a cooking show and prepared themselves a Christmas Eve dinner. They got out flour, eggs, and sugar and made some sort of pancakey cake thing on the griddle while they talked to each other trying to sound like Julia Child. They poured water into their mom's wine glasses and Nate found an expired green food coloring bottle in their junk drawer from Easter. They squeezed some green drops into each wine glass and pretended they were drinking Christmas cocktails. It was one of the best Christmas Eves she could remember. Inspired by this memory,

Emily decided to do her best mimic of Paula Dean, mixed with a faulty Italian accent. "Now first I must find a pot and fill it with water. I need an assistant to tell me where you keep the pots. Anyone?" She looked at both girls.

"Me, me!" shouted Sophie.

"Yes, Sophie?"

"They're in there!" She pointed to the cabinets behind Emily. Emily turned around, opened them, and took a modest pot out.

"Bravo!" she exclaimed as she filled it up with water. Both girls snickered again. She placed the pot on the stove and fiddled with the gas knob to turn it on. She heard a click and then watched as the flames rose and she placed the pot on the stove. "Voila!" The girls broke out in laughter. "Next, I need an assistant to tell me where the milk and butter are!" Katie raised her hand urgently in the air. "Yes, Katie?" She pointed to the fridge behind Emily. "The fridge, you say?" Katie giggled. Emily turned and opened the fridge door and pulled out a stick of butter and a half gallon of milk. "Bravo, Bellissima!" The girls erupted in laughter. "Now I need an assistant to tell me where your measuring spoons are!"

"Me, me!" Sophie yelled, raising her hand.

"Yes?"

"Over in that drawer by the dishwasher!" She pointed. Emily marched over to the drawer and pulled out a tablespoon. "Voila!" The girls giggled. She was really loving all the attention she was getting from them.

"Last but not least, I need to know where a big stirring spoon is!" Katie began jumping up and down, pointing to a canister of spoons next to the oven. "Over there, you say?" Emily looked at Katie pointing toward the spoons. Katie nodded ferociously as Emily picked one out and held it in the air. "Perfecto!" she yelled. The girls exploded in laughter again. "Now I'll pour the pasta in and set a timer on my phone for ten minutes."

She poured in the pasta and set the timer. The girls seemed to be getting bored with her and initiated a fork battle with each other using their plates as shields, so Emily peeked through the cabinets for a pasta strainer. When her phone timer beeped, she took the pasta off and stirred together the cheese mixture, milk, and butter and put it back on the stove. She poured it into the girls' plastic bowls and placed one in front of each of them. "Bon Appetit! Dinner is served!"

"Yayyyyyy!" they both hollered. As the girls dug in, Emily poked around in the cabinets, peeking to see what other food was there since she was hungry. They were bare except for junk food. *Not very healthy eaters, huh?* she thought as she found a bag of cookies for the girls and a protein bar for herself.

After they finished dinner, they each had three cookies. "You're the best!" Sophie exclaimed as she scraped the cream filling from the Oreo.

"I think you're the best!" Emily said as she walked over and gave her a bop on the nose with her finger. "Should we watch a movie now until bedtime?"

"Yeah!" they yelled as they hopped off their stools and ran into the family room. Emily peered at the mess in the kitchen behind her. *I'll clean it up later tonight. The Thomases shouldn't be home until late, so I'll have all night to do it,* she thought.

She walked into the family room and turned on *Frozen* for the girls. Plunking herself on the couch, she reached for her cell phone in her back pocket, which was switched to silent mode.

Not to her surprise, she had ten messages and three missed calls from Hannah inquiring when she'd be leaving to go to the bonfire and spy on Topper.

"I can't talk now," Emily texted back quickly, hoping the girls wouldn't catch her texting and report it to their mom. "I'm putting the girls to bed at eight then will head over around nine or whenever I'm done. Putting phone down now until then."

"Ok hurry," Hannah texted back. Emily rolled her eyes, not sure how she could possibly hurry up the time. She put her phone back in her pocket and cuddled up with the girls as they watched the movie.

The movie didn't end until 8:15, but Emily allowed the girls to stay up a little later so they could finish it. "Okay, girlies, bedtime!" she announced when the final song was playing.

"Awwwww," Sophie whined. "Can we have some gummy vitamins before bed? Mommy always gives a vitamin to me." Emily looked at Katie, waiting for her to confirm as if she was a reliable source to verify this statement. Katie glanced at Sophie and back at Emily before nodding in agreement.

"Um, I guess so," Emily said, figuring one vitamin couldn't hurt them. "Where are they?"

"In the pantry," Sophie directed as she marched into the kitchen, opened the pantry, and pointed to where the vitamins were on the shelf. Emily followed her in with Katie trailing behind her. She grabbed the bottle, opened it and took two vitamins out, handing one to each girl.

"I got the dolphin, my favorite!" Sophie exclaimed, popping the vitamin into her mouth. "Pink shark!" Katie mimicked, popping hers into her mouth.

"You like dolphins?" Emily asked as she screwed the cap back on and placed it in the pantry. "I do too."

"I love, love, love them. I saw them once at the aquarium," Sophie shouted, her eyes glimmering in delight.

"So, so, so cool. I can't wait to hear all about it at bedtime." She grabbed both of their hands and led them upstairs. She glanced into both bedrooms, expecting to see pajamas laid out, but didn't see any.

"Sophie, can you be a big help and tell me where Mommy keeps both of your pajamas?" she asked.

"Yeah!" Sophie exclaimed. She went to her bureau and pulled out her pajamas from a drawer before throwing them in the middle of her floor. Then, she ran into Katie's room. Emily could hear drawers opening and closing and a few minutes later Sophie came back in with pajamas and a pair of Pull-ups for Katie.

"What an awesome helper you are!" Emily said as she gave her a high five. Sophie got herself dressed in her pajamas as Emily dressed Katie.

"You can each pick out one book," she told the girls and they scrambled toward Sophie's bookshelf, scanning the spines of the books. The trio sat on Sophie's bed and both girls squeezed themselves on Emily's lap as she read them two Berenstain Bear books. When she finished reading, she tucked Sophie in first and then carried Katie out on her hip as she switched off her light. She walked into Katie's room and placed her in her toddler bed.

"No!" she cried.

"What's wrong?" Emily asked, having no idea how to put a toddler to bed since she'd never done it before.

"Mommy sings me a song," she informed her, gripping the plush doll in her hands.

"Okay," Emily agreed as she leaned over the bed. She began to sing "Rock-a-Bye, Baby" and softly played with Katie's hair as she watched Katie's eyes close. After singing through five verses, Katie appeared to be asleep. Emily slowly tiptoed out of the room and closed the door gently behind her. She quietly walked down the stairs into the foyer and took a giant sigh of relief. She'd done it. The girls were in bed safely, were fed, and seemed happy. *I'm not half bad at this babysitting thing,* she thought as she pulled out her phone to text Hannah.

37

———◦◦◇◦◦———

When Nate came home that night, he'd encountered Debbie, Charlie, and Emily eating buckets of Chinese food in the kitchen. No one talked about court, and no one talked about the big elephant in the room. Emily was pretty sure her mom told Charlie about the pregnancy test since he was pulling her chair out and catering to her as if she were dying. They'd all squeezed on the couch and watched *Schitt's Creek* on TV after reading one another's fortune cookies. Emily's had said, "A new perspective will come with the new year." She thought of it as a sign of good luck and put it in her pocket.

Before they'd fallen asleep, Emily had heard Nate's voice whisper from across the dark room, "Em?"

"Yeah?" she had whispered back.

"Are you okay?"

"I'm pregnant," she blurted out before she lost her nerve. He didn't reply, but she could've bet he was nodding his head with his eyes closed as he soaked in the information.

"I'm here for you if you need me," he said as she heard him turn toward the wall and drift off to sleep. *If only sleep could come that easily to me*, she thought.

That morning, she decided to nix the Valium and spiked coffee before court. Now that she knew she was pregnant, she just couldn't take them anymore, even if she decided to not keep the baby. She also wanted to be clearheaded during her questioning in case Mindy threw any curveballs at her. Her body felt more nourished after all the food she'd eaten the previous night. She decided to eat breakfast to make sure she didn't throw up all over herself while she was on the stand. When she came into the kitchen, she saw Nate had already made her tea and put a granola bar next to it on the counter. Chuckling, she picked up the granola bar. *Where did Nate get this?* she wondered as she took a huge bite of it.

Charlie strolled out of Debbie's bedroom and sat down next to Emily at the kitchen table. He gave her a nod, poured himself some coffee and lit a cigarette. He glanced at Emily as if suddenly realizing he shouldn't smoke indoors anymore around her and quickly picked up his mug and stepped outside. She heard the shower shut off as Nate finished in the bathroom and she could hear him faintly humming "Somewhere Over the Rainbow." *He'd always loved that song*, she thought. She listened to her mom press snooze on her alarm clock again for probably the fifth time.

Realizing it might be one of her last, she tried to savor the morning in the house with her family. Charlie stepped back into the house, rubbing his hands together from the cold.

"I started the car up!" he yelled toward Debbie's room. "It's cold out there today! We leave in five minutes!"

Emily was grateful to have Charlie there to support not only her, but Nate too. Whatever happened, Nate would need someone to lean on. She shuffled into her room and double-checked herself in the mirror. Black pants, a gray sweater, and black boots, simple. She picked up the fortune from her cookie the previous night and placed it in her pocket for good luck before putting on her thick, black coat.

"I'm ready!" she yelled as she marched into the hallway and peeked into her mom's room. Debbie appeared disheveled as she hopped both of her legs into the pants that she'd worn to court the day before. She got on her hands and knees and searched on the floor for a clean blouse. *Charlie and she must have stayed up late last night,* Emily thought, annoyed that her mom was so hungover for her important day. She went outside and saw Charlie and Nate were already waiting in the car for her. *God bless them,* she thought.

Five minutes later, Debbie ran out of the trailer and into the car with a coffee mug in one hand and a cigarette in the other. Her mascara was smeared, she had dark circles under her eyes, and her hair seemed like it hadn't been brushed in days.

"Jesus, Mom, fix yourself up," Nate directed her as he reached over and handed her a brush. She glanced back at him sheepishly as she ran the brush through her hair. She wiped the makeup from under her eyes as Charlie drove toward the courthouse. As they approached it, Emily saw loads of cars and cameras waiting out front, probably looking for her so they could capture an image of *Keller the Killer.* Charlie steered the car around back and pulled up to the side door as Valerie opened it and indicated for them to jump out while Charlie parked.

Emily headed into the conference room one last time and took a seat alone with Valerie, while Nate and Debbie went into the courtroom to get seats.

"You're looking much better today, Emily," she acknowledged. "Are you feeling better?"

Emily nodded her head. She was glad that her google search showed her that sometimes not eating could make morning sickness worse. She was feeling so much better after eating.

Valerie nodded and then furrowed her brow. "First, I'm going to question Steph and Miss Jelly. That should be easy and simple. Then we'll move on to you. Do you think you can hold it together? Help to prove yourself out of this somehow?"

"Well, it will prove I had no ill intent," Emily said.

"Okay," she continued. "But what you have to worry about is Mindy. She's going to try to squeeze you into saying things that you may not mean to say. Her goal is to make you appear as poorly of a person as possible to the jury. Are you sure you can handle that?"

Emily thought about her question for a minute. "I mean, my life can't get any worse than what it is now, right? I may as well just try. If my testimony doesn't work, then I have to accept what the jury decides, I guess. But I know I'll always regret it if I don't take the stand."

"Okay, your decision, Emily," she said. "Do you need to use the bathroom or eat anything before you take the stand?"

She shook her head. "Let's do this," she said. They both stood and Emily followed Valerie into the courtroom. She sat down next to her and tried to steady her breath as the judge was called in and the jury was sworn in.

"The defense may call its first witness."

"The defense calls Stephanie Martínez to the stand," Valerie said, picking up her notebook from the table.

Emily turned as Steph walked down the aisle wearing black pants and a tan sweater. Her chocolate-colored hair was up in a messy bun, and she was wearing thick-rimmed glasses that she normally only wore in school. She smirked at Emily nervously as she took the stand and then focused back on the clerk as she was sworn in.

"Good morning, Stephanie," Valerie began. "You like to be called Steph, is that correct?"

"Yes," Steph said shyly as she pushed up her glasses.

"How do you know the defendant?" Valerie asked, gesturing toward Emily.

"We've been best friends since elementary school."

"Do you live nearby one another?"

"Yes, we live in the same community. We've seen each other pretty much every day since we were little."

"And what kind of things do you do together?"

"Well, I guess we go get food at Emily's mom's bar she works at. We do our homework together. We play games together. We do our hair and makeup together. Normal girl stuff."

"How would you described Emily's character?"

"She's like a sister to me. We've gotten into our share of fights, I'll admit. But we always make up. Emily has always been like a grown-up. She and her brother have always had to take care of themselves since they never had a dad and their mom always had to work. So, they learned to cook and clean themselves. Emily is the smartest person I know and will probably get into any college she wants with a scholarship."

Valerie paused and looked at the jury. "The person you're describing sounds pretty responsible. Would you use that word to describe her?"

Steph nodded. "The most responsible person I know."

Valerie folded her arms and smiled. "Have you ever known Emily to hurt anyone? To do anything malicious?"

"Emily wouldn't hurt a fly. One time in the fifth grade, I stole a piece of chocolate from the teacher's desk and showed Emily at recess. I didn't tell her I stole it, and we split it in two and ate it. The teacher, Miss McClain, came up behind us and asked who took the chocolate from her desk. I stood there in panic. Emily looked at the expression on my face and then spoke up and said she took it, no hesitation. She ended up losing her recess for a whole week just to keep me from getting in trouble."

Emily blushed, wondering if Valerie had prepped her about bringing a do-good story with her, or if Steph had just thought of that on the spot. Emily remembered when she'd taken the blame for Steph that day. She'd do it again if she could.

"Wow, that seems like a really great friend. Thank you for that special memory, Steph. Have you ever seen Emily cook on a stove before?"

"Sure, all the time. She's made me mac and cheese and pasta tons of times when I've been over her house."

Valerie nodded. "Does she have a gas stovetop?"

"Yes," Steph said, subtly glancing down at the scar on her arm that she and Emily had branded on one another with a fork. Emily wondered if she was going to bring it up to the room, but then figured she wouldn't. It'd probably only make Emily look bad.

"And does she seem to know how to operate it correctly?"

"Yeah, I mean, Emily's been making herself dinner since she was little. She knows how to use a stovetop."

"Have you ever known her to leave a stovetop on by accident?"

"No."

"Thank you, Steph. No further questions." Valerie headed back to her seat next to Emily.

"Does the prosecution have any questions?"

"Not at this time, Your Honor."

"Then the witness is dismissed, and the defense may call in their next witness."

Emily watched as Steph self-consciously got up from the stand, head bowed, and headed back down the aisle. She'd never liked being the center of attention.

"The defense calls Jelica Simmons to the stand."

Miss Jelly entered the room, wearing a pink Raven's sweatshirt, jeans, and purple Converse sneakers. Emily assumed the guards made her take off her Orioles baseball cap when she entered, or she was sure she'd be wearing that as well.

Emily felt a little more relaxed as Miss Jelly took a seat and was sworn in. Seeing her up there was like seeing her grandmother up there.

"Good morning, Miss Simmons. How are you doing this morning?"

"Anyone I can," Miss Jelly joked. "Oh, you said *how* am I doing, I thought you said *who*!" She smirked at the jury and several of them smiled back at her charm. *They're eating her up,* Emily thought.

Valerie smiled too. "Glad to hear, Miss Simmons. Can you tell me how long you've known the defendant, Emily Keller?"

"Since she moved here about ten or eleven years ago."

"That's quite a long time. How would you describe your relationship?"

"Emily, her brother, and her mother are my next-door neighbors. They're like family to me as I have no children or parents left in this world. In the past ten-plus years, I've been there for all of Emily's birthdays, first days of school, and holidays. She's like the granddaughter I never had." Miss Jelly wiped a tear from her cheek, and Emily realized that she, too, had a tear coming down her cheek.

"That sounds like an incredibly special relationship. Can you tell me about Emily's character? Is she the type of teenager you can trust?"

"Oh, very much so. Two years ago, I had both knees replaced. I was out for weeks and couldn't afford one of those fancy rehabs or live-in nurses. Emily and her brother ended up sleeping over and taking care of me day and night for four or five weeks. Emily cooked for me, cleaned for me, walked to the grocery store and got me groceries. She even helped bathe me. She was like my own personal nurse. She did more than I could ever ask for and never requested one penny. I still don't know how to repay her."

Miss Jelly glanced up at Emily, eyes full of tears and mouthed, *Thank you.* Emily's eyes filled with tears. She'd loved taking care of Miss Jelly. She'd loved staying at her house for that month and feeling needed and appreciated.

"That's not something one would think a typical fourteen-year-old girl would do during her free time, is it Miss Simmons?"

"No, certainly not. Emily is one of the most responsible and trust-worthy people I know, regardless of age. I would trust her with my life."

"Thank you, Miss Simmons. No further questions."

"Does the prosecution have any questions?"

"No questions, Your Honor."

"Then the defense may call its next witness." Judge Wilson slammed his gavel down. Emily was up next.

38

————◦◦◇◇◦◦————

Ignoring the mess in the kitchen, Emily headed into the family room, sat down on the couch, and took out her phone. It was 9:15 p.m. and she flinched, knowing she'd be getting some angry texts from Hannah asking what she was doing. Instead of reading the texts, she found Hannah's name in her call log and pressed send. Hannah picked up on the first ring.

"Emily, what the fuck have you been doing?" she yelled into the phone.

Emily cringed and pulled the phone away from her ear. "What do you mean, what have I been doing? I'm babysitting for you, remember?"

She was really beginning to not like how Hannah was treating her. *She's morphing into a mean girl, and I'm starting to feel like she's just using me to dig up information on Topper,* Emily thought.

"You said you were putting them to bed at eight!" Hannah shouted into the phone.

"What difference does it make? I just got downstairs!" Emily yelled back at her for the first time in her life. She could hear silence on the other end of the line as Hannah was processing the fact that Emily actually was standing up for herself.

"Okay, Em," Hannah said, transforming her tone into a sweet, quiet voice. "I'm just really upset about my grandmom and about Topper and I really thought you were going to help me tonight, that's all!"

Emily rolled her eyes at the TV screen. "I'm going to help you, Hannah, I *am* helping you right now since I'm babysitting for you! And I said I would go spy on him even though I really don't feel comfortable doing it."

"Ok, thanks so much, Em. You know how much you mean to me, right?" she said, still using a sweet voice.

"Sure, yeah," Emily lied, just wanting to get the night over with so she could move on with her life and distance herself from Hannah and all her drama.

"So what time are you going over there?" Hannah asked carefully, not wanting to upset her. "It's just I don't want you missing them in case they're there now. They might leave early!"

"I'll leave soon, okay?" Emily replied sternly. "I want to make sure the girls are all the way asleep first."

"Ok, thanks so much, Em!" Hannah exclaimed. "Text me as soon as you leave and then as soon as you get there! I need to be updated at all times!"

"Will do," Emily agreed before clicking off the phone. She was dreading leaving the girls alone in the house, even though she'd installed the baby monitor app on her phone. She opened the app and stared at both girls sleeping in their beds. She wondered how often Mr. and Mrs. Thomas used this app when they were out, if ever. She decided to wait twenty minutes until the girls fell into a deeper sleep to go, and so she flicked through the TV until she got to the show *Intervention*, which was centered on an alcoholic mother. *She seems to be way worse off than my mom,* Emily thought, as she watched the drama ensue as the mother refused to go to rehab. *I wonder if my mom could ever stop drinking if she tried to or if she would need an intervention too?* Emily wondered.

Once twenty minutes passed, she got up and peeked up the stairs. She glanced at the kitchen one last time, deciding that she'd clean it as soon as she got back. She checked that Trixie was still asleep and then tiptoed out the back sliding glass door onto the deck.

She opened her phone and texted Hannah, "Leaving now."

"Great!" Hannah texted back immediately.

Emily snuck quietly down the stairs, past the back of the house, through the neighbor's yard, and around the side just like Hannah and she had done before. It reminded her of the Berenstain Bears book she'd just read to Katie and Sophie where the group of bears snuck out of bed to Spook Hill to see an owl. She glanced down at the baby monitor app on her phone to ensure the girls weren't awake. She decided that if she saw even the slightest movement, she'd run back to the house as fast as she could. I *should be able to get back to their house before anything bad happens, I'm sure of it,* she thought.

Several blocks and fifteen minutes into her walk, she realized the fire station was a farther walk from the Thomases' house than the ten-minute walk Hannah had stated it was. She'd never actually walked there, but in her mind, it didn't seem that far. She thought she was about halfway there a while ago and now it seemed to be even farther away. She stopped and opened her texts.

"This walk is taking way longer than I thought," she texted Hannah. "Do you know how far it is? I've been walking for fifteen minutes."

"Only about 2 miles," Hannah texted back.

"2 miles!?!?!?!" Emily texted, enraged that Hannah hadn't told her the truth about how far it was. "If I had known that I wouldn't have gone!" She glanced around at her surroundings, not sure what to do. She could head back to the house or she could speed walk to the bonfire, take a quick look and speed walk back. She felt so infuriated she even left the girls and risked so much for Hannah in the first place.

"Pleassseeeeeee, Emily!" Hannah texted back. "You're almost there!"

Emily gave a loud sigh and watched as her breath made steam in the frigid air.

"Fine," she texted back. She put her phone in her jacket pocket and ran toward the firehouse. She cut through yards, hearing dogs bark, not caring if anyone saw her anymore. She just wanted to get there as fast as she could. When she could see she was close, she slowed down and caught her breath. She tiptoed in the shadows around the firehouse and stood back as the bonfire glowed from afar. It looked like there were about twenty people around it and a few people were scattered off in the field. *Probably couples going to hook up,* she thought. She leaned against a tree and got her phone out to text Hannah.

"Here," she texted. She glanced around the parking lot at the cars. "Looking for them now. No sign of his truck in the lot."

"Do you see them?" Hannah texted back immediately.

"Can't see that far," Emily squinted, trying to make out the faces around the bonfire, but it was too far away and too dark out to tell who each person was.

"Get closer!" Hannah directed.

I'm really getting tired of her bossing me around, Emily decided. She scurried from the side of the firehouse to a tree closer by as she tried to be as deer-like as possible. Luckily, the moon was a slit and, besides the bonfire and parking lot lights, there was no other light to indicate to any of them that she was spying. She poked her head slowly around the tree she was hiding behind and tried to make out faces but was still having a tough time. She thought she recognized a few people, but no one familiar stood out to her. She didn't see Topper or Madison anywhere.

"They aren't here," she texted Hannah.

"Are you sure???" Hannah texted back.

"Yes, I don't really know any of the people they're all seniors it looks like," she replied.

"Maybe they're coming later," Hannah texted.

"Maybe," Emily responded. "But I can't wait here to find out"

"Or maybe they're in the woods hooking up!" Hannah texted.

Getting frustrated, Emily responded, "Maybe, but again, I can't wait here to find out. It's going to take me 30 minutes to run back to the house." She glanced at the clock on her phone: 10:20. She really needed to head back. She opened the baby monitor app and looked at the two girls slumbering away and let out a sigh. She'd completed her assignment and looked for Topper and Madison. She could head back now and get back to the girls, safe and sound.

"Wait," a text from Hannah popped up.

"Sorry," Emily replied decisively as she put her phone back in her coat. She wasn't going to be her puppet anymore. *I need to get back to the person I used to be who would never have left those two little girls home alone,* she thought. Just as she rounded the curve of the tree to head back, she stumbled headfirst into another person.

"Sorry!" she apologized, looking down as to not to draw any attention to herself.

"Well, well, well, look who we have here," a familiar male voice boomed, and Emily felt a cold, bulky hand grip the back of her neck.

39

TRIAL DAY 5: JANUARY 11, 2019

———◦◦◇◦◦———

"The defense calls Emily Keller to take the stand." The bailiff marched over next to Emily and led her to the witness stand. The court was eerily silent as she took her designated position and the clerk approached her with a bible in his hand.

"Please stand. Raise your right hand. Do you promise that the testimony you shall give in the case before this court shall be the truth, the whole truth, and nothing but the truth, so help you God?" he asked.

"I do," she said, her knees buckling as she stood.

"Please state your first and last name."

The muscles in her arms and neck tightened and she felt herself freeze. *Say your name. Say your name*, she told herself, momentarily unable to speak.

"Emily Keller," she somehow forced through her lungs.

"You may be seated."

Valerie approached the stand and began her questions. Emily scanned the courtroom in front of her frantically and found Nate's eyes. She watched as he nodded at her and smiled encouragingly, giving her a minuscule sense of confidence.

"Good morning, Emily. I want you to understand that you do not have to testify today if you don't want to. Do you understand that you made the choice to do so and anything you say in this court of law can and will be held against you?"

At first, she was so blinded by being in the spotlight, she couldn't see Valerie at all. She could only hear the typing of the stenographer, the sniffling of a woman in the back of the room, and the air-conditioning humming above her. When at last she shifted in her seat, she saw all the faces in the room were turned her way. She breathed deeply and looked at Valerie.

"I understand," Emily replied.

"I must say, it's very brave for a sixteen-year-old girl to take the stand. I can't imagine having the nerve to do that myself when I was your age. I just want the jury to remember that Emily still is a minor, a child in the eyes of the law. It can be a scary thing to do."

Emily blushed, not knowing if she was supposed to say anything back or not but decided to keep quiet.

Valerie continued.

"What grade are you in, Emily?"

"Eleventh."

"Can you tell me what your GPA is?"

She felt her face redden again. "4.0."

"Wow, very impressive. Are you taking any special classes?"

"Yes, AP English, AP US History, AP Calculus, and AP Psychology."

"So, you're a pretty smart girl, huh?"

Emily glanced around the room, not sure of what to say and looked back at Valerie. "I guess so." She shrugged her shoulders.

"Now is not the time to be modest. Have you had any babysitting jobs before babysitting for the Thomases?"

"I've tutored kids around the neighborhood. But my schoolwork has always kept me too busy to have a steady babysitting job."

"So how did you end up babysitting for the Thomases the first time?"

"My friend, Hannah Patterson, asked me to babysit with her."

"Can you tell me how many times you babysat the Thomases?"

"Two times."

"Do you remember the date of the first time you babysat?"

She stared up at the ceiling trying to calculate the date in her head. She remembered it was the weekend before Mr. Thomas raped her, which was October 19, a date always burned in her mind. "It was the second Friday in October. I'm not sure what the date was. I think the 12?"

"And before that time, had you ever met the Thomases before?"

"No."

"Can you tell me what happened the night that you first babysat for them?"

She nodded and began. "Hannah asked me to babysit with her. We got there before dinner and the kids ate and we watched movies and played with them and then Hannah put them to bed. After they were in bed, Hannah wanted to sneak out and meet her boyfriend and his friend in the playground across the street. She said she had an app on her phone where she could watch the kids while they were sleeping so we could make sure they were okay while they were asleep."

"And did you sneak out with her?"

"Yes," she admitted, fidgeting with her fingers. There was a rustling in the courtroom and Emily could feel blood rush to her face. Her heart began to beat faster in her chest.

"And what did you do when you got to the playground?"

"We met with Hannah's boyfriend, Topper, and his friend Chuck in the playground and then Hannah and her boyfriend drove off in his truck. I ended up going back to the house and putting Sophie back to sleep since we saw her wake up on the app and then I fell asleep in Sophie's bed for about an hour." The beating in her chest sped up and then her chest began to ache in pain. *Could I be having a heart attack on trial?* she wondered in a panic as Valerie continued her questions.

"So, Hannah was the babysitter in charge, and she left in a truck with her boyfriend while you went back to the house and took care of the children?"

"Yes," she said, omitting the part about the vodka and smoking. A sour taste seeped into her mouth and her arms felt so heavy, she couldn't lift them anymore. She didn't know why she'd nominated herself to take the stand. She was about to have a panic attack and throw up in front of the entire courtroom.

"Wow, good thing you were there that night and could take care of her. What do you think would have happened to Sophie that night if you weren't there and Hannah had taken off in her boyfriend's truck?"

"I guess I never thought about that," Emily replied, slowly moving her pinky finger to ensure it was still alive.

"Could she have fallen down the stairs, turned on the oven, walked out of the back door or gone into the water?" Valerie asked.

"Yeah, I guess she could have," Emily agreed, swallowing her thumping heart back down her throat.

"So, because you were there, you essentially could have saved the girls' lives?"

"Well, I don't know about that. But I did help her get back to sleep," she responded.

"And the second time you babysat the Thomases was November 9, is that correct?"

"Yes."

"And did you want to babysit them?"

"No, Hannah had asked me to babysit with her again, but I didn't feel comfortable. I said no and then Hannah's grandmother died and she was unable to babysit them that night. My mom ended up seeing

Mr. and Mrs. Thomas at a bar and my mom told them I would babysit for them even though I really didn't want to babysit for them and had already declined." She reddened, knowing that her mom may now just be coming to the realization that it was her, in fact, who had told the Thomases that Emily would babysit for them even though she didn't want to.

"So, the only reason you babysat for them was to help out your friend and help out the Thomases, who were in a bind?"

"Yes."

"And tell me what happened the morning you were planning on babysitting for them."

"I saw Hannah's boyfriend making out with a girl and I texted her and told her. She was really upset and kept begging me to sneak out of the Thomases' house to see if her boyfriend was with the girl at a bonfire, but I told her I was uncomfortable doing it."

"And what got you to finally say yes?"

"She just kept begging and saying it wouldn't take long and I could get there quickly and take a quick peek and run back. I just thought it would take fifteen minutes and I was planning to have the baby monitor app on my phone the whole time so I could make sure the girls were okay."

"So, when you got to the Thomases' house that night, can you tell us what happened?"

She swallowed hard and began to speak, the room spinning wildly in front of her.

40

PAST: NOVEMBER 9, 2018

———◦◦◇◦◦———

Feeling a mammoth, icy hand grab the back of her neck, Emily turned and squinted in the darkness at Chuck's smirking face. He reeked of alcohol and cigarettes, and she grimaced in disgust.

"Chuck," she said his name matter-of-factly, hoping she could say a quick hello and get on her way.

"Why are you leaving so early? I just got here," he said as he forcefully steered her by the neck toward the bonfire.

"Oh, I have to get home," she informed him, not able to come up with a good excuse as to why she was hiding behind a tree.

"Come on, Em, stay for a little," he urged as he continued shoving her toward the fire, his hand still gripping her neck. Emily tried to thrust her body weight back to stop him from pushing her forward, but he was double her weight and triple her strength.

"I really do need to get home," she repeated as they inched closer to the fire and she looked at the faces of the people around the fire, not recognizing anyone she knew.

"Just one drink, baby," he purred as his hand inched its way down from her neck to her butt, as he led her the rest of the way to the fire. They walked to a cooler, and he grabbed two beers and handed one to Emily. She took it from him so she didn't make him angry and held it in her frigid hands without taking a sip.

"I really have to go after this drink." She tried to think of a plan to escape. Chuck took a hefty gulp of his beer and leaned toward her, sloppily trying to kiss her neck. She inched backward and stumbled on a crushed beer can on the grass behind her.

"What's wrong?" he slurred in her ear as he grabbed her sweatshirt. She glanced around the fire nervously at the group of people. Some were in conversation, some were chugging beers, and a couple of girls were giving her mean looks.

"I really do need to be going," she said again as she tried to pull his hands off her.

"Don't be a tease," he whispered in her ear. "You owe me from last time." He put his lips against her neck again and she felt a slobber of spit on her skin.

She cringed and then started to panic that time was passing and Sophie and Katie were alone in the house. *I need to get back now,* she thought. She pulled away from him, deciding that she needed an excuse fast.

"How about we go somewhere private then?" she asked him as she tried to come up with a plan.

"That's what I'm talkin' about," he murmured in her ear as he grabbed her butt. She grabbed his hand and led him toward the side of the firehouse, figuring once they got to where there were no more lights, she could start running. *There's no way in his drunken state that he'll be able to catch up to me, especially if he doesn't know which direction I'm going,* she thought.

She led him to the dark side of the firehouse.

"How about here?" she asked him, trying to sound seductive.

"Perfect," he mumbled as he stopped and began to unbuckle his pants. Before Emily could make a run for it, he lunged toward her and forcefully pushed her against the brick wall. "How do you like it?" he slurred as he fiddled with his belt.

Emily's eyes darted around in a panic. She had led him to this spot and now she needed to do something about it. She looked below her and saw a loose brick on the ground. She had only one way out.

"Take off your pants and lie down. I'll take care of you," she directed him. *Sophie, Katie, Sophie, Katie,* she repeated in her head. She was getting angry. *Why do these guys think they can do this to me? Do I have a sticker on my forehead saying, Rape me? I need to get back to those little girls. No one will ever do to me what Mr. Thomas did to me again. No one.*

"Now that's what I'm talkin' about," he repeated himself as he unzipped his pants and lay down on the graveled lot. Emily bent down and pretended to begin, but instead she grabbed the brick with her free hand.

She glanced up at him to see if he caught on to what she was doing, but his eyes were closed, and his hands were behind his head as if he were basking in the sun.

"Hurry the fuck up," he snapped, keeping his eyes shut.

She stood up slowly with the brick in her hand, not sure exactly what she was going to do with it. *I can't exactly hit him in the head with it, he could die. I don't want to kill him.* She looked down at his growing erection and made a decision. *This is for all you assholes who think you can do what you want to girls,* she thought. *This is for you, Mr. Thomas.* She raised the brick high above her head and threw it down on Chuck's crotch as hard as she could. She squeezed her eyes tightly and held her breath.

"AHHHHHHHH!" Chuck screamed as he curled into a fetal position. Emily turned toward the bonfire to see if anyone had heard him, but everyone seemed to be in the same spots they had been in before. She turned in the direction of the Thomases' house and began to run as fast as she could.

"YOU FUCKING BITCH!" he yelled. She could hear Chuck
stumbling to get up as he tried to run after her. She started to run faster
as she got into the neighborhoods that she'd taken on the way there.

"YOU FUCKING CUNT!" he screamed as he tried to chase
after her, but she could hear his yells and footsteps were getting farther
away. She zigged and zagged through houses until she couldn't hear
him anymore. As she ran through a neighbor's backyard, one of her
feet stepped into a large hole she hadn't see in the darkness. Her body
hit the ground hard. Trying to catch her breath, she glanced down
at her ankle, which was throbbing. Her heart was racing so fast, she
felt like she was going to have a heart attack. Her fingers felt like they
had frozen.

She winced and took a couple minutes to let her ankle rest before
getting back up. She took out her phone, ignoring the texts from
Hannah, and opened the baby monitor app, praying the girls were
okay. She glanced at the screen and saw that both girls were in the
same positions they had been in an hour before. She slowly stood and
began limping slowly back to the house, keeping the baby monitor app
open the whole way home to make sure the girls were okay.

When she finally limped into the playground across from the house,
she let out a sigh of relief. *The girls are okay, I did what Hannah asked, and I
escaped from Chuck unharmed.* Her only worry was what the repercussions
would be with Chuck. Her ankle would heal. She glanced down at her
phone for the time: 12:20. She limped behind the neighbor's house,
back up the Thomases' stairs, and into the house.

The house reeked of burnt pumpkin pie. She'd forgotten to blow
out the candle that was now giving her a migraine. But everything
appeared as she had left it. Sitting down on the couch, she lifted her
sweatpants to peek at her ankle and saw that it was beginning to swell.
She stood up and limped to the kitchen to get some ice and blow out
the candle but decided to check on the girls first. Hobbling her way up
the stairs, she peeked into both rooms and was comforted to see they

were both still in their beds as she had left them. She wobbled into the girls' bathroom, relieved herself, and glanced in the mirror. Her face was flushed from being outside in the cold and her hair was tangled in knots. Picking up a Barbie hairbrush from the sink, she brushed the knots out. Then, she rinsed her face in warm water and patted it dry on the princess towel hanging behind her. As she stepped into the hallway and began to wobble down the stairs, she heard the front doorknob jiggle and feet stumble inside. A fright washed over her. She didn't expect the Thomases would be home until at least after 1:00 a.m. since their wedding was on the Eastern Shore. *Did Chuck follow me back?* She panicked.

"Hello?" she called as she continued to stagger down the stairs carefully, trying to hide her limp.

"Emily?" Mrs. Thomas yelled out with a twang in her voice, indicating she had one too many drinks.

Emily hobbled down the last step into the foyer. "Hi. I was just checking on the girls," she said cheerfully, trying to compose herself. She gawked at the Thomases as they were taking off their jackets. They both had glazed-over eyes and were clearly drunk. Mr. Thomas couldn't seem to get his coat off, and he cursed as he shook his arm furiously.

"How was the wedding?" Emily asked.

Mr. Thomas turned toward her as if realizing for the first time she was standing in the room with him. His eyes moved slowly. He was more drunk than she'd seen him before. "You wanna know about the fuckin' weddin'?" he slurred, angrily.

"Stop, Steve," Mrs. Thomas directed him, and she turned toward Emily to speak as if he wasn't there. "Steve got us kicked out."

"Kicked out?" Emily asked, not knowing people could get kicked out of weddings.

"Some trashy girl with a fake Chanel bag claimed he grabbed her," Mrs. Thomas informed Emily as she bent down to unstrap her shoes. "Clearly, she was trying to get with my man." She looked up and winked. *I doubt that,* Emily thought.

"Lil skank," Mr. Thomas slurred as he finally gave up on getting off his jacket. He stumbled into the family room and plopped himself in front of the TV. "Get me a drink someone, will ya?"

Mrs. Thomas looked at Emily. "What an asshole, but ya gotta love him, ya know?" she admitted as she reached into her purse and pulled out a wad of cash. "I'm getting it!" she yelled to Mr. Thomas as she handed Emily the money. "Ya need a ride home?" she asked, still slurring her words. Emily couldn't even fathom how the two of them could have driven in the condition they were in.

"I just got a text that my mom's pulling up," she lied, hoping Mrs. Thomas was drunk enough not to realize that it didn't make sense since she hadn't known they were coming home right then. Mrs. Thomas nodded.

"Ok, hon. See ya." She staggered into the kitchen. Emily suddenly realized that she never had a chance to clean up after dinner and felt slightly embarrassed, but then again, she never planned to see them ever again. She peered over at Mr. Thomas, who was staring blankly at the TV screen, and she crept out the front door and tiptoed down the stairs. Her only solace leaving the house was that she never had to see the Thomases ever again.

41

———◦◦◦◦◦———

Emily paused and stared at Valerie, her thoughts too distracted from someone crying loudly in the courtroom. It was a minute before she realized the crying was actually coming from her.

"I want to point out that the police officer first to arrive at the scene, Officer Morgan, told us on Monday that both girls were sharing a bed when he arrived that morning. But you say you're sure both girls were in their own rooms when you left?"

"Yes, I'm sure," she said, dabbing tears from her eyes with the back of her hand.

"And what was the mental state of Mr. and Mrs. Thomas when they arrived home?"

"They were both incredibly intoxicated and said they'd been kicked out of the wedding they were at because Mr. Thomas had hit on some girl. He probably shouldn't have been driving."

"Let's circle back to you making the girls dinner. You say you made them macaroni and cheese?"

"Yes." Emily sniffled, thinking back to that night.

"Had you made that before?"

Emily took a deep breath. "Yes, thousands of times. We aren't gourmet chefs at my house, but we know how to make mac and cheese."

"The Thomases have a gas stovetop. Had you ever cooked with a gas stovetop before?"

"Yes. We have one at my house. Propane."

"So, you're very familiar with cooking with gas heat?"

"Yes, very."

"And you know when you're finished cooking with a burner, you have to turn the knob off to turn the stovetop off all the way or it will continue to emit gas?"

"Yes, I do. The trailer I live in is an eighth of the size of the Thomases' house. If we leave a gas burner running, we can smell it right away."

"And did you remember to turn the gas burner off after you made the macaroni and cheese for the girls?"

She blinked as she stared at Valerie straight in the face. "I think so," she admitted. "I've thought about this so many times. I've cooked macaroni and cheese so many times and always turn off the burner. I really do feel like I remember turning it all the way off, but the girls and I were acting out these cooking show scenes and having fun, so I can't remember all the exact facts. But I really do think I turned it off."

"But you obviously never intentionally left it on, is that correct?"

"God no! Why would I do that?"

"Just making sure the jury understands that there was no pre-meditated ill harm planned." Valerie grinned.

Emily felt sick. *How could anyone think I would plan to murder the family?*

"Is there anything else you want to say to the court, Emily?"

Emily looked at the jury. "I swear I would never hurt anyone intentionally. I made the biggest mistake of my life that night by getting peer pressured by a friend to do her a favor when everything in my gut told me it was a bad idea. I didn't even want to babysit for the Thomases in the first place but felt pressured to do it and then didn't want to sneak out and go to the bonfire but felt pressured to do that too. I'm guilty of doing that, I know. But please understand that by no means did I plan to leave those girls alone for that amount of time and I really do think I turned that burner off. I really do. I just really want the jury to understand that yes, I made this mistake, but I'm not a murderer. I'll have to live the rest of my life in guilt and shame, and I feel like that is punishment enough. I ask you if you could please have it in your hearts to understand this and maybe what happened to me can teach other girls my age to not give in to peer pressure."

"Thank you, Emily. No further questions, Your Honor." Valerie grinned and marched back to her seat.

"Does the prosecution have any questions?" Mindy stood up and smoothed out her sleek black hair as she approached Emily.

"Good morning, Emily. I'm so glad you're feeling better after being ill yesterday. I hope you didn't have a bug?" She looked at Emily with a furrowed brow, and Emily wasn't sure if it was a rhetorical question or not. She decided to sit and wait for her to go on.

"You said you've made macaroni and cheese before?"

"Yes, hundreds of times." Emily rubbed her sweaty palms on her legs.

"And which burner did you use to cook the macaroni on at the Thomases' house?"

"The upper right burner."

"And what did you do after the macaroni was finished cooking?"

"I drained it, added the cheese, milk and butter, and stirred it."

"Which burner did you put the pot back on after you stirred it?"

"The bottom right burner."

"I don't remember anywhere in your response you stating that you turned off the stove, is that correct?"

"I'm pretty sure I did. I think I did." Her eyes darted around the room, looking for Nate, but everyone's faces were blurry. She needed someone to assure her that yes, she had turned off that stove. She needed someone's familiar face to look her in the eye and give her some sort of comfort. But all she saw was a sea of hazy faces.

"Would you bet your life on it? Are you one hundred percent sure you turned it off?"

"Not one hundred percent sure, no."

"Not one hundred percent. Hmm. Now, let's talk about that first night you babysat with Hannah on the night of October, what was it, the 12?"

"I think so."

"You said you and Hannah snuck out and met Topper and Chuck at the playground and then she drove off with Topper, is that correct?"

"That's correct."

"And you headed straight back to the Thomases' house to check on the girls when she left?"

Emily hesitated. "Yes, after a few minutes. She asked me to go check on her before she left so I did. I ended up falling asleep on Sophie's bed so I was gone for an hour."

"But you went back out?"

"Yes, I went back to let Hannah know everything was okay."

"Couldn't you just text her everything was okay?"

"I guess I could have."

"And was Hannah there when you got back to the playground?"

"Not yet."

"Who was there?"

"Just Chuck."

"And what did you and Chuck do while you waited for Hannah?"

"Well . . . he kissed me. And sort of tried to force himself on me. But I pushed him off. Hannah drove up just in time so nothing else happened."

"And did you drink any alcohol that evening?"

She hesitated again and looked down at her fingers folded on her lap. "Yes."

"What did you drink?"

She thought about how much she should tell. *Is it perjury to omit how much I drank? Should I tell the truth?* "Well," she began, "Hannah gave me a sip of something from the kitchen before we snuck out. I don't know what it was. And then when we got to the playground, I took a sip or two of the guys' vodka. I'm not really sure exactly how much I drank."

"That seems like quite a lot of alcohol for a thin girl's frame like yours. And did Hannah or the guys force you to drink this alcohol?"

"No, they didn't."

"Did they force you to sneak out?"

"No."

"So, you drank and snuck out all on your own free will, is that correct?"

"Well, yes, but—"

"Is that correct, Miss Keller?" she interrupted Emily.

"Yes."

"Let's talk about the weeks that went by between the next time you decided to babysit for the Thomas family. Did you see anyone in the Thomas family at all during that time frame?" she asked, knowing quite well that Emily had seen Mr. Thomas according to the cameras that had proven she had slept there with Hannah.

"Yes."

"Who did you see from the Thomas family?"

"I saw Mr. Thomas."

"Where did you see him?"

"I saw him at the thrift store down the street from my house." Mindy looked surprised at Emily's response.

"What happened when you saw him at the thrift store?"

"He insisted on paying for some boots that I couldn't afford and offered to drive me home. It made me feel a little uncomfortable, so I asked him to drop me off at my friend's house because I didn't want him to know where I lived."

"Very interesting indeed that he gave you the creeps, but yet you decided to sleep over his house sometime after that. Is that correct?"

"Well, I didn't really decide to sleep over his house. I was at a party with Hannah, and she left me there. I asked her to call me an Uber and she texted Mr. Thomas to pick me up instead. I didn't know he would show up. He took me to his house, even though I asked him to take me home. I had drank too much and thrown up and I just wanted to go home and lie down."

"Drank too much again, huh? Seems like underage drinking is a recurring theme here. Is it true your mother has a drinking problem too?"

Emily stared up at Mindy with startled eyes and opened her mouth in surprise. She was unsure what to say.

"Objection, Your Honor!" Valerie called.

"Sustained," Judge Wilson responded. "Stay on course, Attorney Rosenbaum."

"What happened after he took you to his house? Were the children and Mrs. Thomas home?"

"No, he said they were at their beach house. He told me where their guest bedroom was, and I went upstairs and tried to go to sleep, hoping Hannah would get there soon. She was supposed to get there soon. She had just gone for a drive with her boyfriend, Topper. I really didn't feel comfortable in there."

Mindy paced up and down in front of Emily, deciding what to say next. "And were you . . . intimate with Mr. Thomas?"

Emily stared up at her again, stunned as she felt her face go red. "Well . . . he was intimate with me . . . but I didn't want to be intimate with him."

She wasn't sure how to delicately let Mindy know what happened without totally embarrassing herself.

"So, let me get this straight. You slept with Mr. Thomas and a month later, the night you were babysitting, the whole family mysteriously dies from carbon monoxide poisoning on your watch? Were you getting revenge on an unrequited love? Would he not leave his wife for you? Is that what happened, Miss Keller?"

Emily felt her blood begin to boil. "I didn't want it!" she screamed. "He raped me!" She heard a gasp in the crowd.

"Order in the court!" Judge Wilson shouted.

Mindy stared at Emily for a few seconds, tilting her head to the side as if coming up with a new theory. "So, was it that? Were you getting revenge on him for raping you? Were you punishing him and his entire family for it? Why else in God's name would you go back to someone's house who allegedly raped you? Did you find out that you were pregnant from his child and you wanted to pretend that you could play house like them?"

Emily began to weep into her hands and the clerk walked over to her, handing her a box of tissues. "I didn't even know I was pregnant when it happened!" she yelled. She heard another gasp from the crowd, and she opened her eyes wide again, realizing that she'd revealed too much.

"I didn't know what to do. I didn't tell anyone, and I felt pressured by Hannah and my mom to babysit for him. I said no when they asked me to babysit! I didn't want to!"

"I think the theme of this trial here, Miss Keller, is that you're doing a lot of blaming other people for choices that you made yourself, would you agree? Do you agree that it was ultimately your decision to sneak out of the Thomases' house the night of November 9?"

"Yes, but I felt pressured, I didn't know it would take that long, I swear!"

Mindy nodded her head.

"Yes, we've heard your excuses over and over, Miss Keller. But the fact of the matter is that you, my dear, ultimately chose to babysit for the Thomases on November 9. Nobody made you do it, is that correct?"

Emily glanced up and sniffled, feeling a tear slide down her face. "That's correct."

"And you, my dear, chose to sneak out and go to the bonfire that night, leaving the children alone. No one made you do it, is that correct?"

"That's correct."

"And you cooked the girls' dinner that night and are not one hundred percent sure if you turned off the gas burner, is that correct?"

"Yes, I guess so."

"No further questions, Your Honor."

Emily put her head in her hands and sobbed, completely and utterly defeated.

42

PAST: NOVEMBER 14, 2018

—◦◦◇◦◦—

"So, what'd you do anyways?" Emily's roommate, Kara with a K, asked from the bunk above her. Kara, who'd told Emily she'd been at Lincoln Juvenile Correctional Center for six months, had hot pink hair, tattoos up her arms, and a piercing in her septum.

Earlier that morning, Nate and Emily had taken a walk to The Pit to watch the sunrise. No Instagram or phones, just them.

"Have you heard all the rumors?" Emily had asked him, her face puffy from crying, as she kicked a rock toward his feet. Emily hadn't stopped crying since she'd found out about the Thomas family a few days before. There'd been so much talk and gossip in the neighborhood about their deaths. Rumors were spreading that it was Emily's fault.

"Yeah," Nate replied, kicking the rock back toward Emily. "I try to ignore everyone. You should too."

As Nate and Emily had headed back to their trailer, a police car slowly approached them, and two officers stepped out. Emily knew what they were going to say before they even began to read her the

Miranda rights. The rumors must not have been total lies because the cops believed them. She'd silently cried as the cops cuffed her, Nate shouting that he was running home to wake up Debbie and call a lawyer.

When she'd arrived at the detention center, the intake officer removed Emily's handcuffs, had her remove her shoes and earrings, and had her empty her pockets. She then had Emily walk through a metal detector before handing her an undersized towel with a little bar of soap and miniature bottle of shampoo and ushered her through a two-way door into a room with a large shower in it. After she showered and dried off, the officer handed Emily socks, underwear, a bra, sweatpants, a white T-shirt, and a sweatshirt. She got dressed in her new wardrobe and then followed the officer back into the intake room as the officer got more information before leading her to her pod.

"It's your lucky day," the officer announced as she led Emily to her cell. "Our facility would put you in isolation since you're a juvenile, but today we're at maximum capacity. Looks like you have a roommate."

As Emily stared at the bunk above her, the whole morning seemed like a dream now.

Kara and Emily were in Pod D. Their cell was furnished with a built-in bunk, a desk with a stool, a sink, and a toilet. Kara was already in the top bunk when Emily arrived, so she gladly lay down on the bottom bunk.

"I didn't do anything," Emily said with a sniffle as she stared up at the metal bars of the bunk bed.

"Yeah, sure you didn't," Kara said with a snicker. "You haven't stopped crying since you got in here."

"What'd you do?" Emily asked her as she wiped her eyes with the rough blanket beneath her.

"Meth. Heroin. Fentanyl. Selling. Buying. Using. You name it," Kara said matter-of-factly. "God, what I wouldn't do for some crank right now," she whimpered longingly.

Emily frowned thinking of how troublesome it was that this girl was hooked on such hardcore drugs and had ruined her life. *But then who am I kidding, I'm in the bunk below her,* she thought.

"Knock, knock," a tall prison guard announced in a thick Nigerian accent as he approached their cell.

"My lawyer here?" Kara asked excitedly as she hopped from the bunk above Emily.

"Her lawyer," the guard directed, pointing toward Emily.

My lawyer? Emily wondered as she sat up and placed her feet into the slip-on shoes provided for her. She stepped out of the cell and followed the guard through Pod D into a room similar to the intake room she'd been in earlier that morning. When she walked into the room, she saw Debbie sitting next to a woman wearing a lime green pantsuit with matching lime green nails. Her flaxen-streaked hair and overly done makeup made her look like she was a clown. She had a large notebook in front of her, *probably filled with notes from my case*, Emily thought.

"My baby!" Debbie stood up and gave Emily a hug. "I'm so sorry I wasn't there this morning when those monsters arrested you!" Seeing her mom made Emily automatically break down in tears.

She began to shake as she sat down in the empty chair across from the lawyer.

"Hello, Emily. My name is Valerie Anderson," the lawyer introduced herself. "And I'm going to be your court-appointed lawyer for this case."

"She's going to help us get you out of this, hon," Debbie said, reassuringly. "I've been talking to her. She's real good, okay?" Debbie sniffled and wiped her nose with her hands.

"The state is charging you with manslaughter. Under the common law in Maryland, manslaughter is the killing of another unintentionally while doing an unlawful act, a negligent act, or by negligently failing to perform a legal duty," Valerie read from her notes. *I wonder why Valerie needs to read this from her notes. Doesn't she know this stuff if she's a lawyer?* Emily wondered.

Valerie continued. "I have good news and bad news. The bad news is that the state is charging you as an adult given your age and the nature of the crime."

Emily stared at Valerie with wide eyes. *An adult?*

"She's only sixteen!" Debbie exclaimed, running her hands through her hair.

"Yes, but in the eyes of the law, if a juvenile commits a crime this serious, they can be tried as an adult, and they're pulling out all their bells and whistles. They could charge you with up to ten years of imprisonment."

Emily thought about herself as a twenty-six-year-old sitting in prison. All her friends would be graduated from college, married with kids.

My life is ruined, she thought.

"You said you had good news?" Debbie asked with a gleam of hope in her eyes.

"Oh yes," Valerie said, glancing down at her notes. "The good news is at the bail review, I'm requesting to place Emily on probation under supervision in her home. That means that hopefully, during the trial, she'll be able to stay at home under your guardianship with some sort of an ankle monitor that tracks her whereabouts."

Emily breathed a sigh of relief. "So, I won't have to stay here the whole time?"

"I'm not promising anything," Valerie said, closing her notebook and placing it in a bag on the floor. "Let's see what happens."

"Time's up," the guard announced as he opened the door and peeked his head in.

"We'll see you in two days at the hearing," Valerie said and reached her hand out for Emily to shake it. Emily reached her hand out awkwardly and shook Valerie's hand, her clammy fingers sticking to her lawyers'. "And just a reminder in case you don't know this, no talking to anyone about your case. No one. You hear?"

Emily nodded her head slowly.

"And try to get some rest."

Debbie staggered over and gave Emily a bear hug. "I love you, Em," she whispered. "We'll get through this." She grasped her hands in Emily's and Emily felt something hard slip into her palm as she did this. As the guard led Emily back into her room, she peeked down into her palm and saw a small white pill. She slipped it into her mouth discreetly before the guard turned back around.

43

TRIAL DAY 5: JANUARY 11, 2019

———◇◇◇◇◇———

Emily leaned back in her seat, her face swollen and puffy from crying, as she watched Mindy stand up to give her closing arguments. She wished she had a Valium right then; she felt so naked and exposed sitting there. *No tranquilizing shield of armor. Just me and the tiny baby inside of me.*

"Your Honor, ladies and gentlemen of the jury, let me first thank you for your time and attention this past week," she said as she walked over to the jury, placing her hand on the wooden jury box. "We now know, on the evening of November 9, 2018, that Emily Keller cooked dinner for Kathryn and Sophie Thomas using a gas stove. We know that she used the upper right burner to cook the macaroni and then moved the macaroni to the lower right burner once it was cooked. Miss Keller has admitted under oath that she cannot be one hundred percent certain if she turned that gas burner off or not. She has also admitted to sneaking out of the Thomases' house, leaving the two children unattended and alone for hours. While Miss Keller was out of the house, Kathryn and Sophie were breathing in the carbon monoxide being omitting from the stove that Miss Keller left on. While Miss Keller was at a bonfire, miles from the house, Kathryn and Sophie Thomas were slowly dying in their beds from the negligence of their babysitter. We now know the family of four died from carbon monoxide poisoning. We know who cooked dinner that night: Emily Keller. We know who left the girls alone for hours: Emily Keller. People, let me remind you that manslaughter refers to the unintentional killing of another person. This crime occurs when unreasonably dangerous action results in the death of a person, or persons in this case. These incidents prove without a reasonable doubt that Emily Keller is guilty of manslaughter of the Thomas family. If Emily had not snuck out that night, would she have noticed the smell of gas in the house and then gone to turn it off? Or would she have gone into the kitchen to clean up and notice the burner still on? There are so many what-ifs that night that could have happened if Emily had not been negligent and left those innocent children alone. Those girls would still be alive. This whole family would still be alive." She paused, turning her back toward the jury, and then faced them one last time. "I've demonstrated, with convincing, credible, and consistent witnesses, that the defendant, Emily Keller, was negligent while babysitting for the Thomas family and, therefore, this negligence led to the deaths of Steven, Brandi, Kathryn, and Sophie Thomas. I ask that you return the only verdict that this evidence supports, and fairness demands, a verdict finding the defendant, Emily Keller, guilty of manslaughter. Thank you." She folded her hands somberly in front of her, bowed her head, and walked back to her seat. She courtroom was silent; Emily could swear the jury could hear her holding the deep breath she'd taken.

Valerie rose from her seat and began. "Your Honor and people of the jury, it has been a pleasure to appear before you in this tragic case. I want to thank you for listening to both sides equally as you promised you would do in jury selection. What we've all heard this week is a terrible tragedy. It's a tragedy that Mr. Thomas did not properly install carbon monoxide detectors on every floor, like he legally should have per Maryland law. It's a tragedy that Mr. Thomas did not have the proper venting system over his stovetop like he should have. And it's a tragedy that Mr. and Mrs. Thomas did not go into the kitchen and see the stovetop was on or notice any unusual smell before going to bed on the evening of November 9, 2018. Emily Keller did make Sophie and Kathryn Thomas dinner and has admitted to sneaking out of the Thomases' house on the evening of November 9, 2018, yes. But does that mean she was trying to harm them? Let me remind all of you that Emily Keller is sixteen years old. Who here in the jury didn't make less than smart choices when they were sixteen years old?" Valerie paused and looked a few jury members in the eyes. A couple of them smirked and nodded, as if reminiscing on the stupid mistakes they'd made when they were teenagers. "I want you all to think about whether this one decision that Emily made should cause her to live the next ten years of her life in prison. A girl with a 4.0 GPA who has no criminal history, has her entire future ahead of her. I'm asking for you to return a verdict of not guilty. Thank you." Valerie walked back toward Emily and sat down. Emily glanced up at the jury for just one second, letting them see how empty she was inside. Decision time.

44

JANUARY 12, 2019

———◦◦◇◦◦———

D ebbie and Emily pulled into the Women's Center in downtown
Baltimore as soon as it opened. They'd had to get special approval
from Judge Wilson since Emily could only go to certain locations with
her ankle monitor on. They headed inside, and Emily observed that the
walls were covered with a pastel pink and light green striped wallpaper.
Is this a bad teen movie from the eighties? she wondered.

She glanced at the people in the waiting room and saw that only
about half the seats were filled. Emily hesitated as she saw pamphlets
about safe sex and STDs in stacks on the tables, along with baskets of
assorted condoms.

Debbie casually sat down and picked up an issue of *People* mag-
azine that was sitting next to the condoms. Emily gave her a look, and
Debbie motioned to the front desk. *So much for support,* Emily thought.
She hesitantly approached the front desk.

"You have an appointment?" the woman from behind the desk
asked, without glancing up from her paperwork.

Debbie had made Emily an appointment as soon as they got home from court the day before. "Yes," Emily muttered, placing her hands in her pockets nervously.

"Sign in there," the woman directed her, pointing her pen toward a sign-in sheet on the counter. Emily signed her name with a quivering hand before quickly scurrying back to her seat. She grabbed the first magazine she could find to bury her head in, trying to ignore her mom chewing gum obnoxiously. *Snap. Snap. Snap.* Emily could see the girl across from them give Debbie a disapproving look. Emily nudged her, but Debbie continued to snap.

"Amanda?" she heard the nurse call as the girl sitting across from them got up and headed quickly toward the woman. *I wonder what she's here for. Birth control? Syphilis? Abortion?* Emily pondered.

Debbie reached over and grabbed a handful of condoms and stuffed them in her coat. "Mom!" Emily whispered harshly to her.

"What?" she whispered back. "That's what they're there for!" Emily shook her head and looked back down at her magazine, trying to focus on the ad in front of her for no boil lasagna noodles.

"Emily?"

Emily froze and glanced up at the nurse who called her name and then looked over at her mom. Debbie nodded at Emily, and she nervously rose and headed over to the nurse. She followed the nurse back to the examining room with her mom in tow, who was still snapping away on her gum obnoxiously. *Snap.*

They followed the nurse into a basic examining room where she proceeded to take Emily's blood pressure, heart rate, and weight. She then had Emily undress and handed her a gown to cover herself. Emily waited anxiously for the doctor to come into the room and began to pick at her cuticles.

"I remember when I first went to the doctor when I was pregnant with you and your brothers," Debbie recounted with a smile on her face. "I was so excited. When the doctor put that ultrasound gel on my stomach and I not only heard one heartbeat but three? It was one of the best days of my life." She leaned back in her chair and gazed reminiscently across the room as if imagining the day all over again.

"Wasn't it scary to be pregnant with triplets?" Emily asked her.

"Of course," she admitted. "Everything is scary if you let it be."

Emily sat and thought about that for a second before hearing a light tap at the door.

"Knock, knock," she heard a voice say as a slim, middle-aged woman entered the room wearing a white lab coat. "I'm Doctor Cole," she introduced herself with a warm smile. "And you're Emily Keller?"

"Yes," Emily said quietly.

"You're here to talk about getting an abortion? Is that correct?" she asked as she glanced down at a clipboard of paperwork she was holding.

"Yes."

"When was the first day of your last period?"

"October 5, I think, although I've never really paid that much attention or written it down."

"Do you know when the baby was conceived?"

That was something she did know. "October 19."

"Did you use protection?"

"No," she responded, not knowing how much she should tell the doctor.

"She was raped," Debbie interrupted. "She was raped by a man she babysat for, and she would like to terminate the pregnancy."

Dr. Cole opened her eyes in surprise and wrote something down on her clipboard. "I see. I'm deeply sorry that unfortunate event happened to you, Emily. We can provide you with trauma and psychiatric services on your way out if that is something you're interested in."

"Thanks," Emily replied. "The only thing is . . ."

"She may be going to jail on Monday," Debbie blurted out again.

"Jail?" Dr. Cole asked in confusion.

"It's a long story," Emily tried to explain. "I may be getting in some trouble and unable to get the abortion after this weekend is what my mom is telling you, so we're here to find out how fast this . . . termination . . . can happen."

Dr. Cole gave an uncertain look and put down her clipboard. "Why don't we have a look now and see what we're dealing with before we talk about any specifics. Does that sound okay?"

"Okay," Emily muttered. She lay down while the doctor did a pelvic exam on her and measured her belly.

"Now I'm going to put some gel on you; it may feel a little cold." She squeezed a dollop of gel on Emily's stomach and rolled the ultrasound machine toward them. She pressed the wand against Emily's belly and moved it around as images appeared on the screen.

"It looks like you're about fifteen weeks pregnant," she informed her, moving the wand around. Emily stared as little arms and legs moved around the screen. "And see that?" Dr. Cole asked as she pointed to the screen. "That's the heart beating."

Emily watched in awe at the little thing moving around on the screen, so totally alive yet she hadn't even known it had existed the week before.

Too bad things couldn't be different for you, little one. She placed her hand on the side of her belly, feeling shame for what she was planning on doing to the life inside of her. She glanced over at her mom and saw her discreetly dab a tear away from her eye.

Suddenly, she had a memory flicker in her mind to when she was seven years old. She picked up her present and carefully unwrapped the paper. As she did, she saw the most magnificent baby doll she'd ever witnessed. A little baby girl with a lace dress and pink bonnet. She looked up at Miss Jelly with tears in her eyes, knowing she was the one who'd bought it for her.

"I love her!" Emily exclaimed as she reached out and hugged Miss Jelly. "Thank you!"

"What will you name your little baby?" Miss Jelly asked as she picked the wrapping paper up from the floor and put it in the trash can.

"Fiona," Emily said. "I think I'll call her Fiona." She held Fiona tightly in her arms. "I'll give you the best life ever, baby Fiona."

Emily shut her eyes tightly and focused back toward the doctor, trying to erase the idealistic fantasies she'd once had of having a baby.

"You can wipe your stomach with these and sit up," Dr. Cole directed as she handed Emily a box of tissues. Emily wiped the gel from her stomach and sat up, pulling the gown back down to cover herself.

"Well, I've got good news and bad news for you, Emily," Dr. Cole said.

"Okay," Emily replied, hesitantly.

"The bad news is that tomorrow is Sunday. And you said with your circumstances, you need this performed before Monday. Our clinic requires a twenty-four-hour period after you sign and review documents before any type of abortion, including a surgical/in-clinic abortion, can be performed. So, the earliest you could have this abortion is Monday. But you say you cannot do that. Is that correct?"

Emily glanced down and shook her head no.

"The good news is that recently the Maryland General Assembly approved a bill that would require all state prisons to have written medical-care policies for incarcerated pregnant women with things like prenatal care, abortion access, and labor and delivery. So, you may be able to get an abortion while you're incarcerated, and since you're a juvenile this may be a special circumstance. If I were you, I'd talk to your lawyer if you do get convicted and see what she thinks."

Emily looked at her, surprised by this information but still feeling defeated. "Okay, thank you for all your help," she said.

"You're welcome." She paused and looked at Emily with sympathetic eyes, placing her hand delicately on Emily's forearm. "And if you end up not getting convicted, give us a call and make an appointment for next week."

Emily's eyes welled with tears. The doctor's touch made her feel like someone cared about her. Like someone wasn't judging her for once. "Okay, I will. Thank you, doctor."

"Thank you so much, Dr. Cole," Debbie said, reaching out her hand as if conducting a business transaction.

Now it's the waiting game to see if I'll be calling her next week for the abortion or having it in prison, Emily thought as she rubbed her belly with her hands.

45

———◦◦◇◦◦———

Emily woke up to the smell of coffee brewing, banishing the dream of Sophie and Katie swinging with her on a hammock from her head. Sophie had whispered something to her. Something important, yet it was just on the edge of her recollection.

The girls had been happy. She'd been happy. She glanced at the alarm clock and saw that it was 10:45 a.m. *I haven't slept this well in who knows how long,* she thought, stretching her arms up above her head. She glanced over and saw Nate's vacant bed neatly made. Rising up, she put on her worn teddy bear robe that was starting to rip in the front.

As she walked out of the bedroom, she saw that Nate and her mom were both in the kitchen. She could heard the news playing on the TV and heard her name mentioned. As soon as Nate saw her, he clicked off the TV and turned up the volume on the compact radio in the kitchen, which was playing an old Taylor Swift song. Emily looked at the kitchen table and saw bagels, cream cheese, scrambled eggs, and bacon strips. Nate and Debbie both grinned at her eagerly and she grinned back, humbled by their effort.

"Juice?" Debbie asked as she reached into the fridge and pulled out an orange juice carton.

"Sure," Emily said as she pulled a chair out and sat down next to Nate. "You guys didn't have to do all this, you know. This is too much."

"Yeah, we did, Em," Nate informed her.

Debbie shuffled over and handed Emily a glass of juice before serving Nate and her eggs and bagels. Emily reached across the table and grabbed a big, burnt piece of bacon, just the way she liked it. She closed her eyes and took an enormous juicy bite of the bacon, feeling a flood of heaven enter her mouth.

She couldn't remember the last time her mom cooked it for her. Nate, passing on the bacon, made himself a cream cheese bagel and took a big bite.

"How are you feeling?" he asked, hesitantly. "Do you want to talk about anything?"

Emily thought about it for a second. "No," she admitted honestly. "I'm scared. I'm nervous. But what is there for me to do but wait? I just want this all to be over, no matter what they decide. If they find me guilty, at least I won't have to worry anymore over what will happen."

"We'll fight it, hon," Debbie assured her, trying to uplift her. Emily observed as her mom lifted her glass of orange juice with a shaky hand, almost spilling it. *Nate must have asked her not to drink this morning.* Emily grinned at her and took a bite of her eggs. She heard a knock on the door and glanced over as Steph walked in, holding a bound book in her hand.

"Steph!" Debbie said, excitedly. "Come join us! Have you eaten?"

"I ate early this morning, but I could eat a little something more," she said as she took the seat on the other side of Nate. "I just wanted to stop by and say hi before your big day tomorrow," she said. *You mean you came here to say goodbye before I'm sent to prison,* Emily thought.

"I made you this." She reached over and handed Emily a scrapbook. On the cover she wrote the quote: *A friend is someone who understands your past, believes in your future, and accepts you just the way you are.* Emily opened it and found it was filled with pictures of them through the years next to magazine cuttings and quotes. She saw photos of them at The Pit, photos of them playing dress-up with Nate, photos at her mom's bar, and photos on their first day of school each year. Emily's eyes welled up in tears. When she flipped to the last page, she saw a final quote: *When you follow the crowd you lose yourself, but when you follow your soul, you'll lose the crowd. Eventually your soul tribe will appear, but do not fear the process of solitude.*

"Thank you so much," Emily said, holding the book against her chest. "This really means so much to me and it's so good to know that I have a friend that's always been there for me, even if we may have veered off for a little while there." Steph blushed as she took a bite of her bagel. "There's something I need to replace this with," Emily admitted more to herself than anyone else. She got up and headed to her room, retrieving the vision board hiding underneath her bed. As she glanced at the cutouts of the celebrities she'd never met, she realized how stupid it was for her to want to be someone else. She lifted her knee and cracked the board in two and then headed over to place the board in the trash can. "Sorry about that," she said to Steph. "I just realized I was searching for something I had here all along."

The door opened again, and Charlie bounced in carrying a dozen donuts and a container of coffee. "What's up, dudes!" he bellowed as he closed the door behind him. "Who wants some sweets?" He put the coffee down and opened the large container of Bayside Donuts filled with an assortment of delicious-looking donuts. Emily's mouth watered looking at them. "I'll cut each one in half so everyone can try a couple!" He passed out the various flavors: Oreo, maple, Reese's peanut butter, and even Old Bay chocolate. Emily tried a bite of each one. Before she could say how full she was, she heard a knock on the door and Miss Jelly came in carrying her famous Berger cookie pie.

"Miss Jelly!" Charlie yelled from across the room. "Gimme a big ole piece of that pie!"

It was becoming clear to Emily what this was: a going-away party and last meal all in one. She decided to savor the day as she cut herself a sizable piece of Berger cookie pie.

As they sat around the table, reminiscing on old times, Debbie's cell phone rang from the kitchen. Charlie glanced at it and hollered, "Looks like it's Emily's lawyer, Valerie. Guess you should get this." He got up and handed Debbie the phone and she stood up and walked into the family room, away from their chatter. Emily scooted her chair out and looked over at her mom, who was pacing the family room with the phone to her ear and the other finger pressed to her opposite ear to cancel out the noise.

"So, at nine a.m. still? Uh-huh. Okay, we'll be there." She ended the call and headed into the kitchen with her eyes open wide. Nate and Steph saw her approach and slowly stopped their conversation.

"What'd she say?" Emily asked urgently.

"She said the jury will not be announcing a verdict tomorrow. Something happened. They have new video footage and will be showing it to us at nine a.m. She said they'll explain tomorrow, but whatever it is, it's big and has transformed the whole course of the trial apparently."

Emily stared at her, trying to brainstorm what video footage the cameras could have possibly gotten that they hadn't already seen and how it could possibly alter any outcome of the trial.

"Em," Debbie said. "She acted like the case may be dismissed."

46

—◦◦✕◦◦—

Emily hit send on her email from the school laptop that she'd been working from during her home supervision period. All her teachers were graciously sending her schoolwork through email, even though they weren't required to. She reached down and scratched at the scab that'd formed under her ankle monitor.

"You finish your feminist essay?" Debbie asked as she walked out of her bedroom, still wearing her clothes from the previous night. Nate was in school still, so Emily had the delight of spending the afternoons with her mom until he got home.

"The feminist and sociological approaches to literary analysis? Yes, just sent it in. I've finished all my work now. Ready for winter break," she admitted before thinking, *what kind of winter break do I really have to look forward to? I'm confined to my trailer by my ankle bracelet. I have no friends besides Steph. Everyone in the world thinks I'm a killer. And maybe I think I am too. I can't sleep and when I do sleep, my dreams are filled with the faces of Sophie and Katie. Sometimes they're alive, hugging my legs and giggling. Sometimes they're dead, lying in their beds.* Emily had started taking a white pill before bed every night. Sometimes when she woke up crying from nightmares about Sophie and Katie, Debbie would hand her a brown pill with the white pill. That combination made her sleep dreamless.

Debbie headed into the kitchen and poured herself a vodka orange juice. Her shaky hands lifted the cup to her lips and she took a sip. She carried the drink back to her room and closed the door behind her. Emily rolled her eyes and closed her laptop.

Since she'd finished her schoolwork, she got back into bed and went back to sleep, or at least tried to. She knew she was depressed. She felt a heaviness in her heart that couldn't be lifted and was tired all the time.

At three o'clock, Nate and Steph entered through the front door, laughing giddily about something. Emily opened her bedroom door and peered out into the family room.

"Em! Where are you?" Nate called as he shook off snow from his coat.

Emily wrapped her arms around her body, trying to keep warm as she stepped into the family room. She began shivering from the frigid air they'd let in from the cold December wind.

"Right here," she mumbled as she squinted at the bright white blanket of snow behind them. She'd been keeping the drapes and blinds in the house closed because she wanted darkness. Because of this, some days she didn't even know what it looked like outside. She hadn't even known it had snowed.

"Look at all the snow!" Steph exclaimed as she reached her hand out the door, letting the snowflakes fall onto her pink mitten.

"Wow," Emily gawked, trying to join them in their excitement.

"We have another surprise!" Steph emphasized as she pulled at Nate's hand and they disappeared outside. Emily waited a minute for them to come back and heard something being dragged through the snow.

"Look what we got!" Nate yelled. Just then, Debbie came out of her bedroom appearing more refreshed since she'd had her drink.

"What'd you get?" she asked as she peered toward the door.

"A Christmas tree!" Nate proclaimed as he dragged the snowy tree into the family room.

"Christmas tree?" Debbie shouted in excitement. Normally every year, they decorated their house with tons of cheesy Christmas decorations. But this year, it just didn't feel right.

"Listen, I know this is a hard time right now," Nate admitted. "But Christmas is in a few days, and I'd like to decorate a tree with my family tonight." He glanced back and forth from Debbie to Emily, grinning earnestly.

Emily thought about it for a minute. *The past month has been hell. I guess a little tree decorating would be a nice distraction. It may be my last Christmas at home for the next ten years.*

"I'll go look in the closet for the ornaments," she said with a smile. "Can you help me, Steph?" Everyone beamed.

"I'll go get the tree stand," Nate said in excitement.

"I'll go get eggnog from the store and call Charlie!" Debbie volunteered as she skipped toward the door.

47

———◦◦◇◦◦———

Debbie pulled up to the courthouse at 8:45 a.m. and dropped Nate and Emily off while she searched for a parking spot with Charlie. Emily had been up all night speculating what could possibly happen that morning. Now that she had a glimmer of hope, it'd be harder to accept if she were proven guilty. Valerie was standing at the door with a huge grin on her face and led them into the conference room. There was a TV set up in the corner that hadn't been there the week of the trial.

"So, you heard the news from your mom that there's been new evidence found?" Valerie asked Emily as she took a seat at the end of the table.

"Yeah," Emily replied. "Why aren't they presenting this in court? I don't understand. What's going on?"

Debbie trudged in with Charlie, both smelling like cigarettes, and they sat down at the table with everyone.

"So, what's the scoop?" Charlie asked, clearly excited to be in the back room and in on everything for the first time.

"Were you aware that Mr. Thomas had a hidden camera inside of the house, Emily?" Valerie asked. Emily stared at her blankly.

"Inside?" she asked. "No. Where?"

"He had a hidden camera in a big taxidermy bear in the family room that I guess no one knew about but him. Apparently, a family member just found footage on his phone from it that we were unaware of because it was not installed by the same security camera company as the one that installed the outside cameras."

"Daddy killed that mean bear with Uncle Tommy in Alaska and Tommy killed a cheetah in Africa," Sophie whispered in her ear. Emily stared at her lawyer, dumbfounded. "I remember my first time babysitting and he pointed out that bear and said something about how it watched over the house or something." It was all starting to make sense.

"So, the bear's camera has views of the family room, foyer, and most of the kitchen the way it's set up. We were able to view everything that went on the evening of the ninth, as well as evidence of his several affairs, including with Hannah the babysitter."

Emily nodded her head, soaking in the information. "But what did it see that would change anything that happened that night?" she asked her. Valerie leaned over and turned on the TV. On the screen, Emily saw the Thomases' family room, foyer, and kitchen from the bear's eyes.

"Wild," Charlie proclaimed, stretching out his arms behind his head.

Valerie pressed a button and it fast-forwarded through Emily entering the room, sitting with the girls watching TV, and making them dinner on the night of November 9. "Now, it's hard to tell from this far away, which is why we have a program that allows us to zoom in." She pressed another button and zoomed in on the kitchen as it showed Emily taking the macaroni pot off the stove and turning the knob off.

"See that?" Valerie directed, pointing at the screen. "It shows you almost certainly did take the macaroni from the stove and turn the burner off."

"Boom!" Charlie yelled.

"But I still could have maybe not turned it all the way? Maybe I turned it halfway and left it on?" Emily asked, still not convinced of her innocence.

"Well, there's more," Valerie promised as she pressed another button, fast-forwarding the tape through the night to when Mr. and Mrs. Thomas arrived home. Emily viewed the tape as it showed her walking down the stairs and saying goodbye as Mr. Thomas staggered into the kitchen and Mrs. Thomas took off her coat. Mr. Thomas stumbled around in the kitchen and poured himself a shot before putting the macaroni pot back on the stove and turning the knob. He staggered over to the pantry and took out a bag of Doritos, opened the bag, and poured them into his mouth. Mrs. Thomas stumbled in and poured herself a drink. The footage showed them sitting in the kitchen for a bit longer as he reheated the macaroni and then scooped the noodles straight from the pot into his mouth without taking it off the stove. After a few minutes, he and Mrs. Thomas hobbled into the family room and sat on the couch.

"So, *he* turned the stove back on!" Debbie yelled.

"Yes," Valerie said. "It looks like after you left, Mr. Thomas reheated the macaroni and cheese and put it back on the stove. He turned the stove back on and must have left it on."

Emily wept in relief. "So, I didn't kill the girls?" she asked.

"You didn't kill them, honey," Valerie explained. "And you know how I know?"

"How?"

Valerie pressed play and Emily watched as the footage showed Sophie shuffling down the stairs with her blankie in her hand, rubbing her eyes as she headed over to the couch. Mrs. Thomas marched over to her, picked her up, and carried her back upstairs. Mr. Thomas then staggered across the room and picked up Trixie from the dog bed and began to cuddle with her on the couch.

Emily stared at the screen with raised brows and relief.

"The girls were alive and well when you left, Emily. You didn't leave the stove burner on. Mr. Thomas did."

"So, what does this mean now?" Nate asked, sitting up straighter.

"It means the prosecution has dropped the manslaughter charges. They now have no evidence at all that you had anything to do with the death of this family. Did you leave while babysitting? Yes. Could minor charges be brought up for that? Sure. But this case has been dismissed. You're innocent."

Emily bent over with her head between her legs and sobbed tears of joy, sadness, grief, relief, and guilt.

48

———◦◦◇◦◦———

"Do you want milk in it?" Nate asked. Emily sat in the family room with her legs resting on the couch as Nate fixed her a hot tea from the kitchen. Her mom had opened the kitchen window and the air coming through felt like it had purified the atmosphere.

"Milk?" Jeremy, Nate's new boyfriend, asked in disgust. "Lemon only."

"You're such a tea snob," Nate teased before giving him a kiss on the cheek. Nate and Jeremy had been dating for about a month and they were attached at the hip. They'd met at a record store in Hampden, both ogling a Bob Marley original vinyl. Emily thought their obsession with one another was cute.

"Lemon sounds nice," Emily shouted to them and grinned. She watched as her mom scooped ranch dip out of a container and placed baby carrots around a paper plate. She heard a tap on the door as Steph and Miss Jelly came in, each carrying platters of food. They handed their dishes to Debbie before heading over to Emily.

"Smells good!" Emily yelled from the couch. "What'd you bring?"

"I brought baby spinach salad, pigs in a blanket, and Chex mix," Steph revealed proudly.

"I cooked my Berger cookie pie, my peanut butter cheesecake, and my baby pizza bagel bites," boasted Miss Jelly. Emily's mouth watered.

"I can't wait to try them all!" she exclaimed as she stood up.

"Oh, you stay right there, dear. We'll make you a plate," Miss Jelly ordered. She filled up a plastic plate to the brim and handed it to Emily.

Emily beamed as everyone gathered around her, holding their baby-themed food on their laps.

"Am I late?" she heard Hannah's voice shout as her head popped out from behind the front door. She was carrying two cups filled with milkshakes from Emily's favorite ice cream shop, Pete's. "I have Oreo milkshakes!"

"Yum!" Emily moaned, her belly rumbling. Hannah handed Emily her milkshake before bending down and embracing her friend in a bear hug.

"Hi, boo," Hannah whispered as she gave Emily a kiss. "Long time, no see."

Emily chuckled. They'd just seen each other at the previous night's SASA, Sexual Assault Survivors Anonymous, meeting. Along with Emily's weekly AA and NA meetings, she'd been going to the sexual assault meeting with Hannah three times a week.

"Forgiving her will help your recovery. Holding onto resentments is like drinking poison and expecting the other person to die," her sponsor told her when Hannah had reached out to Emily shortly after the trial had ended. Emily had been hesitant at first to accept her apology.

But she went to a SASA meeting and watched as Hannah admitted to the group that Mr. Thomas had raped her. And Emily decided, why not heal together?

She came to terms with the fact that she couldn't blame Hannah for everything. She'd made her own decisions; Hannah never forced her to do anything. Emily's sponsor helped her realize her own involvement in her decision making, and she'd taken accountability for her choices. No more skeletons in anyone's closets.

Steph walked over and gave Hannah a hug before offering her a drink. Emily could see Hannah's sleeve lift up as she hugged Steph, showing the scars on her wrists, now almost completely healed.

"So, should we start?" Debbie asked, standing up in front of the group.

"We should," Emily agreed, sitting up straighter. Debbie marched to the kitchen, grabbed a thick stack of folders, and handed it to Emily.

Emily picked up the top folder, turned to the first page, and read to the group.

"Candidates 1: Chris and Evelyn Shank from Western Maryland. Looks like she's a teacher, and he's an engineer. They've been trying for seven years and have been unable to have a baby. They have a pug and like to hike and camp on the weekends."

"That seems like a good one," Steph said as she bit into a baby carrot.

"He looks a little weird to me," Debbie said. "Who goes hiking for fun? Let's see the next one."

"Okay," Emily said, rolling her eyes at her mom's pickiness, as she selected the next folder. "John and Luke Grant. They've been together for fifteen years and married for five. John is an interior designer and Luke works for a nonprofit. They live in Bolton Hill and have a beach house in Rehoboth. Looks like they do well financially. They have no pets and have wanted a child for ten years but have had no luck adopting."

"Let's see some stats," Nate said, pushing aside his corn salsa. Emily passed the folder to him. He looked at it quickly and passed it around, while she watched her family and friends flip through the pages to help her decide her baby girl's future parents. After the charges were dismissed, she didn't have the heart to have an abortion. She felt that she *had* to give Sophie and Katie's baby sister a chance for a better life. Better than Emily could give her and better than Mr. Thomas could give her.

"Are they drinkers?" Debbie asked hesitantly. "Make sure you find that out." Debbie took a sip of her club soda and set it down as she reached for the folder. She and Charlie had been going to AA meetings for two weeks now and Debbie was beginning to think she was holier than thou. Emily was proud of her, though. No. More than proud.

"I'll check," Emily said, smiling. "So put this in the maybe pile?"

"Yes, maybe," Miss Jelly instructed. Emily put the folder in the maybe pile and moved to the next couple.

"We'll find the perfect one for our girl," Emily proclaimed confidently. *I can do this one thing right.*

"Emawee," she heard Sophie whisper. She felt Katie nuzzle her head against her shoulder and smiled, feeling Katie's spirit warm up her body. She rubbed her belly, feeling Fiona kick her leg out, and felt a sense of peace for the first time in her life.

EPILOGUE

"Did my mistakes make me a bad person? I don't know. I know that I could've killed the Thomas family with one wrong turn of my hand. There was no happy ending for the Thomas family. The only thing I could do was give my baby the best life possible. A fresh start with a new family," Emily told the group as she rubbed her flat belly, trying to remember the feeling of Fiona kicking inside. "And maybe try to give myself an okay life too."

She glanced up at the clock and realized she'd spoken for the whole hour, giving no one a chance to share. She watched as the women around her applauded. Nikki wrapped her arm around Emily's shoulder and punched her bicep.

"You're so strong," she whispered.

I don't feel strong. But I guess I don't feel weak anymore either, she thought.

"Would you like to end the meeting by reading *Just for Today*?" Darlene reached over and handed Emily the reading.

Emily took the paper and read, "Just for today my thoughts will be on my recovery, living and enjoying life without the use of drugs. Just for today I will have faith in someone in NA who believes in me and wants to help me in my recovery. Just for today I will have a program. I will try to follow it to the best of my ability. Just for today, through NA, I will try to get a better perspective on my life. Just for today I will be unafraid. My thoughts will be on my new associations, people who are not using and who have found a new way of life. So long as I follow that way, I have nothing to fear."

"Thank you for sharing today, Emily. I hope to see everyone again next week. Keep coming back!" Darlene announced.

"Time's up, ladies," the guard announced. "Let's go."

Emily stood up and gave her goodbyes. "You ready?" Darlene asked as she put an arm around Emily's waist.

Emily glanced around the room at the inmates lining up to go back to their cells. "I am," she said and she headed with Darlene toward the exit.

"Your probation for child endangerment is over now that you've hit your year. You don't have to come back here every week if you don't want to," Darlene informed Emily as they exited the building.

"I know," Emily replied. "But I probably still will. I get just as much out of this as they do."

"Me too, kid," Darlene agreed. "Me too." They strolled out of the detention center into the freezing cold toward Darlene's car. "It's supposed to snow tonight." Emily gazed up at the sky and took a deep breath. She could smell the snow coming.

"And once the storm is over you won't remember how
you made it through, how you managed to survive.
You won't even be sure, in fact, whether the storm is over.
But one thing is certain. When you come out of the storm you
won't be the same person who walked in."

Haruki Murakami

———◦◦◇◦◦———

ABOUT THE AUTHOR

Kathleen wrote her first story in the third grade, an assignment for writing class about a mysterious door hidden in a stairwell. She's loved writing ever since. She received her master's in Reading Education from Towson University and a bachelor's in Elementary Education from University of Maryland, College Park. She is a member of the Maryland Writers Association, the International Thriller Writers, and the Author's Guild. When she's not writing or selling real estate, she enjoys spending time with her family, traveling to the Outer Banks, and of course, reading anything she can get her hands on. She currently lives in Baltimore, Maryland, with her husband, three children, and a Sussex Spaniel.

ACKNOWLEDGMENTS

———◦◦◇◦◦———

I started to experiment with alcohol at an early age, and so understand firsthand the effects that peer pressure can have on a teenage girl. When I think back to those years, I sometimes wonder: *What if?* What if I had made this choice or that decision? There were so many terrible outcomes that could have occurred in my life. I wanted to write this novel to show my readers a "what if."

I've had the premise of this novel in my head for the past fifteen years or so. Writing has always been a passion of mine, but I've continually put it on the back burner. In 2020, my husband decided to take a giant leap in his career. With two toddlers, a newborn, and a full-time job, I finally thought to myself, *What better time to write this novel than now? If not now, then when will I ever write it?* And so, I took a giant leap also and picked up my pen . . .

Thank you to my trusted early reader, dear friend, and fellow author, Twig George. Thanks for being kind, even when my first draft was vastly different from the final product (and not in a good way).

Thanks to my editor, Elana Gibson. Your thoughtful edits have elevated this novel in every way.

My gratitude to the amazing team at CamCat Books, especially: Sue Arroyo, Helga Schier, Meredith Lyons, Laura Wooffitt, Maryann Appel, and Abigail Miles.

Dawn Fredrick, thank you for being my advocate.

Reba Buhr, thank you for doing an amazing job giving my characters life.

Thank you, Judson Arnold, for your legal expertise on Maryland law.

For reading my drafts and providing invaluable help and insight, thank you to: Alyssa Matesic, Gerrie E. Summers, Jessica Bell, and Jenn Weede.

Thank you to these amazing authors for giving me advice and knowledge on the writing industry: Donna Bertling, Timmy Reed, Vanessa Formica, and Kathryn Williams.

Thank you to my earliest editor as a child and the smartest person I know, my dad. You may be able to finish the Sunday *New York Times* crossword puzzle before lunch, but I can still beat you at Wordle once and a while.

Thank you to my mom, who has always supported me in all my mistakes and endeavors in life.

Thank you to Josh, my guiding light and rock. I love you.

To Gavin, Paige, and Porter. The greatest blessing of my life is being your mama.

And to all the readers, friends, and family members who have helped me along the way, thank you.

If you or someone you know has a substance abuse problem, cutting problem, or has been the victim of sexual abuse, here are resources to get help:

———∞∞∞∞———

S.A.F.E. Alternatives (Self-Abuse Finally Ends)

Organization dedicated to helping people who self-harm, with a helpline at 1-800-366-8288 (1-800-DON'T-CUT). http://www.selfinjury.com Referrals for therapists and tips for how to stop. 1-800-273-TALK A 24-hour crisis hotline if you're about to self-harm or are in an emergency situation.

SAMHSA National Helpline 1-800-662-HELP (4357)

Operated 24/7, the Substance Abuse and Mental Health Services Administration (SAMHSA) National Helpline provides information and referrals if you or a loved one are facing mental health and/or substance use issues. The confidential service does not provide counseling, but can direct you to helpful resources, treatment facilities, and support groups in your area.

Crisis Text Line Text 741741

The Crisis Text Line serves anyone in the United States with this confidential and free 24/7 text line, connecting you with a trained crisis counselor.

Childhelp National Child Abuse Hotline

1-800-4-A-Child or 1-800-422-4453

Dedicated to preventing child abuse, this 24/7 hotline is staffed by professional crisis counselors and translators who provide help and emergency/social service referrals in over 170 languages. Online chat with a trained professional is also available through the website.

Rape Abuse and Incest National Network (RAINN)

1-800-656-HOPE (4673)

With both phone and online chat options, the 24/7 RAINN helpline provides access to support from trained staff, who can help direct you to a local health facility with experience caring for survivors of sexual assault, as well as resources for healing, recovery, long-term support, and more.

National Alliance on Mental Illness (NAMI) HelpLine

1-800-950-NAMI (6264)

The NAMI HelpLine is a nationwide peer-support service, not a crisis line. It provides information, resource referrals, and community support if you or someone you know are living with a mental health condition.

If you liked
Kathleen Fine's *Girl on Trial*,
please consider leaving a review
to help our authors.

And check out another great read
from CamCat:
Jeff Wooten's *Kill Call*.

CHAPTER ONE

ON AUGUST 9 AT 1:32 IN THE MORNING, Hanna Smith is going to die.

Thirteen days. That's all she has.

She stands less than a hundred yards from me, texting in front of Markle's, a designer jeans store. Two bags stuffed with clothes hang from the crook of her left arm, a huge purse on her right.

She's in workout clothes, and her long blonde hair is pulled back in a ponytail. She's seventeen and goes to Miller's Chapel. I go to Bedford with the rest of the public-school kids. It's Saturday afternoon and the mall is packed. People swarm around me as I sit on a bench in the middle of the promenade. Somewhere a baby is crying.

I feel ya, kid.

I don't want to be here. It feels way too stalker-ish. That's not what I am. This whole thing feels wrong, but Dad says it's important, so here I am, trying to be cool. I don't feel cool. I feel like there is a huge spotlight on my head and everyone is staring. Only no one is actually staring at me.

I'm not antisocial, but I hate crowds. It's probably because of what I am.

I lean back, trying and failing to be nonchalant. I'm bad at this. Hanna's in her own world, hammering away at her phone with her thumbs.

In thirteen short days, Hanna Smith is going to die.

But only if I'm not there to save her.

A life for a life.

It's the only way.

My phone vibrates in my hand, and I jump, almost dropping it. I check the text, trying to be chill. Nothing to see here, just a dude sitting in the mall on his phone.

PARTY NXT SAT—B thurrrr!!!

It's a huge group text from Jacoby Cole. My phone buzzes with replies before I manage to mute it. How do people type so fast?

"Hey, Jude."

I flinch at the sound of my name and look up.

Molly Goldman smiles down at me, her hazel eyes bright. "Did you get Jacoby's text?"

I glance over at Hanna, but she's gone. She was standing there for ten minutes, and I take my eyes off her for a second—

"Jude? You okay?"

I look up at Molly. "Sorry. I was just—yeah, Jacoby's text. Just got it. Guess you did too?"

"Yep. Bet you're dying to go, huh?"

Molly and I have been friends since elementary. She knows I'm not the party type, or—in general—the social type. The short bark of laugher that escapes me is a little much.

"You bet, can't wait."

Molly sits beside me, pushing a lock of curly red hair out of her face. "You waiting for someone? Not sure I've ever seen you here."

I glance one more time to where Hanna was. Still gone. I should go, but . . . Molly.

I've always had a thing for Molly, but I've been in the friend zone, well, since forever. "Football starts next week," I say. "I need new cleats. Coach thinks we can win state."

"I've heard," Molly says.

"Yeah, right. Lucas." Lucas is Molly's boyfriend, my teammate, and a grade A dick. Next year he'll be playing college football somewhere big. I don't even know if college is a possibility for me.

We sit in silence for longer than is comfortable. I clear my throat. "Lucas decided where he's going to college?"

Molly hesitates. "No, but, well—just so you know, Lucas and I aren't seeing each other anymore."

I clear my throat again, for real this time. "What happened?"

"Not sure I want to talk about it."

"Yeah, sure," I say.

"So what have you been up to this summer?" she asks.

"Eh. Working with Dad, roofing, off-season football . . ." *Planning my first kill,* I add to myself. "You know, the usual." I can't help but laugh at the absurdity of my words.

Molly elbows me. "What's so funny?"

"It's nothing."

"It's something. And now you have to tell me."

For a fleeting few moments, I consider throwing it all away. Letting it all out, telling her everything. The dreams, what they mean, what Dad is, what I am. It's ridiculous. Molly would think I was crazy. Sometimes I think I might be.

All this goes through my head in seconds, but it's long enough to be odd. I shake my head and shrug, trying and failing to think of something to say.

"Awkward silences are fun," Molly says, "but I want you to use your words, Jude."

"Well, awkward silences are kind of my thing, and I hear you're single now." I hesitate, not sure where that came from. Since the dreams started six months ago, life has been stressful.

Molly's smiling though, obviously not offended. "Honestly, I appreciate you not giving me a pep talk about Lucas."

"Not a chance of that, "I say, surprising myself again.

Molly laughs for real, and I smile. It feels good to talk and laugh, and I do have a question now. I take the leap. "Can I ask you something?"

"Oh, this sounds interesting. Asking permission. Go on."

"Ah, never mind."

"Too late, now you have to ask."

I hesitate for just a second and go for it. "Why Lucas Munson? I never understood."

I'm expecting the standard. *He's nice, he's cool, he's interesting,* but Molly surprises me. "You know your problem, Jude?"

"*My* problem? I thought we were talking about Lucas."

"He asked, Jude." Molly's eyes measure me.

He asked.

"Uh," I say. "That's it? He asked? It has to be more than that."

Molly shrugs. "Sure, but it has to start somewhere."

Life is strange. Never thought I'd come to the mall, a place I hate, to definitely not stalk a girl, to be hit on by another girl. And not just any girl. Molly Goldman is flirting. *With me.* It doesn't seem possible, but she *is* flirting.

I swallow and force the next sentence out of my mouth. "You want to come . . . help me pick out some cleats? We can go to the food court after. Mall pizza is, surprisingly, not horrible. I mean if you don't want to, it's cool. I thought, you know, why not?" I clamp my mouth shut, not trusting myself to speak anymore.

Molly searches my face for a second, her eyes narrowing, as if trying to read my thoughts. I meet her eyes, but it isn't easy. After a lifetime, she smiles. "Okay, sure. I've already eaten, but yeah, why not? I can hang for a while."

"Cool." I laugh, standing up as nonchalantly as I can.

It's not easy. I'm so self-conscious of every movement now. It's like some evil scientist has control of my body, making my palms sweat.

I take two steps, smiling back at Molly . . . and run straight into Hanna *Freaking* Smith.